I tapped on Clarita's door and when she didn't answer, I opened it and looked in. Her black-clad form lay stretched upon the bed, and I thought for a moment that she was weeping. But when I spoke her name, she sat up and stared at me with dry, ravaged eyes.

"Why did you lie?" I asked her softly. "Who was it who went along the hillside that day?"

For an instant I thought she was going to strike me. Her thin hand with its flashing rings came up, but I stood my ground and it fell back to her side just short of my face.

"You are like your mother," she whispered. "You ask for killing."

# BOOKS BY PHYLLIS A. WHITNEY:

*Published by Fawcett Books*

*Phyllis A. Whitney*

# The Turquoise Mask

FAWCETT CREST • NEW YORK

A Fawcett Crest Book
Published by Ballantine Books
Copyright © 1973, 1974 by The Phyllis A. Whitney Trust

ISBN 0-449-23470-3

Selection of the Doubleday Bargain Book Club, September 1974

This edition published by arrangement with Doubleday and Company, Inc.

All the characters in this book are fictitious, and any resemblance to actual persons, living or dead, is purely coincidental.

Manufactured in the United States of America

First Fawcett Crest Edition: February 1975
First Ballantine Books Edition: December 1982
Twenty-fourth Printing: August 1992

# The
# Turquoise
# Mask

# I

I had set my "arguments" out carefully on my drawing table. Every item was significant and to be considered soberly if I was to make a right decision. To act meant stepping into something completely unknown and facing what I had been warned against, while not to act meant continued loneliness and the frustration of never knowing the truth.

Across the street from my third-story window, New York brownstone fronts shone with a bronze gleam in the spring sunlight, and East Side cross traffic was heavy. I wouldn't miss New York. There was too much that was painful here. But New Mexico was foreign to me and it held a possible threat.

A little way off in the room my telephone waited mutely on an end table, and I knew that it could either reproach me forever or hurl me into action and doubtful adventure. As always, my instinct prompted me to the bold stroke, but I was trying to use the caution my father had always urged upon me. Too much spirit was as bad as no spirit at all, he used to say, and I was too ready to be headstrong. Now I would try to think before leaping.

But I had to decide.

There they lay, side by side—the objects that would

help me in my dilemma. There was the small, carved wooden road runner. The silver-framed miniature painting of a woman's face. The advertising brochure that carried illustrations by me—Amanda Austin. The snapshot taken twenty years ago, showing my father and mother and me when I was not quite five. A glossy page torn from a fashion magazine. My father's pipe with the crust of its last smoking still black in the bowl. The bracelet Johnny had given me—gold, set with sapphires, my birthstone. A slave bracelet, he had called it once, teasing me as he admired it on my wrist. That was why I'd placed it here— as a reminder of something I must never again forget.

Last of all were the two letters from Santa Fe, where I was born and which I had left shortly after that snapshot was taken—after my mother's death, when my father had brought me East to grow up in his sister Beatrice's house in a small New Hampshire town. I could return to her any time I wished. Aunt Beatrice would welcome me with stern kindness and no sentimental nonsense. She had never approved of my mother or her family. She had never accepted that one quarter of me that was Spanish-American, and she might very well wash her hands of me if I went to New Mexico. It wouldn't matter a great deal. She had never been what I thought of as "family." I suppose I had some romantic notion, gleaned from childhood reading, of boisterous, all-for-one, and one-for-all *families*. That was the experience I had never had.

I picked up the pipe with the blackened bowl and held it in my fingers as though I held my father's hand. I had not wanted for loving there. But he was gone—recently, suddenly. We had been happy together in this apartment. His work as an engineer often took him away for weeks at a time, but we were always glad to be together when he returned—companionable and content with each other, as far as we were able, and in spite of our different temperaments. He had lost my mother long ago, and I had lost Johnny because Johnny had walked away no more than a year ago. Now my father was gone too and the apartment was empty. My life was frighteningly empty. There were friends, of course, but now, suddenly, friends weren't enough.

I had to fill my life with something new, with something that would belong to me, in spite of all the warnings that had been given me.

My father, William Austin, had been a kindly, gentle man, though he had a good deal of New England stubbornness in him. Only once had I seen him furiously angry. One summer when I was ten years old I had gone rummaging in an old trunk and I'd found the very miniature which now lay on my drawing table. The bright, smiling face of the girl in the painting fascinated me. I could not miss the resemblance to my own face, and I took it at once to my father to ask who she was.

Never had I seen him so angry as when he'd snatched the small picture from me.

"That was a woman I once knew," he told me. "She was worthless—wicked! She is nothing to you and you are not to go snooping among my things!"

His unfamiliar anger frightened me, but it also raised a response of indignation and I stood up to him.

"She's my mother, isn't she?" I cried. "Oh, why won't you tell me about her? I want to know!"

He set the picture aside and held me so tightly by the shoulders that his hands hurt me. "You look like her, Amanda, and that's something I can do nothing about. But you're not going to be like her if I can help it. Not ever!"

His hurting hands raised my own anger and I sobbed with rage. "I *will* be like her! I *will* be like her if I want to!"

He shook me then until the angry sobs choked in my throat and I looked at him with terrified eyes. When he saw how he had frightened me, he turned away, and I will never forget the strange words he muttered: "That dwarf! That damnable dwarf!"

The words had no meaning for me then, but I'd known better than to ask questions.

Anger had spent itself in both of us. We drew apart

and for a few days we watched one another uncomfortably, until the soreness and the astonishment faded and we could once more turn to each other lovingly.

The miniature vanished and I never saw it again until I had come upon it recently among my father's things. He had called her wicked, but once he must have loved her, and he had never brought himself to destroy the portrait.

Always after that outburst of temper between us he had watched me warily, as if waiting for something to surface. But we'd never raged at each other again, and he went out of his way to be gentle with me. Now I reached across the table to pick up the round, framed miniature. She had been very young, hardly more than a girl, when this was painted. Doroteo, her name had been. I had only to hold the miniature up beside my own face in a mirror to see the resemblance. Not that I was any duplicate of the girl in the painting, for she was a beauty, with dark eyes, a great deal of thick black hair, and a smiling, sensitive mouth. I had the same black hair, and I wore it long in a heavy coil at the back of my head—in secret imitation of the portrait. I had the same eyes, the same sun-tinted skin, but my mouth was wide and my chin less rounded. I was no beauty.

Her face did not seem to me a wicked one. Spirited, yes, with a laughing mischief in the eyes—but not dangerous. I couldn't see her that way. I was spirited too, with a temper that was sometimes hard to control, and a determination that wanted its own way. But these things didn't make me wicked, though I suspected that they came from her.

I had never been able to get my father to talk about her or her family out in Santa Fe. When I wanted to know how she had died, he told me shortly that it was in a fall, and would say nothing more. His very silence told me there was more. From the time when I was very young I had sensed some horror about my mother's death— some devastating truth that he did not want me to know. Now perhaps there would be a way to find out. Though the question was, how wise would it be for me to know?

I wondered if my grandfather had painted the minia-ture, for I knew at least that he had been something of an artist, and that he had done some carving in wood. I set my mother's picture down and picked up the small, hum-orous carving of a road runner.

The bird stood upon a diamond-shaped block of wood, perhaps three inches long from its bill to its feathered tail. It was executed with a minimum of detail—merely shaped, with a forked tail and arrowed lines here and there which gave the effect of feathers. Tiny indentations marked its small round eyes and nostrils, a slashed line indicated the opening of the beak. Yet so skillful were these touches that the humorous whole was magically suggested. The figure had been carved of some clean white wood, but I had played with it as a child until it was smudged with gray, rubbed in with grime. I'd loved it dearly. It was a toy I used to take to bed with me at night—not soft and cuddly, but still somehow comforting.

I turned it over, knowing what I would find etched into the base of the under side. *Juan Cordova,* the scratched-in letters read. Once when I was eight, I had asked my father who the Juan Cordova was who had carved the road runner. I think he hadn't wanted to answer me, but we were honest with one another in most ways, and he finally told me. Juan Cordova was my grand-father in Santa Fe. He had given me the little carving when I was very small.

After that, my father had sometimes spoken of Juan Cordova, and his disliking had been intense. He was a tyrannical man who had ruined every human relationship he had touched, my father told me, and I was never to go near him for any reason. This of course made me more curious than ever.

The carving led me to the next in my collection of "arguments"—that dog-eared page torn from a magazine. I'd come across it when I was cutting out paper dolls one day when I was ten. The name at the top of the ad that ran down the entire page had arrested my attention.

CORDOVA, it announced in great block letters, and I had read every word of the ad eagerly.

CORDOVA was a shop in Santa Fe. It was one of the fine shops of the world, and it was owned and run by Juan Cordova. The ad spoke of his being an artist and craftsman himself, and a collector of fine articles, not only of Indian work, but of treasures from Spain and Mexico and the South American countries. There was a photograph of a portion of the shop's windows and I had looked at it many times and tried to examine in detail the carvings and ceramics and silver displayed in that window. To me, the ad said, "Come to Santa Fe." All through my childhood I had made up fantasies based on that ad and the fact that Juan Cordova was my grandfather. There was nothing frightening about it, as there was about the picture of my mother.

What else was left?

The snapshot—not very clear—of three people, with a low adobe house in the background. A man, a woman, and a child. The man was my father when he was young. The woman, my mother, wore her black hair wild at shoulder length and her face smiled gaily from the picture. With one hand she touched the shoulder of the child I had been. Whenever I looked at the small picture, it was as if something pulled at me—as if I could somehow step backward in time and recapture what it had been like to be nearly five and have both a father and a mother, a grandfather, and perhaps other relatives. But I could remember nothing of that time at all.

The letters were left, the bracelet, the brochure, and one other thing that was not tangible. I chose my grandfather's letter first and read it through once more, although I already knew it by heart.

> *Dear Amanda:*
>   *It has recently been brought to my attention that William Austin is dead. Come to see me. I want to meet Doroteo's daughter. They tell me that I have not long to live, so it must be soon. You can*

*take a plane to Albuquerque, where your cousin,
Eleanor Brand, will meet you and drive you to
Santa Fe. Wire me your flight number and the time.
I await your response.*

*Juan Cordova*

There was something imperious about the letter. It
issued commands, rather than made a request. Still, a
dying man might feel he had no time for pleading, and it
meant something to me that he wanted to see his granddaughter. I would have to act soon, or be too late. My
father had not liked or approved of him, and he had
felt that Juan Cordova had damaged my mother. He
had never wanted me to see any of that side of my family.
Was I to heed him?

The second letter was from a grandmother whose name
I had never known until I'd found her letter hidden
away in my father's desk in a sealed envelope. It was
dated three years ago, but he had never told me of its
coming. My eyes followed the strong script down the page.

*Dear William:*

*I am very ill and I want to see my granddaughter
before I die. Besides, there is much we should talk
about. You have misjudged Doroteo cruelly, and
that is something which should be mended. Please
come to see me.*

*Katy Cordova*

But William Austin, for all his kindness, his gentleness,
had a stiff New England spine. He had not gone to see
her, and I'd lost that chance to meet my grandmother.
I had no idea whether she was still alive, but I thought not,
since my grandfather had not mentioned her in his letter.
Even more than I wanted a family of my own, I wanted
to know the truth about my mother and why my father
had "misjudged" her. Now, like his wife, Katy, Juan
Cordova had written me near the end of his life, and I

felt that this time the request could not be ignored. Still I held back, doubting myself.

What must I do? How must I choose?

I picked up the brochure I'd illustrated and flipped through its pages, considering. This was the way I earned my living. As a free lance I was moderately successful and I illustrated ad copy of all sorts, but what I wanted to be was a serious painter. My father had always encouraged me, given me something special in the way of independence, of reliance on myself. He had encouraged me to develop my talent and had sent me to art school. Painting was as much a part of me as my very hands. I had a certain talent, but I wanted to do something more with it, and that was the quality in me which Johnny Hall had never understood.

This brought me to the bracelet. I slipped it over my wrist and let the sapphires shine in the reflection from the nearest window. When he had gone away, I'd tried to give the bracelet back to him, but he had dismissed the idea lightly.

"Keep it," he'd insisted. "Keep it to remind you of what you're doing to your life."

Johnny had seemed such a safe love in the beginning. He was gay, lightheartedly adventurous, breezily dominating. He was absorbed in Johnny Hall, and since I was absorbed in him too, everything was lovely. Yet falling in love had not happened suddenly in that dangerous way my father had warned me against.

"Never let your heart run away with your head," he'd told me in my growing-up years. From the things he said, I gathered that he and my mother must have fallen in love with each other instantly—with that attraction which must be magical when it happens, and at the same time dangerous, because it may not last. I was safe enough. Such attraction had never happened to me. The beginning with Johnny was slow, gradual. We had come to like each other, to enjoy being together, and then had warmed to a closer relationship that promised a happy marriage.

If it had not been for my work and my painting! They were always getting in Johnny's way. I had deadlines to meet that spoiled his plans. It grew so that he did not even want me to take a sketchbook along when he went on outings. He wanted all my attention for himself. It was all right to earn my living with my little drawings, but that wouldn't be necessary after we were married. Then I would never need to pick up a drawing pencil or a paintbrush again, except as a sort of minor amusement.

"But I want to paint!" I told him. "I want my work to be good enough to be recognized."

He laughed and kissed me. "You'll get over all that when you have me to look after. I'll make name enough for both of us, and you can be just as proud of me as you want to be. I'll eat it up!"

By that time I was thoroughly in love, and tried to think in terms of compromise. As a matter of fact, he gave me very little time to think at all. He swept me along on a gay, impulsive, overweening tide of his own desires and wishes. My father was doubtful and a little sad, but then, he would lose me when I married. I tried to be what Johnny wanted, not talking about my work, hiding it from him.

The breaking point came when a small gallery showing was arranged for some of my work. I'd done a collection of paintings in various neighborhoods of New York, including a Chinatown scene, children playing on a Harlem street, a boy and girl standing in the stern of a Staten Island ferry, watching its wake, with the Manhattan skyline in the background. There were a number of other scenes as well, for I'd enjoyed sketching and painting all around New York, even though Johnny thought it silly.

When the show was actually put on, it shocked me that he should resent it and be jealous of my work. He sneered at a modest review in the *Times,* which was remarkable to receive at all, and pointed out that Amanda Austin was pretty nearly as unheard of as before.

That was when I began to assert myself and produce

my sketchbook as I hadn't done before, even though I could see Johnny cooling before my eyes. He didn't want a career girl in his life, or even a wife who worked. He was old-fashioned and Victorian, and I began to cool a little too in the face of that realization. So when he walked out, I let him go. And when he was gone, I had for a little while a feeling of marvelous release and escape. I would never let myself in for a dominating male again. But I missed him just the same. I hadn't cooled as much as I'd thought, and there were times when I nearly phoned to tell him he could have everything his own way, if only he would come back. Something fiercely self-preserving kept me from calling.

Now a year had gone by and I was trying to ignore the ache of emptiness in me. I had my work, and I didn't want to fall in love again. I had a few men friends, but they were only that and I could take them or leave them, but it was all growing terribly flat—meaning nothing.

What I needed was a change of scene—a whole new way of life. I took off the bracelet and tossed it on the table. I wouldn't go on being lacerated because of an old love that hadn't worked out.

There was still one more thing to be considered. The intangible thing that was perhaps the strangest of all. That was my fearful nighttime dream. A frightening, recurring dream that verged on the edge of nightmare, and sometimes haunted me into the daylight.

It was always the same. There was a hard, bright light from the sky, and smudged charcoal-dark against that blue stood a tree. A very old tree, with black, twisted branches that seemed to reach toward me—as if the leafy ends were hands that would grasp and injure me. Always there was horror in my vision of the tree. A sense that if I stared at it long enough the ultimate terror would seize and engulf me. But I always woke up before whatever threatened me could happen. As a child, I'd sometimes wakened screaming, and my father had come to soothe and comfort me. As I grew older, the nightmare came less often, but it still troubled me, and I wanted to know its source. Was there such a tree out in Santa Fe? If I found the reality, would I understand the terror and be free of it?

Still—the dream was not the deciding factor. It was my grandfather's letter, the words my grandmother had written, and the miniature of my mother that made up my mind. I wanted to know the truth about Doroteo Cordova Austin—what she was like and how she had died. If there was some hidden tragedy there, I wanted it to be hidden no longer. As it was, I had roots on only one side of my family. On the other side there was empty soil that gave me an uneasy feeling. If there was darkness, it was a part of me, and I wanted to know about it. How could I understand myself when I knew nothing at all about half of my forebears? They had formed me too, and there had been times in my life when I felt an affinity to something other than my Aunt Beatrice's rock-bound New England, or my father's usually gentle ways. Sometimes there were storms let loose in me. Sometimes I too had an instinct toward that same highhanded imperiousness that showed itself in my grandfather's letter. There seemed to be a suppressed passion in me, something that needed an outlet now lacking.

So what was I? Until I knew, how could I offer myself in any sound human relationship? I had often surprised both Johnny and myself, and didn't know why. Now I must find out.

I reached for the telephone and dialed the number of an airline which flew into Albuquerque.

## *II*

Outside the airport building there was a glare of afternoon sunlight where cars and taxis stopped to let out passengers or pick them up. I stood beside my bags, not far from the end doors and the baggage area, as the wire from my cousin Eleanor Brand had instructed me. No one had been there to meet me, and no one had come since I'd arrived, though others from my plane had already collected their baggage and gone.

I waited a little impatiently, with a traveler's anxiety. I had no idea what Eleanor would look like, and since I was standing in the appointed place, she would have to find me. I paid little attention to a woman, probably in her forties, who came rushing through a door, stopped abruptly, and stood looking toward the baggage section.

That is, I paid no attention to her at first, except for a quick glance which told me she couldn't be Eleanor. Somehow I expected Eleanor to be young. But when she continued to study me fixedly, I grew uneasy. This was more than the casual interest of a stranger, and I looked at her again, meeting her gaze with my own.

She had short, rather deliberately brown hair and hazel eyes with the beginnings of crinkle lines about them. She was not very tall, but she wore her smartly tailored tan slacks well. Her citron-yellow blouse set off the strand of turquoise and silver she wore about her neck. One sensed a woman who tried a little desperately for a semblance of youth.

When she realized that I too was staring, she seemed to recover herself and gave me a half-apologetic smile as she came toward me.

"You're Amanda, of course. You couldn't be anyone but Doro's daughter. I'm sorry I stared, but you stopped me cold and I had to take you in. The resemblance is startling. I couldn't help wondering how much you're like her."

Such frankness left me at a loss and I felt a bit prickly over being so openly examined.

"Are you Eleanor—?" I began.

"No, I'm not. Though I suppose I'm a second cousin or something." She led the way toward an exit door. "I'm Sylvia Stewart, and my husband and I live next door to your grandfather. Have you been waiting long? I got off to a late start because they didn't call me until the last minute and it's an hour's drive from Santa Fe. There's trouble at the Cordova house. Eleanor has disappeared. Completely gone. God knows where. Her bed wasn't slept in last night, and Gavin, her husband, was away until this morning, so he didn't know. Here's my car. Wait till I open up and put your bags in back."

I watched her store my sketchbook along with my two bags. I'd had no time to ask questions and I contained myself until Sylvia Stewart was behind the wheel and I beside her. At least she was a relative of sorts, and I could begin to learn about my family from her.

"Have they any idea what has happened to Eleanor?" I asked as we pulled away from the curb.

She gave me another studying look that seemed to weigh and consider, as though my appearance troubled her and she was searching for some conclusion about me. The insistence of her scrutiny made me uncomfortable because something I could not understand seemed to lie behind it.

Her shrug was expressive and probably critical. "Who's to tell what would happen to Eleanor? Maybe she's been kidnaped, murdered—who knows? Though I expect that's too much to hope for. She's probably gone off somewhere on her own just to drive Gavin mad. She's rather like your mother for doing the unexpected. That's the wild Cordova streak that Juan is so proud of."

I hardly knew how to meet this torrent of haphazard information, and I gave my attention to the city outskirts we traveled through. Everything was bathed in a glare of bleached light, and I remembered involuntarily the light in my recurrent dream—blazing sunlight reflected back at the sky from the earth colors—dun and ocher—all around.

No. Sand. The color of sand—of pale mud. The earth, the buildings, everything but a hazy cobalt sky was the color of sand. The landscape was a shock to eastern eyes accustomed to granite and concrete, or suburban greenery. Yet I liked the high intensity of light on every hand. It seemed familiar, and not just because of my dream.

"I never knew my mother when I was old enough to remember her," I said. "Apparently you did?"

"I knew her." The tone was dry, enigmatic. "I grew up with her. I grew up with all of them—the Cordovas, that is."

"It's strange to be coming here to a family I know nothing about."

Again she turned her head with that openly searching glance. "You shouldn't have come here at all."

"But why not—when my grandfather wanted me to come?"

"Oh, I don't suppose it could have been avoided, really. If you hadn't come, Paul would have gone to see you in New York."

I was completely at sea. "Paul?"

"Paul Stewart is my husband. You may know his books. He's writing one now that you may be a part of. That is, you could be if you remember anything about the time when you lived here."

The name of Paul Stewart was vaguely familiar, but I didn't know his books, and I didn't see what I could possibly have to do with whatever he was writing now.

"I don't remember anything," I said. "Nothing at all. Why should it matter when I was only a small child then?"

There seemed to be a visible relief in her response to my words that puzzled me all the more.

"Probably it doesn't. Anyway, Paul will tell you about it himself. I'm afraid I can't prevent that. Though I'll admit I'm against what he intends."

This seemed a blind alley. "How ill is my grandfather?"

"His heart is bad. Mostly he stays close to the house these days. To add to his troubles, there's a clouding of his vision, so that he can't see as sharply as he used to, and glasses won't help. Of course he's been threatening to die for years—to get people to do as he wants. But this time it's for real. The doctors don't know how long he may last and he's not a very good patient."

"Then I'm glad I've come in time. I haven't any other family. I don't even know whether my grandmother is alive. I know nothing about her."

"Katy died nearly three years ago." There was a softening in Sylvia Stewart's slightly brittle tones. "Katy was wonderful. I'll love her always. You know, of course, that she was an Anglo?"

"I don't know anything," I said.

"It's like your father to do that—isolate you, I mean." The softness was gone. "He told your grandfather off pretty thoroughly before he left. Though it was thanks to the Cordovas—to Juan—that the scandal about your mother was at least minimized and never erupted into the full-scale horror it might have become. Her death devastated Juan, and Katy's heart was broken. Everyone adored your mother."

There was a hint of bitterness in her last words, and I shrank from asking this tart, gossipy woman about my mother's death. I didn't like the words "scandal" and "horror." Whatever had happened, I wanted to learn about it from a more sympathetic source. It came through rather clearly that Sylvia Stewart had not liked my mother.

"What was your relationship to Katy?" I asked.

"Her sister was my mother. My parents died when I was fairly young, and Katy took us into her family and into her heart—my stepbrother, Kirk, and me. It never mattered to her that Kirk wasn't related by blood. She was just as good to him as to the rest of us. Just the same, there wasn't any nonsense about her. Katy came from Iowa farmlands and she hated adobe walls. But she loved Juan and she put up with them without complaining. After your father took you away, Katy used to send you presents and write you letters. But they were all returned and she had to give you up."

Until just before her death, when she'd written again, I thought, and I mourned her sadly. How could my father have done this to her and to me? No matter how much he had disliked Juan Cordova, he shouldn't have kept me from my grandmother.

"Katy could love without spoiling," Sylvia went on. "In that way she was different from Juan. He has always spoiled everything human he's touched with what he calls affection. He loved my stepbrother, Kirk, more than his own son, Rafael. I suppose they were two of a kind. But I'd rather be loved by a man-eating tiger! That's what's the matter with Eleanor. You can hope he'll spare *you* his affection, Amanda."

This was something I'd have to find out for myself, and I didn't mean to let this woman, second cousin or not, prejudice me against my grandfather. I drew her attention casually away from Juan Cordova.

"I suppose there are other relatives living?"

She was willing to talk. "Eleanor and Gavin Brand live in the house. When Gavin married Eleanor some years ago, he wanted them to have a house of their own. But old Juan wouldn't have it."

As quickly as that, we were back on the topic of

my grandfather. I let her go on.

"Eleanor didn't want to move out anyway. She wanted to stay close to Juan so she could influence him. Gavin had to listen when it came to the house, since he's employed by Juan—though I'd say Juan is about the only one Gavin would listen to. Of course he should never have married Eleanor, but he was mad about her, the way men so easily are—just as they were about Doro. Are you like that, Amanda?"

The bitter note was in her voice again and I glanced at her. She was looking straight ahead at the road, and she seemed not to care whether her words distressed me.

"I've never thought of myself as a *femme fatale*," I said coolly. "Tell me who else lives in the house."

She waved a hand toward the window on my side of the car. "Don't miss the scenery, Amanda. That's Sandia Peak out there. The Sandia Mountains guard Albuquerque the way the Sangre de Cristo range guards Santa Fe."

I looked out at the massive bulk that made a close backdrop to the city, but it was not scenery which interested me most just now.

"I don't even know how many children my grandfather had—only that my mother was one of them."

"She was the youngest. Clarita was the oldest. Clarita —never married."

There seemed a slight hesitation in Sylvia's words, and again that bitterness I didn't understand. But she went on quickly.

"Clarita's still there in the house and it's a good thing your grandfather has her. Most things depend on Clarita these days. Then there was Eleanor's father, Rafael, who married an Anglo, as your mother did. You'll notice Katy had nothing to say about their names. They were all Spanish, thanks to Juan.

"When Rafael grew up, however, he would have nothing to do with being Spanish-American. He rebelled from all that Spanish heritage your grandfather dotes on. He wanted to be all Anglo and he wanted to raise his daughter that way. But when Rafael and his wife were

killed in the crash of a small plane, Juan took over as
always. So Eleanor moved into Juan's house and she's
been very close to him. Closer than she ever was to
Katy, in spite of the efforts Katy made with her. Eleanor
always had her own self-interest at heart. You might
say her first attachment was to her grandfather when she
was small, and then to Gavin Brand, who was always
in and out of the place. Now, who knows?"

Sylvia threw me one of her sidelong looks, and I suspected that she was testing the effect of all this upon me.
I said nothing, and she went on without restraint, as if she
were somehow eager to warn me away from my family.

"From the time she was in her teens, Eleanor was
bound she was going to have Gavin for a husband, and
she succeeded in snaring him." Tartness had turned cor-
rosive in her dislike for Eleanor.

"What does Gavin do for my grandfather?" I asked.

"Everything! Mark Brand, Gavin's father, was Juan's
partner when CORDOVA was first opened, and Gavin grew
up in the business. Now that his father is gone, he's
manager and chief buyer, since Juan can no longer get
around very much. Gavin tries to hold Juan to a little
sanity. It's really he who's held the store together."

I told Sylvia about the page I'd torn from a glossy
magazine—that ad about CORDOVA—and of how I'd made
up stories about it to amuse myself.

Sylvia shook her head. "Watch out for CORDOVA,
Amanda. A long time ago it became the beast that rules
the Cordovas. When we were young, we all knew the
store came before any of us. Oh, not with Katy, but always
with Juan. It's the monument on which his life is built.
Gavin's rebelling though. There's a war going on between
them over more than Eleanor. Gavin may not be pleased
to see you here. You may be a threat."

I couldn't see how that was possible, but I let it go.

"You don't seem to like anyone connected with the
Cordovas," I said.

I heard the soft gasp of the breath she drew in. "I
wonder if that's true. Maybe I haven't much reason to

like them—though they're my family as well as yours, and I grew up with Clarita and Rafael—and Doro. I suppose I hate to see Doro's daughter walk into the lair. Are you sure I can't persuade you to turn around and fly back to New York?"

I wondered why it should matter to her so much whether I stayed or left, but I didn't hesitate. "Of course not. You've made me all the more eager to know them—and make up my mind for myself."

She sighed and raised one hand from the wheel in a helpless gesture. "I've done what I can. It's up to you. I'd like to get away from Santa Fe myself and never see another Cordova. But Paul likes it here. It's good for his writing, and he's the only one I really care about. He's lived in the house next door since before your mother died. When I married him he wanted to stay there."

She was silent after that, and I gave my attention to the straight, wide highway we were traveling at seventy miles an hour, the city left behind. Mesa country stretched on either hand—the color of pale sand, dotted with juniper bushes. A tree was a rarity, except where there was a stream bed with its sprouting greenery. Uneven hill formations sprang from the dusty ground, and always in the distance there were mountains. Sometimes the near hills bore slashes of dun red and rust and burnt orange, and the always-present juniper grew like green polka dots up their sides.

I felt again that stab of familiarity. The brilliance of the light, the sand color, the wide sky above, the sense of space all around, as though the land ran on forever—all these were known to me. I had seen them before. A sense of excitement stirred in me, a feeling that I was coming home. This would be a wonderful landscape to paint. It was as if I had been born with an affinity for it. It invited me, belonged to me.

"I think I remember this," I said softly.

Sylvia Stewart threw me a quick look and I sensed again some anxiety in her. The speed of the car lessened briefly as she gave me her attention.

"Don't try to remember, Amanda. Don't try!"

"But whyever not?"

She would not answer that and gave her attention again to her driving.

The air was clear and intoxicating to breathe as we climbed toward high Santa Fe. There was little traffic at this hour and the straight road arrowed north into the distance, with now and then a crumbling adobe hut by the wayside, but no real habitation anywhere.

Recently, there had been a welcome rainstorm, and when the Sangre de Cristos came into view—the very foot of the Rockies—there was snow along the peaks. Below them the roofs of Santa Fe were visible. Anticipation began to quicken.

Once we were within the city limits, the approach turned into the usual honky-tonk that mars the outskirts of most American cities. There were the cheap hamburger stands, the gas stations, and motels.

"Pay no attention," Sylvia said. "This is an incrustation, not the real Santa Fe. We live up near Canyon Road where the artists hang out. It's an old part of town. But I'll drive you through the center first, so you can have a taste of the old city. As we'll tell you frequently, this town was founded ten years before the Pilgrims landed and it's the oldest capital in the country."

I knew that. I had always loved to read about Santa Fe. Now, however, I had a curious sense of a city set apart from the world. Where I had lived, you could hardly tell where one town ended and the next began, while all around Santa Fe stretched the wide mesa country, and behind it crouched the mountains, shutting it in, isolating it. I had a feeling that once within its environs, I was leaving all the life I knew behind, and this was a feeling I didn't altogether like. Foolish, of course. Santa Fe was an old and civilized city. This was where the conquistadores had come after marching through all those empty miles of desert. This was where the Santa Fe Trail had ended.

So it was that I came into city streets with a mingling

of homecoming, anticipation—and a curious apprehension. I supposed I could thank Sylvia Stewart for the latter, and I must get over it as quickly as I could.

We left the wide road as the streets narrowed and twisted. The buildings were the color of adobe, whether real or simulated, so there was again that glow of dull earth color drowsing in the sun. In the plaza that was the heart of the town the green of trees relieved the eye, and as we circled the central square, Sylvia pointed out the side street down which CORDOVA was located. Then she drove out of the plaza and past the Cathedral of St. Francis —that sandstone building with the twin towers that has the look of France about it. I knew of Archbishop Lamy who had erected it, and about whom Willa Cather had written in *Death Comes for the Archbishop.*

"My bookshop is down that way." Sylvia pointed. "My assistant is taking over today. You must drop in and see me soon. Now I'll take you home."

*Home!* Suddenly the word carried a ring of new meaning, in spite of my trepidation. For me it meant the end of a quest. I too was a Cordova, and no matter what Sylvia had said about them, I was eager to know my family.

We turned up the Alameda near where the Santa Fe Trail had once ended and followed a strip of green park above the dry bed of the Santa Fe River. We drove up the narrow spine of the hill that was Canyon Road, past studios and art galleries. Here the old adobe houses that had once been Spanish residences crowded close together, separated only by rounded adobe walls that enclosed houses and hidden patios. On Camino del Monte Sol we turned off and then took another turn down a narrow lane of old houses.

"There ahead—the one with the turquoise window trim and gate," Sylvia said. "That's your grandfather's house. Ours is beyond, where the next wall starts. Juan's is older than Paul's and mine—more than a hundred years."

I wanted to stop and search for recognition, but we

were past. Sylvia's next words brought disappointment.

"I won't take you there first. You'll come to our place and meet my husband. Then I'll phone Clarita and see if she's ready for you. Everything was in an upheaval when I left because of Eleanor."

Just past the Cordova house a garage faced on the narrow road, and Sylvia drove into it. From the back a door opened upon a bricked patio and we walked through. Adobe walls, shoulder high, shut out the street, and Sylvia led me across the patio and through a heavy wooden door into a long, comfortable living room with Indian rugs scattered over the floor, and a collection of Kachina dolls on two rows of shelves.

"You'll probably find Paul out in the *portal*." Sylvia gestured. "Do go out and introduce yourself. I'll be along in a moment. Tell Paul I'm calling Clarita to let her know you're here and find out if Gavin has finally done away with Eleanor, as she deserves."

I went through the door she indicated and out upon a long, porchlike open space that was level with the patio it edged. In a rattan chair at the far end sat a man who was probably in his late thirties—certainly younger than Sylvia. His thick hair, sun-bleached, rose in a crest from his forehead and grew long at the back of his neck. He wore a beige sweater against the cool May afternoon and his legs were encased in brown slacks. He heard me and turned, rising from his chair.

He was tall and lean, with a thin, rather bony face, intent gray eyes, a long chin, and a straight mouth that moved into a slight smile at the sight of me. It was a face of considerable character and I liked what I saw. But there was more than that. Something unforeseen happened in that arrested moment of time. It was as if we looked at each other with a heightened awareness. An awareness that came from nowhere and was electric in its recognition. It was as if he had said, *I am aware of you and I'm going to know you better*.

I remembered that he was Sylvia's husband, and I had to break that arrested moment with its unexpected undertones of attraction. It made me self-conscious and suddenly wary. I tried to erase it by being flippant.

"Hello," I said lightly. "I'm Amanda Austin, Juan Cordova's long-lost granddaughter. Sylvia told me to come out here and wait until she's phoned to find out whether Gavin Brand has finally done away with his wife."

I expected him to laugh over the foolish words, but instead the faint smile vanished and he bowed his head gravely.

"How do you do, Miss Austin. I'm afraid you've made a mistake. I'm not Paul Stewart. I'm Gavin Brand."

I could feel the awful sensation of bright, burning blood rushing into my cheeks. My tongue felt numb and my body stiffened. There was nothing I could say, no amends I could make.

After a moment of hideous embarrassment for me, he went on coolly. "As it happens, I'm rather concerned about Eleanor. I came over here to talk to Sylvia and Paul, to see if she might have dropped any sort of clue that would lead us to her."

I could only stammer a hapless apology. "I—I'm sorry."

His nod was as grave as before and he seemed to remove himself to some remote plane that I could not reach. I would have no welcome to the Cordova house from Gavin Brand and it was my own fault.

The appearance of Sylvia and the man who must certainly be her husband, Paul, rescued me from trying to say anything more. Sylvia seemed surprised to find Gavin here, and I caught the uncertain look she gave Paul.

"Hello, Gavin," she said. "I didn't know you were out here. I see you and Amanda have already met. Amanda, this is Paul."

Her husband came toward me, his hand outstretched. Though he moved as lightly as a cat, he was a big man. His hair, a sandy gray, was thinning at the temples, and his eyes were a color I couldn't define. There was something oddly like a challenge in the look he gave me, and I sensed an inner tension in him so that he made me as immediately uneasy as Sylvia had done.

"I've been looking forward to meeting you," he said, and there seemed some special intent in his words. His look questioned me as it searched my face, and I felt at a loss to meet it. He went on at once, fortunately expecting no response. "You'll be welcome at the Cordovas'. Old Juan's been looking forward to your coming. Indeed, we all have. May I say you look very much like your mother. I remember her quite well."

Sylvia broke in hastily, as though she did not want him to talk about my mother. "Gavin, I've just spoken to Clarita. Word came in after you left the house. Eleanor's car has been found at White Rock on the road to Los Alamos."

"White Rock?" Gavin seemed baffled. "Why would she leave it there? Do either of you have any idea?"

Sylvia shrugged. "As well there as anywhere else when Eleanor takes a notion into her head."

Paul seemed to be thinking, but before he had anything to say, I caught the look he exchanged with Gavin Brand, and I could almost hear the antagonism that crackled between the two men. It was clear that they did not like each other.

When Paul Stewart spoke, it was almost grudgingly. "That White Rock branch of the road is also the way to Bandelier. I've heard her talk about the caves there with enthusiasm—as a hideaway. Once she suggested I use them for background in one of my books, and she's talked about what fun it might be to spend a night in one of those caves. It's possible she may have gone there."

"It's wild enough for Eleanor," Sylvia said, "and she's always gone for the outdoor life. Sleeping bags and all that."

"As a matter of fact, her sleeping bag is gone." Gavin seemed to be thinking. "At least it's a lead. I'd better get out to Bandelier and have a look."

"Then may I go now to see my grandfather?" I asked Sylvia.

She shook her head. "Not right away. Though Paul will

take your luggage over soon. There's more to come. Gavin, you know that small pre-Columbian stone head that Juan had in his private collection? I understand it's been missing for a week. Now it's turned up—on a bureau in your room."

Gavin stared at her and I saw how chill his gray eyes could become. "It wasn't there a little while ago."

"Clarita found it," Sylvia said, sounding waspish, as though she might be enjoying this. "She went straight to Juan to tell him, and the old man is furious. Now there's a new uproar going on. I think you'd better wait awhile before going to the house, Amanda."

Paul said smoothly, "They'll find out how it came there, of course."

"It can wait." Gavin did not look at him. "I want to find Eleanor before I deal with anything else. I'm going to drive out to Bandelier at once. It's a long shot, perhaps, but it's the only one I have at the moment. Sylvia, if there's any further word, will you phone the park rangers out there and have them give me a message?"

She nodded a bit grimly, and I stood helplessly by while Gavin strode across the *portal*. As he passed me, he paused and turned around with a speculative look.

"You can come with me," he said with calm assurance. "You shouldn't see Juan now. Eleanor's your cousin and I may need a woman along when we find her."

I didn't believe his reasons. He wanted to get me away from Sylvia and Paul. What he'd given me was more command than request, and clearly he expected no refusal. This was the last thing I wanted to do. I had no wish to be in the company of this cool, remote man to whom I'd been so instantly attracted, and whom I'd insulted so cruelly. It seemed, however, that I had no choice. He expected me to come and his will dominated my own, whether I liked it or not. At least going with him would be better than an idle marking of time.

"I'll come," I said, as though he had been waiting for my assent.

We went out of the Stewarts' house together and he

seemed very tall at my side. The crest of his sun-bleached hair shone in the clear light as we crossed the patio, and I thrust away the memory of that first attraction. He couldn't have been more distant if he'd existed on another planet.

# III

Gavin took the road to Taos north out of Santa Fe. He drove at the maximum speed with an assurance that commanded the car as he had commanded me. I reminded myself that this was exactly the sort of man I did not like.

I had not expected to be traveling again so soon, and I regretted the further postponement of my meeting with the Cordovas. But thanks to my foolish words to Gavin, which had put me at a disadvantage, and his own rather highhanded commandeering of my company, here I was on the way to a national monument called Bandelier, of which I'd never heard before.

Most of the time we were silent, and once or twice I stole a sidelong look at my imperturbable companion. It gave me pleasure to dislike him, but at the same time the shape of his head, the planes of his face intrigued me as a painter. My fingers itched for a pencil so that I could catch an impression of that forceful head on paper. I wondered if I could paint him. I wasn't at my best in portraiture, but an interesting face always challenged me.

His voice broke into my thoughts. "I suppose you wonder why I took you away from the Stewarts so abruptly?"

"I did wonder—yes."

"I didn't want to leave you there for Paul to prey on."

"Prey on? What do you mean?"

"You might as well know—he's writing a book, and he wants to pick your memory, if he can."

"Sylvia said something of the same thing. But how can anyone pick a five-year-old child's memory? What sort of book is it?"

He stared grimly at the road ahead. "A chapter will deal with the Cordovas—specifically with your mother's death. How much do you know about that?"

I could feel myself tense. "I don't know anything, really. You see, my father would never talk about her or tell me what happened to her. All I know is that she died in a fall. That's one reason I've come here. Somehow, it's terribly important for me to—well, to know all about her. All about the Cordova side of my family."

He glanced at me and I met his look, to find unexpected sympathy there, though he went on without commenting on my words.

"Your grandfather is very much against Paul's writing about the Cordovas. And I agree with him. It will do no one any good to dig up an old scandal at this late date. You least of all."

I didn't like the sound of this. "Sylvia talked about a scandal too. But what scandal? If there is anything to do with my mother—scandal or not—I want to know it. Why shouldn't I?"

"Better let it rest," he said. "You'll only bruise yourself."

"I don't care about that—I want to know! This is maddening!"

He threw me a quick look in which there was a certain grim amusement. "The Cordova stubbornness! It sticks out all over you."

"Perhaps it's only my New England side," I told him.

Neither of us spoke for a while. When we turned off the Taos road toward the Jemez Mountains which rose beyond Los Alamos, we had the snow-crested Sangre de Cristos at our back, and I studied the landscape with the same interest I'd felt on the trip from Albuquerque. This was a different world from the one I was used to.

I was glad I had done some map studying before I'd left New York and knew something about the locality. Well over on our right appeared a massive, curiously black mountain, standing alone, with its sides rising straight up to the flat mesa of its top. I watched it intently as we drove parallel with it. Memory seemed to stir and a name came to me from nowhere.

"Black Mesa," I said, surprising myself. The name was not one I had noted on a map.

"So there are things you remember?" Gavin said.

"I keep having flashes of familiarity, so that I feel I've seen this country before. As of course I have. I must have made this trip with my parents when I was small."

We were driving through mesa country and the hills ahead were like sandy ships riding a juniper-green sea. Sometimes their tops were crowned by spiked pinnacles of rock and there were often caves in the sandstone. Perhaps all of this was known to me, though I had no further flash of recognition as I'd had with Black Mesa. But I could not relax and give myself to an enjoyment of the scene. Always there were questions to be asked.

"Did you know my mother?" I spoke the words into the silence that was broken only by the rush of the car.

"Yes, I knew her," he said, but offered nothing more, frustrating me further.

"My father would never talk about her," I repeated doggedly. "It's strange to have grown up without any memories or knowledge of Doroteo Cordova Austin."

"At fifteen, I found it hard to understand what Doro saw in your father," Gavin said. "He was her opposite in every way."

I wondered if he were prodding me to indignation, but he seemed too uninvolved for that, too indifferent.

"Can you remember me?" I asked.

"Very well." His straight mouth softened briefly. "You were an engaging little girl and very like your mother."

For just an instant I relaxed toward him. No matter what denials I'd made to myself, something in me wanted to like this man. His next words dampened my own softening, and I knew he would not for long make concessions to the past.

"It's too bad engaging little girls have to grow up," he said.

The words seemed simply an opinion calmly expressed. He was not taunting me, but he cared nothing about how I might feel. The earlier flash of sympathy I'd seen was gone, and I moved away from him in the seat, disliking the twinge of hurt I felt, and wanting to show my resistance to anything he might say. He didn't seem to notice, and we said nothing more until we reached White Rock.

"This is where Eleanor left her car," he told me. "I won't stop now to check with the police. If she went to Bandelier, it's possible she thumbed a ride from here."

It was a sand-colored New Mexico town, quickly lost in the landscape, and we were away on the winding road to the park.

"Do you know why she's gone off?" I asked, still prickling from his remark about growing up.

"She'll probably have a good many reasons," he said. "What the real one is I'd better not try to guess."

"Sylvia spoke about a wild Cordova streak in Eleanor that my mother had too. That sounds like nonsense to me—a wildness in the blood and all that."

"Juan will tell you it's anything but nonsense. But can't you speak for yourself? You're a Cordova."

"I like to think that I'm fairly well balanced," I told him.

"My congratulations." His tone was dry, and I was silent after that, my anger beginning to boil. I could not like Gavin Brand, and my sympathy for my cousin was increasing. I wouldn't even accept Sylvia's estimation of her until I had a chance to judge for myself.

After several miles, during which I simmered down a little, we reached the admission booth to the park, where Gavin stopped to pay an entry fee. He asked the man in the booth if he had noticed a tall woman with long fair hair who might have checked through with someone else yesterday.

The attendant shook his head. "Too many people come through for me to remember. There's probably been a lot of girls with long blond hair. I don't keep track."

"Doesn't the park have a closing time?" I asked as we drove through the entrance. "Don't people have to get out then?"

"The place is enormous, with miles of trails," Gavin said. "And there are always campers staying overnight. I don't think they make a head count when day visitors leave."

The road wound downward toward the bottom of the canyon and high cliffs rose on either hand, tree-covered on one side, steep volcanic ash on the other.

"Why is it a national monument?" I asked.

"The Indians were here until around 1500. You'll see the ruins of their dwellings and kivas. It's all being carefully preserved."

And he was being carefully polite—the courteous guide.

"But if there are miles of trails, how will you find her?"

"Paul thinks the caves interested her most, and they'd offer shelter. We can have a look at some of them. It depends on how far she'd be willing to wander off the main path, whether we'll find her or not. If she's here, I suspect it won't be far."

"But if she really wants to hide—"

"*If* she really does," Gavin said quietly, "then she can elude us. But I suspect that by this time, if she's here, she'll want to be found. Paul was pretty ready with information about where she might be. It could have been planted."

I did not understand in the least why Eleanor Brand

had suddenly run away from home to spend the night in so unlikely a place. Or why any information about her would be "planted."

However, I knew he would explain none of this. There had been an edge to his voice when he spoke Paul's name, and I decided to be bold, asking my question swiftly.

"Why don't you like Paul Stewart?"

He gave me a look that said this was none of my business, but he answered. "Dislike can be a complex matter. For one thing, he has an avidity for stirring up trouble. Stay clear of him."

Perhaps I would, or perhaps I wouldn't. In any case, I meant to go my own way.

The sun was out now, but the air was chilly and I was glad I wore a sweater.

"Doesn't it get pretty cold here at night?" I asked.

"Decidedly. But Eleanor could manage if she chose."

I wanted to ask why—why? But his manner held me off.

Near the small building of the Visitor Center, Gavin parked his car and we got out. He glanced at the low-heeled shoes I'd worn for travel and nodded.

"You'll be all right. It's not a difficult path or very long."

The narrow road had been paved for comfortable walking, and it wound into the open along the floor of the canyon. Again I had the sense of a world wholly new to me. The canyon ran straight, with steep cliffs going up on either hand, wooded on one side, bare rock on the other, so that it was as if one walked into a wide slash in the earth, shut in on both sides, protected. On our right the sheer cliffs rose toward the sky and at their base in the pockmarked volcanic rock were caves that Indians had used. There were dozens of these and one could climb to them only over rough ground.

Gavin saw the direction of my gaze and shook his head. "If she's here, she'll probably choose the easier way. We'll follow the trail." He seemed assured in his knowledge of her and not particularly worried.

There were the ruins of kivas along the path—those buildings which had once been used as meeting places for religious and ceremonial rites. There were stone ruins in the ground where the ancient pueblo of Tyuonyi had encircled a central plaza. It had once been three stories high, accommodating a hundred people or more, Gavin told me. At another time I'd have been more interested.

The trail turned toward the base of the cliffs and began to climb until we were edging along just below the caves and reconstructed cliff dwellings. For the first time I grew a little breathless at this slight exertion, responding to the unaccustomed altitude. Gavin noticed and slowed his pace, not without a certain consideration.

Now he stopped before each cave and looked inside. Where a wooden ladder was propped against the cliff, he climbed up to peer through the opening. We had mounted fairly high above the canyon floor, and there were occasional steps cut into the narrow, rock path. The cliff face was uneven, with indentations or sections that thrust outward, so that the trail turned like a string twisted across its surface. Only once did other visitors pass us, coming from the opposite direction, and the floor of the canyon, far below, with its winding stream and groves of trees, seemed empty. The vast reaches of Bandelier could swallow hundreds. We began to alternate now. I took one cave, and Gavin the next, so we could increase the speed of our search.

It was I who found her. At first, when I climbed the short ladder to look into shadowed cavern depths, I saw nothing. Then something at the back moved and I glimpsed a face peering from a sleeping bag on the rocky floor.

"Eleanor?" I said.

There were sounds at the back of the cave as she came out of her bag. But she did not approach me. She merely sat crosslegged upon the bag, staring at the patch of dark I must have made against the brightness outside. I could not see her clearly in the dim light.

"Who are you?" she asked, and I heard for the first

time the light, rather musical voice that belonged to Eleanor Brand. It was a voice which lent itself to mockery.

I told her I was her cousin Amanda Austin, but she cut me short with a wave of her hand that seemed imperious.

"Is Gavin there?"

"Of course," I said. "I've been helping him look for you. He's been concerned."

"Has he really?" Here was more mockery, and she still made no move to come out of the cave.

I waited helplessly on the ladder as Gavin crawled out of the next cave and came toward me. When I gestured and descended the ladder, he went up it at once, calling to her through the opening.

"Come out, Eleanor. The game's over for the moment. So roll up your bag and come out."

Her soft laughter, issuing from the cave, had a faintly vindictive sound, but I could hear her preparations as she rolled up her bag. Gavin backed down the ladder, and she came to the rocky lip of the cave and tipped her sleeping bag over, letting it drop to the path. Then she backed out, her short alpine hikers finding the rungs of the ladder, blue jeans, thick blue pullover sweater and long blond hair coming into view, until she stood on the path beside us, and I had my first view of my cousin Eleanor.

She was older than I by five years or more, I judged, and for all her unconventional position at the moment, she was a poised and confident woman. And a very beautiful one, with her violet eyes and thick lashes, her full, slightly pouting lips, and that fine hair cut in bangs across a smooth forehead, falling in a sheen over her shoulders. It seemed untangled, as though she might have been calmly combing it recently. She paid no attention to Gavin, but looked straight at me, still mocking, hardly friendly.

"So you're Doro's daughter? How much like her are you?"

It was not a question I could answer, and I made no attempt to reply. She was not really interested in me anyway, in spite of her attempt to ignore Gavin.

He spoke to her curtly. "You were supposed to meet Amanda at the airport at Albuquerque. Sylvia had to go in your stead."

"I supposed she would. Juan should never have asked me to go in the first place. Why should I be happy about Amanda's coming, considering the plotting he's likely to do? So I went off by myself for a while. To state my independence and let you all worry a little. I had a lovely night. There were a million stars, and all those Indian ghosts were stirring down there in the canyon. I'm sure I heard their drums."

Gavin ignored this flight of fancy. "There is such a thing as consideration," he said.

She laughed softly again, maliciously. "Have I ever bothered about that?"

Gavin remained unmoved by what seemed a deliberate effort to irritate him.

"Are you hungry?" he asked her.

"Of course not. I had sandwiches and cans of orange juice. I've finished everything up."

"You planned well," he said dryly. "My arrival is properly timed."

"You can never let me go, can you? You always come after me!" Tall as she was, she was not as tall as Gavin, and she tilted her head back to look up at him with a look that challenged and provoked.

"Your grandfather was worried. He wanted me to find you."

"I thought he would be. That was a bang-up fight the three of us had yesterday, wasn't it? Maybe you'll both begin to think about what *I* want now."

Gavin turned away from her. "Let's get back to White Rock. We can pick up your car there and phone Santa Fe."

I had the feeling that this woman had the power to hurt him, and I felt an unexpected pang of sympathy for Gavin. I'd known what it was like to be hurt by someone you loved.

He went ahead of us along the cliff's face, carrying Eleanor's sleeping bag, and she gave me a small smile filled with malice and triumph as she went after him.

I followed uneasily behind. Something stubborn stirred in me, stiffening my resistance. It looked as if I would have to stand against them all. Well, Juan Cordova had asked me to come, and only he mattered.

When we were in the car heading for White Rock, no one spoke. We sat in the front seat, with me in the middle, and the miles of curving road wound away in heavy silence. What was unspoken throbbed beneath our quiet.

At White Rock we picked up Eleanor's abandoned car, and a change was made. She and I were to return in her car, while Gavin followed us in his own. I would have liked to protest this arrangement because I felt an instinctive reluctance to be alone with my cousin Eleanor. Even more than the others, she seemed to oppose my coming, and her uninhibited frankness about this left me thoroughly annoyed. Gavin, however, was ordering us both, and this was not the time to argue. At his biding, I got reluctantly into the passenger's seat of Eleanor's car, and he went around to the driver's side to speak to her.

"You'd better go straight back to Santa Fe," he said. "Amanda has been traveling most of the day, and I'm sure she'd like a rest." His manner toward her was withdrawn, remote, but I sensed that it covered some deep emotion—whether of anger or frustrated love, I couldn't tell. His guard of indifference hid a deeper seething, I was sure. What would he be like if he exploded? More likable, perhaps—more human?

Eleanor smiled at him brightly and he walked away to his own car. Without waiting for him to get in, she switched on the motor, and by the time we turned onto the highway we were going fast, and Gavin was nowhere in sight behind us. Eleanor seemed to relax a little, her hands assured on the wheel. I noticed the diamond-set platinum band on her left hand, and the large turquoise and silver ring on her right. They were beautiful hands, with long slender fingers, the sinews hidden by smoothly rounded flesh. I hid my own utilitarian hands in my lap. Mine were working hands, square, with spatulate finger-tips. It didn't comfort me to know they were an artist's hands.

My cousin threw me a sudden questioning glance, bright with reckless promise. "We don't have to go back to Santa Fe, you know. There's a choice of roads. Gavin will be wild if we're not back at Juan's by the time he gets there. Shall we provoke him?"

The prospect of driving aimlessly about the country-side with this woman who didn't like me had no appeal, nor did it seem anything but pointless for her to defy Gavin and our grandfather any further.

"I think we'd better go back," I said. "I want a room of my own and a bed I can stretch out on."

Her lips curled in a smile that dismissed me. "I didn't think you'd pick up a challenge. And I suppose we do have to go back. I don't mind making Juan angry—but not too angry. Why did you come with Gavin to look for me?"

"He asked me to."

"Of course," she said. "Women usually do what he asks. But why did you come to Santa Fe? Whatever possessed you to say 'yes' to Juan's letter?"

"I suppose because I wanted to know the other half of my family."

This seemed to strike her as amusing. "You'll regret that soon enough. Juan will want to know what I think of you. What shall I tell him?"

"How can you tell him anything?" I was beginning to feel tired, and her behavior was increasingly outrageous. Any sympathy I might have felt was now on Gavin's side. No wonder he tried to remain distant and untouched. "You don't know me yet," I pointed out, a bit sharply. "There's nothing to tell."

She smiled secretly to herself, and I let the matter go,

though I could not help wondering what she might find to tell Juan Cordova.

By the time we reached the main highway, dark clouds were boiling up over the Jemez Mountains behind us, but Eleanor only shook her head when I commented that it looked like rain.

"Clouds often come up like that, but we seldom get much rain. We need it badly."

Far ahead across the countryside a whirlpool of dust rose in a spiral like a miniature cyclone, spinning along above the junipers. A dust dance, I thought, and knew that the phrase had again come, unbidden, out of memory. I had seen those spirals before and been fascinated by them. I glanced at the woman beside me.

"I don't remember you at all," I said. "Can you remember me?"

"I can remember your sitting on Grandfather Juan's knee. I can remember being jealous. But that was when we were babies, of course. I don't need to be now."

Yet she was, I thought. She deeply resented his sending for me.

"I wonder what's happened since I've been gone," she went on. "What have you heard?"

"I haven't been to the house yet," I told her. "Sylvia Stewart took me next door, where I met Gavin and her husband, Paul."

"Gavin at Paul's house? That's quite mad. They don't like each other."

"Gavin was concerned for you. And it was Paul who suggested Bandelier's caves to him."

"Good for Paul. I really didn't want to stay another night. But I had to let him find me dramatically."

"Why did you go off in the first place?" I asked her bluntly. "Why stay there at all?"

She seemed not to resent my questioning. "That's complicated." Again there was the sidelong look. "Mostly I had to give Gavin and Juan a chance to cool off and start worrying about me. They're both a little afraid of me, you know. They don't dare push me too far."

I wondered if the quarrel she referred to had in any way concerned me, but I didn't ask. Eleanor had wanted news and I volunteered the only bit I had in order to see her reaction.

"It seems that Aunt Clarita found some sort of pre-Columbian stone head in Gavin's room. Sylvia said it had been missing for a week."

The light laughter came again. "That's lovely! Though I'm glad I wasn't there or they might have said I'd planted it. Juan will be furious. What did Gavin say?"

"Merely that he'd have to look for you before he gave his attention to anything else. I'm afraid I don't understand what all this is about."

"You don't need to," Eleanor said. "You won't be staying in Santa Fe long enough for it to matter."

I was silent, not knowing how long I would be there, and not liking the way she had put it. There seemed something that was almost a threat underlying her words —and I wouldn't be threatened.

"He's very hard to please—Grandfather Juan," she went on. "You'll irritate him like everyone else, and he'll soon send you away. I'm the only one he can tolerate these days. I'm the only one he listens to. Except perhaps Gavin. But he'll stop listening to him soon. Gavin's grown too highhanded, too overconfident. This stone head, for instance."

"But of course he didn't take it," I said.

"Of course he took it. He's been slipping things out of the store for the last year or so. I suppose he has a market where he can sell them. Juan's got to wake up about him sometime."

I didn't believe any of this, and my sympathy for Gavin increased. His wife was completely vindictive toward him, and I wondered how much he was hurt by this.

Eleanor was silent for a time, and I made no further effort at conversation. When she spoke again, her question startled me.

"I supposed you've learned by this time why Juan has brought you here?"

I hesitated. "I thought he wanted to see Doroteo's daughter."

"Oh, that's the angle he'll undoubtedly play up. The daughter of his favorite child and all that. He's been rubbing it in with the rest of us. But there's a better reason than that. If you don't know, you soon will."

"Is it something to do with Paul Stewart's book?"

"So you've heard about that? I'm the one who put Paul up to it, really, and now he's determined to carry through and write it, no matter how Juan Cordova feels. Grandfather's furious."

"Then why do you want to see this book written?"

The mocking little smile was on her lips again. "Family scandals don't bother me. And this annoys Juan. After all the hushing up he's done over the years, he doesn't want it all dug up again now. But I don't mind. It may give me a lever over him."

"Hushing up of what?"

"You mean you don't know?"

"I don't remember anything, and I'm getting tired of all this hinting and secrecy. What on earth is it all about?"

"I could tell you, but I won't. Not after the orders Juan has laid down. No one is to talk to you about it until he does."

By this time I was thoroughly discomfited and angry. It was clear that my mother had been involved in something quite dreadful, and I could only cling for reassurance to the thought of Katy's letter and what she had written my father. But I didn't want to tell Eleanor about that, and open myself to more derision.

"Anyway, I haven't any memories about Santa Fe to tell anyone," I said.

"If that's true, Paul will be disappointed. But it's hard to believe you don't remember anything. Perhaps it will begin to come back, once you're in a familiar place."

I thought of the tugs of unexpected recognition I'd

already felt, and wondered if this was true.

By this time the outskirts of the city were coming into view and from the northern approach there was less honky-tonk than from the Albuquerque direction. I was relieved to find our journey ending, as I felt an increasing distrust of Eleanor, and a growing conviction that if she could injure me with Juan Cordova, she would.

In a short time we were driving through Santa Fe streets at a more decorous speed, and I tried to rouse myself in preparation for the encounters that were to come. After all that had happened since my arrival, I felt emotionally drained, and it was difficult to recover any sense of anticipation. If anything, a feeling of dread had replaced all eagerness.

We took a wide avenue that led uphill to the Canyon Road area and found our narrow lane with its adobe houses. The Cordova garage, with room for several cars, was tucked into a corner of the property where it abutted on an adobe wall. I got out of the car and looked around, wishing I could recapture my first feeling of excitement at sight of the house.

The afternoon had grown late, but turquoise-trimmed windows and painted gate still shone in bright sunlight, and rounded adobe walls encircled the house in smooth, pale ivory. Deliberately, I put everything else from my mind and thought of painting, of color. Ivory wasn't right. Flesh? No, that was too pinky. Pale apricot, perhaps? If I painted any of this I would try earth colors— red and yellow ochers and Venetian red. Perhaps a touch of viridian green for the shadows. Eleanor's voice brought me back from the thought of painting, made me stiffen for the next test.

"Has our adobe put you into a trance? Come along and I'll take you to Aunt Clarita."

We went in at the front, by way of the turquoise gate. The house seemed low and not particularly impressive— small to house a family—but that was its deception. I was to learn later that it had grown by addition to addition over the years, so that it ambled into many rooms and passageways, gaining its own individuality and character, as well as a sense of secrecy—of concealment behind closed doors and outer walls.

Eleanor led me across a narrow yard, through a carved wooden door and into the Cordova living room. I had come home to my beginnings, and I had no feeling now that there would be welcome for me here. Instead, adobe walls seemed to close me in tightly, shutting out sunlight, enveloping me in a cool gloom, holding me prisoner.

I tried to shake off such fantasy as I stood looking about the room. Nothing imprisoned me. I was quite free to walk away any time I wished. It was foolish to feel a faint prickling up my spine—as though there were something in this house for me to fear. Something hidden deep in old memory.

# IV

The room was long and cool, with white painted walls and the contrast of dark wood. Overhead, the bare pine beams that supported the flat roof, and which I would learn to call "vigas," were dark brown stripes against the white ceiling, each ending in a wooden corbel where it met the wall. Navajo rugs, black, crimson, and gray in their striking patterns, were scattered across a polished red brick floor. The corner fireplace was adobe, rounded and smooth like the outdoor walls, with a crude, narrow mantel. Beside it along one wall stretched a built-in *banco,* a typical fireplace bench, piled with cushions of henna and pine green. Beside the chimney hung a long strand of red chili pods, drying and decorative, and within the fire-bricks of the hearth white piñon logs were piled, waiting to be lighted. Two dark leather chairs had been drawn up before the fireplace, with Indian rugs tossed over their seats and backs. All the furniture had a dark, Spanish look, with considerable use of leather and deep carving. From the center of the ceiling hung an ancient wrought-iron chandelier on a chain, casting a soft light in the cool, dim room.

All around on shelves and small tables were skillful wood carvings of desert animals. Probably they had

49

been created by Juan Cordova, but they were not like my amusing little road runner. Each seemed to be performing some cruelty, however natural to the species. A horned toad had a half-eaten winged creature in its mouth. The tarantula looked fearfully alive. I turned my attention quickly to a painting of the Sangre de Cristos that hung upon one wall, the high snow peaks shining in the sun, and a girdle of evergreens climbing the slopes below. Here there was no threat of death by a predator.

My impression was of a room wholly southwestern in character, yet I recognized nothing about it except for some vague haunting of disquiet which existed in me. I tried to tell myself that I had come home. Very soon I would meet my mother's sister, my mother's father. Eleanor and Gavin did not matter. I waited not only for some greeting, but for a recognition within me that did not come. There was no easing of that barely perceptible pulse of anxiety that seemed to beat at the back of my mind, carrying in it something close to fear. There was some memory here, after all, but I did not know with my mind what it was my senses remembered.

Eleanor said, "She'll have heard us. She'll be here soon."

Doorways with carved wooden arches led off from this central room, and in one corner were steps that mounted to a little balcony at half-level, with a closed, recessed door beyond it. As I glanced toward the door it opened. A woman came out on the balcony and I saw Clarita Cordova for the first time.

She was tall and very thin, not having turned to plumpness with the years, as many Spanish women do. She was dressed almost wholly in black, even to her stockings and black buckled shoes. Only at her throat fine ivory lace in a modern ruff offered relief and threw reflected light into her narrow face. Her hair was as black as mine, and she wore it pulled severely down from a center part and wound low at the base of her neck. From her ears hung an unexpected touch of color in dangling turquoise and silver that danced whenever she moved. She looked wholly Spanish. If my grandmother Katy's blood had come down to her, it did not show outwardly.

It was not her appearance, however, which made the most impression on me, but the manner in which she stood on her small balcony and stared at me with narrowed eyes, as though she weighed and judged me— for whatever reason I could not tell. I was reminded of the manner in which Sylvia Stewart had stared at the airport, measuring me. All of them questioned me silently, resented my presence, and held secret their thoughts about me. I tipped my chin, staring back, resisting the strange sense of some mental pressure this woman put upon me. I would not be downed by these Cordovas. It was my grandfather who wanted me here. And I wasn't Spanish—I was from New England. Perhaps that was one of the things I would discover about myself.

Almost gleefully, Eleanor let the moment grow long before she spoke. "Aunt Clarita, this is Amanda. This is your sister Doro's daughter." There was something overly dramatic in her tone, as though she meant to torment the older woman in some way with my presence.

Clarita gave me a slight nod of recognition and then looked at Eleanor. It was a strange look—both affectionate and despairing, as she spoke to her in Spanish. Eleanor shrugged her indifference and answered in English.

"I chose to go away. I'd had enough of all of you. That's all there is to it."

Clarita came down the steps into the room. "We will talk later," she said to Eleanor, and her attention turned again upon me. Once more I felt that sense of pressure, a sense that something I did not understand was required of me. "So you are Doroteo's daughter?" She held out her hand to me, though the gesture did not seem wholly welcoming.

"And you are my mother's sister," I said, taking her hand. It was thin, with jewels on the fingers, and it released mine at once.

A pretty young Spanish-American girl came into the room and Clarita spoke to her.

"Rosa, you will take Miss Austin to her room, please. Your luggage is there waiting for you, Amanda."

The girl smiled at me with a flash of white teeth and stood waiting.

"You are tired, Amanda?" Clarita said. "You would like coffee—something to eat?"

"No, thank you. Just to wash and rest for a little while. My grandfather—how is he?"

Clarita's dark eyes were large and placed deeply beneath the bony structure of her brows. When her heavy lids closed over them, the sense of pressure upon me seemed to lighten.

"He is not well today. Eleanor has disturbed him. It is best if you do not see him at once."

I was no longer impatient to see him, but all too willing to postpone the meeting until I felt rested and stronger. The experience of meeting Clarita had further dampened any eagerness I might have felt. My father had been right. Nothing about this house or family reassured me. There was something ominous in the very air—some warning that was part of the walls and dark vigas, of those omnivorous carved creatures my grandfather had made.

"Go with Rosa then," Clarita said, gesturing toward the maid. "There is time to rest before dinner. We have given you our one upstairs room. It belonged to Doroteo when she was young. Eleanor, I wish to speak with you."

I went with Rosa through an arched doorway into another room that seemed an extension of the living room, except that a passageway toward the rear of the house branched off from it, evidently leading to bedrooms, and at one corner a flight of narrow stairs rose toward an open doorway above. Rosa climbed the stairs, and I followed.

Here was welcome contrast to the dark room downstairs. This was a high place of windows—windows on three sides, set deep into thick adobe walls. A bright room with white walls, overhead vigas, and a splash of color where a Navajo blanket hung against the white.

Over the small, rather narrow bed was a framed painting of mesa country—rather good. I liked the shadows across the sunny land, the chiaroscuro of light and dark. Had that picture been here when my mother was a girl? I thought not—its execution was too modern. The very brush strokes belonged to today.

Yet this was my mother's room. It had known her as I did not. The views from the windows were those she had seen. I moved from one window to the next, looking out, and a whisper of familiarity went through me again. Perhaps long ago someone had held me up to those windows and I had delighted even then in the beauty they framed. The Sangre de Cristos with snow on their crests were visible from one side, the more distant Jemez Mountains which I'd approached with Gavin that afternoon were on the other. A third window looked out upon the surprise of a large patio behind the house, and gave onto a vista down the hillside into an arroyo. Something quivered in me, like the kindling of old fear. What was it everyone expected me to remember?

Rosa motioned to where my bags and painting gear stood near a wall. "All is ready for you. This is best room. It is better than downstairs." Her smile wavered and she gave an odd little shiver.

"I'm sure it is," I said. "Thank you."

Perhaps I understood what she meant. Up here I was above those outer walls that sealed in the Cordovas. Up here I was free—except when I looked out toward the arroyo. That was when something stirred that led to horror. I didn't want to recapture that feeling, whatever it was, and I turned quickly away.

Rosa went out of the room, leaving uneasiness behind her. I tried to shake it off. I mustn't give in to some absurd and unhealthy haunting.

The bathroom was in a passageway near the foot of the stairs, and when I had taken a few things from a bag, I went down to freshen up. From the door to the living room I could hear the murmur of voices, speaking in Spanish again, and I suspected that Eleanor was being reproached for her escapade. I could imagine how casually she would dismiss any lecturing from Clarita. Yet her aunt, in spite of her severity, had seemed to show an affection for my cousin.

The bathroom had been remodeled and it sparkled with decorative Mexican tiles. There was a wide mirror over the wash basin and I looked into it as I brushed my hair and recoiled the knot at the back of my head. Cool water freshened and rested me a little, and I felt better with a touch of lipstick to make me look courageous. Now I would lie down on the bed that had been my mother's, and see if I could renew myself before the ordeal of dinner. But I was not to do that right away.

When I climbed back up the flight of stairs to my room and went through the door I had left open, it was to find Eleanor standing in the center of the room, obviously waiting for me. She had changed from wrinkled jeans and pullover to violet linen that matched the color of her eyes. Her windblown bangs had been fluffed, and her hair had been brushed to a smooth sheen and hung down her back nearly to her waist, longer than mine. I had no wish to see her, but here she was, and I was aware that she appraised me, just as I did her.

"You're all Anglo, aren't you?" she said. "In spite of all that black hair. Juan won't like it."

"What difference does it make? My mother was his daughter."

"Just as my father was his son. But I'm the one who is all Spanish in temperament, in spite of the fact that I'm fair. Juan knows that Spain is in my blood and he's proud of that."

I found it hard to carry on any sort of conversation with her. "Does he permit you to call him by his first name?"

"Permit? What is that? Sometimes I do and sometimes I don't. Oh, don't think I call him that to his face. Not the hidalgo. We all have to play to his delusion."

I wished she would go away. I had no desire to discuss our grandfather with Eleanor Brand. But I might as well find out all I could if she wanted to talk.

"What delusion is that?"

She shrugged lightly. "That he comes down straight from the conquistadores—a son of old Spain. He forgets the children of Montezuma with whom the conquistadores mated. Don't expect to find this a typical Spanish-American family, Amanda. Chicano is not a word that is used in this house."

"And does Clarita share this—delusion, as you call it?"

"She's Spanish to her fingertips. You'd never guess that Katy was her mother. But it doesn't get her anywhere with Juan. He thinks she's a poor thing for a Cordova."

I hadn't thought her a poor thing. I'd sensed a good deal of Spanish pride in the woman, as well as some dark force that I didn't understand.

"Why did you come to my room?" I asked Eleanor.

She moved about gracefully in her violet frock, glancing at the picture over the bed, looking out the window toward the arroyo. When she turned back to me, I thought for a moment she meant to say something pertinent, but she only shrugged again.

"Go away, Amanda. Don't stay here. No one wants you. Not even Juan. He'll only use you if you stay. He'll play with you—the way those carved monsters downstairs play with their victims. He's carnivorous, really."

"Aren't you being melodramatic?" I said.

Her eyes narrowed a little as she looked at me and her mouth had a tight, drawn set that had a hint of cruelty. I wondered if that was a trait of Juan's too, revealed in those carvings.

"We're a melodramatic family," she told me. "We are always at stage center. Go away before we hurt you."

"Whether I stay for a while or not is between Juan Cordova and me," I told her. "It's being made perfectly clear by everyone else that I'm not wanted here. But it's my grandfather who asked me to come. And he's the one I want to see."

"You may harm yourself by staying."

"Harm myself? How?"

"You'd better remember all that wild Spanish blood that flows in the veins of the Cordovas. It's better if you don't find it being used against you. It will do you no good."

"But I have some of that Spanish blood. It surfaces at times."

She looked at me as though I had said something significant. "Then you do have it too? The blood of our legendary dwarf?"

"What are you talking about?" I demanded.

But she had finished with her purpose in coming here. With a flick of her fingers she turned away and went out of the room, moving as gracefully as a dancer.

Until she had gone lightly down the stairs, I stood quite still, looking after her. Then I went to close the door. There was no bolt or key, or I would have locked it. When it was shut, I flung myself upon the bed, longing for rest and quiet and a stilling of the throb that had begun in my head.

*Dwarf*—there was that frightening word again. But I didn't know what it meant, and I must not think of it now. I closed my eyes and tried to drift into nothingness. I didn't want to think about the lack of welcome for me in this house. And I didn't think of it. With my eyes closed I saw—unexpectedly—Gavin Brand's face, with its marked cheekbones and straight mouth, his fine head crowned with thick, fair hair that grew to a point at the back of his neck. And then I remembered that same face a moment later when he had turned cold and remote and ready to dismiss me as someone he did not care to know.

But I didn't want to think about Gavin either. I didn't want to think of anything. I could only wait and see how events developed. I could only wait for the meeting with my grandfather. It was he who had sent for me, he who wanted me here. I must have faith in that fact. None of the others mattered. I had already given up my fantasy of a close, warm relationship with my family. I couldn't imagine any genuine warmth between me and Clarita. Nor with Eleanor. Of them all, I really liked Sylvia Stewart best. But she too had warned me away, and apparently her husband was engaged in a writing enterprise that was stirring up the Cordovas, and which concerned me because it concerned my mother. I was being plunged into some strange maelstrom that seemed to have surfaced at my coming. My mother was involved, and something hung over this house which had not died with her death. Juan Cordova must tell me what it was.

My thoughts stopped surging at last, and I fell wearily asleep. When I awakened, Rosa was tapping at my door to tell me that dinner would be served shortly. Daylight had faded and the lights of what must be Los Alamos twinkled against distant mountains. The breeze that came in the windows was cool.

I rolled off my bed, found a light switch and went to look in the dressing table mirror. It was an old mirror, its silvering marred, and I knew my mother must once have looked at herself in this glass. Strange that a mirror and the spaces of a room which had known a human body intimately could bear no trace of what was gone. There was a yearning in me to reach out to the woman who had borne me and find her again in this house where she had grown up. *She* would not have set herself against me or tried to send me away. But I could only find her through those who remembered her. That was my mission now. To discover her, to penetrate the mysteries, the shadows, and find my mother, whatever she had been. Only then would the odd feeling of terror subside, and I'd be free to go home when I pleased.

I unpacked a few things hurriedly and hung them up. The wrinkles weren't too bad. I put on a cowrie shell print with a coral belt and was ready to go downstairs.

The big dining room was at the far end of the house from the living room, on a horizontal plane with the street, and kitchen and pantries opened off it. I followed the sound of voices into a room that had the usual dark

vigas overhead. A long, linen-covered refectory table
was set with heavy silver and fine crystal, and the Spanish
chairs had dark leather seats and tall backs, ornate with
carving. Against the white walls hung several good paintings. I recognized one of John Marin's floating land-
scapes, and two others belonged certainly to the private
world of Georgia O'Keeffe—sand and bones which suited
this country where she had made her home, not far from
Santa Fe.

The family stood about waiting for me, with glasses
in their hands, and I paused in the doorway for a moment,
studying them. Clarita with her dark eyes and her black
dress and turquoise earrings. Eleanor with that brightly
malicious look upon her, and Gavin, standing a little
apart from the two women, his manner as detached as
though he hardly knew them. I was relieved to find in
myself nothing of the sense of attraction that had flashed
through me when I'd seen him earlier today. He was
only my cousin Eleanor's unfortunate husband and he
meant nothing to me.

Clarita saw me first. "We thought it best to let you
sleep," she said, and moved to the head of the table,
motioning me to a chair at her right. Gavin went to the
far end, opposite Clarita, while Eleanor sat across from
me. There were great stretches of empty table between
us.

When we were seated, I spoke to Clarita. "Grandfather
doesn't join you for meals?"

"He prefers to eat alone in his room," she said. "Rosa
takes him a tray. Tonight he is particularly upset because
of Eleanor." She threw her niece a despairing look and
busied herself with serving the food.

Eleanor, still in her violet linen, with the inevitable
New Mexico silver and turquoise about her neck, looked
subdued for the moment and rather watchful. Once or
twice I caught her gaze upon me in speculation, and at
other times she watched Gavin as if she were not altogether sure of his reactions.

Clarita, clearly trying to do what was proper, made

conversation by asking if I knew about Santa Fe's Fiesta, which was held in September.

"That's when we burn Zozobra," she explained. "He's the monster figure that represents gloom. There will be music and fancy dress on the floats and much excitement. Visitors come from everywhere."

"That's something for you to see, if you're an artist, Amanda," Eleanor put in. "I noticed your painting gear. But of course you probably won't be here by that time."

No one at the table wanted me to stay that long, and I said nothing.

Gavin paid no attention to this idle interchange. He was intent upon his own thoughts, as was clear when he spoke abruptly into the new silence.

"This is the first time we've all been together since Eleanor got home. I want Amanda to hear this too. Who put that stone head in my bedroom today?"

A moment of further silence met his words, and I could feel tension in the air. Then Clarita spoke.

"It was I who found it. I think we know how it came to be there."

I had a feeling that Clarita and Eleanor were closing forces against Gavin, accusing him.

He returned Clarita's look coldly. "There's no doubt about who is behind these tricks, but I hadn't expected you to back Eleanor up."

Clarita's manner was as distant as his. "We have a guest," she pointed out. "This is not the time for such discussion."

"Our guest is one of the family," Gavin said flatly.

Eleanor's soft laughter mocked him, and I wished myself well away from such family feuding. I wanted no family like this one.

Unexpectedly, it was Eleanor who drew the conversation onto safer ground by asking me about my painting.

A little stiffly I told them about my work and my wish someday to be a real painter. Surprisingly, Clarita showed an interest.

"My father was something of a painter at one time,"

she said. "And Doroteo liked to sketch."

I snatched at that. "I want to know about my mother. Do you have any of her sketches?"

Again silence fell upon the table and I was aware of Gavin's eyes upon me, faintly pitying. Why pity? I wondered. Rosa came to serve the plates as Clarita filled them, and for a little while we were busy with our meal. My unanswered question hung in the air until Eleanor leaned toward me across the table.

"This is a house filled with secrets, Cousin Amanda. You'd better not go dragging them out of the shadows. Of course you could hardly know that Aunt Doro's name isn't often mentioned here. Least of all to our grandfather."

This was something I didn't mean to accept, and I looked around at them all defiantly. "But I mean to mention it. That's one of the reasons why I've come here —to learn about my mother. My father would never talk about her either. Yet I have a right to know. All I've been told was that she died in a fall, but I don't even know how or where."

Clarita choked and put her napkin to her lips.

With a too innocent air of concealing nothing, Eleanor spoke to me openly across the table. "There was a picnic outdoors. Several of us were there that day. I can't remember very much, but I've been told that, at least. Katy was there, and Sylvia—though she wasn't married to Paul Stewart at that time. Gavin was there too, though he was only fifteen. The trouble is most of us didn't see what happened. It was all out of our sight." She fluffed her fair bangs with a childish gesture that did not match the wisdom of her eyes.

Clarita stared at her niece with an air of stunned horror, until Gavin reached out and placed a hand on his wife's arm. "That's enough, Eleanor. You're upsetting Clarita, and you know Juan's wishes."

"But why?" Eleanor asked quickly. "Why shouldn't Amanda be told what happened? Aunt Clarita needn't be upset. She didn't even go to the picnic that day. She was ill and couldn't come, and Juan wasn't there either."

"It might have been better if I had gone," Clarita said hoarsely. "Perhaps it would never have happened if I had been there."

"But how did she fall? How?" I persisted.

Clarita recovered herself. "We will have no more of this subject. Do you understand—all of you? And I will not have my father disturbed with questions, Amanda. What happened nearly killed him, and I will not have him made ill over it now. You are here because he wanted you to come. Only for that. But there must be rules about your meeting him. You are not to ask him anything about the death of your mother. If he chooses to speak of it himself, that is something else."

I felt again that force she possessed. It put a pressure upon me and I found it hard to resist, as her will bore down upon me, defeating me. Juan Cordova was apparently Clarita's charge and she would protect him at all costs. I was ready to give in until she pushed me too far.

"You will promise me this," she insisted.

I recovered my own will and shook my head. "I can't promise," I told her, and Eleanor laughed as if she approved.

"You can see Amanda is a Cordova," she said.

Clarita ignored her. "It will not make you happy to learn about your mother," she assured me.

Gavin made an effort to draw the lightning away, and I was briefly grateful to him as he began to talk about the firm of CORDOVA. Until I found that this too was a dangerous subject.

"Paul is going to put in the Penitente display you asked him to loan the store, Eleanor," Gavin said. "I'm not sure it's a good idea."

Eleanor nodded with no great enthusiasm. "He wants to advertise the book he's written on the subject. And Grandfather was pleased. He'd like to turn the store into a museum anyway."

"Which he can't be allowed to do," Gavin said, and

I heard the grim note in his voice.

"*You're* not likely to stop him," Eleanor taunted. "He'll do as he pleases. But it's interesting to see you standing against him after all these years. Amanda, how much do you know about our albatross?"

"CORDOVA is scarcely an albatross," Clarita broke in. "We live and eat well because of it."

"And who comes first in any crisis—the store or us?" Eleanor sounded angry. "You know very well that the store has been held over us all our lives. We can't do this, and we can't do that, because the store might suffer. My parents ran away from it, but after they died Juan brought me back here. And I was foolish enough to marry a man who is owned by CORDOVA."

"Eleanor!" Clarita said warningly.

She paid no attention. "Oh, you'll feel it too, Amanda, if you're here long enough. It's Juan Cordova's life and blood, and he cares about none of us as he does about all those treasures he's collected for the store. It ruined your life, Aunt Clarita, because he could never spare you from the work you did for him. He made you a slave to it, and it kept you from having any happiness of your own. But it's not going to ruin my life!"

"No one but you can ruin yours," Gavin said grimly.

Eleanor turned her interest back to me. "Don't ever accept any part of it, Amanda. If you do, it will destroy you, just the way it destroyed your mother."

"That is ridiculous," Clarita said, but she looked a little pale, as though Eleanor's words had got home to her.

"Why?" Eleanor persisted. "Amanda's father wanted to take Doro and the baby away from Santa Fe. You told me that, Aunt Clarita. But Juan said if she went away he'd leave her no share of the store and his fortune. So she stayed. And look what happened to her! Wait till he tries to buy you, Amanda. The way he's bought Gavin and me!"

"Be careful," Gavin said evenly. "You go too far, Eleanor."

By this time we had reached dessert, but I could eat

nothing more. The meal had been disastrous, and Eleanor's efforts to mock everyone and stir up emotional storms left us all upset and antagonistic.

I don't know whether she would have subsided or not, for at that moment Rosa came into the room looking excited. She spoke in Spanish to Clarita, and I saw my aunt close her eyes, as if against the inevitable. Then she opened them and looked at me.

"Your grandfather is asking for you," she said. "I will take you upstairs to see him, but you are not to stay more than ten minutes."

Again Rosa broke in with words in swift Spanish.

Clarita sighed. "He wishes to see you alone. There's nothing else to be done. You will have to go to him now."

This was what I had been waiting for—yet with the moment upon me I felt frightened and unready. I cast a quick glance around the table, seeking for help, for reassurance. Eleanor was eating a piece of fruit with an air of concentrated unconcern. Clarita, clearly disapproving, restrained herself with difficulty. Only Gavin looked at me with some consideration—where I had expected none.

"Don't be afraid of him, Amanda. Don't let him intimidate you."

While this hardly sounded promising, at least it helped me to brace myself against the coming interview. This was what I had come here for, and I must make up my own mind about my grandfather. All the others had disappointed me. Clarita, Eleanor, even Sylvia, would never seem close to me as relatives. But Juan Cordova remained.

I pushed back my chair from the table and the others rose with me.

"Rosa will take you to him," Clarita said. "Remember that he is ill. Don't upset him or stay very long."

The little maid threw me a quick look and hurried off through connecting rooms toward the other end of the house.

"Wait a moment," I called after her. "I want to get something from my room."

While she waited, I ran up my private flight of stairs and took the little road runner from one of my bags. Then I rejoined her.

"I'm ready now."

She took me to the foot of the steps which led to the small balcony off the living room.

"Better you go up alone," she told me.

I hesitated for a moment, looking about that south-western room with its dark Spanish furniture and bright Navajo rugs. But all I saw was the carved tarantula on the table near a lamp. It looked ready to move, to pounce. Yet the same man had carved my amusing road runner, and it was reassuring to feel its outlines hard in my hand.

I reached for the railing and mounted the balcony steps.

# V

The door of Juan Cordova's room stood open and I stepped through the gloom. At the window, draperies were drawn and no lights burned. Only a glow from the balcony behind me picked out general shapes. The room was a study, not a bedroom, and across it I discovered a man's straight figure seated behind a desk. He did not droop as a sick man might, but sat facing me with a manner of pride and assurance.

"I am here," I said hesitantly. Now that the moment was upon me, I found myself both fearful and hopeful.

He reached out a hand and touched a switch. The gooseneck lamp on the desk beside him was bent to turn full upon me and it was as though I were lighted suddenly by a spotlight. Shocked and startled, I stood blinking in the glare, unable to see the man behind the lamp, and disturbed that he should do such a thing. With an effort, I recovered myself, and I walked out of the circle of light and around the desk. Any possible moment of sentiment between us in this first encounter had been lost, and clearly that loss was deliberate. There would be no affectionate welcome for me from my mother's father. Indignation erased my shock.

"Is this the way you always greet visitors?" I asked.

His chuckle was low, amused. "I like to see how people react. Come and sit down, Amanda, and we will look at each other in a kinder light."

He stood up and touched another switch that lighted an amber glow overhead. Then he turned off the glaring lamp and waited for me to seat myself in a leather chair near his desk. As I sat down, I hid the road runner carving beneath my hands in my lap. Bringing it here had been a sentimental gesture, and this was clearly no time for sentiment.

In the softer light I studied him boldly, still prickling with resentment from his cruel greeting. Juan Cordova was tall, I noted, as he sat down, retying the sash of the maroon silk robe which hung loosely upon his spare frame. His gray hair was brushed close to a finely shaped head, and his face was lined and drawn by illness, though the proud beak of the nose denied all weakness and somehow reminded me of a falcon. It was an infinitely proud face, its expression not a little arrogant— with a falcon's arrogance—even to the posture of his head and the way he held his leanly carved chin. But it was the eyes, most of all, that arrested my own gaze, almost absorbing me into the fierceness of his look. They were eyes as dark as Clarita's, as dark as my own, but they glowed with an intensity of spirit that gave no quarter to age or illness or weakness of vision, and made an almost palpable effect upon me.

My own eyes dropped first because I had, instinctively, to protect myself from some strange emotional demand he seemed to make upon me. I had felt this before— from Clarita and Paul—some inner questioning. It was a demand that had nothing to do with affection. If I had expected to find an old man, beaten by illness, someone whom I might pity, I was quickly disillusioned. No matter what his body had done to him, his spirit was invincible and I could see why those around him must fear him a little. I had hoped that I would be wanted by him, and his look told me that I was—not because he had love to give, but because he had a purpose in bringing me here. In these few moments I stiffened against him, aware that this was a man I might need to battle.

"You look like her," he said. It sounded more accusation than praise.

"I know," I agreed. "I have a miniature you painted of my mother when she was young. But she must have been beautiful and I am not."

"It is true you are not like Doroteo in that respect. *No importa*—the resemblance is there. You have the family hair, thick and lustrous, and I like the way you wear it. I wonder how much you are like her in spirit?"

I could only shake my head. "How can I know?"

"You are right. *Quién sabe?* You do not remember her, of course?"

"No—I wish I could. I don't even know a great deal about her because my father never wanted to speak of her. I've even been told not to talk about her to you."

Something in those fierce eyes seemed to flinch for just a moment, and then the very flinching was dismissed.

"It is still painful to think of her, speak of her. But now that you have come, I must face my own pain."

He used a certain formality in his speech, as though he had grown up accustomed to another language, seeming thoroughly Spanish. Clarita's speech was rather like her father's, I realized, perhaps copied from him.

I waited, having nothing to offer. His pain was none of my affair, since he had not chosen to greet me warmly as belonging to his family.

"If your father would not speak of her, Amanda, perhaps he was more willing to speak of me?"

"To some extent, yes."

"He had no love for me."

Again I was silent, agreeing, and again Juan Cordova chuckled. There was bitterness in the sound and no mirth.

"I remember our parting. I will never forgive William for taking you away, but I can still understand how he felt. Now I suppose I am to prove myself to you—prove that I am not so evil, so wicked as he portrayed me?"

"I expect you will do as you please, Grandfather."

Oddly, he seemed to like my resistance. "You interpret me well already. And you will have to take me as you find me. I will pretend nothing. I am quite likely all the things he has told you I was. But we must get to know each other on a basis of our own. Why did you accept my invitation to come here?"

I made a small, helpless gesture. "I've already been asked that several times. It seems to be part of the Cordova arrogance to invite me here, and then demand why I've come."

"I do not deny that we can be arrogant. But you could have refused to come. Especially with your father's warnings."

"I had to see for myself. One half of my family I know very well. The other half is a blank page. Naturally, I want to fill it in."

"Perhaps you will not like what you find."

"That seems quite possible. I've hardly received a warm welcome here, but I'm beginning to learn about the Cordovas, and what being a Cordova means."

That seemed to rouse his indignation. "You don't know the least beginning of what it means to be a Cordova!"

"What I've learned, I don't want to be."

He smiled at me thinly, his face lighting briefly. "You have a certain arrogance yourself, Amanda. You are instinctively more Cordova than you know."

Impatient, and moving in angry denial, I sprang up from my chair. On the wall behind him hung a narrow mirror in which I glimpsed myself—and was astonished. The stranger in the glass looked proudly Spanish with her black hair and flashing dark eyes, and there was nothing of humility in her. I hadn't known I could look like that, and I turned away from my reflection, rejecting it.

"If there is evil in me, then it lives on in you," Juan said slyly.

I knew he meant to torment me and I stood up to him. "All right—I'll accept that. But I think there was no evil in my mother. The miniature you painted tells me that she was gay, perhaps a little reckless, but not wicked."

"Sit down," the old man commanded. "Tell me what you know about her death."

I took my chair again, shaking my head. "Nothing. My father told me only that she died in a fall."

"And no one here will tell you the truth. As I've told them not to. I wanted you to come to me."

"I've come. And now I'll put it to you directly. Is it true that she died in a fall?"

His thin hands were clenched together on the desk before him, and he stared at them for a moment before he looked back at me, his face expressionless and deeply lined.

"Yes, she died in a fall. But first she killed a man. The law calls her a murderess, and then a suicide."

It was as if I had been suddenly frozen in my chair. My muscles tightened in rejection of his words, my hands were clenched about the carving of the road runner as tightly as his own were clasped on his desk. My breath seemed locked in my chest. Only by a terrible effort was I able at last to move, to cry out.

"I don't believe that! I will never believe it!"

There was pain in his voice. "That is what I said in the beginning—that I would not believe. But of course there was a police investigation and the result left us no choice. Clarita saw what happened. She stood in the window of the room you now occupy and she saw it all. Even I had to accept the truth in the end."

"Katy didn't accept it," I said.

His look sharpened. "What do you mean by that?"

"My grandmother wrote my father a letter before she died. She said he had misjudged my mother, and she wanted him to bring me to visit her. He never told me about the letter. I found it among his papers after he died, but I didn't know what it meant."

"Katy did that?" He seemed both astonished and outraged. "She should not have acted without consulting me."

"Would you have told her not to write?"

"But of course. I would have known it would be no use. Your father would not change. Katy wanted to deceive herself up to the end. She wanted to believe what was not so."

"Could she have had some reason for believing it wasn't so?"

The fierce, dark eyes examined me, probing as though his clouded vision sought for clarity. "I wish I could think that. She had only a mother's heart. She had the love she felt for a daughter."

"Perhaps there's wisdom in love."

He answered me in a tone more gentle than I had heard from him. "I loved Doroteo too. As she loved me. We were very close, your mother and I. That is why I have sent for you to come here."

I believed him. And yet I didn't quite believe him. That air of gentleness was uncharacteristic. Surely if he had brought me here because he loved Doroteo, and thought with any warmth of her daughter, he would have greeted me differently. My uncertainty strengthened me and hardened me against him as I spoke my thought.

"I can't believe you sent for me because of any love for my mother."

Again he spoke in sudden anger. "You know nothing of me!"

It no longer mattered whether he kept me here or sent me away. It didn't matter at all, I told myself. I had been terribly shocked, and there was still a trembling within me. Tears burned in my eyes and I hated my own weakness.

"I already know that you're arrogant, and perhaps a little cruel," I told him, blinking weakness away furiously.

His own anger seemed to die. "You are more like Katy than like Doroteo. They both had spirit, but Katy would fight for more. Perhaps you have possibilities. I can offer you nothing but hurt when it comes to the past, though perhaps there were extenuating circumstances. I have tried to believe that."

Possibilities? I didn't like the sound of the word. What

use he had for me, I didn't know, but I would be on guard against anything that might violate my own feelings. Now, however, was the moment to learn as much as I could.

"Who was the man my mother is supposed to have killed?"

"His name was Kirk Landers. He was the stepbrother of a second cousin of yours—the woman who brought you to Santa Fe today. Sylvia Stewart. They both grew up in this house because Katy took them in when their parents died."

I tried to digest this, remembering Sylvia's uneasiness with me. She must have felt a reluctance to meet the daughter of the woman who was supposed to have killed her stepbrother.

"What were the extenuating circumstances?" I asked.

Juan Cordova sighed deeply. "That is a long story. Shall we save it for another time?"

He looked suddenly tired and old, and I remembered Clarita's warning not to stay with him for long. The effect of that shocking revelation he had made still seethed in me violently, but I must not push him now in his illness.

"I'd better go," I said. "I've tired you."

One long-fingered, aristocratic hand reached out to rest on my arm. I could feel the strength of his fingers. If there was weakness in this man, it was not something he chose to accept.

"You will stay with me until I say you may go."

My private resistance to such male authority stirred in me, but he was old and ill, as well as domineering, and I let the command pass with only a small effort to deny it.

"Aunt Clarita warned me that—"

"Clarita is sometimes a fool! She will do as I say."

Even though he knew her so much better than I, I had the sudden feeling that he underestimated his older daughter. Clarita had more to her than surfaced in her obedience to her father.

"Tell me," he said more gently, "do you remember

anything at all about the day your mother died?"

"I don't remember anything of that time. Since I've come here, I've had a few flashes of recognition. But these seem to do with places, not people. I suppose the people I might remember have all changed in twenty years."

"It's probably just as well," Grandfather said. "Paul Stewart is planning to write a book about famous murders of the Southwest."

So that was the answer—a book about murder! This was what they had been hinting at, and why no one had wanted to come right out and tell me what his book was about.

"You mean he is going to—to include—" I faltered to a stop.

"Yes. He means to write about Doroteo and Kirk."

"But that's dreadful. He should be stopped. Can't you—"

"I have tried. Without success. Naturally, I don't want these happenings resurrected at this late date. It can only hurt those who are living. The affair has been mostly forgotten, except by us. Now he will renew interest in it, and we will have to live through it all over again."

Sorrow seemed to crush him, and for the first time I felt a sympathy for him. In spite of his arrogance, he had suffered too, and my coming here must be a goad to old pain.

"Sylvia told me that Paul would have gone to New York to see me, if you hadn't happened to bring me here."

"Yes. He is questioning anyone who was present at the time of the tragedy. I suppose even a five-year-old might have memories that he could find useful. But now you can tell him that you remember nothing, and he'll have to leave you alone. Perhaps it will help if you can be as discouraging as possible."

"I'll certainly try, if he questions me," I promised.

"Now tell me something about yourself," he said. "What do you do? What do you want to do?"

"All I want to do is paint."

He laughed softly, delightedly, the bitterness gone, the mood change instant, and in its suddenness unnerving. My own emotional transitions were made less quickly.

"So there is such a thing as heritage! The strain has come down through the family. Along with other things less pleasant. I am an artist manqué. So I give myself to the collecting of the art of others. As an appreciator and critic, I have few peers. Doroteo had the talent too, but she would not work at it. She did not care enough."

"I care. I work very hard. It's the way I earn my living, though mostly in small ways. I've had a showing of my paintings at a gallery in New York, and I've even sold a few. I'm already eager to paint in Santa Fe."

"Good—this is a fine country for painters, and a town that is kind to them. What is that you've been fondling in your hands ever since you came in? It looks like a carving."

I remembered the figure of the road runner and handed it to him across a corner of the desk.

"You made this for me when I was very small. I've kept it ever since. It was the toy I took to bed with me at night when I was young and sometimes frightened."

He took the carving and turned it about in his hands. I knew he was sensing the smoothness of the wood with his fingers, noting the indentations of the carving. His love for wood as a medium was evident in the sensitivity of his touch, and perhaps too his sorrow because he could no longer create, as once he had done. I felt a bond of understanding with him, because I too wanted to create.

"Yes, I remember this," he said. "I remember the high hopes I had for you as Doroteo's daughter. You loved me quite innocently then. Without wanting anything from me." Sudden suspicion came into his voice, and my brief sense of a bond was broken. "What do you want from me now?"

These changes of mood ruffled me, but on this I could answer him readily. "Nothing except what you want to give, Grandfather."

The look he returned was arrogant, proud—it gave

me no relief. "There is little I can give you. But there may be something I want of you."

"I'll give it, if I can," I said.

"You are like Doroteo. Generous. I am surrounded by those I can no longer trust. Those who are my enemies. I suffer over this. But then—the essence of your true Spaniard is his ability to suffer. To suffer and to laugh. But laughter turns to mockery after a time."

He seemed to go into a brooding silence, and I tried to draw him from it.

"I would like to know something about my grandmother," I said gently. "What was Katy like?"

His expression softened and he opened a drawer of his desk and took out a picture in an oval frame—another miniature. "This I painted too, before any of the children were born."

He handed me the picture and I saw again the gift he must have had for portraiture. The young face that looked out at me had strength and character. She was a woman who might have hated adobe walls, as Sylvia Stewart had said, but she'd have loved her husband with a loyalty that would permit no weakness. Her hair was fair, like Eleanor's, and she wore it short in the picture and fluffed youthfully about her ears, yet there was maturity in the blue eyes and a forcefulness about the chin. Here was a woman who had been able to cope.

*My grandmother,* I thought, and felt a stirring of recognition in me. She was not a stranger to me. I could recognize kinship, even though I resembled her outwardly not at all.

He took the picture back from me and put it away. "She did not look like that as I remember her. I wanted her to have long hair, and she grew it for me. Her hair was thick and heavy as the gold it resembled. She wore it high on her head, and it gave her a look of poise and assurance. She could have been a great Spanish lady— my Katy."

Katy, from the farmlands of Iowa! Had she ever expected to play the role of a Spanish lady?

"I wish I could have known her," I said.

Juan Cordova made a sound of distress that carried anger in its depth. "She had the right to know you. Your father took you away."

"I suppose he did what he thought was best. He wanted me to grow up in a different environment."

"And away from me."

The words were flat, certain, and I did not contradict them.

"Enough of all this," he went on. "I have no time for sentiment. No time for the past. The present is short and there is much to be done. We must make plans."

I suppose it was sentiment I had come for, but I was beginning to see that I would not have it from Juan Cordova. I could only wait to hear about his plans.

He was silent for a few moments, thinking, and as I waited uneasily, not trusting any plans he might make for me, I looked about the room. There were the inevitable white walls, the brown vigas that graced every ceiling. Burgundy draperies were drawn across the windows, but since the room was only a little higher than the floor of the living room, it could not have looked out upon any distant view, as my room did. There was a door which led into the darkness of a bedroom beyond. And all about, set on bookcase shelves and small tables, were the treasures of a lifetime. My eye was caught by the handsomely carved and painted figure of a bullfighter swirling his cape. On a lower shelf stood a buff-colored pottery bowl with brown buffalo pounding their hoofs as they ran endlessly from hunters around its circumference. It looked as if it might be old and valuable. Here, however, were none of those frightening desert creatures I had seen downstairs. Perhaps Juan Cordova himself played their role, and I wondered if I was the victim upon whom he would next pounce. I put the uneasy thought aside and let my gaze move on about the room.

On the walls were hung paintings of Santa Fe scenes —the Cathedral of St. Francis casting the shadows of its twin towers across a stone walk; a row of adobe houses that might belong to this very neighborhood; a scene on the Alameda and another in the sun-speckled plaza. Undoubtedly these had been painted by local artists, and they made me want to find my own scenes, try my own conception in color of what I saw.

"I have decided," my grandfather said abruptly, and his voice was strong, assured, banishing all weakness. "There are things you will do for me at once."

A warning of resistance stiffened in me, but I answered quietly. "I'm waiting, Grandfather."

"First you will speak to Clarita." His tone was harsh, commanding. "She guards me like a dragon because the doctor has said I must conserve my strength. There is to be no more of that. You are to come here to me whenever you wish, and without waiting for her permission. Tell her so. Then you will tell Eleanor that she is no longer needed to accompany me when I walk in the patio. From now on, you will come with me on my walks. As for Gavin—you will tell him that he is to take you through the store and show you all that is important for you to know. You will now become one of the family, and you are to learn the store, Amanda. He will teach you. If all this is clear, you are to go at once and begin."

My gasp must have been audible. It shocked me that I should be brought in from outside and set above everyone in the house. Such an act was anything but just, and I didn't mean to be so commanded. Setting out to anger members of my new family with these highhanded orders was not for me. What he planned, I didn't know, but I suspected that it wouldn't be something I'd want. What I had wanted from the Cordovas had another value.

"No," I said. "I won't do any of these things."

There was a small silence as though he listened to the echo of my words without fully understanding them.

"You said?" he murmured.

"I said I wouldn't go about giving orders to the people in your household. If I'm to visit here, I want to be friends with them. I'm certainly not going to set myself above them and tell them what to do."

Perhaps it had been a long time since anyone had spoken so to Juan Cordova. I saw the angry flush mount in his face, saw the tightening of his hands into fists where they lay before him on the desk. He lost his temper.

"You will do as I say, or you may pack up and go away at once! I will not endure such foolishness. Your mother betrayed us all. Your father was a fool—stupid and mindless in his behavior. I have not forgotten or forgiven the words he spoke to me before he left, and I will not tolerate disobedience from his daughter. You will not go the way of Doroteo. Or—if that is the pattern—you can leave at once."

I pushed my chair back and stood up. I was trembling and my muscles were tense as my own rage spilled out.

"Then I will pack up and go! The only reason I came here is because I love my mother. Even without knowing her, I love her. If some injustice had been done her, I wanted to set it right. And I won't listen to words against my father. How could someone like you possibly know his worth and his goodness? He was so far above any of the Cordovas that—that—" I choked on my anger and there were tears of rage in my eyes. As I started for the door, I shoved my chair aside so furiously that it fell over on the floor with a bang. I didn't care. I was through with this dreadful man.

His sudden ringing laughter brought me to a halt before I reached the door. Juan Cordova was laughing. I turned about in further outrage and stared at him.

"Wait," he said. "Come back here, Amanda. I am pleased with you. You will do, as none of the others will. The Cordova strain comes through. You are a young, wild thing with a temper. You are a part of me and of your mother. Come—sit down, and we will talk more quietly."

The unexpected gentleness of his voice warned me. He could not be entirely trusted. Yet the tone of it hypnotized me. With hands that still shook, I righted the chair and sat down in it. I had no intention of forgiving him easily, no intention of trusting him, but something in me did not want to run away.

"I'm waiting," I said, and hated the way my voice trembled.

He rose from the desk and bent toward me. His long fingers touched the weight of my hair at the back, moved lightly down my face, as though the artist in him sought for deeper knowledge than the eyes could give, reached my chin and tipped it upward. I sat frozen, resenting his touch, finding it more possessive than loving.

"I remember the small Amanda," he said. "I remember holding her in my arms. I remember reading to her of Don Quixote while she sat on my knee."

He was trying to beguile me. "Don Quixote when I was less than five?" I said.

"But of course. The meaning of the words is not important to a child. It is the interest of the adult and the music of the sound." I did not move, and he sensed the resistance in me, drew away, sat down. Not hurt, but still amused, and obviously pleased because he had so upset me. He was a dreadful old man—wicked and quite dangerous.

"Now we will talk again," he said. "All the things I've stated to you must be done, but you are right. It would not be good to antagonize the household yourself. I will take care of my orders. The others are used to the outrageous from me, as you are not, and they cannot run away—as you can. So I have them where I want them. At least, you are good for me. I feel more alive at this moment than I have in months. You may go now. And tomorrow we will begin."

"I'm not sure I want this," I said. "What is it you wish of me?"

"That depends on what you have to give. It will be best, however, if you do not go stirring up old fires, old wounds. All that could be done about your mother's death was done at the time. Let it rest, Amanda, and do not bother yourself talking with Paul Stewart. Now, good night."

"Good night," I said. But I did not promise that I would let the matter of my mother's death go. I had not been told everything yet, by any means.

I went through the door and out upon the landing. Only Eleanor sat in the living room below. She had a book in her hands, but I didn't think she was reading. She looked up at me wih a searching glance.

"You were shouting," she said. "You must have made Juan very angry."

"He made me angry," I said sharply. "I think I'll go to bed now. I'm very tired—after all the graciousness that's been extended to me by the Cordovas."

"Of course," she agreed, unruffled, and rose smoothly from her chair. "I'll come with you and see if everything is right in your room."

I had no wish for her company, but there was no way to discourage her. She followed me up the flight of stairs to my room and waited while I opened the door.

Someone had lighted a lamp on the bed table, and the shaggy white rug on the floor nearby glowed yellow. Something rested in its center that did not belong there. I bent to pick it up.

The little object lay heavy in my hand, and I saw that it was made of some black stone formed roughly in the shape of a mole, with a pointed snout and rudimentary legs. Bound to its back with sinew thongs were an arrowpoint and several colored beads, including a piece of turquoise that had been threaded onto a thong. These things looked old and were stained with some brownish color. Strangely, I felt a revulsion toward whatever they represented. There seemed no reason for so strong a flash of repugnance, but the feeling was there. Atavistic. This was some sort of Indian relic, I was sure, and it had not been left in my room for any but an evil purpose.

I looked at Eleanor and saw that her gaze was fixed with bright interest on the black stone I held.

"What is it?" I asked.

She raised her shoulders in a slight shiver. "It's an Indian fetish. That's probably dried blood on the back. There's a ritual where the fetish is fed blood."

In my hand, the black stone felt cold and heavy as a threat. But I refused to let the matter of its presence go.

"Why is it here?"

"How would I know? Someone must have put it there. Let me see."

She took the thong-wrapped stone from me and examined it closely. "I think it's a Zuni fetish, and I know where it came from. It's been missing ever since Gavin brought home several fetishes to exhibit in the store. Genuine fetishes are hard to come by these days because no self-respecting Indian will sell anything so personal. I think this is a hunter's fetish. It's supposed to bring good luck in the hunt. Gavin told me it was a rare one because it's in the form of a mole. Moles belong to the nether regions and they aren't highly thought of as fetishes, so there aren't many of them. Still—a mole has its virtues. It can burrow in the dark and lay traps for larger animals."

She was all too well informed, and there was mocking intent in her words.

"But why would someone leave it here?"

"Perhaps it's a warning, Cousin. Perhaps you are the prey." There was an odd light in her violet eyes that did not reassure me.

"And who is hunting me?" I challenged.

Her hands moved gracefully and I was reminded again of a dancer. "Who knows the hunter until he strikes? It could be any of us, couldn't it?"

I stared at the black stone mole in her hands. "Why should I be anyone's prey?"

Eleanor laughed softly, and I heard the ruthless echo of Juan Cordova in the sound. "Isn't it obvious? I heard some of what our grandfather said to you. He means to use you against us. He means to try to frighten us."

From the living room below, a voice called up the stairs. "Is anyone at home? I've been wandering around without finding a soul."

"That's Paul." Eleanor's eyes lighted with a pleasure I did not like. "I'll give the mole back to Gavin, Amanda. Don't worry about it. Or"—she paused—"perhaps you *had* better worry about it." Then she moved toward the door. "I expect Paul wants to talk to you."

I shook my head. "Not now. I don't want to see anyone tonight." I'd had enough of the Cordovas, and in particular of Eleanor. "Good night," I said in firm dismissal.

For a moment she regarded me intently, but I didn't waver and she shrugged as she went toward the stairs. At the last minute she turned back with that bright look in her eyes.

"You really aren't afraid, are you, Amanda?"

I met her look, asserting my own courage and dignity. The small victory was mine, and she ran lightly down the stairs. From below, as I closed the door softly, I could hear the sound of voices—low, conspiratorial.

Was I afraid?

I hadn't come here with any wish to be used as a weapon for some veiled warfare that might be going on in this house, a weapon with which those who might oppose Juan Cordova could be subjugated. But neither did I mean to be threatened by those who opposed him. I would not let either side use me, and there was nothing to keep me from going home at once, if I chose. There was nothing to hold me here—except my own will. Was the wish to stay stronger than the desire to run?

Once more I had the feeling of adobe walls closing in on me, holding me a prisoner. Had Katy ever felt like that? And how had my mother felt, here in this room? Nothing I had learned about her seemed like the behavior of a prisoner—she who had grown up happily in these walls. Yet she had died, and a man had died too—they said because of her.

Feeling a little sick, I went to a window and spread the

curtains that had been drawn across it. A cool night wind touched my face and under starlight the snow on pointed peaks glistened against the deep, dark blue of the sky. At least this room was above the walls. Here, at least, I was not closed in. Except by my own thoughts.

A past that had always seemed distant and something to be gently unraveled—a story to give me pleasure and a new knowledge of myself—now seemed imminent and threatening. I had been in this house at the time when they must have brought them back to it—Kirk Landers and my mother, Doroteo, both dead. Yet I had no memory of loss, of suffering. Whatever existed deep in my consciousness was smothered in a mist through which no light penetrated. I did not want to remember that time in order to help Paul Stewart with his book, but now that I knew there must be something hidden in me, something lodged in the recesses of my own mind which had experienced a time of tragedy, I wanted to seek it out for myself, bring it into the open, know it for whatever it was. Katy had known—something. Or discovered something later. If I stayed here, could I perhaps find out what it was? Could I free my mother's memory of that dreadful stamp of murder and suicide? How futile was such a wish?

I couldn't know until I had stayed for a few days, at least, and had learned everything I could about the past. There were so many gaps that were still not filled in, and I still knew nothing at all about what dreadful thing had risen to cause violence between my mother and Sylvia Stewart's stepbrother.

No, I could not leave right away. Not even if some threat to me existed in this house. What had happened long ago was all going on still. It had not ended with my mother's death, and perhaps my coming had stirred sleeping terrors. I must stay and find out. For myself I must allay them.

# VI

Weariness enveloped me the moment I was in bed. I fell soundly asleep and heard nothing of the whisperings of a strange house. It must have been well into the early, dark hours that the dream began to take shape in my sleeping mind. I knew with a sense of dread that it was coming, yet I was chained by sleep, unable to waken and protect myself from the vision that grew in my mind.

The tree was there. That dreadful, haunting tree—so enormous that it hid the sky, reaching upward with twisted black branches. I cowered close to the ground, staring up into that sickly green canopy that held all horror, that enclosed me in frozen terror. The thing was alive with movement, trembling, writhing, reaching toward me. In a few moments it would grasp and smother me with that awful green. Already, I could hardly breathe. A heavy limb lowered itself slowly, moving with a strange life of its own, to rest upon my chest and I struggled to fight it away, to cry out, to scream for aid that I knew would never come in time.

I sat up in bed struggling with the bedclothes, fighting for my breath. My nightgown was soaked with cold perspiration and the sharp breeze from the window chilled me into consciousness. I did not immediately know where I was because the familiar horror lingered. I could see the tree as though it grew within the walls of my room, and I fought to free myself of the clinging vapors. As always, there was a sense of loss in me, of abandonment.

I had been on feared and well-known territory. As a child I had dreamed of the tree and when I awakened screaming, my father had held me in his arms to soothe and quiet me. Yet his arms never obliterated that terrible sense of loss. I could never tell him how bad the dream was—how frightful. Sometimes it was hours before I knew I was safe with him in a real world, and there was no tree, no black limbs to twine about me and stop my breath with the smothering green of their leaves.

Even now that I was grown and awake, the sense of terror returned to me in waves, and it was a long while before the haunting faded and I was able to sleep again.

When I awakened the next time, the sun was up, but I felt drained and weary, as I always did when the nightmare had returned. Somehow I knew that I had come close to the source of the dream. I had come to the place where the tree waited, and I must find it in reality this time. Only when I knew why it haunted me would I be free of it.

When I came downstairs, the cook was still in the kitchen, though no one was left at the table. She served me cheerfully enough, and my appetite returned as I drank hot coffee and revived a little.

In bright daylight, I could put the dream away and face a present that, while not wholly attractive, was at least real and could be dealt with, as the dream could not. I would see Juan Cordova as soon as possible and try to clear the air between us. I would let him know that I would not be used for some purpose which might be unfair to others in his family, and I would also persuade him to tell me the full story of my mother's death.

The still disturbing puzzle of the mole fetish which had been left in my room remained, but I supposed this too would be made clear eventually. There were those who did not want me here, but I would not be frightened off like a child. The word "evil" which had come to me last night was only something to make me smile by daylight. I was not without courage, and I would stand up to whatever must be faced. I'd come here to learn who I was, and I wouldn't go away until I knew.

When I'd finished breakfast, I went into the living room and approached the short flight of steps to my grandfather's room. Clarita stood on the balcony.

"I'd like to see my grandfather," I told her.

She loomed above me, a black figure, with her thin arms folded across her body, and her aging face looked down at me in disapproval.

"That isn't possible this morning. Your visit yesterday excited him too much. He isn't well and he can see no one."

Her concern for her father seemed genuine, but she was still the guardian dragon, as he'd called her. Though he had given me instructions as to what I must say to her, I would not give her his orders. She had a right to tell me what I might do in this house, and I couldn't oppose her. I would see him eventually because he would ask for me. I would wait till then.

I went up to my room, feeling restless and at loose ends, and got out my sketchbook and a pencil. These always served me when I needed release from tension. I let myself out through a rear door to the patio, finding the air marvelously clear and bracing, the morning sky pure turquoise. Behind the house, the garden was surprisingly spacious, stretching down an incline toward the back. It was not, however, a garden in my sense of the word. There were areas of bluestone, where nothing grew, and there was little grass. Since such a small amount of rain fell that constant watering would have been necessary to keep anything growing, no great effort had been made to provide flower beds. There were clumps of cholla and other cactus, and the native gray-green chamiso bushes one saw everywhere. Fluff from a cotton-wood tree floated to the ground, whitening an area around its base, and a path wound downhill toward a small building on the lower level of the property. Beyond it was a rear gate which must open on the hillside. Around all of this ran the adobe wall, shutting in the Cordovas, sealing them away from the world. They had, indeed, had secrets they wanted to conceal behind their walls.

The small building at the bottom of the property offered a contrast to the rest of the neighborhood. Though the walls were adobe, redwood had been used for the roof and it slanted to a high peak, like the roof of a church, so that I wondered if it might be a chapel of some sort. Its construction was modern and graceful, appealing to the eye, and it drew me, so that I walked down to view it more closely.

The typical carved wooden door was closed, and thick curtains covered its windows, unlike the windows of a chapel. A nearby rock, flat enough to sit upon, gave me a perch, and I sat down and opened my sketchbook.

In a few quick lines I caught the outline of the building, blocking in a cottonwood tree nearby and a clump of cholla by the front door. I made notes about the colors I might use and took the liberty of sketching in the rise of a mountain above the adobe wall, though none was visible from this angle. For me, the interest of painting, the satisfaction, was never in copying a scene exactly, but in creating my own impression of what I saw, finding a dimension caught only by me, selecting and rejecting, searching for an expanded vision, until the result pleased me, existed as mine.

I did not notice the nearby gate in the side wall, or hear it open until Sylvia Stewart called to me.

"Good morning, Amanda."

Apparently this gate led into the Stewarts' patio and the two families moved back and forth to visit each other as they pleased.

She wore fawn slacks and an amber sweater, and her hair with its deliberate shade of brown was brushed straight back from her forehead. I found myself looking at her through my new knowledge, wondering whether, because of her stepbrother, she resented me as Doroteo's daughter. All the time we had been together yesterday she had known what was said about my mother, and I had not. But there seemed no particular uneasiness in her this morning.

"May I see what you're drawing?" she asked, and came to look over my shoulder.

I had turned another page, to make a careful study of a cottonwood tree, but now I flipped back to my drawing of the chapel-like building.

"Juan will like that," she said. "Though you ought to put in his pride—those climbing Castilian roses against the wall. They're the only flowers the Cordovas give much attention to. Do you know what it is you've drawn?"

"It looks like a chapel."

"In a way, it is. To Juan it's quite sacred. He keeps his private collection of art treasures there. Most of them are paintings from old Spain. Rumor has it that one of them is a Velázquez. But there are other things too. Sometimes I suspect that not everything has been legitimately come by."

She laughed wryly and I did not comment. It was one of her typically barbed remarks.

"I suppose you've seen the collection?" I asked.

"Of course—since I'm counted as one of the family. But he shows it to very few people, and it's his own private passion that he's not given to sharing. Don't try to walk in. There are burglar alarms everywhere. You have to know the right combination or you set them off."

"Did the pre-Columbian head disappear from here?"

"Not exactly. It belongs here, but I understand that Juan had given permission for it to be put on display in the store with a special exhibit. It's from that exhibit that it was taken. If it's true Gavin is to blame, he could easily have picked it up from the store."

"But why would he do a thing like that?"

"I don't think he did. I suppose you've met all of our family by now? How do you like them?"

"I've hardly had time to get acquainted," I said.

Closing my sketchbook, I stood up from the rock, and at once she gestured toward the gate in the adobe wall. "Do come over and visit Paul. He's been waiting to talk to you, and you might as well get it over with."

I looked at her questioningly.

"By this time you've been told more about the book he's working on, haven't you? Its subject, that is?"

I answered her evenly. "If you mean has my grandfather told me about my mother's death—he's given me the bare facts. I know what's supposed to have happened, and that your stepbrother died. I don't think I can accept his account."

"Not accept it?" Sylvia was clearly startled.

I tried to explain. "I can't accept it—emotionally. My grandmother Katy wrote a rather strange letter to my father before she died, and said that he'd misjudged my mother. What do you suppose she meant by that?"

Sylvia walked off a few steps, her back to me. My words had somehow disturbed her.

"Before she died, Aunt Katy left me something for you," she said. "She told me if you ever came here I was to give it to you."

Eagerness alerted me, but I felt impatient with Sylvia.

"Then why didn't you tell me? Why didn't you give it to me yesterday? Perhaps she's left me some message that will clear up her letter."

Sylvia came slowly back to me, her expression faintly pitying. It was the same look I had seen in Gavin's eyes at the dinner table last night, and I resisted it, waiting for an answer to my questions.

"I had the package with me when I met you," Sylvia said. "But you knew nothing about your mother's death, and I didn't want to throw everything at you at once. It was better to wait a little. Now you're going down a blind alley, Amanda. Don't deceive yourself with fantasies. What happened, happened. I never liked your mother, but all that has nothing to do with you. I'm trying to be fair about that and not let old emotions mix in because it was my stepbrother who died. I suppose they've told you that Clarita saw the whole thing?"

I nodded, waiting.

"There's no getting around that. Once Clarita fancied herself in love with Kirk, you know. That was when we were all around twelve and thirteen, and used to go out to the *rancho* for holidays and weekends."

"The *rancho?*"

"Yes—the *Rancho de Cordova*. It belonged to Juan's father—your great-grandfather. He raised horses and we used to love to go there. It's a ghost place now. Juan doesn't keep it up, though he employs a married couple who stay at the hacienda. Of course Clarita got over that childhood infatuation. By the time Kirk died she was in love with—someone else. She didn't even like him by that time."

I thought with a feeling of shock of Clarita, who had seemed to me eternally middle-aged. It was hard to imagine her a love-sick girl. Now, because of my mother, Clarita too might hold old prejudices against me.

"Of course Doro was in love with Kirk too in those *rancho* days," Sylvia went on. "I grew up with them. I saw the whole thing from the beginning."

I didn't want to think of my mother in connection with any man but my father.

"I don't believe I'm making up fantasies," I said. "But perhaps all the truth hasn't come out. That's what I want to know."

"Then come and see Paul. He knew her too, though he was outside the family then. I'll have to be running along soon. My bookshop usually opens at nine o'clock, but I'm late today."

Juan Cordova had told me not to trouble myself by talking to Paul, but of course I would pay no attention. I hadn't felt strong enough to face Sylvia's husband last night, but I could manage it now. There was nothing in the way of memories I could give him, though there might be something he could tell me. Besides, I wanted whatever it was Katy had left for me with Sylvia.

She moved to the gate in the wall as I packed up my painting gear.

"You might as well know that I hate what Paul is doing," she said over her shoulder. "I agree with Juan that all of this should be left alone. But my husband is a strongly determined man, and he seems to have a bit between his teeth about this. I blame Eleanor. She likes to stir up trouble and annoy Juan, and she's convinced Paul that he'll be doing history a favor with this book. I've heard her tell him that he mustn't pay any attention to Clarita or Juan's feelings. Or mine, for that matter. Of course it's not really to anyone's interest for him to write it. Not even Paul's. But he likes to play with fire."

She had grown oddly excited as she spoke, and only quieted herself when she saw I was staring at her.

I left my painting things beside the stone I'd perched upon and joined Sylvia at the gate. Before we went through, she put a hand on my arm, halting me.

"Be careful, Amanda. I have a feeling that all those heated emotions Doro stirred around her like a whirlwind have never quite died down. The repercussions can still damage those who are living. You among them."

It was a strange warning, though I'd felt something of the same thing myself. I didn't try to answer her as I went through the gate between the two gardens. How could I be careful when I didn't know what it was that I must guard against?

We crossed a patio that was smaller than that of the Cordovas' and stepped into the Stewarts' living room, with its brilliant Indian rugs and rows of Kachina dolls. At the far end a door stood open on Paul's study. He was pacing about his desk restlessly and he looked around when he saw me, his face, with its wide cheekbones and cleft chin, brightening as though I were a gift Sylvia had brought him. For the first time I noticed that his eyes were the pale yellow-green of chrysolite, with an intensity in them, a probing quality in their gaze, as though he sought to draw out some inner significance that might be hidden from him. My instinct to resist such probing was strong now. I wasn't sure what I must defend, but I was on guard against him.

"Hello, Amanda," he said, and came toward me with a step that was buoyant for so big a man. "How are you settling in with the Cordovas?"

"I've met them all," I said carefully, avoiding the demand upon my will that seemed to light his strange eyes.

"As I've told you, Amanda doesn't remember anything," Sylvia said quickly. "It's as though everything is being told her for the first time."

"Come and sit down," he said, drawing me toward a living-room chair with a blue-and-brown rug flung across it.

Sylvia made a futile gesture toward delay. "Do look at that chair covering before you sit down, Amanda. Juan gave it to us one Christmas years ago. The things he finds for the store are superb. That indigo color is hard to come by, and the brown isn't dyed. It's the natural color of the sheep."

I duly examined this treasure before I sat down. Sylvia's slight flutter seemed uncharacteristic, but I hadn't seen her in the presence of her husband for long before. In any case, my main attention was given to Paul.

"They've told me about your book," I said bluntly. "I don't like what you plan to do. In any case, I can't be of help to you. There's nothing at all I can remember of that time."

"I didn't expect it to be so easy," Paul said. "Such memories are apt to be deeply buried. You'd instinctively try to protect them from view, forget them—wouldn't you? But perhaps they can be coaxed to emerge."

My sense of wariness increased. There had already been small flashes, an edge of memory, though I wouldn't tell him that. And my dream had come again last night, brought on, undoubtedly, by the impact of these once known surroundings. Nevertheless, if I were to remember something terrible, I wanted to share it with no one, least of all with this man who seemed avid for such knowledge.

"I don't want to remember, that's true," I told him. "Nothing has come back. I have no recollections of my grandfather's house, of the patio garden—nothing. And no one I've seen has brought back any feeling of recognition. My cousin Eleanor, Aunt Clarita, my grandfather are all strangers to me."

"You see, Paul?" Sylvia said, almost pleading with him.

He turned his head with its sandy-gray hair to look at his wife, and thus presented me with his profile. Strangely, it did not seem to match the rather engaging look he displayed full face. Seen from the side, he wore the profile of a faun—sharp-featured, playful, hinting of dangerous delights. I could well see that he might hold a fascination for women.

The look reproached Sylvia now, though he went on calmly, losing nothing of that deeper intensity I'd glimpsed in him.

"The surfacing of memory is a fascinating phenomenon. I've seen the forgotten emerge from hiding bit by bit until a picture became clear that was not clear in the first place. I'd like to try this with you, Amanda."

Underlying the calm assurance of his manner, I sensed excitement—some quality that courted danger. As Sylvia had suggested, this was a man who would play with fire for the fun of it. I sensed in him a tendency to enjoy the macabre, and I knew that whatever happened, he must not be allowed to write about my mother. Why Sylvia should be so concerned about Paul's project, I didn't know, but I could understand why my grandfather did not trust this man.

Sylvia broke in again, and I heard strain in her voice. "No, Paul—no. Let her alone. Don't do this. It could be dangerous."

He glanced at her with those pale eyes and she seemed to shrink back from his look. "Dangerous to whom, my dear?"

"To—to all of us. I mean emotionally, of course.

Please let her be, Paul. You have enough material for your book without the Cordova affair. And I don't want to upset Juan and Clarita. Or Gavin, for that matter."

He came to sit in a chair opposite me, leaning toward me with all his intensity turned in my direction. "Someone is always upset in these efforts. Obscure relatives threaten to sue. Indignant letters are written. I've been through it before with other books. Since I deal mostly with facts, it all comes to nothing. Besides, the Cordova case is what set me off on the idea of doing this book in the first place. This is one murder I was close to. I knew all the actors personally. I was there at the time. Most of the people involved are still at hand, even though the two main actors are gone."

"You weren't close to it—you weren't!" Sylvia cried.

"If you mean that I wasn't actually there when it happened, that's true. But I must have arrived ten minutes later—which is close enough. And I remember everything."

"Then I don't think you need to bother about the nonexistent or hazy memories of a five-year-old," I said.

He looked at me with a certain amusement, as though I had said something funny. "You don't know, do you? You really don't know?"

"I don't know what you're talking about."

"Then perhaps we ought to tell her. Don't you think so, Sylvia?"

"No—no, I don't!" Sylvia cried. "It's up to them to tell her the whole story."

"And color it as they please?"

"That's Juan Cordova's right."

He shrugged and leaned back in his chair. "I'm willing to wait. There's plenty of time."

His quiet certainty that I would talk to him eventually disturbed and angered me. "It doesn't matter whether you wait or not. Even if I should remember anything, I wouldn't talk about it. I've already told you that."

"Not even if what you might remember should change

the story about your mother? What if it should exonerate her in some way?"

I stared at him. "What do you mean?"

"Nothing at all. It's just a possibility that we can't overlook." He made a bland gesture with his hands which was belied by that tantalizing light in his eyes. "As Sylvia has suggested, we'll wait for the time being. I'm always here if you should want to talk to me. Does that satisfy you, Sylvia?"

Almost imperceptibly she relaxed, though she didn't answer him, but looked at me instead. Her interest now lay in changing the subject.

"Did you find out yesterday why Eleanor ran away?" she asked.

Since Paul had seen Eleanor last night, it seemed strange that Sylvia had not been told her story. However, there was no reason why I shouldn't talk about this, and I gave an account of our finding Eleanor in the cave and bringing her home. "She seems to have wanted to get away from her family—"

"And worry them to death," Sylvia put in.

"Gavin's a brute," Paul said.

What had Eleanor told him? I wondered, and felt unexpectedly indignant.

Sylvia contradicted this at once. "He's not a brute at all. You know him better than that. Eleanor wants a divorce, so I wouldn't put it past her to try to goad Gavin. There's a whole nest of hornets being stirred up. Juan is bound that she's not going to leave Gavin and he's using every card he can play to keep them together."

Was I one of the cards? It seemed likely.

"What does Gavin want?" I asked.

"Eleanor, of course," Paul said. "She means money and the control of the store to him. He'll never let her go unless she forces his hand. She's finding herself helpless in a difficult situation, so she takes imprudent courses."

"She's about as helpless as a tarantula," Sylvia snapped, sounding like herself again. "But let's stop talking about the Cordovas. It's not pleasant for Amanda. I've some coffee perking in the kitchen. I'll go and get it. Show her a copy of *Emanuella,* Paul. I've always thought it was your best book."

Paul smiled, and I was not sure I liked the smile. It seemed to take too much for granted—as though he assumed that I would side with him in any controversy, and that if he waited long enough I would come over to his way of thinking.

"Sylvia is prejudiced," he said when she'd gone. "Against Eleanor, I mean." He leaned toward me, and I felt again the submerged intensity in this man that filled me with foreboding. "You're a lot like your mother. You take me back to another time. Before all the trouble. Would you be surprised to hear that I once thought myself in love with Doro? Foolish, of course. She was already married, and Sylvia was the right woman for me."

Perhaps she heard him as she came back into the room with a tray of coffee cups and set it down on his desk. Perhaps he had intended for her to hear. I did not like or trust Paul Stewart, and I hoped that my mother had ignored him.

"He hasn't shown you the book," Sylvia said, and when she had poured our coffee she went to a bookcase and took down a volume in a mustard dust jacket. "Take this along and read it sometime, Amanda. It's semi-nonfiction. Paul based the story on old Spanish history. We went over to Spain when he was doing the research and stayed awhile in Madrid. As a matter of fact, it's Cordova history. At least of that branch of the family which stayed in Spain."

I took the book from her, interested in the family connection. When I flipped open to the copyright page, I saw it had been published a few years after my mother's death.

I had taken only a few sips of coffee when Eleanor came brightly through the door. Her hair was brushed to a sunny shine this morning, and her tall person looked beautifully trim in a dove-gray trouser suit.

"I've been looking for you, Amanda," she told me. "Grandfather wants to see you at once. So you'd better hurry."

I took another sip of coffee and stood up. "Thank you, Sylvia. I suppose I'd better go. Did you say you had a package for me?"

Sylvia remembered and jumped up. She ran out of the room and was back in a moment with a lumpy brown envelope.

"Here you are. I almost forgot. Katy was very weak when she gave me this, but she managed to whisper a few words. She said, 'Tell her to go to the *rancho.*' "

I took the envelope and moved toward the door. Both Eleanor and Paul had watched this interchange, but neither Sylvia nor I explained.

"Come back soon," Paul said, and his look seemed to challenge me with that amused assurance, as though he knew I would be back.

Eleanor gestured with a careless hand. "You know the way. I needn't go with you. I'll have some of that coffee, Sylvia, if you don't mind."

Sylvia turned away to pour the coffee, and in that instant I saw the quick exchange of looks between Paul and Eleanor. What I saw I did not like. Some pact, some understanding existed between them, and I had a feeling that it had to do with me.

The gate stood open in the adobe wall and I went through to pick up my painting gear and go into the house. Clarita was in the living room, talking to Rosa. When she saw me her eyes went carefully blank, and she made no effort to stop me as I set down my gear and the small package on a table. The book *Emanuella* I took with me. Perhaps I'd ask Juan about it. Evidently she had received her own orders by now and liked me none the better for them. I wished I could reassure her, but there was no way to do it at the moment.

As I mounted the steps to the balcony, I heard voices and I approached the doorway hesitantly. Gavin was there with my grandfather. Juan Cordova sat behind his desk, white-faced, his eyes closed, his lips thin with tension. Gavin stood above him, and I heard his words as I reached the door.

"This isn't something you can order as you please," he said grimly. "We've been over this ground before, and I won't be changed."

"Grandfather?" I spoke quickly, not wanting to hear what was not intended for my ears.

Gavin turned his cool look upon me and I found myself wishing that he might have been an ally, instead of one more antagonist. There were matters I might have consulted him about, if I were able. But he turned his back, dismissing me, and walked to a window, where the burgundy draperies had been drawn aside to let in New Mexico sunlight.

"Come in, come in, Amanda," Juan Cordova said testily. "Where have you been that it took so long to find you?"

I went to stand before his desk. "I was next door with Sylvia and Paul."

He stared me down with his fierce, falcon's look. "I told you not to talk to Paul Stewart."

"I know. But I didn't promise you not to. However, you needn't worry that I might help him with his book. There isn't anything I can tell him. He said something strange, though. He wondered if anything I could remember might help to exonerate my mother."

"Exonerate? I hardly think that is his purpose. But we will speak of this again. Now sit down for a moment. I've been talking to Gavin about you. I want him to show you the store this morning. It is necessary for you to learn as much as you can about what it means to the Cordova family."

I didn't like the implication. "Why?" I asked as I sat in the chair beside his desk.

The heavy lids closed over his eyes as though he found it difficult to deal with me. He looked anything but kind.

"The store is part of your heritage. You must learn about it."

"I've heard it called an albatross," I said, and drummed my fingers lightly on the book Sylvia had loaned me.

Gavin turned from the window. "It's all of that, if you let it be. But you're forewarned. All right, Juan—I'll do as you ask. If Amanda is to go through the store, we'd better start now."

"One moment, Gavin," Juan said. "Have you learned anything more about the pre-Columbian head someone put in your room?"

"I didn't expect to," Gavin said. "All these happenings are meant to look bad for me, and no one is going to admit anything. I can only count on your trust in me."

"To a certain extent you may count on it," Juan said. "To a certain extent. I'm not sure who can be trusted any more. But shortly after I've spoken to her, you will take Amanda to the store and introduce her to the best of it. She and CORDOVA may be important to each other."

I stood up, speaking hastily out of embarrassment. "Of course I'd like to see the store—as a visitor. I've known about it since I was a little girl and it has always fascinated me. Isn't it possible for you to come with us?" I said to my grandfather.

I could hear the weariness of ill health in his voice as he replied. "Not today. Leave us alone for a moment, Gavin. I want to speak with Amanda."

Gavin went out, but there was an angry glint in his eyes that did not promise well for our tour of the store. He had never been an ally, but this talk of showing me CORDOVA might make him an enemy.

My grandfather beckoned me closer. "I want you to do something for me in the store. I go out very seldom these days, and I have an errand for you. You are to notice one display case in particular while you are in the store. You will find it on the second floor—a tall glass case containing articles of Toledo steel. Locate the cabinet. Look at it so that you can find it again. Do you understand?"

"I don't understand at all," I told him. "But I'll do as you wish."

"Good. I will explain another time. Now go and join Gavin. But report to me when you return. I want to know what you think of CORDOVA. And—listen to me carefully, Amanda—you are to say nothing to Gavin about the cabinet. Do you hear me?"

"I hear you," I said. "I'll do as you wish."

Some strange relief seemed to wash over him. He smiled at me with a certain air of triumph, as though he had not been sure he could bend me to his will, and was pleased that he had. I suspected that I had been bested in some way I did not understand, that I was being made sly use of. But the matter didn't seem important, and in this case I would do as he wished.

I went down to the living room where Rosa was busy working and Clarita had disappeared. Gavin waited for me.

"I'll put this book of Paul Stewart's and my other things in my room, and get my handbag," I said, holding up the volume.

Gavin looked at it with distaste. "It's a good thing your grandfather didn't notice what you've got there. He long ago ordered every copy in the house of that book to be given away or thrown out. He won't be pleased about your reading it. He doesn't feel that Stewart did well by Emanuella."

"Then I shan't tell him," I said, and hurried up the stairs to my room.

Now the book interested me all the more, but I had no time for it at the moment. I tossed it down on the bed, glancing quickly at the white rug where the fetish had lain, relieved to find nothing there. I liked that episode less every time I thought of it. But now what mattered was Katy's package. That could not wait. I ripped open the sealed flap and looked inside. All the envelope contained was a small blue jeweler's box of the sort that might hold a ring. There was no paper, no message. I pressed the catch and the lid of the box opened. Inside, tucked into the satin slit where a ring might have rested, was a tiny brass key. Nothing else. I had been left a puzzle to which I had no answer, except that I had been told to go to the *Rancho de Cordova.* There was no time to ponder over this now, since Gavin was waiting, and I was eager to see the store for myself.

Juan was right—it was a part of my heritage, whether I liked it or not, and it would tell me more about the Cordovas. Gavin was clearly reluctant to be my guide, and I found myself regretting that. He mustn't become my enemy. If he didn't so obviously disapprove of me, he might have helped me when it came to the things I wanted to know. I might even have told him of Paul Stewart's effort to put some pressure on me to remember what had happened at the time of my mother's death. But I couldn't do that unless I broke through the barrier Gavin held against me.

For the first time, I wondered if that was possible. In spite of the way Juan's words had antagonized him, perhaps, as he showed me about the store, I could find a way to allay the suspicions he held against me, whatever they were. I needed a friend badly, and I went downstairs to join him with a new intent in me, a new purpose.

*VII*

CORDOVA fronted spaciously on a street that branched off from the plaza. I saw that only a portion of its glass windows had been photographed in that ad I had long ago torn from a magazine. The wide store front was impressive, and there was an elegance, a luxury about the windows with their exotic treasures discreetly displayed.

Gavin opened a glass door and let me precede him into the shop. It was an old building, and I had an immediate sense of great space, high ceilings that lost themselves in upper gloom, of polished counters and wall shelves that followed long aisles to the rear of the store, all handsomely arranged to attract the eye and tempt those who might appreciate the beautiful and unusual.

Daylight penetrated only a little way past the front windows, and the vast interior was illumined by artificial lighting. Inside, visitors moved about decorously, and women behind the counters waited on customers with grave courtesy. A hush that shut off traffic sounds from outdoors gave the shop an aura of restrained and almost awesome dignity. It was not a place in which boisterous behavior would be tolerated, any more than such behavior would be endured in a museum. Juan had apparently made an elaborate effort to turn CORDOVA into a shrine for the rare objects he worshiped. I found the effect a little oppressive and somehow it made me feel irreverent, contrary.

"Does anyone ever laugh in here?" I asked Gavin.

Apparently he had been waiting for my first reaction, and I had surprised him. His smile came slowly.

"So you aren't going to be intimidated, after all?"

I stood before an ancient Spanish chest with heavily carved drawers and wrought-iron pulls. On top of it stood a bowl of beaten brass from Guyana, and several carved trays and boxes made of rare Paraguayan woods, all labeled with discreet small signs.

"It's not that I don't appreciate all these beautiful things," I said, "but I can't help thinking of what Eleanor said about CORDOVA—that it was always put above the human beings connected with it. So that now, when I'm here, I have a feeling of resistance to its—well to its smothering perfection."

Gavin reached past me to touch the surface of an exquisitely carved bowl. "The man who made this knew how to laugh. He was close to the earth, perhaps ignorant by our standards, but he could create beauty with his hands. Juan knows nothing about him. He has always been interested in the product, not the man, except as the artist can be used. For the purist, that may be the way to look at it."

"But you're interested in the artist apart from his art?"

"Yes—perhaps because I've traveled a lot and come to know some of the people who sell us their work. It's not disembodied for me, since I care about th craftsman who is alive and working today. A good man of the things we carry here have men and women behin them who live in Spain and Mexico, or in the South an Central American countries. I've come to know som of their families and a good deal about their person skills and talents. When my father used to go abroa for Juan, he always looked for sources, instead of dea ing with some middleman. I've done the same thing. Craftwork *is* a living thing."

His head with its thick crest of fair hair was held high, so he could look all about him, and his gray eyes saw more than mere objects, wherever he looked. I liked him better for his explanation, and my brief sense of irreverence faded.

We moved on past a rug with a Kachina design in brown and white and black, displayed against a nearby wall, and I paused before a Mexican sunburst mirror next to it, looking at Gavin behind me in the round of glass. For the first time since I had met him, he seemed alive and concerned, instead of being far away and always on guard. It was interesting to see his eyes take on warmth and excitement when he was involved in the things he cared about. Perhaps this was the man I had sensed in that moment when I had first seen him and felt that breath-stopping attraction I couldn't quite shake off.

"Are you and my grandfather at odds about the store?" I asked.

At once his guard was up again. "I work for him," he said curtly, and moved on to a table graced by an intricate wrought-iron candelabrum, with fine Indian pottery arranged around it. Against the wall beyond leaned a stack of great, carved doors of Spanish colonial design, such as I had already seen at the Cordovas' and the Stewarts'.

"Those doors are made in the city," Gavin said. "They're known everywhere as Santa Fe doors."

He was again the guide Juan had instructed him to be, and I had lost my tenuous contact. I could only follow as he turned down the next aisle and paused before a cabinet with a glass front. A sign indicated that these objects belonged to pre-Columbian times and were being loaned to the store for exhibit. There were bits of stone, shards of pottery, and ornamentation from ancient buildings. One piece was a stone head with bulging, exaggerated features, broken off at the neck, but otherwise intact.

"Is that the head that disappeared?" I asked.

"Yes—the one I'm supposed to have stolen."

"Why would anyone play such a trick on you?"

He gave me a distant glance. "It's hardly your concern."

Prickling indignation swept me and I would not be intimidated by Gavin Brand either. "Grandfather seemed to think that everything about CORDOVA was my concern."

"Why?"

"I suppose because I'm one of the family and should know about such things. What else? Surely Grandfather doesn't believe in any robbery when it comes to that stone head, does he?"

"There was a robbery. Someone took the head out of this locked case. Someone who had access to the key that's kept in the store."

He moved away, indifferent to what I might believe, continuing our tour of the first floor. Now and then he paused to explain something casually, or stopped to point out some article with an admiration that shone through his indifference toward me. I felt increasingly resentful of his attitude. All his barriers were up, and my wish to break through them was obviously futile. Yet I didn't want to accept this as final defeat.

We reached the back of the store and a corner where articles of woven grass were displayed. The scent of the grasses was fragrant and all pervading. There was no one about back here, and when Gavin would have moved on, I stopped him.

"Please let me apologize for that ridiculous remark I made when we first met. It was stupid, but I wish you wouldn't go on holding it against me."

At least his look focused on me, though he seemed surprised. "I'd forgotten all about it. It was never important."

"Then why must you—" I began, but he broke in on my words, suddenly willing to be frank.

"Juan brought you out here to use you, and you're stepping right into his trap. I suppose it will serve you to step into it, but you might as well know that I'll oppose you all the way. There are prior rights."

I stared at him in outrage, so furious I couldn't speak. I didn't understand his talk about traps or about my willingness to be used. Too angry to answer him, I moved on to the next display, unable to examine it calmly.

"The better things are upstairs." He was my impersonal guide again, grimly doing his duty. "A good deal of what we show down here is for the tourist trade. Or else it consists of imported objects that Santa Feans buy."

There was a strong smell of leather as we walked through a section given over to Spanish leather goods— belts and pocketbooks, and even boots and saddles. Near the front of the store, a wide flight of stairs rose toward the floor above, and I mounted them beside Gavin, still seething. But at least I remembered Juan's words—that it was up here I would find the cabinet of Toledo steel, the case he had instructed me to notice for some reason he hadn't explained. I would take care of my mission as soon as I could, and then I would turn my back on Gavin and the store.

At the head of the stairs a glass-enclosed ceramic flamenco dancer waited to greet us, and beyond her the floor turned into a museum of fine arts and crafts. Here much of what was displayed was fabulously expensive, exquisitely wrought. This was CORDOVA, restrained in its presentation of superb workmanship, less crowded than the floor below, yet stamped somehow with the same arrogant confidence that characterized Juan Cordova. There was no entreaty to buy, for here that function seemed a privilege. For the first time, I began to sense the element of proud family that ruled both the store and the Cordovas.

"I could never belong to all this," I said impulsively. "It would try to dominate and rule, wouldn't it? It would have to be possessive. You'd have to give your life for it."

Gavin glanced at me with mild curiosity. "I didn't expect you to understand that."

I thought with resentment that what he expected of me had little concern with reality. But in spite of the effect the store might exert upon me, I was quickly lost to the rich fare it presented on every hand. The artist in me was beguiled in spite of myself.

Hand-embroidered shawls from Spain were glorious and I stopped to finger silken fringe and study the design of great, embroidered blossoms. This was like painting on silk. Brilliant blankets and rebozos and ponchos from Bolivia caught my eyes as I moved on, only to be drawn along to the next display of a stunning suede jacket from Argentina.

"There's nothing machine-made here," Gavin informed me. "Behind everything you see there's a craftsman or a woman talented at design and needlework." His tone had warmed again, though not toward me. "Juan has let me have my hand up here, and none of these things are confined in a museum. Because we can sell them, we help to keep these crafts alive and their creators productive."

The anger he could so quickly arouse in me was dying. I could understand the importance of finding the artist a market, and I touched with respect an inlaid box of exquisite woods from French Guiana.

"Even though it's possessive, CORDOVA is more than I thought," I said. "Sylvia Stewart called it the beast that ruled the family. And I can see the enormous amount of effort and expense that must go into keeping it alive. But perhaps it's worth it."

"It's worth it if we keep our feet on the ground and don't get lost in clouds of antiquity, which is what Juan, more and more, seems to want. He buys museum pieces he would never sell. He gets carried away by the idea of collecting and displaying, instead of selling. But this isn't a musty museum—it is something to keep men and women earning and productive, to preserve skills that might be lost. It must be kept *alive*—not allowed to die in the dust of a mere collection."

There was a passion in this man—a love for hand-wrought beauty, but also a belief in the worker behind it that I found myself relishing.

"What will happen to the store when Juan dies?" I asked.

He answered me curtly. "Eleanor will inherit it. That's the way his will reads."

"What about Clarita?"

"She's taken care of in other ways. Though I don't think Juan has ever been fair to Clarita, considering all the work she's put into the store. She used to manage this entire floor and she knows CORDOVA as Eleanor never will."

"Another one who's given her life to it? Perhaps CORDOVA is omnivorous like Juan. What will Eleanor do with it, if she inherits?"

"That remains to be seen. She'll hardly be possessed by it." His tone was dry.

"But of course you'll continue to manage it, buy for it?"

"There's no guarantee of that."

"If Eleanor has any sense—"

His look told me that once more this was none of my business, and I broke off. I could see how there might well be some sort of war going on under the surface in Juan Cordova's house.

We walked on past other displays, but I was beginning to feel sated, as one does sometimes in a museum. There was too much to see, too much to absorb. If it was possible, I would come back here again. I wanted more, but not now, and I wondered with a certain self-distrust if I too was beginning to be possessed by the store's power to absorb the Cordovas.

As I passed a shelf, my eye was caught by a carving done in some reddish-brown wood and I stopped to look at it more closely. It was about eight inches high—the head of an Indian woman with wide cheekbones, a nose with flared nostrils, and a generous mouth. The lines

were swift and modern, suggesting, rather than ex-
pressing, detail. I took it in my hands and felt the
smooth grain of the wood like satin under my fingers.

"How beautiful!" I said. "Where did this come from?"

Gavin thawed a little. "A woodcarver in Taxco did
that. He's part Indian and supremely gifted. The only
trouble, from our viewpoint, is that he carves very few
pieces. He doesn't care about money, and he'll work
only when the vision comes to him and he can produce
something superb."

I set the carving regretfully back on the shelf. I would
have liked to own it for myself, but I didn't trouble to
look at the price label glued discreetly to the base. I
knew what it must cost.

"How lucky he is to do only the work he really cares
about," I said, thinking of my brochures, my drawing
for advertising projects I often didn't care about. "Sometimes I've wished—" but I stopped, remembering that
Gavin Brand would not care what I wished.

"You want to be a painter, don't you?" he said.

I was surprised that he would comment. "More than
anything. But no matter what I might wish, I have to
work at jobs that are often less than creative."

"And probably good for you. My Taxco friend is an
exception. Ivory towers don't work for most artists.
Or for the rest of us, for that matter. Men need to
be engaged in life. Otherwise our viewpoints become des-
iccated and narrow."

As Juan Cordova's had? I wondered. Gavin was involved with more than the mere perfection of all this
rich merchandise which the store presented. How much
was he involved with Eleanor, and how much was
Eleanor concerned with what lay outside herself?

But again, this was none of my business.

"Don't let anything stop you. Be a painter," he said,
and moved on to the next display.

I heard him in surprise. He had cut through to an
understanding I hadn't expected of him. He had not

softened toward me particularly, but he respected what
I must do.

"You haven't seen my work," I said. "How do you
know that I shouldn't be discouraged from going ahead,
that I shouldn't be stopped?"

"No one should be stopped. You can create for your
own satisfaction, if for nothing else."

"That's not good enough. That's the ivory tower bit.
I suppose I want to say something in my work that
someone else can see and enjoy. If there's no one to
appreciate, you're only looking in a mirror."

He smiled at me—for once without suspicion or disliking, so that his face lighted and lost its somber quality.

"You're right, of course. This is the thing Juan is
forgetting. He has created CORDOVA, yet he's becoming
a miser about it. He wants it all for himself and his
family—like that art collection of his. He's forgotten
what is fundamental—the sharing and appreciation of
art by many. Will you show me some of your work
sometime?"

"I—I don't know," I said. I was suddenly both hopeful and oddly shy. Gavin had taste and perception. He
would be honest, and if he didn't like what I showed
him, it would hurt me. It would matter.

He didn't press me, but allowed me the right of uncertainty, and I was unexpectedly grateful.

"Here is something you must see," he said, and we
stopped before a glass counter in which fine silver and
turquoise jewelry was displayed against a background
of black velvet.

"These are things from the Southwest," he told me.
"From some of our best Indian craftsmen. Your grand-
father said you were to choose whatever piece you like.
He wants you to have something in turquoise from
CORDOVA."

I was touched and pleased, and I bent over the glass,
searching. The girl behind the counter drew out a tray
and set it before me so that I could finger the lovely
gleaming rings and brooches and pendants. I did not

want a ring or necklace; so I finally picked out a brooch, inlaid with turquoise, jet and coral, and outlined with the points of a silver sunburst.

"This one, I think," I said. I pinned it to the shoulder of my blue linen and the girl brought a mirror on a stand, so that I could see how it looked.

"A good choice," Gavin approved. "That's Zuni work and of the finest."

I was turning away from the counter when a tall cabinet in the center of the floor caught my eye. I walked over to it at once to look at the swords and knives it displayed. *Toledo Steel,* the card in the case read. I could not imagine why my grandfather had wanted me to locate and remember this case, but I looked around to check it against other displays, so that I could find it again.

Gavin seemed uninterested in such cutlery. "You've just about seen the store," he said, turning distant again. "Have you had enough? Do you know all about CORDOVA now?"

"As you very well know, I couldn't learn all about it in months of study," I assured him. "But I'm glad to make a beginning."

Apparently my choice of words was unfortunate. His face was expressionless, all feeling suppressed. "Yes—you're expected to go on from here, I gather."

We were walking down an aisle and there was no one nearby to overhear. I spoke to him quickly, bluntly.

"What is it my grandfather expects of me? What does he want?"

He answered me with careful indifference, as though the words he spoke did not matter. "Perhaps an heiress. Perhaps only a weapon to threaten us with." He might have been speaking of the weather.

"But I don't want to be either of those things!" I cried. "I don't want anything from him, except perhaps an affection I'm not likely to find in his house."

He didn't believe me. His silence was skeptical and I went on heatedly, even though I knew it was no use.

"Certainly I don't want to threaten anyone. Though

someone seems to be threatening me." I told him abruptly about the mole fetish which had been left in my room yesterday.

He seemed unsurprised. "What can you expect? If you're determined to stay here, you're sure to stir up antagonisms. Juan will use you, as he tries to use everything he touches."

"Perhaps I won't let him use me."

"Then there's no point in staying, is there? Why do you want to stay?"

"Why do you want me to go away?" I countered. "What are you afraid of? I don't really know my grandfather yet. I want to know him for myself, not just through the eyes and prejudices of others." There was still more to it. There was the matter of my mother, but I didn't want to tell him how I felt about that, and have him laugh at me. "If my staying here is Cordova stubbornness, then let it be that way."

"The stubbornness of Spain or New England?" he said. "There's not much to choose between, is there?"

To my surprise he was not wholly mocking. He might dislike and disapprove of me, but I had the feeling that he had, strangely, begun to respect me. Nevertheless, I resented his calm assurance as he strode toward the stairs ahead of me, obviously relieved that his guide duty was over, taking it for granted I would follow. All that was contrary in me resisted, and I turned down an aisle I had not seen and came to a halt before an open display case.

The key was in the lock of the door which stood ajar, as though someone must be working on the display, and the contents of the case took my startled attention.

In the center was a crude, two-wheeled wooden cart with spikes protruding all around the upper edge. It was filled with large rocks upon which sat the figure which had startled me. It was made of carved wood—the skeleton of a woman with a wig of scrawny black locks, and a bow and arrow fixed in her bony hands. Her eyes were hollows and her teeth grinned eerily in her skull's face.

"Attractive, isn't she?" said a voice behind me.

I turned in surprise, to find Paul Stewart at my shoulder, holding up a vicious-looking three-pronged whip in one hand. When I stared at the whip, he gave the thongs a little flick with the fingers of his other hand.

"This is a *disciplina*. Just part of my Penitente collection," he said. "Of course you've heard of the Penitentes of the Southwest? I offered to loan my collection to Juan for the store, and he was pleased. So I've brought these things over and I've been arranging them. How do you like the lady in the cart?"

His pale, chrysolite eyes turned from me for a moment to look down the aisle, and I saw that Gavin was standing a little way off, clearly waiting for me with some impatience. I stayed where I was.

"What is she?" I asked Paul.

He bent his big frame and carefully arranged the whip to best effect among the other articles in the case.

"She's *La Muerte*. Or Doña Sebastiana, if you wish. That's what they call her. You'd better pray to her for a long life. That arrow poised in the bow is intended for some nonbelieving bystander. She's sitting in one of the death carts they pull in their processions. The stones that fill the cart make it heavy, so that those who pull it punish themselves."

"You've written about all this, haven't you?"

"Yes. I found it fascinating. I've been into Penitente country a good many times and managed to get myself trusted enough so they'd talk to me. That whip is one they use for self-flagellation. The wooden clackers are *matracas* and they can make a hideous noise. The flints down in the corner there—the *pedernales*—are used to inflict surface wounds, and you'll see there's a candle lantern and a crucifix. The sect is dying out to some extent, but *Los Hermanos*, The Brothers, still exist back in the hills. They're Hispanic in descent and Catholic, of a sort, though the Church has denounced their practices."

Near the center of the case Paul Stewart had taken care to display several copies of the book he had written and I read its title, *Trail of the Whip*. Doña Sebastiana herself graced the jacket, and Paul's name was in black letters across the bottom.

"I'll loan you a copy, if you like," he said.

I shivered slightly. "I still have *Emanuella* to read, and I think she'll be more to my taste."

"I'm not so sure," Paul said. "You may find out too much about the Cordovas in those pages."

"The Cordovas are what I want to know about," I said lightly, and turned to walk toward Gavin.

Gavin stood near the stairs, and he made no comment as I joined him. I sensed that Paul Stewart's presence in the store was not something he liked, and if the choice had been his, he might have dispensed with the Penitente display. I sensed, too, disapproval of me because I had stopped to talk to Paul. But Gavin was not my keeper and I would do as I pleased.

We went down to the lower floor and out to the side street, where he had left his car. On the way to the house I tried to unbend my resentment enough to thank him.

"I'm sure no one else could have told me as much about the store as you have," I said. "I appreciate your taking the time."

He gave me a casual nod without speaking, and his very silence dismissed me. He had simply been doing what Juan Cordova had ordered him to do. I had arrived nowhere with my foolish hope that we might become better friends during my tour of the store. In fact, part of the time I wasn't sure I wanted him for a friend anyway.

He let me out at the turquoise gate and said he was returning to work. When I crossed the narrow yard to the unlocked front door, there was no one about, and inside the house I climbed the steps to my grandfather's rooms, knocking on the door. He called to me to come in. I entered, to find him lying stretched out on a long leather couch, a cushion propped beneath his head, and his eyes closed.

"I've seen the store," I told him. "You asked me to come back afterwards."

He gestured toward the chair beside his couch, his eyes still closed. "Come then and sit down. Tell me about it."

I tried haltingly to obey, but my impressions were too recent, too many, and I hadn't begun to digest them. I found myself quoting Gavin, speaking about the store's use in helping so many skilled craftsmen to keep working.

He shrugged this aside. "We are not a charitable institution. Fine work is well paid for. Tell me what you liked best."

I told him about the wood carving from Taxco and he opened his eyes to look at me approvingly. "Ah, yes—the Tarascan woman. Beautiful. I wanted to bring her home and keep her in my study, but Gavin would not permit me."

"Permit you?" I echoed in surprise.

He smiled at me slyly. "These days Gavin must be my eyes, my hands, my will. It doesn't do to oppose him too much. Did you find something in turquoise for yourself?"

I touched the pin on my blouse. "Yes. Thank you, Grandfather."

"Come closer," he said, and reached out to touch the pin, sensing the inlay with his fingers. "Zuni. A good choice. Did Gavin help you?"

"I chose it myself," I told him, and couldn't help the slight tartness that crept into my tone. I was not leaning upon Gavin.

"And did you see the case of Toledo steel?"

"Yes. I know where it is. Why did you want me to see it?"

"Later, later," he said testily. "Tell me what you think of Gavin?"

This was not a question I wanted to answer and it took me by surprise. I formed my words cautiously.

"He seems to know everything about the store. He made a very good guide."

"I know all that. What do you think of *him?*"

Since he would allow no evasion, I tried to answer honestly.

"He seems to understand the man behind the craft. He believes that art should be a living thing—something with meaning for the living. And in the case of craftwork, a living for the creator."

"He has been lecturing you, I see. But you're still talking about the field in which he's an expert. What do you think of him—of Gavin himself?"

Again, I tried to be honest, though this was not a subject I wanted to discuss. "I think I would like him if he permitted me to. But he doesn't like me. He believes that I mean the Cordovas some harm."

There was a wicked glee in the old man's laughter. "They are all sure of that. I have poured poison in the ant heap and they are scurrying to save themselves."

"I don't like to be regarded as a household poison."

His glee included me. "They don't know what I am going to do about you, and I've frightened them badly."

"I didn't come here to frighten anyone. I don't like this role you've thrust upon me."

"Why did you come then?"

It was the old question, and he had not understood my reasons. The attraction of a family for someone who had no family was beyond his comprehension.

"I came because of my mother," I said. "I know now that there's something I need to remember. Grandmother Katy left me a small ring box containing a key. She gave it to Sylvia to keep in case I ever came here, and she left me a message too. She said I was to go to the *rancho.*"

He flung back the light covering and sat up on the couch to stare at me in astonishment. "What does this mean? Sylvia has been like a daughter, yet she has never told me of this. Why?"

"I'm afraid you'll have to ask her."

He sat there pondering. "Before she died, Katy tried to tell me some wild thing of which I could make nothing."

"Then she knew something!" I cried. "She really did know something. What if Paul Stewart is right and some memory of mine might be used to exonerate my mother?"

"It is all so long ago." He shook his head in unhappy memory. "It is not an experience I want to go through again."

"But you loved Doroteo."

"That too was long ago. Now I am an old man, beyond loving or being loved."

"Then I'm sorry for you," I said.

He rose from the couch, and his height gave him dominance over me. His height and his arrogance.

"I want pity from no one. Mine is an enviable state. I have all that I want, and there is no one who can inflict pain upon me."

"And no one who can bring you joy?" I said.

"You speak your mind like a Cordova. What do you intend to do with this key and ring box?"

"I'll get someone to take me out to the *rancho*. Perhaps something there will help me to remember."

He moved to the chair behind his desk, pulling the maroon silk of his robe more tightly across his chest.

"If there is a real need for you to remember, perhaps I can help you. But not if you mean to talk about these things to Paul Stewart."

"How can you help me?"

"I will think about this and we will speak of it again. If there should be a way to change our beliefs about what happened with Doroteo and Kirk Landers, that is something I would like to explore. Doroteo was my beloved daughter, and Kirk was more like a son than Rafael. Perhaps he loved me more than my own son did, and he loved Spain. He should have been born to me."

This was a new view of Kirk, and I listened in mild surprise.

"Never mind," he went on. "I have little faith that the past can be changed. And now there are more urgent matters pressing upon me. You have made a beginning with the store, Amanda. We will go on from there."

I didn't care for the sound of that, but he reached for papers on his desk and nodded a cool dismissal. He wanted nothing more of me now. On my way down to the living room, I realized that he still hadn't told me why he'd sent me to look at the cabinet that held swords from Toledo.

No one was about, and I stood upon a Navajo rug and looked around thoughtfully. Nothing spoke to me with a clear voice. The room with its cool gloom seemed strange to my eyes—all white walls and brown vigas and Indian ornaments. Yet something hovered just beyond the edge of vision—something that waited to pounce. I remembered the mole fetish and Eleanor's hinting that I was the hunter's prey. But I wouldn't accept that. I would not play mouse for Juan Cordova or prey for a hunter. I would stay here only long enough to find out what I wanted to know about my mother, and then I would turn my back upon adobe walls and encroaching mesa, get away from here forever.

As I walked toward the stairs to my room, I wondered why this decision filled me with no relief. Was there, after all, a spell exerted by mountains and desert, and adobe-colored towns? Something seemed to draw me, hold me here, yet whatever it was pulsed faintly with a sense of danger at the same time. What if Doroteo had not, after all, pulled the trigger of that gun which had killed Kirk Landers? What if she had not killed herself? Was there someone still living—someone who knew the truth and would be on guard against me if I meddled with matters that were thought settled and long buried?

The house was very still, yet I never had the sense of being alone in it. There were too many windows and passages, too many rooms opening one out of another. Was I being watched, as was so easily possible? I turned about quickly and caught a faint movement at a door that led to the patio. For an instant I was prompted to run to the door and see who was there—but I did not. An odd prickle of panic went through me and I fled up the stairs to my room, wanting only to close my own door between me and the rest of this silent, watching house.

But when I reached my room, I saw that it would do no good to close the door. Once more, Eleanor waited for me. She wore dove-gray trousers and a sleeveless turquoise blouse, and she sat cross-legged in the middle of my bed, with the book *Emanuella* open on her knees.

"I've been waiting for you," she said. "I see that someone has loaned you *Emanuella*."

"Sylvia said I should read it."

"She's right—you should. Though it may frighten you badly. It did me. Do you know who Emanuella was?"

I shook my head, wondering why Eleanor had come to my room.

"Legend has it that she was an ancestress of ours. Rather a notorious one, because of all her affairs at the court of Philip IV of Spain. Paul learned about her after he married Sylvia, and he went to Madrid to do some research on her before he wrote the book. Grandfather is proud of what he claims is the line of descent and he makes a lot of it. Emanuella was supposed to have a passionate disposition and a temper that we're all expected to inherit. But when Paul wrote the book, Grandfather was furious because he claimed she was a little mad. Her cousin Doña Inés wound up in a madhouse. Do you suppose the strain really comes down to us, Amanda?" Her eyes were bright and wide, with that appealing air of innocence that I didn't trust. I knew there was nothing innocent about her intent.

"I shouldn't think so," I said carelessly. "It would be a pretty diluted strain if it did."

"Velázquez painted the mad one—Doña Inés," Eleanor went on, tossing the book aside on the bed. "Velázquez himself is a character in Paul's story. Has Grandfather old you any of this, Amanda?"

"No," I said. "And I'm afraid it all sounds too remote as a scandal to get very excited about."

Eleanor uncurled herself and stretched out her legs in their gray trousers. "Not so remote, perhaps. Grandmother Katy took it seriously. I think she used to watch all of us for signs of the wild strain that Grandfather is so proud of. Only he won't call it madness."

"From what I've heard of Katy, she sounds too sensible for that."

"I remember her very well," Eleanor said. "She wasn't always calm and sensible. When I was small I can remember her walking in the patio and wringing her hands together as though there was something she couldn't bear. Once when she didn't know I was near I heard her talking to herself about being trapped in silence. I've always wondered what she meant."

I wondered too, and thought of the little key I'd put away in my handbag. Was that trap of silence about to be sprung open? Was I to be the instrument? I walked to one of the room's three windows and stood looking through the deep recess, down into the patio. I could imagine Katy walking its paths with a warm sun beating upon adobe walls. Eleanor came quietly to stand beside me.

"From here you can see the place where the family used to picnic," she said softly, slyly. "Do you see where the hillside dips into the arroyo beyond our back wall?" She pointed. "There's a very old cottonwood tree down there that gives a lovely shade. And there's a place where the hillside levels out beneath it. Do you see where the path winds down to the clearing?"

My gaze followed her pointing finger and I remembered my earlier uneasiness when I'd looked out toward the arroyo. I could see the path she indicated, and the clearing itself in the midst of that green growth that sprang up wherever there was a trace of water in New Mexico.

"Yes, I can see it," I said.

I would have turned from the window, but she put her hand on my arm to hold me there, and I felt malice in her grip.

"Your mother died on the ledge below the clearing." Her voice was light—and deadly. She meant to wound, to torment. "Because of the juniper bushes it's hidden from those who were there above at the picnic. But you can see the ledge from here. There are rocks along the hillside, forming the ledge. Do you see them?"

I could only nod, my throat constricted. The pressure of her fingers hurt my arm.

"That's where they struggled—your mother and Kirk Landers. Though he was away in Taos when it happened, Mark Brand, Gavin's father, was visiting here at the time and he had a gun. Doro must have gone into his room to get it, and everyone thinks she went down there to kill Kirk Landers."

"I don't believe that," I said tightly.

Eleanor shrugged graceful shoulders and took her hand away from my arm. "What difference does it make whether you believe it or not, when it really happened? I've heard Paul say that Doro was like Emanuella. She was in love with men. Many men. But she had a passionate nature and she couldn't bear to be—what's the old fashioned term?—spurned. She was in love with Kirk when she was young, but he went away and changed. So she killed him."

My breath was coming quickly and I could feel the perspiration breaking out on my cheeks and neck.

"What if none of this is true? You said they couldn't be seen from the picnic ground above."

"That's the angle that interests Paul. But you forget there was a witness—Aunt Clarita. She'd stayed home since she had a headache. But she got up for fresh air and she stood at this very window and saw the whole thing. She saw Doro fire the gun, while Kirk struggled with her. There was blasting going on in a nearby lot that day, so no one heard the shot. But Aunt Clarita knew when it was fired because she saw Kirk fall and your mother fling herself over the ledge into the arroyo. She could swear to all this later and there weren't any who would doubt Aunt Clarita's word."

The light, breathless voice at my side was still for a moment, but I was aware of the air of triumph with which she awaited my reaction. I felt a little sick and somehow angry as well. Stubbornly, I refused to accept.

"You wanted to know, didn't you?" she went on. "No one else would tell you the truth, but I think it's only fair that you should know the details of what happened. Of course, it's too bad the other witness couldn't be coherent about what she saw."

"There was a second witness?"

"Yes. Hasn't anyone told you? *You* were there on that ledge with your mother. You saw everything that happened and you were a lot closer than Clarita. But you were too terrified to talk. Gavin says you were speechless for quite a while after what happened. Your father was away that day, and it was Gavin who found you crying your heart out, and he brought you back to the house. Everyone else was too busy with the tragedy to think about you until you could be taken to Grandfather. All that part I saw, because Gavin brought me along too. Oh, he could be kind enough in those days. Not the way he is now."

Because I was shivering and the breeze felt cold, I moved back from the window.

"You came to my room for some reason?" I asked, knowing how stiff I sounded.

"Yes, of course. And I've told you what I came to tell you. Now you know everything that happened, so you can go back to New York and not worry Grandfather any more."

She turned from me with a light flick of her fingers that dismissed me, and went out of the room. Whatever malice she'd intended had been accomplished. I didn't want to look out that window again. I closed my door against further unwelcome guests and threw myself upon the bed. Eleanor wanted me gone, and that was why she had told me. But I couldn't accept her story. I still rebelled against the published version of what had happened, yet I had only my own instinct about my mother to guide me. Even my father had believed the worst of her. Only I, who knew her so little, believed in her. I flung an arm across my eyes to shut out the bright Santa Fe light.

*I* had seen what happened. I had seen it all—and I knew and remembered nothing. Or perhaps some instinct in me still remembered the truth and this was why my belief seemed unshakable, so that I had to stay and uncover the past.

# VIII

I must have fallen asleep, for when I awakened it was nearly time for lunch. Something hard lay on the bed beneath my hand and I saw it was the book by Paul Stewart. I sat up and stared at the back jacket, where a photograph of the author had been used.

The picture must have been taken years ago, for he looked youthfully handsome and more like a faun than ever. His sharp-featured face with those pale eyes gazed out at the world with an expression that seemed to invite danger. He was hardly the ivory tower writer, but looked like a man who enjoyed living, and who might court danger for the sheer satisfaction of defeating it. Only a few years before this picture was taken, he had—as he'd told me himself—been in love with Doroteo Austin. Yet he had married Sylvia. And now he chose to bring to life the circumstances under which Sylvia's stepbrother had died, and which his wife opposed having resurrected. Besides all this, some relationship seemed to exist between Sylvia's husband and Gavin's wife. Eleanor too seemed to be stirring something up, and I had again a feeling that the past hung over the present, dangerously imminent and involving all of us. Perhaps involving me especially, because of whatever lay buried in the memory of the child I had been.

I was sharply aware of the window that looked down upon the arroyo and drew me toward it with invisible threads. There was something down there which compelled me, and inevitably I would have to obey the summons. But not now. Not yet. Nevertheless, I went to the window and looked out.

At once my attention was fixed on the patio below. Near the gate which joined the Cordova and Stewart properties, Paul and Eleanor stood talking. They were in open view and there was no reason why they should not be there, yet there was something that suggested the clandestine in their interest in each other, in their whispered conversation. If I'd had to title the picture they made, I'd have called it *The Plotters,* and I wondered why that impression was so strong.

A memory flashed into my mind of Paul as I had seen him today in the store with the *disciplina*—that three-pronged whip of the Penitentes—in his hand. He had startled me unpleasantly then, and it wasn't hard to imagine his using the whip. Though not, I thought, on himself.

As I watched, Paul turned from Eleanor and disappeared through the gate to his own house. She, with a small, secret smile on her lips, ran across the patio to the garage, out of my view. As I stood there, I heard a car start, heard it move out of the garage and down the road.

Beyond patio and wall the path Eleanor had pointed out led along the hillside above the arroyo. Abruptly I faced my room. I was not yet ready to deal with what awaited me down there. Before I answered that summons, I wanted to talk to Clarita. Both Juan and Eleanor had told me she'd seen what happened, but I wanted to hear it from her own lips. I wanted to watch her face and listen to the tone of her voice when she told me.

When I was ready for lunch I went downstairs apprehensively. I wasn't anxious to face Eleanor again so soon, or for that matter, any of the rest of the family.

However, neither Eleanor nor Gavin was there, and only Clarita sat at the head of the table. As I took my place, she regarded me with her curiously intent look, though her words were casual enough.

"We are having only an omelet. I hope that will suit you. Often I lunch alone, and I prefer something light."

"That will be fine," I said. This was my opportunity, and I began to wonder how I might bring up my question. I knew I must move with care, since this was a subject she abhorred. Her guard must be down first, and that might be difficult to achieve.

The omelets arrived, and were made with tomatoes, green pepper and onion, lightly browned, with the edges firm. I found I was hungry and I ate with relish and relief, since the others weren't there and there need be no crosscurrents of hostility. However, nothing in my aunt's manner gave the opening I wanted, and I said nothing of what was uppermost in my mind.

Again Clarita wore her favorite black, with little concession to fashion. Only her dangling turquoise earrings gave her a touch of elegance and did not look foolish against her thin cheeks. She had the same manner of pride that characterized Juan Cordova, and which she had probably learned from him.

"You visited CORDOVA this morning?" she asked, when the omelets had been served.

"Yes. Gavin took me all around the store. There's more on those shelves than I could see in a lifetime."

Her look grew distant, remembering. "I used to know all of it. I trained the women who work on the second floor. As my father trained me. If I had been a man, Gavin would never have been put in charge over me. But my father doesn't believe in the business ability of women."

Her words carried a hint of hostility toward Juan, which I hadn't expected. For the first time I was aware that underlying her concern and care for her father, lay something else—an antagonism—that seldom surfaced.

"Surely you'd proved your worth to him in the store,"
I said.

"Gavin knew my worth. He always consulted me, as
his father used to do before him. I had a certain influence when I worked for CORDOVA."

"Why did you stop?"

The rings on her fingers flashed blue and amber light
as her hands moved about the table. "I am no longer
interested in such things."

Her answer allowed of no questioning, but it seemed
to hide more than it revealed. I ate in silence. We had
little to talk about. But at the end of the meal she surprised me.

"I have something to show you in my room. Will you
come with me?"

She rose from the table and I followed her into the
long, bedroom wing and through the first door. No sun
fell through the windows into Clarita's room, and it
had a muted, austere look. The blanket on the narrow
bed was an Indian weave in brown and white, and on
the floor nearby lay a shaggy brown rug. The rest of the
floor was of dark, wide boards, richly polished and bare
of any covering. On the wall above the bed, Clarita
had hung a row of very old *santos,* those pictures of
saints that were commonly seen in the Southwest, and
on a shelf were two *bultos*—saints carved in the round
and also clearly old. On a table near a window, various
small objects had been collected, and she waved me toward them.

"These belonged to your mother," Clarita said. "I
came upon them in the storeroom and I thought they
might mean something to you."

I approached the table hesitantly because of unexpectedly quickening emotion. Emotion so sudden and shattering that I didn't know how to cope with it. These
were feelings long buried, yet able to rise and devastate
me. For an instant the old dream-vision of a tree was
sharp in my mind, and I swayed as if I were dizzy.

Clarita was watching. "Is something wrong?"

The child which had risen with such sudden passionate grief, subsided, sank below the surface, and I managed to recover my adult self.

"I'm all right," I said. But the child had frightened me.

On the table lay a pair of silver and turquoise earrings of exquisite design. Zuni work again, with the typical inlays of coral, turquoise, and jet in the form of small winged birds that must once have graced Doroteo's lovely ears. There was a long-toothed Spanish comb with a high curved back that might have held up a mantilla, and I could almost see her wearing it—gay in Spanish dress. The small prayer book fell open when I picked it up, to reveal pressed rose leaves between the pages, and I set it down with hands that were quick to tremble. Last of all was a single satin baby shoe, embroidered in pink. I picked up the shoe and my eyes filled with tears that were a release and a relief.

"Are these the only things of hers that are left?" I managed the words.

Clarita nodded. "They are a few things my mother packed away in a box when everything else of Doro's went out of the house."

"Why? Why were her things sent away?"

"Your father wanted to keep nothing of hers. And my father ordered everything to be given to charity. He wanted no reminders of her around. But Mother stole out a few things and set them aside. She said they were for you. But I had forgotten about them until now."

I couldn't stop my tears. The impact of emotion had been too great, too unexpected. Grandmother Katy had thought of me again with these small treasures that had been my mother's. Clarita stood silently by and let me weep. She offered me no sympathy, no kindly understanding, and her eyes were bleak.

When I'd dried my tears, she spoke to me without emotion. "They are for you to keep. I would not want my mother's wish to be forgotten. Here is the box she packed them in." She brought a small sandalwood case from under the table and gave it to me.

I picked up earrings, comb, prayer book, and shoe, one by one, and placed them on the nest of cotton in the box. Having wept, I felt a little steadier, less vulnerable to the frightening child that haunted me. Touching them seemed to bring Doroteo a little closer to me as an adult, and in coming closer, her demand upon me was all the greater—the demand I had put upon myself. Somehow I must talk to Clarita.

"The shoe is badly embroidered," she pointed out critically. "Doro had no skill when it came to sewing, and she would not apply herself. Our mother could teach her nothing."

All the more reason I would treasure the small shoe which she had tried awkwardly to embroider because it was for me. I closed the box. This was the moment for the next step.

"Thank you for thinking of these things, Aunt Clarita," I said. "Now I wonder if you will do something more for me?"

Though her expression did not change by a flicker, I sensed that she was immediately on guard—and I wondered all the more what secret it was that she guarded. I went on resolutely.

"Will you tell me what it was you saw that day when you stood at the window in Doroteo's room? When you saw what happened between her and Kirk?"

Clarita turned toward the door, offering me her stiff back and the heavy black coil of hair on the nape of her neck, the twinkling earrings.

"I have already told you that these things we do not discuss."

"But they are being discussed," I said gently. "My grandfather has told me that you saw what happened. And so has Eleanor. What I want—what I have a right to as Doroteo's daughter—is to hear this from you. Please tell me."

I half expected her to walk out the door and leave me standing there, rebuked, but instead she whirled toward me with a violence that left me startled. I had not thought her an emotional person.

"You might as well know that I was not fond of Doroteo. Sylvia was more a dear younger sister to me than your mother ever was. I owe nothing to you as Doro's daughter. If you have heard what happened from both my father and Eleanor, then you know all there is to know. I did not grieve when Doro died."

"But you grieved for Kirk," I said, and stood my ground.

She came close enough to put an angry hand on my arm. "I did not grieve for him! Once, long ago, Doro and I loved him when he was a young boy. And I hated your mother then because he liked her best. Later it was different. But I do not wish to talk about these things. I have suffered enough. Remember that you are the daughter of a woman who committed murder, and you have no rights in this house."

The violent emotion that shook her frightened me, but I would not step back from her touch.

"You forget something," I said. "You forget that I too saw what happened. I was there. Closer than you. Close enough to see and hear as well."

The shock of my words made her drop her hand from my arm, and step back from me. For just an instant I saw open fright in her eyes. Then her guard was up again, all emotion erased, her face as expressionless as usual, her eyes bleak, but unrevealing.

"So what did you see? What have you to reveal that would be any different from that which I saw very clearly with good eyesight?"

"Nothing," I said. "Nothing yet. But perhaps there will be a way of remembering. My grandfather has said he'd try to help me remember, if that's what I wish. Aunt Clarita, were you really in Doroteo's bedroom that day when it happened? Did you really stand at her window?"

Nothing moved in her eyes, her face. She simply walked to the door and stood aside, gesturing me through. There was nothing to do but walk past her and back to the living room. She did not follow me, and I stood in the cool, dim room, feeling shaken by a confrontation more extreme than I had expected or intended. Clarita would tell me nothing more now, but she'd already told me one thing. She had told me of her youthful disliking for my mother and her consequent lack of any liking for me.

Adobe walls were tight about me. Beyond them mountain and mesa seemed to close me in. For a little while I had to escape. I wanted to tell someone what had happened to me. Gavin, I thought. I would go downtown to the store again and see if it was possible to talk to Gavin. Yet I knew in the same breath that I would not. We hadn't ended our morning as friends. He wouldn't welcome the sight of me, and he was too closely involved with the Cordovas to listen to me with any sympathy. But I had another cousin—Sylvia Stewart. Tart of tongue though she might be, she had more honesty in her than the others, and she might be willing to listen to me as no one else would. Sylvia would be in her bookstore downtown.

I took the sandalwood box to my room, and stopped there long enough to clip on my mother's earrings. The small winged birds seemed to flutter at my earlobes, and the Zuni work matched my grandfather's gift of the brooch. When I'd picked up my handbag, I ran downstairs and went out through the front door. The little key was with me again, though when I'd have the chance to use it, I didn't know.

Perhaps I could have had the use of a car, if I'd asked, but I didn't want to speak to anyone in that house in my present mood. The central plaza downtown was no great distance and I could find my way along Canyon Road and down the Alameda.

Walking calmed me to some degree. When I reached the plaza, dreaming in cool May sunshine, with its white wrought-iron benches and its memorials—a center of quiet, while traffic moved all around—I paused before the

nonument trying to focus on everyday things. There was
a plaque and I read the words.

TO THE HEROES WHO HAVE FALLEN IN THE BATTLE WITH
SAVAGE INDIANS IN THE TERRITORY OF NEW MEXICO

I wondered what New Mexico Indians thought of this
plaque. But of course these words belonged to another
century and different thinking.

I left the plaza, crossing to the long adobe building
that was the Governor's Palace which now housed a
museum. On the sidewalk, beneath protruding brown
vigas, Indians sat against the wall, displaying turquoise
and silver jewelry spread before them on squares of
cloth. Passers-by stopped to examine their wares, while
the Indians, both men and women, regarded them im-
passively, urging nothing upon them. Hunched beneath
shoulder blankets, they waited for whatever might come.
Both "heroes" and "savages" were gone and these Pueblo
Indians regarded the rush and avarice of the Anglos with
a quiet, superior wisdom. It was a scene I would like
to paint.

Walking about the square, I found the street Sylvia
had indicated when she drove me through town on my
arrival, and I moved slowly past the windows of small
shops until I came to one which displayed books. When
I stepped inside, I found Sylvia busy with a customer.

Her short brown hair was slightly rumpled and she
looked at me through dark-rimmed glasses, gave me a
nod and a signal to wait. The shop was small, with a
single window at the back, and it was crowded with
bright-jacketed books. They stood in neat rows on wall
shelves and were piled in orderly fashion on a central
table. In an alcove there was a desk and typewriter,
where her assistant was working.

I found the books by Paul Stewart easily, since his
wife had given them prominent display. I found *Emanuella,
the Trail of the Whip,* and several others. I was brows-
ing through a volume on the Pueblo Indians, when the

customer left, and Sylvia came over to me.

"How are things going?" she asked.

I put the book back on the shelf. "I'm not sure. I've just had rather a row with Aunt Clarita. She gave me some things that had belonged to my mother and I asked her to tell me exactly what she saw that day when my mother died."

"Did she tell you?"

"No. She seemed terribly upset and she wouldn't talk about it. I did something rather foolish. I reminded her that I'd been there too that day, and that I had seen everything that happened."

Sylvia gasped. "Do you mean you've begun to remember?"

"No—not at all. But Clarita looked positively frightened for a moment, and then she turned into stone again. I think she's hiding something."

Sylvia picked up a book and blew imaginary dust from its top a little too casually. "That's unlikely, I should think."

"I even asked her if she was really there at the window where she could see what happened."

"You *have* stirred her up! Clarita is the most under-estimated member of the Cordova family. There's a lot more to her than she ever shows the world. Juan always discounted her and let her know it, yet she's held that household together and been a loving mother to Eleanor. When we were young, she was very good to me, and I'm fond of her."

"She said you were like a sister to her."

"Katy appreciated her quality of loyalty and her sense of duty, but I think she guessed too that Clarita, when she was young, had a passionate nature. There was a time when she was blindly in love with Kirk—but that changed with the years, and a good thing. Only Juan, I think, kept his affection for Kirk—perhaps because Kirk tried to pattern himself after Juan Cordova. Sometimes I found it hard to take that Kirk was more Spanish than Spain. We fought a bit because he didn't want me to marry Paul."

But it was not Kirk who interested me most at the moment. I wanted to talk about Doroteo first, and I dared a question in the face of this outpouring. "Was Paul really in love with my mother at one time, as he says?"

Sylvia shrugged a little too elaborately, and I suspected that there might be certain matters on which she too would not be altogether honest. Perhaps in self-deception?

"I think that was a little fantasy he developed while he was writing *Emanuella*—that he had once been in love with Doro. All the way through writing that book he admittedly saw Doro in Emanuella. But it hadn't any reality in fact, as far as I know."

Her voice had turned a little hard, and when a customer came into the shop, she hurried from me, as though relieved to end our conversation. She hadn't, after all, been a satisfactory person to talk to. The interplay of all those emotions which had dogged the Cordovas and those involved with them was a complex thing.

While she was busy, I stepped to a rear window and looked through glass upon an unexpectedly pleasant vista. The building which housed Sylvia's shop ran around the hollow square of a large patio. There were trees and shrubbery growing there, and brick walks crossed one another. On a stone bench near the center, Paul Stewart sat writing in a notebook.

He was not a man whose company I enjoyed, and I hadn't liked the way he wanted to study me, extract from me those buried memories. I'd wondered besides about his relationship with Eleanor. But now there were things he could tell me, and I might do a little extracting myself.

Back in the shop's alcove was a door to the courtyard. "May I go outside?" I asked Sylvia.

She nodded and I went through the door. There was the pungent scent of juniper warming in the sun, and snowball bushes displaying their white puffs. Iris grew along a walk and birds sang in this quiet place where traffic sounds were muffled and distant, and a blue sky arched overhead. Running part way about the hollow of the patio was a sheltered walk, with a wooden gallery overhead, and offices and shops opening off it. Again I had a sense of enclosure, of a place that tried to shut out the world. A Spanish family had once lived here, treasuring privacy, turning its back on all that lay outside. But increasingly, I didn't like being shut in.

I walked toward Paul, my footsteps echoing on brick, and he looked up at me, smiling, though his eyes appraised and questioned.

"Am I interrupting?" I asked, glancing at the notebook.

He flipped it closed. "Not at all. I needed to get away from my typewriter and do some thinking. Have you been visiting Sylvia's shop?"

"Yes. I've even been looking at some of your books. Is there one you can especially recommend?"

"I only know what the critics tell me. I'm a masterful writer to some, too fanciful in my nonfiction for others. Of course, I'm half fiction writer deliberately. I let my imagination go with *Emanuella*. It's really a novel."

"Your wife says you had my mother in mind when you were writing that book. What was Doro like?"

He answered with a slight edge to his voice. "She was unforgettable. Beautiful, and a little wild. Perverse, tantalizing. Mercurial. All the things Emanuella must have been. Are you any of these things, Amanda Austin?"

I shook my head, smiling back at him, though it was as if we dueled, and I thought once more of a faun with all its whimsicality and mischief-making ability.

"What you're describing sounds like my cousin Eleanor."

"Possibly. But Eleanor is her own woman."

"And I think my mother was not very much like her."

"Have they told you yet?"

I knew what he meant. "That I was there when it happened? Yes, Eleanor took care of that."

"I made her see that she must. You couldn't really

begin to remember until you knew that. Now it will
surface. Will you tell me what you discover?"

I didn't think I would, but I evaded a direct reply,
because I wanted him to answer me.

"You've told me a little about my mother. What was
Kirk Landers like?"

He seemed to answer carefully. "Women thought him
pretty dashing, and he enjoyed that. He wanted to masquerade as a Spanish *caballero,* a young Spanish don. I
can't say I cared for him."

"Sylvia says he didn't want her to marry you."

"He had a prejudice against me. I'm not sure why.
I think Juan sent him off with a bribe to get him away
from Doroteo until they both grew up, and then Doro
married your father—which didn't please Juan very
much. Of course when Kirk came home, his nose was
pretty much out of joint, with Doro married, and Clarita
no longer looking at him in adoration."

Paul fingered the hinges of his notebook and his smile
had a secret look, as though he glimpsed a joke he didn't
mean to tell me. When he looked up, there was speculation in his eyes.

"In any case, Amanda, there's a way to help you
remember, if you'll let me try."

I didn't trust him at all, but I was curious to know
what he meant. When I merely waited, he flipped open
his notebook again.

"I've been sitting here jotting down bits and pieces
out of my memory, trying to reconstruct what happened,
and recall where everyone was at the time. But I'm not
getting anything significant. I've thought of going back
to the actual place where the picnic was held, to see
what might return to my mind. Will you come with me?"

Even though he took me by surprise, I didn't hesitate.
There were things this might tell me, and I already knew
I had a rendezvous with that particular spot.

"When?" I said.

"What better time than now? My car's outside, and
we can drive there directly. Unless someone looks out

of that high window, no one at the Cordovas' needs to know we're there."

"All right," I said. "Let's go back through Sylvia's shop. I'd like to tell her what we plan to do."

He seemed to hesitate, as though he'd rather have gone directly through the archway to the street. Then he came with me as I started across the patio.

The shop was empty of customers, and Sylvia was un-packing a carton of brightly jacketed books. Her eyes went to Paul's face, and in that look I knew how much he meant to her.

"We're going to see what we can resurrect from the past," he told her. "We're going back to the picnic place to see what we can learn."

That odd, dancing light was in his eyes again, and Sylvia looked her alarm, as though this was something she feared. However, she offered no objection. Perhaps she knew objecting would do no good. She went quickly to a small artificial tree set on a counter and hung with tiny squares. From it she selected one and brought it to me.

"You must have an *Ojo de Dios*. To protect you against evil."

Her tone was light, but I sensed meaning beneath the surface, as though she was warning me. The piece I took from her was hardly an inch square, made of two crossed sticks, wound about with strands of colored yarn to form a pattern in red and green and white. In the center was a spot of black.

"What is it?" I asked.

She seemed anxious to hold me there talking, and she explained in detail, while Paul moved restlessly about the shop, examining book titles.

"The Zapotec Indians make one of these for every child at his birth. They cross two twigs and wind yarn about them, beginning at the center—for the years of a child's life. There are bright colors and dark, for the gay and the sad. The years go very quickly there at the beginning, but they grow longer and slower at the outer edge. They used to hang one on the wall to represent all the years of a life. Nowadays they're regarded as good luck charms against evil spirits. That black spot in the center is the Eye of God—the *Ojo de Dios*. Put it in your bag and keep it with you."

I saw now that above a bank of bookshelves hung a row of larger squares of the same sort, made of various colored yarns. I thanked her and dropped the little token into my bag, but somehow I felt uneasy. Why should she warn me against Paul? She stood close to me, watching, and she said something odd for a woman who seemed as practical-minded as Sylvia.

"That's an evil place he's taking you to. I wish you wouldn't go."

Paul heard her and laughed. "There's no such thing as an evil place. There are only evil people."

"Not my mother," I said.

He smiled at me and that strange gleam was back in his eyes. "No, not your mother. Perhaps she was reckless and wild, but not truly evil."

"Kirk was reckless too," Sylvia said quickly, "but he wasn't evil either. In spite of everything."

"Then that leaves no one who was evil." Paul seemed to challenge her.

For an instant there was fright in Sylvia. I could sense it in her tightened lips, in the look she gave him. Then she reached out to touch my arm.

"Don't let him torment you with all this. Let what's gone be forgotten."

"Come along, Amanda," Paul said curtly, and the look he threw his wife was not one of affection.

But I had ceased to pay attention. I'd known all along that the arroyo would summon me, and the moment was here. This was what I must do.

## IX

We drove back to the Stewarts' garage, and on the way Paul had little to say. I was aware of the occasional glance he turned in my direction, aware again of something in him that probed and searched. For what? What compulsion drove him that he *had* to know about the past?

From the house we went on foot, and he led the way out to the rear where the hillside curve followed above the arroyo. He pointed out that there were other ways to reach the picnic place from above, but this diagonal path which ran behind the Cordova wall was quicker.

"It's the path you and your mother took that day when she was hurrying to meet Kirk," he said.

His will was pressing upon me, exerting a force that I had to resist. If I wasn't careful, he would make me "remember" something that had never been.

"How do you know that Doroteo went out to meet Kirk?" I asked.

"They think she'd taken Mark Brand's gun from his room. She must have had it with her. She must have known she would meet him."

I shivered in warm sunlight, and let him lead the

way. The path we followed meant nothing to me. There seemed no memory here. Cottonwoods and poplars grew thickly above the dry arroyo, where water would sometimes rush furiously, coming down in a spill from the mountains. There were the usual clumps of chamiso and juniper. We came quickly upon the open space beneath a cottonwood tree, and stood in its shadow, looking around.

Paul's hand was on my arm, its pressure light, but somehow compelling. "This is where they used to picnic. Can you remember it? Can you remember anything?"

I could only shake my head. The place was strange to me. It was not familiar as the mesa country seemed beyond Santa Fe. Perhaps something in me, always on guard, had buried the memory of this hillside so deep in my consciousness that it was forever blocked from rising.

A steep, rocky path led from the clearing to the ledge below—a ledge that was out of sight of the picnic place because of the brush. Paul led the way again, and I followed him, my sandals slipping on the rough earth as we went down. The ledge below gave way in turn to a steep bank sloping to the bottom of the arroyo, and as I reached it something in me quivered—and was still. For an instant, memory had fluttered, only to be rejected by whatever it was that stood so relentlessly on guard.

How quiet everything seemed. There was no noise of blasting now, but only a faint whispering as breezes touched the treetops and wild shrubbery. I was aware —as though I stood on some dangerous verge—but I was still untouched.

"This is where it happened," Paul said softly.

Stepping to the edge of the steep bank, I looked down, and now I was shivering and a little sick. This was not because I remembered, but only because of all I'd been told of what had happened here. I turned about slowly, my eyes searching the nearer ground, and then seeking what lay farther off.

Up the hillside I could see adobe walls that surrounded

the Cordova house, and I could see that one high room which had been my mother's, standing up above the lower roofs. I could see the window from which Clarita had looked that day—the window of what was now my room. Hillside and house and window were all as they had been long ago. Only I was not the same. I had been a small child then. I was a woman now. A woman who could remember—nothing.

As I stared at the window, something moved beyond the glass, and I knew someone was watching us. But the light was wrong and I couldn't see who it was. It didn't matter. Let them worry that I had come here, if they chose.

Paul no longer touched my arm, and he had stepped back a little to let me be alone. I turned toward him and saw that pale yellow-green of his eyes, felt the pressure his will once more exerted upon me.

"Tell me what you're thinking," he said. "Tell me what you see."

"I don't see anything except what's here. It all seems strange to me."

He was watching me closely. "Let me remind you. Your grandmother Katy and Gavin were in the clearing above when it happened. Eleanor was with them. She was about ten at that time. Two or three neighbors had joined them. Juan was at home because he never liked picnics and he wasn't well that day. Clarita wasn't feeling well either, and she was lying down in Doro's room, which was more airy than her room downstairs. At least that's the story she tells. Sylvia and I were just leaving the house. We came along the lower path, and Kirk must have been waiting for Doro right here when she arrived. Doesn't any of this come back to you?"

Nothing did. There had been only that quiver of memory when I'd looked down into the arroyo, but it was nothing clear that I could recognize and account for. Paul Stewart's presence disturbed and distracted me. How could I remember anything with that intense demand he put upon me?

"Why does it matter so much to you for me to remember?" I asked. "A child's recollections can't mean anything. Not in so young a child."

"I'd like something fresh for this section of my book, of course," he told me. "But if you can't remember, you can't."

"Perhaps it would help if I could stay here alone for a little while," I said.

"If you like. I'll go back to my typewriter. You know the way home." He was almost curt now—as though he had satisfied himself about something and had no further use for me.

I nodded and he went back along the hillside by the way we had come. Immediately, I was closed in by a pocket of silence. City sounds were far away, and few cars came along the quiet lane above.

What had it been like to be five years old on that long ago day and stand here on this hillside with my mother? What had I seen and heard? Surely I must have been terrified, shattered, hysterical. Yet there was no emotion in me except for that which conscious knowledge provided. This was the place where my mother had died. She had fallen down this steep bank into the arroyo, and the fall had killed her. But first she had deliberately raised the gun she'd brought with her and had shot Kirk Landers.

No! There was something wrong. Something I could not believe in what I'd been told. Since this ledge where they had stood revealed nothing to me, I climbed back to the clearing, and this time I faced the cottonwood tree that I had only walked beneath before. At once a piercing, terrifying sense of recognition flashed through me. This was the tree of my nightmare. It was tall and spreading and thickly leaved, its branches gnarled with age. It commanded the hillside and it must have seemed a giant to the little girl I had been.

Nearby stood a weathered wooden bench, probably left by those former picnickers, and I sat down on it abruptly because my knees were trembling. This was where I must have sat as a child, facing the tree. I had stared at it in my desperate state until I saw it above all else, and it had marked me with a haunting—the symbol of something terrible that a young mind had washed away.

This was the beginning of memory and I was frightened. The tree of my dream was centered in some mirage of horror and I could feel the misty visions sweeping back upon me in waves of vertigo. I put my head down upon my knees and let the dizziness wash over me. My handbag was under my cheek, and I could feel in it the shape of the sketchbook I took with me everywhere. Let me exorcise the tree by drawing it, I thought. Let me register its reality so that I would not dream of it in terror ever again.

As I reached into my bag the little "Eye of God" Sylvia had given me came to my fingers. I held it for a moment, half smiling. Let its spell against evil work now, if ever it did.

Then, with my pencil in hand, and the sketchbook open on my knees, I began to draw, shaping the gnarled form of the tree—the trunk and the branches, the foliage that had seemed to reach out to smother me in my dream. The drawing that took shape on paper was more like my nightmare than was the real tree. Its limbs seemed to writhe as if with eerie motion, its leaves appeared to flutter in a raging wind.

I closed my eyes to shut out the horror that seemed embodied in what I had drawn, and at once there was new motion before my eyes. Shadowy figures struggled and fought each other for their lives, and horror had a color—the color of scarlet, of blood. But nothing was clear. There was no real remembering.

Sounds reached me from the path above. Someone was coming down from the direction of the road. Someone real in a real world. I could not bear it if Paul had come back. He must not see me like this—on the verge of dreadful discovery, my hands wet with perspiration, so that the pencil was slippery in my fingers, and my mouth was dry. I opened my eyes reluctantly and looked at the man who stood before my bench. It was Gavin Brand.

He must have seen terror in my face. Quietly he sat beside me on the bench and looked at my open sketchbook.

"You've caught more than the image of a tree," he said. "You've caught the spirit of it. When I was a small boy, I used to think that some trees were alive, as men were alive. I used to think there were trees that could menace me."

I began to breathe in deeply, steadying myself. "I remember this tree," I said. "Sometimes I've dreamed about it in a nightmare. It's a dream I've had all my life."

"I can understand its haunting you. I was here, you know. I brought you up from the ledge below and got you to sit on this bench for a while. I had to leave you because there was need for help. I climbed down into the arroyo with Paul Stewart and helped to bring your mother up. Nothing could be done for Kirk. When I came back, the way you looked frightened me. You'd stopped crying, and you were sitting there staring at that tree with a fixed look that was hard to break."

"I must have imprinted it on my memory, while I wiped out everything else."

"It's likely. Katy was concerned about you, but she was trying to see to what must be done, and carry on in spite of her own shock. She asked me to take you and Eleanor back to the house."

I could say nothing. He was telling me the whole terrible story, and it left me shaken—though I could not feel that I'd been there. Gently he reached out and took one of my damp hands into his.

"This is the way I held your hand that day. You clung to me and didn't want to let me go. When you went to sleep that night, you wanted me to sit beside your bed for a while. You were so young and frightened, and I suppose I was frightened too. I'd never come up against violent death before. Something pretty ghastly had happened to people I knew. I'd always liked Doro. She was gay and a bit frivolous, I suppose, but she was kind, too. She never hurt anyone."

He broke off with an exclamation, staring at me.

"Those earrings you're wearing! Your grandfather gave them to her. She had them on the day she died. I remember those little birds at her earlobes when we brought her up from the arroyo."

His hand about my own steadied me, comforted me. I reached up with my free hand and touched coral and turquoise. But I did not pull the clips from my ears. They made me feel as though I were coming closer to Doroteo.

"Thank you for telling me all this," I said. "I don't remember, really. Perhaps I don't want to remember. But sometimes the curtain lifts a little and when it does I feel dizzy and terrified. Yet I've got to face it. I must remember. I know that I saw someone struggling, but I don't know for certain that it was my mother and Kirk."

"It must have been," he said. "There was no one else there."

I tried to steady myself, tried to thrust terror away and return to a real and present world.

"How did you happen to find me here just now?"

"I was looking for you. I went up to your room, and when you weren't there, I looked out your window and saw you here with Paul. I didn't like that. You should stay away from him. He means nothing but mischief. So I came along by the upper road."

I drew my hand from his and wiped it with my handkerchief. It was good to be looked after for a while, but I couldn't let him dictate to me whether or not I would see Paul Stewart. If Paul was on my road to discovery, then I would of course see him.

"Why were you looking for me?" I asked.

A slight smile touched his somber face. "A guilty conscience, perhaps. I've been thinking over some of the things I said to you this morning. I was too harsh and

I felt it might be in order to tell you I was sorry. Since I had to come back to the house from work to see Juan, I looked for you."

"You were fair enough," I said. "If you thought Juan was going to use me in some way against Eleanor, you'd have to protect her."

He said nothing, and there was silence between us. I was feeling calmer, and somehow safer. Once, when I had been a child, Gavin had protected me, and now I had again a feeling of security in being with him. Since he wasn't being harsh and critical, I could relax and let down my guard. Perhaps he was the one who could help me.

"Will you take me to the *rancho?*" I said.

"The *Rancho de Cordova?*" He was surprised.

I told him then about the message from Katy and the small package she had left for me with Sylvia. I had no idea what I must search for at the *rancho,* but sooner or later I must go there, and perhaps it would be best if Gavin could take me, rather than one of the others.

He didn't hesitate. "I'll stop at the house and phone the store. Then we'll go out there. I don't know what you can hope to find, but I'll take you, if you wish. Katy must have had some intent in mind. She was a wonderfully sane and sensible person."

I closed my sketchbook upon the nightmarish drawing of the cottonwood tree, and stood up, turning my back on the real tree.

"Thank you. I feel better now. I'm ready to go."

He nodded his approval, and I thought how kind he could be when he was not condemning me.

We took the short-cut path along the hillside to the back gate of the Cordova house, and there were no more twinges of memory to trouble me. Inside, Clarita was not about. I waited in the living room while Gavin made his call, and then we went out to his car and drove away from Canyon Road.

The highway led south out of the city, in the direction of Albuquerque, but in a little while we turned off on a road that led toward Los Cerrillos, The Little Hills. Again there was empty country and straight roads. I settled back in the seat and let the wind from the open window blow in my face. After my experience in the clearing, I wanted only to be quiet for a little while and renew my forces. Gavin seemed to understand and there was no idle conversation between us on the half-hour drive away from Santa Fe.

I was almost drowsing when Gavin spoke to me. "There's the hacienda ahead—the *Rancho de Cordova*. Most of the land has been sold and it's not what it was in the old days when Juan's father was alive."

Juan's father—my great-grandfather, I thought.

He pulled the car up to a curb before a long, low adobe building. Francisco and Maria, the couple Juan had placed in charge of the hacienda, came to the door to welcome us. They knew Gavin, of course, but had come here since Doroteo's day, so they did not remember my mother. They greeted me warmly, however, as a granddaughter of Juan Cordova.

We stepped into the dim, cool *sala*, where strings of chili and Indian corn hung from the vigas, and the furniture was dark and shabby and old. Gavin explained that I wanted to see the place and asked permission to show me around.

*"Está bien,"* Maria said, with a wave of her hand, offering me the house.

As we stood at a window, looking out into an empty courtyard, he told me a little about what the *rancho* had once meant to the countryside.

"There was always fighting in the early days. And when the Pueblo Indians attacked Santa Fe, most of the Spaniards in the area were killed. Settlers out here came to the *rancho* for protection. Later, when the Spaniards were gone, Union troops sheltered here when they were fighting Rebel forces."

I looked out at the empty courtyard of bare earth, baking dry and cracked beneath the sun. A long *portal* with wooden pillars stretched along one side of the open space, and at the back was a building of adobe bricks.

"Once that was an army barracks," Gavin said.

I could look out and see phantom horses and men stirring the dust, see my great-grandfather moving among them with that pride of bearing that Juan Cordova, his son, would also carry. New England's chill rocks seemed very far away, and I knew that I belonged to this place of sun and dust as well.

"It sleeps now," Gavin said. "Few of us come here to visit. But when Clarita and Rafael and Doroteo and Sylvia were young, it was never quiet."

"And Kirk?" I said.

"Yes, of course. I only remember him after the time when he came back—just a little while before his death. I suppose I knew him when I was a child, but I have only a vague memory of him as rather wild and dashing—dramatic. I was younger than the others, and I was only a small boy when they all used to come out here. I've been told that Doro was a great rider, though a little reckless. She and Kirk used to ride together. Eleanor and I rode too, when we came out here as children. But all that's gone. Juan keeps no horses here now."

We turned from the sunlight of the empty courtyard and Gavin led the way into the long, shadowy house and down a corridor, off which many rooms opened.

"I don't know what to look for that might be unlocked by so small a key," Gavin said. "Will you let me see it?"

I took the ring box from my bag and sprang the latch. The little key was tucked into its satin nest.

"Perhaps a jewel case," I said.

He nodded. "We might as well begin here—with what used to be your mother's room."

I stepped across the sill and looked about. The room was empty of belongings, impersonal. Dust covers had been thrown over the bed and there were no rugs on the floor, or pictures on the wall. All traces of Doroteo Austin had long been removed.

Moving about the room, I opened empty drawers and examined the graceful rosewood desk. In only one drawer did I find something that brought a flicker of recognition. It was a glass paperweight and when I picked it up snowflakes flew over mountains that resembled the Sangre de Cristos, and over the twin church towers of St. Francis.

"I believe I used to play with this when I was little," I said. "Do you suppose anyone would mind if I keep it?"

"I'm sure not." Gavin's tone was kind.

He seemed a different man from the one I'd toured the store with this morning. For some reason I didn't wholly understand, he appeared to have accepted me without the rancor and suspicion he had harbored toward me earlier. In the same way my own resentment toward him had faded because he had indeed become the friend I'd needed. With a new, quiet assurance I felt I could talk to him when the time came—and he would listen. Such knowledge brought with it a warmth that was comforting.

Since there was nothing here in my mother's room that could be unlocked by a tiny key, we went on to the next door, which Gavin opened for me.

"This was your grandmother Katy's room whenever she came to the *rancho*."

I stepped past him eagerly and came to a shocked halt. Someone had been here ahead of us. As though one of those whirlwinds had struck it, everything in the room had been stirred about in great haste and without any effort to replace the things which had been moved. The room was still furnished, and little effort had been made to dispose of the possessions of the woman who had once occupied it. What was here had been thoroughly disturbed.

Drawers were turned out, their contents left on table or floor. Boxes in a closet had been unpacked, and ever the bed had been stripped. While I stood looking about in astonishment, Gavin summoned Maria. She came quickly to look past us into the room, exclaiming aloud.

"But only yesterday I cleaned in here, Señor Brand. Everything was in order, nothing like this!"

"Have you had any visitors at the *rancho* since then?" Gavin asked.

The woman shook her head vehemently, then paused, looking around for her husband. When he came down the hall she spoke to him in voluble Spanish. He nodded, seemed to agree about something and then shrugged eloquently.

Gavin explained for my benefit. "Earlier this afternoon, a little while before we arrived, Francisco heard a sound in this part of the house. When he came into the hall to investigate, he saw nothing. The doors were closed, and all was quiet, so he didn't look into any of the rooms, believing he must have been mistaken. Now he remembers that a little later he heard a car moving away from the hacienda. But when he went to look out a window it was already well in the distance and he couldn't recognize it."

Maria started into the room, greatly distressed and anxious to tidy everything up. I stopped her quickly.

"Please," I said. "Can you let it be for now? I would like to look at some of these things myself before you put them away."

She glanced at Gavin for his consent and then gave me a troubled nod before she went out of the room.

My efforts were desultory. In such confusion, I didn't know where to begin. I found myself picking up a sewing box that had been my grandmother's, poking in among scissors and spools, before I set it down and turned to something else. Nothing I touched required a small brass key to open it. In neither room had I found a jewel case. Nevertheless, I kept on halfheartedly, knowing that someone had been here ahead of me, and that probably whatever could be unlocked by such a key was already gone. My hands moved almost absently among Katy's things, but my mind was busy.

"As far as I know," I told Gavin, "only three people knew about this. Sylvia gave me the envelope sealed, but perhaps she could have opened it in the past and sealed it up again. And I told Clarita and Juan. No one else, until I told you."

"If Sylvia knew, Paul could have known too."

"Yes, and Eleanor, I suppose. But then why wouldn't one or the other of them have investigated here at the *rancho* sooner?"

"Perhaps nothing became crucial until the key was put in your hands."

Most likely, it was Clarita who had come here, I thought. But I let the matter go and went on with my fruitless search.

A large cardboard box had been half emptied, and when I poked through the contents which had been dumped on the floor, I came upon a Mexican costume that a man might have worn. I held up the tight trousers of dark blue suede, trimmed with silver buttons down the sides, and started to pick up the embroidered, braid-trimmed jacket, when Gavin took the things from me without ceremony.

"You don't want these," he said, and thrust them away on the high shelf of a huge armoire.

I wondered at the abrupt removal, but I was emptying out the rest of the box and my attention was distracted. Something made of wood, like a hollowed bowl, fell out and skittered across the floor. I reached to pick it up, turned it over in my hands—and without warning was caught by a wave of cold terror that washed through my fingertips.

What I held in my hands was a carved wooden mask, and I could only stare at it in a frozen state of shock. The entire face had been painted a smoky shade of blue, with the features outlined with great skill in silver and turquoise inlays. The eyebrows were curves of tiny turquoise stones above the eyes outlined with turquoise and silver. The nostrils were silver slits, but it was the mouth that was most arresting. It was in the shape of an oval—the open shape of a scream—and again the outline was done in silver and turquoise. Staring at the blue face, I could feel my own mouth round to that screaming shape and it was all I could do to suppress the sound that surged in my throat.

From across the room Gavin saw and came to me at once.

"What's the matter, Amanda? What's happened?"

When I couldn't answer at once, he took me by the shoulders and held me gently, and I saw warmth in his eyes and sympathy. "Something's frightened you again."

"Yes!" I held up the mask with hands that shook. "It's—like the tree. I've seen this before and it's part of the nightmare— it's connected with that time."

Gavin took the blue mask from me and examined it. "I've seen this before too—when I was small. Long before your mother died. It seems to me—yes, it used to hang on a wall here at the hacienda. I can remember the very place out in the *sala*."

"But how can *I* remember it?"

"Don't try," he said, and I had the feeling that he knew more about the mask than he was telling me.

I paid no attention to his warning. I *had* to remember, and I took the mask back from him, studying it, forcing myself to meet its evil, slitted gaze.

The mouth seemed to shout at me from the blue face, crying out in some silent agony that matched my own. Whoever had created this mask had meant it to agonize, and I could agonize with it.

"I can't remember," I said. "It's just that I have a terrible sense of horror and danger. But I know it has something to tell me."

A smaller cardboard box lay on the bed, with a leather book in it. He dumped out the book and put the mask in the box, closed the lid over that dreadful blue face.

"There—it's out of your sight for now."

I reached for the box. "I'll take it back to the house with me. There's something about it I've got to remember."

"All right," he said. "If you must. And now—here's the brass lock for your key."

He picked up the leather book that had fallen on the bed and held it out to me. I saw at once that it had a brass hasp with a small lock in it. Without ever taking the key from my bag, I knew it would fit. But there was no need. One end of the hasp had been ripped from the leather, and the book was no longer locked.

"It must be a diary," I said as I took it from him.

When I raised the leather cover and looked at the flyleaf, I found Katy Cordova's name written there in the same strong script I had seen in the letter she'd sent my father. The year of the diary was the year of my mother's death.

As I flipped through them I found the pages thick with that same writing. Here was the answer Katy had left for me. Here was the answer to everything.

A little feverishly, I turned the pages, reading dates, looking for the month of my mother's death—which was this very month of May, though I didn't know the date. When I came to the passage about the picnic, I began to read eagerly, forgetting Gavin, forgetting the room about me. Yes, she had written of her plans for the day—she had set down the names of those who would come. My eyes skimmed as I turned the pages and came abruptly, shockingly, to the end of the diary. Only a core of torn edges remained at the central binding. Whatever else Katy had written for that time and the rest of the year had been ripped from the book.

I held out the leather volume to Gavin. "She was writing about the picnic. She must have written about what happened—but it's all gone, torn out. Someone came here—probably today—and tore out these pages. Someone who is frightened."

Gavin took the book from me and stared at the rough edges where only a word or two of script remained. "It looks as if you're right. But don't count too much on what was written here, Amanda."

"I'm counting on it—I am! Those pages have to be found."

"If there's anything revealing in them, they've been destroyed by now."

Limp with disappointment, I sat down on the bed. Now what was I to do? Where was I to turn?

"Perhaps we'd better go back to town," Gavin said. "I've put off an appointment until late afternoon, but I do need to be back for it. And I think this is all we can do here."

I agreed, my thoughts rushing ahead. "Yes—I'll go back now. I'll talk to Grandfather. I'll show him the mask and the diary. If I can only get him to believe what I believe, perhaps he can help me."

"What do you believe?" Gavin asked gently.

"That my mother didn't kill anyone. And perhaps she didn't fall by intent down the bank. Perhaps someone pushed her because she witnessed what happened."

Gavin shook his head at me regretfully. "I'm afraid you're fantasizing. You're hoping for too much."

I snatched the diary indignantly back from him. "This is the evidence! Katy wanted me to know. She felt I had a right to know."

"To know what? Don't you think that if your grandmother had known that Doro was innocent she would have cried it from the hilltops? I remember Katy. I remember her courage. And I remember how much she loved your mother."

"She might not if the truth would injure someone else she loved. She might figure that it was better to save the living than to exonerate the dead. But she still wanted *me* to know."

"Come along," Gavin said. "We'll turn this mess over to Maria and get back to town."

We told Maria and Francisco *Hasta la vista* and I went with him. I knew he was growing impatient with me, but I didn't care. I was on my own headlong course, and I didn't mean to let anything stop me.

# X

When Gavin left me at the house and drove back to the store, I went at once to Juan Cordova's study, taking with me the box that contained the mask and the diary. Clarita was not about to interfere, and his door was open.

"Come in," he called when I appeared.

I placed the box on his desk. "Here's something I want you to see."

He did not look at the box because as I came close he was staring at me. "Where did you get those earrings?"

"Clarita gave them to me. They belonged to my mother. Gavin says you gave them to her."

"Take them off!" he said harshly. "Take them off!"

I understood his pain and I slipped off the Zuni birds, dropped them into my handbag. Then without preliminary I reached into the box and drew out the mask, to place it before him. This time I knew what to expect, and I felt less of a tendency to panic with terror at the sight of it.

"Do you know anything about this?" I asked.

For an instant, the sight of the mask seemed to bring him some unwanted memory, and a grimace of pain crossed his face. But he thrust it aside and picked up the mask, examining its detail with his fingers.

"I've wondered what happened to this. An Indian friend made it for me long ago when the children were young. They were always fascinated by it, and we used to keep it on a wall out at the *rancho*. This is particularly fine work, though of course not traditional. It was made for no ceremony, but because my friend was an artist and wanted to create something original. Where did you find it?"

"In Katy's room at the *rancho*," I said. "Gavin drove me out there because of the message she left me. When I found this, I recognized it."

There was no change of expression in that face that reminded me of a falcon. He merely repeated my words. "Recognized it?"

"I don't know why I know it, but I do. And it frightens me. I thought perhaps you could tell me why."

"Why should it frighten you? You must have seen it on the wall at the hacienda when you were small, but as far as I know, you never had any fear of it. Our own children used to play with it sometimes when they were little—even though it was forbidden. I didn't want a work of art damaged, but you'll find a few nicks in the wood and in the blue paint, as well as a stone or two missing. I can remember one day when I caught Kirk Landers leaping around with it on his face. In those days he had a gift for pantomime, and he could be very amusing." Juan sighed deeply.

None of this meant anything to me.

"I went down to the arroyo," I told him. "Paul Stewart took me there. He thought I might remember something if I saw the place where—where it happened."

"And did you?"

"Only the cottonwood tree. I can remember that. Everything else seems wiped away. Why did Grandmother Katy choose that place for a picnic anyway? Why not eat outdoors more comfortably in your own patio?"

"The walls—she wanted to escape the walls out on the open hillside."

"I've felt that way too—a little," I admitted. "But now I want to remember about that place. You told me you'd try to help me. When will you begin?"

His smile was meant to be kind, but it seemed a little fierce. "Why not now? Sit down, Amanda, and relax. You're wound up with tension."

I put the mask back in the box. Later I would show him the diary. "If you don't mind, I'd like to keep the mask for a while. Perhaps it will encourage something to come back to me."

"You may keep it for now," he said.

I sat in the chair opposite him and waited. For a moment or two he seemed lost in his own faraway thoughts and there was a sadness in the downward droop of his mouth. He closed his eyes, and when he began to speak he did not open them.

"As you may know, I didn't go to the picnic that day. When Gavin brought you back to the house, Katy had already come to tell me what had happened. I had been ill and she wouldn't let me go out to that place afterwards, though she had to go back. I sat here in this room and grieved because I had lost my daughter under terrible circumstances and lost a foster son as well. Gavin brought you to me here. You were white-faced and no longer crying, though your cheeks were streaked with tearstains. You sat on my knee and leaned your head above my heart and we tried to comfort each other. Do you remember any of this?"

I closed my eyes, like Juan, and tried to seek out memory. Could I recall strong arms about me, a strong, adult heart beating under my cheek? The vision seemed very real, but I didn't know if this was memory.

"After a while you began to babble a little. You said your mother had fallen and someone was covered with blood. I held you and tried to talk to you. I told you your mother would never have willingly hurt anyone, but she must have been maddened by anger with Kirk."

I opened my eyes. "Were these the extenuating circumstances you mentioned?"

"Yes, perhaps. I couldn't explain it all to a child, but I had sent Kirk away when he got the idea that he wanted to marry your mother. She was too young for marriage, and he was too young for responsibility. I told him he must go away and prove himself. When they were both older, we would see. When he came back, nearly ten years had passed and Doroteo had married William Austin. He was not the man I would have chosen, but she was happy with him. I had to recognize that. Then Kirk came home and he would not believe that he had to give her up. He'd undoubtedly had affairs in the meantime, but something brought him back to Doroteo. She wanted none of him and she had our hot Cordova temper."

This was not the story Eleanor had told me—of Doroteo using that gun because she had been "spurned." But this story seemed closer to the possible truth.

"Don't you remember?" my grandfather said.

"Remember what?"

"Something happened between them one day, when she was angry with him. He had said he would go to your father and tell him of their love for each other when they were young. By then, I think, it would not have mattered to William. But your mother was furious and she struck Kirk in the face. You were there, Amanda. You were in the living room, which is not so very different now from the way it used to be."

The sound of a slap seemed to echo out of the past. As if through a mist I could see a beautiful and angry woman flinging out her hand. I had been frightened, but she hadn't been angry with me. When the man had gone from the house, she had caught me up and held me close to her. Almost I could remember some flower scent she had worn.

"You are remembering, aren't you?" Juan Cordova said.

I brushed my hands before my eyes. "A little, perhaps. Something."

"Good. Then we have made a beginning. You mustn't

try too much at once. We'll attempt it again another time."

"But remembering a slap doesn't bring back anything of that time on the hillside."

"It's a beginning, and it gives you something to tell Paul. I gather that you're talking to him in spite of my wishes?"

"Why should I tell him that?"

"He must understand that Kirk was tormenting your mother. That he drove her to what she finally did. If he must write this book, then I would like him to be gentle with Doroteo. You must remember that Paul knew her in those days. He knew about her wild temper—the blood of the dwarf that has come down to us."

I stopped him with an outflung hand. "There's that phrase again—'blood of the dwarf'! Eleanor used it to me, and my father once mentioned a dwarf. What does it mean? You must tell me."

"Yes," he said. "It's time you knew." He opened an upper drawer in his desk and took out a ring of two keys, examining them with his fingers, as though he could distinguish them better that way than with his eyes. When he came to some conclusion, he dropped the ring back in the drawer and closed it.

"Not now," he said. "We will go after dark, when no one will be watching. After dinner tonight you will come to me here and I will show you something. You have the right to know all our family secrets. Perhaps they will be your responsibility someday. But I am tired now. Come to me later. *Por favor.*"

I couldn't let him off as easily as that. "I'll come, but there's something else I must show you now."

From the bottom of the box I took Katy's diary and set it before him. I didn't need to ask if he knew what it was—he recognized it at once and drew it toward him, opened the flyleaf to look at the date of the year.

"This has been missing," he said. "She kept diaries for many years—before Doroteo died, and up to the time when she became ill. After Katy was gone, I read them all. But the book for this year was not among them. You found it at the *rancho?*"

I nodded. "It was in a box with the mask and other things."

"I asked Clarita to search for this book, but she never found it. Or at least she told me she had not."

I opened the book to the last pages, where the leaves had been torn out, leaving only jagged scraps at the center.

"We think this was done today. Has Clarita been away from the house?"

He fixed me with that fierce gaze. "She has been here all afternoon. She looked in on me several times. Clarita would not do a thing like this."

"What would I not do?" Clarita asked from behind me.

I turned my head as she came into the room. For once she did not look like a middle-aged Spanish lady. She had put on cinnamon brown slacks and a dark red blouse, and she wore no jewelry. The effect was different, younger, and somehow less subservient to Juan Cordova.

He answered her words coldly. "You would not, I think, go out to the *rancho* and disturb your mother's possessions. You would not tear pages from her diary."

"Naturally not. This has been done?" In spite of her denial, I sensed tension in her.

"Tell her, Amanda."

I obeyed. "Since Katy had left me a message to go to the *rancho,* and left me a key, Gavin took me out there today. We found this book with the hasp of the lock torn loose and the last pages ripped out. The pages which must have told about the picnic and my mother's death."

"Such pages would not matter," Clarita said. "She knew only what was known to all of us from the beginning."

"I have told Amanda that you were in the house all this afternoon, and that you looked in on me several times."

"That is true." Clarita spoke with dignity and assurance, but I did not know at all whether she was telling the truth or whether Juan might be shielding her. Something had made her tense.

"I found one other thing out there," I said, and took the turquoise mask from its box, holding it toward her.

Her gasp was one of repugnance, and she took an involuntary step backward.

"The mask disturbs you?" Juan asked, quickly alert.

"You know very well why it does," she said. "It was found there that day. The day when Kirk and Doro died. The child was holding it. My mother took it from her. Later she packed it in a box with other things and removed them to the hacienda. I have not seen this again until now. It is a thing of ill omen, Amanda."

"I know," I said. "I had an immediate feeling of fright when I saw it."

"No one has told me of this." Juan sounded irritable. "The mask was always hung on a wall at the *rancho*, but the last time I went there it was gone, and I did not ask about it. How could it have come to the picnic place?"

If Clarita had any notion, she didn't betray it. She simply reached past me to pick up the diary from the desk, and she would have carried it away if I hadn't stopped her.

"Please, Aunt Clarita. I'd like to read the pages that are left, if I may. I know so little about my grandmother. And this book would cover part of the year when I was five."

She gave it up to me reluctantly, and I put it and the mask into the box I'd brought from the *rancho*.

"I'll go to my room now," I said. "Is there anything else you wanted of me, Grandfather?"

There was nothing, and Clarita stood away from the door to let me by. Juan spoke as I went out.

"You will remember our plans, Amanda?"

I told him I would remember, and I would come to his study after dinner.

The afternoon was already growing late and shadows lay long across my room when I returned to it. On the bed Paul Stewart's *Emanuella* still awaited my attention, but I was not ready to dip into its pages. My grandmother's diary interested me more because it had to do with the past which pressed with a growing threat upon the present.

I sat down in the chair by a window and began to skim through the pages. Katy had expressed herself vividly, and there were passages I would read with more care at another time, but now I was filled with a strange uneasiness that made me read as though I awaited some revelation. It was as if I stood before a curtained doorway, knowing that it was within my power to fling the curtain aside in time to witness something terrible that was happening beyond. Yet my hand could not move to push aside the curtain. Somehow my will and my vision were blocked. Perhaps this book would give me the power to open that curtain.

Katy had loved life and loved her family, yet she had worn no rose-colored glasses with which to deceive herself. She had lived in a real world in which she made allowances for those she loved, permitting them to be themselves—not always approving, but always loving. Her love for Juan, her husband, came through her words, yet she could be exasperated with him at times. Clarita she worried about and prayed for secretly.

Once she wrote, "Clarita is doomed to unhappiness. I have no use for the man she loves and I do not think he will marry her." She couldn't have meant Kirk at the date of the writing, and I wondered who the man had been whom Clarita had loved in her adult years.

Doroteo was Katy's joy, and she delighted as well in her two small granddaughters, Eleanor and Amanda.

Where she wrote about us, I read more carefully, taking sustenance from the words. Her affection for me— for Doroteo's daughter—came through warmly in the strong script, and tears burned my eyes as I read. Here was the family I had sought. If only this darling grandmother had lived long enough for me to know her after I was grown.

When she wrote about Eleanor, however, there was something a little strange, something pained and off-key, as though she forced herself. The affection was there, but there was something else beneath it—a sadness, a fear, a regret?—that made me wonder if Eleanor had shown disturbing traits even as a small child.

She wrote of Kirk Landers' return to town and there was distress and uncertainty in her words, giving way to relief as she seemed to realize that whatever Doroteo had once felt for Kirk was over, and that Doro would never be turned from her husband. But she fretted about Kirk in these pages. She and Juan had loved and raised him as a son, as his stepsister, Sylvia, had been their daughter. But now Kirk was disturbing the climate of a happy family because he was so unhappy himself. Juan was trying to guide and advise him wisely, and he was the only one Kirk seemed to listen to.

I turned the page and Paul Stewart's name leaped at me from the script. Kirk didn't want Paul to marry his stepsister, and one day there had been a violent quarrel between them, in which Kirk had given Paul a dreadful beating. It had been Katy who'd found them fighting down in the lower patio of the Cordova house. She had managed with difficulty to break up the fight—and not before both men had gained a few battle scars, though Paul's hurts were far worse than Kirk's. Katy's writing became a bit erratic as she told of what had happened, and she closed the episode with these words, "Such angry wounds won't easily heal. Juan mustn't know. He has been ill, and he is still weak. He loves Kirk deeply, and I won't have him upset by Paul."

There was a space of a few days after that in which she didn't write. Then came the time of the picnic, and the preparation for it. A dull passage that was more a listing than anything else—of food to be prepared, of guests to be invited. But there was something wrong in the very writing, because Katy was one to make the prosaic come to life, one to lace her own sense of humor into words with keen perception. There was none of that now—only the wooden setting down of words that might have been a cover for seething emotions she did not want to express.

Then the time of the picnic arrived, and the words suddenly ended, leaving me once more frustrated and questioning, because there were no more pages to be read. Fingering the bits of torn paper at the center of the diary, I found here and there a meaningless word that remained. And one not so meaningless—a word standing by itself near the bottom of what had once been a page. The word "mask."

I sat with the book open in my lap, trying to force that curtain back. But only mists swirled before my eyes and something in me resisted all memory. I had seen something too terrible to be endured by so small a child, and all my forces of self-protection had worked through the years to keep it buried. Now the curtain would not stir. Only through a crack now and then had I glimpsed whatever lay behind the present. Juan himself had helped me more than anyone else, and I must go to him again at another time, but my probing had left him exhausted and I must move gently there.

What was it about the mask?

I went to the box, which I'd left on my bed, and took out the blue carving. I was getting used to it now, and the immediate reaction of terror had faded. But I knew it meant something to me—something agonizing, like its silent scream.

On a sudden whim, I carried it to the dressing table that must once have been my mother's, and sat down to face myself in the glass. With hands that were not quite steady, I raised the mask and placed it before my face. Through the slitted eyes of turquoise and silver I could just make out the mask in the glass, with my own hair sweeping back darkly above the line of blue. The quiver of terror returned. The mask was evil. It intended evil.

The rounded mouth shouted silent obscenities at me. I was I no longer. I was the victim, toward whom evil was intended. I was the hunted.

From across the room Sylvia's voice startled me.

"Since your door's open, may I come in? Clarita said you were up here."

I stared at her in the glass, my vision narrowed by blue slits, and there was an instant in which I seemed unable to stir. Then I removed the mask, laid it upon the rosewood surface before me, and turned around to face Sylvia. I still couldn't speak.

She took my silence for invitation and came toward me across the room. "You're white as a sheet. Have you been frightening yourself with bogeymen?" She reached past me and picked up the mask. "Blind Man's Buff," she said softly.

"Clarita said they found me holding it the day my mother died," I told her.

She nodded, her own expression guarded. "Yes. I remember. Oh, not that you had it—I don't remember that. I was too concerned about Kirk and Doro to think of anything else. But I know Kirk had taken it with him when he went to that place."

"Why? Why did he take it?"

"He didn't explain anything to me. I only know that he was wildly upset, and he went rushing off along the hillside by way of the lower short cut. Doro must have followed him, taking you with her. I didn't want to go that way. I was frightened about what might happen, and I hurried along the upper road to find Katy, who'd gone ahead with one of the picnic baskets. I didn't know where Paul was and I went alone."

A vague questioning stirred in my mind, though I didn't know what it was I questioned—only that something she had said didn't match something I already knew.

"Why did you mention Blind Man's Buff?" I asked.

She set the mask down as though she didn't like the feel of it and turned toward the window chair. "Mind if I sit down? It's a long story. Do you really want to hear it?"

"Yes. I want to hear everything I can."

Light from the window fell upon her insistently brown hair and showed the small lines about her eyes that had begun to make themselves evident. She lowered darkened lashes, shutting out the room, as though she were making a voyage backward in time.

"When we were small, we used to play Blind Man's Buff out at the *rancho,* and whenever we could sneak that mask off the wall without being caught, the one who was 'It' put it on. It made the game all the more scary, and you couldn't really see very well with it on, so it was as good as a blindfold. Of course playing with it was forbidden, because it's a valuable piece. But it fascinated us and added to our fright in being chased by whoever wore it. By the time we were twelve and older, we didn't play such games any more—except out at the *rancho,* where they'd become a sort of ritual. Kirk used to put on the mask and chase Doro. I thought myself too old for such nonsense, and so did Clarita. Paul wasn't around then, of course. He bought the house next door after we were all grown up."

"Who else was there?"

"Sometimes Gavin, though we thought him too young in those days. Rafael was there, of course."

"Eleanor's father?"

Sylvia took her hands from her face and looked at me. "Yes. Eleanor's father. He was always there. He made trouble even then."

"Rafael? No one has said much about him before. Except that he wanted to be an Anglo and he got away from the Cordovas as soon as he could. I hadn't heard that he was a troublemaker. Perhaps Eleanor takes after him."

Sylvia seemed to shake herself, as though some confusion had risen in her mind, and she wanted to be free of old memories. "I don't want to talk about all this. It's gone. Buried. It needs to be forgotten."

But I didn't think anyone was forgetting it. That was the trouble. It was a long while before her hesitation to speak about Eleanor's father returned to me and brought an answer.

In any case, I didn't urge her further. Here and there the bits and pieces were being given me that would eventually add up to the whole—the truth that I was seeking.

I motioned toward the diary, where it lay on my bed. "I went out to the *rancho* today. With Gavin. That's where I found the mask—and an old diary of Katy's as well. It covers the months up to the time of the picnic. The rest has been torn out."

In Sylvia's quiet I sensed an alertness, as though she waited.

"There was a fight, wasn't there?" I went on. "Between your stepbrother and Paul Stewart? Katy wrote about it."

"I—I think there was something of the sort. I was away on a visit at that time."

She didn't want to acknowledge the fight, for some reason. I had the feeling that she was evading her own knowledge of it as something she could not face—or wanted to forget.

"It doesn't matter," I said. "None of this helps me. I've only a crumb or two more to tell Paul."

She made an effort to recover herself. "That's what I came over to hear. Paul sent me to find out whether anything more was stirring yet."

I wasn't going to tell Sylvia the thing Juan wanted Paul to know. Since Kirk was Sylvia's stepbrother, she might try to block those "extenuating circumstances." If I talked to Paul at all, I would tell him myself.

"What happened after—they died?" I asked. "Did you stay on with the Cordovas?"

"Of course. It was my home. I couldn't blame the others for what Doro had done. And Paul was living next door. By that time we were interested in each other. Well, I'd better be getting home—since you haven't anything more to contribute to the book right now."

I wondered at her concern with something she disapproved, but let it go. When she had disappeared down the stairs, I stood for a few moments in the center of the white rug where the Indian mole fetish had lain, looking after her. The question she had aroused was stirring in my mind. Now I knew what it was.

Sylvia had said that she'd hurried along the upper road to look for Katy at the picnic place. Alone. She'd been upset because Kirk had left the house carrying the turquoise mask. But earlier Paul had told me that he and Sylvia had come late to the picnic together. The two stories didn't match, and I wondered which one of them was lying. If he hadn't been with Sylvia, where had Paul been that day, and when had he arrived at the picnic?

I went back to the dressing table and picked up the mask. Its silent cry of anguish was an enigma in itself. There were too many questions. Why had Kirk Landers gone along the hillside carrying it? And what had it meant to Doroteo Austin?

# XI

Soon after I left the dinner table that evening, I went to my grandfather's study and found him waiting for me. There was a change in him—a quickening that made him seem more alive and fiercer than ever. At once I was wary. Whatever he intended, I was not sure I would want to accommodate him.

*"Buenas tardes,"* he said eagerly. "Now you will tell me where each one is."

"I don't know. They all went off in different directions. But they aren't sitting around downstairs, if that's what you mean."

"No matter," he said. "Come with me, Amanda."

He rose from his desk and stepped into the darkened room behind him—the bedroom I hadn't seen until now. A lamp near the big, four-poster bed came on at his touch and I went into the room for the first time.

It was all dark brown against the white of the walls, from the high, carved posts of the bed, to the bed covering and a dark Spanish rug on the floor. Beside a carved table stood a monk's chair, square-wrought, with dark leather across the back, and a crimson velvet cushion over the stretched leather seat. The arms were square-cut and broad, and I could imagine Juan sitting in it as though it were a throne, ruling his domain.

There was nothing Indian in this room. The only relief which offered rich color was a great painting that occupied most of the wall opposite the bed, where he could lie in comfort and look at it. Though why anyone should want such a picture for a bedroom where rest was essential, I couldn't guess.

Fire flared at the painting's center, climbing toward a storm-angry sky and beginning to envelop the man at the stake. Hooded figures with crosses upheld marched about the fire, and a little way off an old woman stood wringing her hands—perhaps suffering for her son who was being burned by the Holy Inquisition.

My grandfather saw the fixed direction of my gaze. "A fine painting and very old. The artist is not known, but I found it long ago in a shop in Seville."

"It seems a strange choice for a bedroom."

He stared me down with proud arrogance. "That scene is part of Spain, part of the Spanish character. We cannot shrug our heritage away in gentler times."

"I'm not sure I like that Spanish heritage," I said. "I haven't any taste for torture in the name of religion."

"I accept what is in my blood, Amanda. And so must you. There are times when one must rule by the brand and the scourge. Come with me."

The falcon's untamed ferocity was upon him again, and I shivered inwardly. I would hate to bring my grandfather's anger down upon me.

I'd wondered why he'd brought me to this room, and now I saw. He went to a door that I had thought was a closet, and opened it upon stone steps running down into darkness, at the end of which was a faint radiance.

"A secret passageway?" I asked lightly.

His tone reproved frivolity. "I do not like a room in which there is only one exit. Nor did the men who built this house. Step carefully now. The light is dim."

He went ahead of me with confidence, since poor vision did not matter here. He knew his way, his hands touching narrow walls on either side as he went down the steps. I followed with less confidence, letting one foot feel for each step as I went down. There were not many steps before the passageway leveled and moved toward the dim bulb which hung from the ceiling at the far end. There Juan Cordova stopped before another door. Before he opened it, he put his ear against the wood panel, listening to whatever lay beyond.

"I think there is no one there," he said.

Under his hand, the door opened quietly, and I followed him into the softly lighted patio. The passageway had not taken us outside Cordova walls, but only by a direct means to the patio.

I offered him my arm, but he had brought his stick and he moved down the flagstone walk without faltering, and I walked at his side. Ahead of us, at the lower end of the patio, rose the small adobe building with the peaked redwood roof that held the Cordova art collection. I knew where we were going now, though I didn't know why our going there should be secret—something concealed from the rest of the house.

A dim lamp burned in the upper part of the patio, its rays barely lighting our way to this lower end. The small building was a dark shadow among other shadows, and thick curtains had been pulled across its windows. I felt a tensing in me as we neared the door—as though I approached some revelation that was to be dreaded. Perhaps this was a feeling I'd caught from my grandfather's manner, since it was as if he approached some blood rite that was half mystical in nature.

At the door he took out the ring of keys he had brought with him, and as his hands moved over a square metal box near the door, he seemed to stiffen.

"The alarm is already off," he said.

At the low sound of his voice, a portion of shadow detached itself from a patch of chamiso and came toward us.

"What are you doing here, Clarita?" Juan's tone was irritable.

She emerged into dim light, wearing black again, as

she had at dinner, her face pale under starlight. "I have been watching. Watching *him*." She gestured toward the adobe building. "You need no key. He is in there now."

Juan uttered an exclamation of annoyance and pushed the door wide. Whatever his intent toward secrecy, it had been defeated.

"Who is there?" he called sharply.

From around a bend that led into a wing at the far end of the central room, Gavin Brand came into view.

"What are you doing here?" Juan asked in quick suspicion.

"You know I have keys," Gavin said. "There was someone around outside a little while ago. I wasn't quick enough to catch him. He got away from me."

"Got away?" Juan challenged skeptically. "In this enclosed space?"

"He managed." Gavin was curt. "Perhaps through the back gate, though there was no one in sight on the hillside when I looked out."

Or through the side gate into the Stewarts' yard? I thought, though I said nothing. There was no reason for such a suspicion, and I wondered why it came to mind.

Clarita drifted into the room behind us. "Perhaps it was I you heard? I have been here for a little while, watching you."

"I came in to check whether everything was all right," Gavin said, paying no attention to her. "As far as I can tell, nothing has been touched. No one has broken in or taken anything from the collection."

I'd stood back a little during this interchange, looking about the interior of the building. It was strangely like a church, with its high cathedral ceiling raftered to a peak overhead, and a chapel-like hush in the room when the voices stopped. One felt a sense of that awe which was reserved for the mystical—as if this were a place of worship. As perhaps it was—Juan Cordova's worship of the art men had created. I remembered that Sylvia had said he collected these things for his own passion and pleasure, and did not readily share them with others.

On shelves along a portion of wall were sculptured pieces and fine carvings from Mexico and Central and South America, as well as ancient Indian pottery from all the Americas. But mostly there were Spanish paintings—not all of them from earlier centuries.

I recognized a Picasso from the blue period—a man and woman standing on a beach at the water's edge, with gray-blue ocean and sky all around, and blue reflected in the sand under their feet, in their very clothes. There was a gypsy study by Isidore Nonell, who had influenced the young Picasso—a swarthy-complexioned girl against a green wash background. The impressionist Sorolla had lent his sunlight effects to a woman in a head scarf walking among the flowers of a sunny park.

In spite of his clouded vision, which kept him from seeing sharply, Juan Cordova knew every item in the room, knew its place and its history, and he paused to tell me about this art he had acquired over so many years. He was clearly not pleased that Clarita should be here or Gavin, since for some reason this was a tour he had wanted to conduct alone with me, without the knowledge of the household. But he bore up under the circumstances and gave his attention to the paintings and to me.

I had exchanged a single glance with Gavin, and found him oddly guarded and not like the sympathetic man I'd met at the picnic place and who had driven me out to the *rancho*. He did not want me here, and I wondered why.

"I have been thinking," Juan said, his eyes on the wall of Spanish pictures, as though he strained to see them. "Perhaps the time has come when I should share some of my treasures with the world. In my own way."

Gavin was silent, waiting, and I sensed resistance in him. Clarita seemed to hang on her father's words.

Juan went on. "I have decided to select five or six Spanish scenes and display them at the store. Gavin, you will have a space cleared for them, so they can be hung well apart."

"The insurance problems will be enormous," Gavin said flatly, "and there is no space."

"Then you will put away wall hangings, rugs, weaving, so you can make space."

"We are not a museum." Gavin was angry but controlled. "The craftsmen you would displace depend on our sales for their living. If you want these things shown, loan them to a museum."

"They must appear under the Cordova name," Juan said harshly.

"Articles have been taken from the store lately," Clarita put in. "Perhaps it is wiser not to risk what is valuable."

Juan ignored her, starting down the aisle. "We will speak of this later, Gavin. Come, Amanda, there is more for you to see."

There was nothing to do but go with him, though my sympathy lay with Gavin's intention for the store.

Before a portrait hung halfway down the room, my grandfather paused and touched my arm lightly. "It is there before you. Look at it well. That is Doña Emanuella. Unfortunately, she was not painted by a great artist, but the portrait is good, adequate. It conveys her personality, her likeness."

I looked up at a painting which had been done rather in the manner of Velázquez, though the artist had far from his mastery. He had portrayed a dark girl in a black lace mantilla, with a cluster of pink flowers pinned to the round neck of her yellow court dress. The gown came snugly in at a waist that seemed all the more slim because of skirts which flared widely over an underframe at each side, in the seventeenth-century style of Philip IV's court of Spain.

She stood half turned, and with one hand she seemed to beckon with a full-blown yellow rose. Her mouth had a sulky look, though gaiety danced in her eyes. I could imagine that I looked again at a portrait of Doroteo

Cordova—and perhaps to a lesser extent and with a little more imagination, at my own face.

"You see the resemblance?" Juan asked.

"I suppose I want to see it."

"And a resemblance to yourself?"

I was silent, and unexpectedly, Gavin spoke for me. "Yes, for herself too. There's a chance likeness there. I saw it the first time we met."

Had that been part of the reason for the current of recognition that had leaped between us on that first meeting? Was it because he had seen Emanuella and Doroteo in me, rather than recognizing me for myself? I felt somehow disappointed.

"There was passion in Emanuella," Juan said. "Spirit. Fire."

"I am none of those things," I said hastily, wanting to stand on my own ground.

"Are you so sure?" Gavin said. "Perhaps you're all of them more than you recognize. Not that I believe these characteristics have come down to you from a legend."

I glanced at him in surprise and saw the guarded look was gone, and in his eyes was that same warmth that had existed briefly at the *rancho* this afternoon. Because the look disturbed me, I turned away, knowing I might be too ready to respond. That way lay danger.

Juan did not see this interchange, all his attention given to the portrait, as he peered to see its detail, but I heard Clarita's faint sniff of disapproval. She was staring at me with a high flare of color on her cheekbones and a challenge in her dark eyes. I gave her look for look, while Juan went on speaking of Emanuella, and Clarita's eyes turned away first, though with an air of proud disdain.

"Emanuella was a great beauty and she married young and was mother to several children," Juan went on. "I've always thought her reputed immorality overrated. She was a little wild but not wicked."

"Paul Stewart seemed to think otherwise," Gavin said.

"Stewart!" There was distaste in Juan's voice. "He fell in love with her picture in his writer's way and he wrote about her to suit himself. Just as he was half in love with Doroteo."

"He has never had a woman worthy of him," Clarita put in irrelevantly, and I glanced at her in surprise. Clarita—Paul? Was he the man Sylvia had hinted about?

"He's supposed to have done a good deal of research on Emanuella in Spain," Gavin said.

"Research!" Juan was emphatic. "He colored his facts. He made her what she never was. Amanda, you can be proud of the bloodline that comes down to you from that glorious woman."

He really believed in that bloodline, I thought, and I looked up at the sulky, beautiful face with its crimson mouth, lightly tinted cheeks and smoothly combed black hair, glimpsed beneath the fine lace of the mantilla. For just a moment I felt close to my mother. Then the sense of nearness fell away and I was looking into the face of an enchanting stranger. It was romantic to think that some bit of this glamorous woman had come down to me, but I didn't really believe it. She belonged to another world and another time.

"When you speak of the bloodline, you can't forget the other portrait," Clarita said tartly. "The Cordovas must claim her too as a relative. Inés as well as Emanuella."

"I am not likely to forget." Juan gestured and we moved on to look at more pictures.

There was a portrait of Cervantes, in which a strange yellow-green light glowed from the landscape behind him, touching his long thin face and the ruff about his neck. Next came a bullfight scene, with a fallen matador and blood streaking the sand of the ring, and then one of Spagnoletto's scenes of torture and martyrdom that would have made a good companion piece for the Inquisition painting in Juan's bedroom. I preferred the following painting of a Spanish street on a misty, rainy night, with a glowing nimbus shrouding the street lamps.

Before this I stood for a long while, studying the effect the artist had achieved so well with his pigments.

There were others, but Juan Cordova grew impatient. 'Enough of all this! You can come back another time, Amanda, and look to your heart's content. Now we will see the masterpiece."

Strangely, Gavin hesitated. "Must she see it?"

"But of course she must. Perhaps it will be her heritage someday."

Clarita made her odd little sound of distaste, and Gavin glanced at me with sympathy. "Don't let it give you bad dreams at night."

I was curious now, and when Juan moved on toward the hidden wing, I walked at his side.

The portrait dominated a small alcove. If the building was given over to the mystical worship of beauty created by gifted painters, this was the central image before which one did homage.

The painting hung against one white wall, framed in gilt and nearly life size. Unmistakably the incomparable artist, whose work I had seen in museums and in reproductions, had painted this and it was dramatic in its impact. The subject was a woman gowned in dark bottle green which had been banded with strips of creamy white. Like the dress of the other portrait, her skirts were extended widely at each side over a hidden frame, but this time the waist was thick, the woman stunted. The size of the dog which lay at her feet with its ears cocked told her true proportions. She was a dwarf, with flowing dark hair and a flat, pushed-in face. There was a strange serenity about the face, yet the dark eyes that looked straight out of the picture had something frightening about them.

"The dwarf," I murmured, and felt a sense of shock. But surely the relationship to Juan was only, as Eleanor and Gavin said, a legend.

"Yes," my grandfather said. "Doña Inés. She was cousin to Emanuella and a maid of honor to Maria Teresa, the Infanta."

"Velázquez," I said. "No one else could have done this."

Juan Cordova looked pleased. "I'm glad you recognize a masterpiece. Yes. Velázquez painted it. It is the famous lost painting of one of the dwarfs he liked to portray in Philip's court."

"But how did you ever—?"

"Come to possess it?" Juan Cordova chuckled, and the sound was sly, wicked. "That is nothing we need to go into now. It has had many travels before coming into my hands. Eventually it will be sent back to Spain. But for now, it is the portrait of an ancestress and I treasure it for many reasons."

"Not all of them pleasant," Gavin said. "Perhaps you'd better tell her the story, since you've gone this far."

If there had been friction between them a short while ago, Juan seemed to have put it aside, but I did not think he would have forgotten.

"Inés was a fiercely passionate woman," Grandfather said. "And apparently she adored the cousin she could not resemble. She murdered one of her cousin's lovers—or at least a nobleman she thought was Emanuella's lover. She stabbed him to death in his bed one night. An attendant apprehended her and she was sent to prison. She was never executed because she went completely mad. So now you have the story of our famous dwarf. That, too, is the blood that comes down to us."

I stared at that strangely serene face, with the eyes that suggested madness, and I could not help shivering. I remembered my father's voice speaking of that "damnable dwarf."

"Any such strain—if it ever existed—has obviously long since been diluted," Gavin said. "Don't worry about it, Amanda."

"It is there," Juan Cordova contradicted coldly. "The passion, the fury, the lack of restraint. It crops out in all of us again and again. In myself. In Doroteo. In Eleanor. Even in you, Clarita. About Amanda, I do not know."

I looked up at the portrait with a growing sense of dismay. What Gavin said was surely true, yet I remembered the way my father had watched me, the way he had fought any signs of temper in me. But there was no reason to be afraid. No real reason.

"I'm not like that," I said.

Gavin reached out a hand and turned off the light that gave the painting its individual illumination. "I'll admit it's haunting. But you'll throw it off as soon as you turn your back on it, Amanda. Your grandfather has too much of an obsession with these supposed female ancestors."

"I am proud of them," Juan Cordova said, and I knew that, strangely, this was true. He actually took pride in fancying this wild strain in himself and in others of his blood.

I was aware of Clarita there beside him, her dark gaze on the portrait with a certain avidity, as though she had, in this too, patterned herself after her father, worshiping at the shrine of the dwarf.

"Perhaps you encourage the strain to exist," I said to Juan. "If your children grow up haunted by that picture and its story, every small loss of temper might be frightening. Or—it might become something to indulge."

Gavin agreed. "Exactly. That's what has happened to Eleanor. Juan has encouraged her to indulge herself in wildness because he's proud of this supposed strain."

"The strain is there." Clarita echoed her father. "We cannot escape it." In the bright lighting that illumined the rest of the paintings, her face seemed stark, colorless—a Spanish portrait in black and white, with the eyes shining darkly in her pale face.

The old man did not look at her. "This is not so," he said in response to Gavin. "It isn't possible to encourage what isn't there. The strain is visible in all the Cordovas. But in Eleanor it is only a youthful unruliness."

"Then it's time for her to grow up," Gavin said. He sounded hard again and unrelenting. This was the side

of him I did not like. He would approve and encourage—
up to a point where a woman wanted to go her way.
Then he could be as domineering as my grandfather. My
feelings toward him were ambivalent, and in either phase
I could feel the other side near. He would never be for
long the kind and sympathetic man I had known this
afternoon.

I turned away from the now unlighted picture of the
dwarf Inés, leaving it to its own demented gaze, and
moved out of the wing. My steps echoed on the tile
floor and Juan Cordova must have heard me, though he
stayed where he was, speaking earnestly to Gavin. Clarita
stayed with them. I didn't want to hear any further
arguments between them, and I returned to the painting
of Doña Emanuella and looked up into those dancing,
provocative eyes. There was no madness there.

At the other end of the room the voices rose a little,
but I paid no attention.

How had Emanuella felt about her cousin, the dwarf?
Had she loved her, been kind to her? Or had she suffered because of her? How much had Paul Stewart un-
covered in the research he had done in Spain? I wanted
to dip into his book and read his account of these two
women who had existed so far back on my family tree.

Now the voices intruded, rising in heat, and I became
aware that Eleanor was the subject of their contention.
When I glanced in their direction, I saw that the two
men had come around the corner of the wing and stood
in full view. They had forgotten me, but Clarita had not.
She remained a little apart, staring down the room in
my direction as though she willed me to turn away,
commanded me not to listen. I began to listen with full
intent.

"We can't stay together any longer!" Gavin cried.
"It's impossible. Eleanor doesn't wish it and neither do
I!"

"Eleanor doesn't know what she wants," Juan protested.

"Do you think that's true of me?"

"I think you have a responsibility."

"Not any longer. Eleanor wants to be free of all restraint. She doesn't want the trust fund you've set up for her. She wants the money itself in her own hands. But if you give it to her—"

"I will not give it to her," the old man said. "You know in your heart you cannot leave her. But if your marriage breaks up I will change my will and leave everything to my other granddaughter, Amanda."

His voice was strong, assured, and it carried with no effort at concealment. It carried to the open doorway where Eleanor had suddenly appeared, her face white, her eyes blazing. She had heard it all, and I thought in sudden alarm—or did I imagine it?—that there was a look of the dwarf about her, for all her golden perfection as contrasted with that dark, stunted figure.

If she saw me, she gave no sign, but rushed past me down the long room, to stand defiantly before Juan Cordova, a tall, slender figure, with her hair falling over her shoulders.

I was suddenly aware of Gavin, his attention not upon Eleanor, but upon me—challenging me in some way, any warmth toward me gone from his face, so there was only a waiting coldness there. But this was no time for me to probe whatever he expected. Eleanor held stage center.

"You can't do this, Grandfather!" she cried. "I won't stay with Gavin. I hate him! I'm the one you should think of now—not Amanda. I'm the one you must take care of."

Juan moved toward her, his expression proud and unrelenting. "You will always be taken care of—modestly. But if you leave Gavin, everything will go to Amanda."

She flung herself upon him, pounding clenched fists against his chest so that for an instant he staggered under the impact. Then he righted himself and held her to him, stilled her beating hands, soothing her until she quieted. I was stunned by this outpouring of emotion. In the face of it any words from me would have been feeble indeed. I stayed where I was in silence.

"Perhaps you've only a little while to live!" Eleanor wailed, clinging to him with a childlike appeal I could not believe was real. "And when you're gone there will be no one to look after me. There will be only what you leave to take care of me."

He spoke to her in soft Spanish and there was the sound of endearment in his tone, yet I felt sure that he promised her nothing. Gavin walked past them stony-faced, and came in my direction. There was no kindness in him.

"Why haven't you said something to stop this?" he demanded. "I thought you were the one who wanted nothing from him. But of course if you stand by and do nothing, everything will fall into your hands, won't it? The store, the money—everything CORDOVA stands for."

I felt outrage rising in me and a deep wounding as well, though this I thrust aside and would not accept. In no way had I meant to be used like this by my grandfather. Gavin was wildly unfair, and I wouldn't be driven away or stopped in my real purpose because of his words or because of Juan Cordova's machinations.

"Go away, Amanda," Gavin said in the same cold fury. "Leave Santa Fe!"

I remembered wryly the time when I had wondered if he might not seem more human if he ever exploded. Now the explosion had come and it was deadly chill—inhuman.

Nevertheless, I stood up to him. "I wouldn't have come here in the first place if I'd known I'd be used like this. But now I won't be driven away."

My words seemed to echo into a sudden silence. For a moment the chapel-like hush lay upon the room and Doña Emanuella looked mockingly down from her place on the wall. Then Gavin gave me a last look and went out the door. When he had gone, Juan put Eleanor from him and came quickly toward me down the room, his stick tapping on the tiles, but used very little for support. Excitement had given him strength.

"Of course you will not go away, Amanda. You are the one I can trust. There is just a little time left for me, and you must stay with me."

I couldn't answer him warmly. What he had done was unforgivable. "I've told you why I mean to stay," I said. "I won't leave until I've found out the truth about what happened to my mother. I think it's beginning to come back to me, a little at a time, and for me nothing else matters."

He gave me a long, searching look and nodded gravely. Then he went past me out the door. There was much to be said, but this was not the time to say it.

Eleanor came running from the back of the gallery, but she didn't follow him immediately. She paused instead to stare up at the painting behind me.

"That one doesn't belong to me," she said of Emanuella. "She is all yours—and your mother's. It's the other one I belong to. The wild, mad one. Perhaps you'd better remember that."

She went past me out of the room and left an echoing silence behind her. The lighted gallery was quiet, yet the atmosphere of awe and worship which Juan Cordova so carefully cultivated was gone, and the air seemed to pulse with the unrestrained emotion that had flowed through it with Eleanor's passing. Here, tonight, something had been unleashed that would not quickly be restrained again. Something of it had touched all of us. I felt shaken by its surging—and more than a little alarmed.

I had forgotten Clarita, until she moved at the back of the gallery, and came toward me with her air of calm arrogance.

"It has begun again," she said as she came opposite me. "I have been waiting, and it has begun."

"What has begun?" I demanded.

Dark eyes were strangely expressionless in her pale face. "It is the death march. If you are very still you can hear the footsteps. They are the footsteps of Inés, coming down to us over the centuries. I have heard them before." She came close to me. "I have heard them along the hillside, when your mother died. You had better save yourself, Amanda."

She was a little mad too—like all of them—and I stepped abruptly away from her.

"Go back to the house," she directed. "Go quickly through the dark. I will lock up here."

I had no desire to linger in her company, and I went out the door into the cool Santa Fe night. Stars seemed very bright, and the dim patio lamp could not rival them. Ahead of me the house glowed with lights, and I walked toward them, hurrying. It was a night in which to slip swiftly past clumps of shadow and regain as quickly as possible the safety of walls and rooms, of warm color and lighted lamps.

No one was in sight when I stepped indoors, though I could hear Eleanor's voice sounding from our grandfather's study. What they had to say to each other, I did not care. None of his plans concerned me, because they were not acceptable to me, no matter what Gavin believed. But as I went up to my room, the sense of wounding returned, and once more I thrust it away. I wouldn't be caught by such a trap again. He was easy to hate, but he would also be more than easy to like. To love? The thought made me angry with myself, and I dismissed it at once. I was a stronger woman than that.

When I was in my room, I turned on a lamp beside the shabby armchair, picked up the book by Paul Stewart, and settled down to read. Now I wanted to know about Emanuella. And about Doña Inés.

# XII

The story of *Emanuella* was a fictionized version—"as based upon . . ." so there was no telling which parts were fact, and which fiction. Nevertheless, I read eagerly, and some of the time I could not fling off the feeling that I was reading about my mother.

Paul Stewart had been skillful in bringing his characters out of the past and his scene to life. Emanuella was all fire, completely alive, yet with a certain sweetness about her. Everyone seemed to adore her and she lived on adoration. How much of this was research, I wondered, and how much of it was Paul's memory of Doroteo?

But as the narrative continued, a note of brilliant wickedness was introduced into the depiction of the heroine. "Brilliant" in the sense of being vivid, glittering, dramatic—revealing all too clearly that the author himself, if he had been in love with Emanuella-Doroteo, saw her as provocative in her very iniquity. Had this been my mother? I couldn't believe it, and I could see why the book had angered Juan, and why he did not want Paul to touch the subject of Doroteo again.

I read on, trying to put the thought of my mother from my mind. The story re-created a lively picture of Philip's court, with mystery and a sense of horror emerging as Inés stepped onto the scene.

It had been King Philip's whim to bring to Madrid from abroad whatever dwarfs he could find to amuse him. Often they were jugglers, tumblers, jesters—a motley, entertaining crew. And the young Velázquez, new to the court under the patronage of King Philip, found them interesting subjects for his early work. There was one dwarf, however, who was no jester, but cousin to a lady of the court, daughter of a nobleman. She was Doña Inés, feared a little, perhaps, but respected, and assigned as lady in waiting to the Infanta. Maria Teresa loved her and made her a playmate and confidante. Perhaps she was more nurse than anything else. For all her stunted size and abnormal appearance she was a woman of dignity and power. Yet Paul drew her in his story as evil, and my flesh crept as he described her fatal devotion to the cousin who was all that she was not.

It was growing late, but I read on. The house about me was very still and from my high room I could glimpse the distant lights of Los Alamos, and on the other side I could see by starlight the Sangre de Cristos. Santa Fe was asleep, but I was not. Once I put my book aside and went to look down into the dark patio in the direction of the Stewarts' house. There lights burned, and there was a distant sound of voices. Paul Stewart, who had written these pages, and his wife, Sylvia, who had gone with him to Spain when he was doing his research, must still be up. In the stillness the woman's voice held a note of disquiet, as though she might be agitated, disputing something.

I turned back to my reading. Emanuella had married well—a gentleman of Madrid, and her children were healthy and beautiful. But there was always a restlessness upon her. Her husband's adoration no longer seemed enough. When a younger man, newly come to Philip's court, began showing more than a little interest in her, she responded. He was handsome, rich, with a wandering eye for women. Emanuella was caught, and Inés, ever watchful, saw what the outcome would be. Her beloved cousin might well risk her marriage, injure the children, whom Inés adored, and the husband who was devoted to her. She counseled Emanuella against this young Don Juan, but of course she was not listened to.

All through the narrative Paul pointed up the taint of wild blood in the family of the cousins. A trait inherited and perhaps exploited when it was convenient. There were storms of temper on Emanuella's part and much excitability. Strangely enough, Inés carried this trait of character with more control and dignity than her cousin showed. Only now and then did she explode in wild anger, and then everyone was far more afraid of her than of Emanuella.

In the face of threat, Doña Inés knew what she must do. While one of the palace guards was sleeping she stole out and took the dagger from his belt. Her hands were small, but powerful, and there was strength in her handling of the weapon. She crept into the room where the young man lay sleeping and stabbed him to death. Only then did her control shatter and she began to scream.

When a guard rushed into the room, he found her there, screaming, bloodstained—and quite mad. It was when she was imprisoned that Velázquez painted her. Serenity had been restored because she no longer knew or cared who she was, had no knowledge of what she had done. So that calm, misshapen dwarf's face looked out of the picture, but the eyes were entirely mad.

I sat with the book open upon my lap, haunted by this tale of horror Paul had written so vividly. It all came too close to home. I had wanted to know what made me, what I had descended from, but I didn't want to believe my mother was like Emanuella, or that the blood of Inés still flowed in the veins of the Cordovas—as my grandfather was determined to believe. On any family tree there were all possible combinations of traits if you went back far enough. There was madness and sanity, and good and evil. But the affairs Paul Stewart had written about had nothing to do with me.

Yet, coming unwanted, there was a vivid picture in my mind of Doroteo with a gun in her hand as she went to that place where she would find Kirk Landers. If she had lived, would she have gone mad afterwards, as Inés had done?

I closed the book sharply, and the slap of sound was startling in my quiet room. The story had put an unwelcome spell upon me—as though I must, after all, believe that murder had been done in the recent past. But I would not accept the murderer, as others had labeled her.

Then in that silent room, as if it were a living presence, a gift from the past, a new thought occurred to me, and it pointed clearly to Doroteo's innocence. A woman who went out with a gun in her hand to commit a murder did not take a loved child with her to witness violence. All the doubting fell away from me. How simple, and how clear an answer. Now my course was plainer than ever.

Someone knew the truth. How was I to find that person and make him talk to me? Whether retribution was done at this late date or not, I didn't care a great deal. But I wanted to know the truth as Doroteo's daughter, and I wanted her immediate family to know.

Paul's book could tell me nothing more, and I put it aside, picked up my sketchbook and pencil and began to sketch idly. I was drawing the tree again, shaping it as I remembered it from recent reality—not from my dream. The branches no longer seemed grotesque, but merely ancient, and the leaves were dry and dusty from the long drought, but not like bony fingers that reached for me. I began to feel a certain reassurance as my pencil moved on the page and what came to life on paper was only a very old tree—not the embodiment of evil. It soothed me to draw the real tree instead of the one that belonged to nightmare, and I even began to feel a little sleepy. In a moment I would go back to bed, but first I would compare my new sketch with the one I'd made in the clearing.

I flipped over the pages to the earlier drawing and knew at once that this was a mistake. I should never have looked at my drawing again tonight. In a rush that enveloped me the sense of horror was back. My eyelids felt heavy, the drawing began to swim before my eyes, and the lights in the room began to pulse. Now I was seeking some hazy, dream-laden answer, trying to see with a child's eyes, trying to return to the terrible past the tree represented, all sense of ease vanishing. Behind my lids weaving pictures moved and there were figures to be seen as if through mist.

Some sort of struggle was going on and I sensed again the terrifying stain of scarlet spilling across my vision. Before young, frightened eyes, forms struggled together in the mists. Not two people—but *three*. I could not recognize who they were. But there were shapes that seemed to writhe in some dreadful death dance. There seemed a tremendous noise inside my head —the sounds of nearby blasting, perhaps. Then another explosion. Afterwards, the hillside was quiet and the three were gone. There was only that frightful mask left on the ground beside the small child who watched, weeping, and who reached down to pick it up.

The fog seemed to swirl like a blown veil before my eyes. Then light flashed through bright zigzags through the mist—and I was fully awake and in the present. The room about me was bright and quiet. The drawing of the tree lay upon my knees, and now it was only a sketch I had made, a thing without life of its own.

Yet I remembered something. Three. There had been three. Or was any of this rational? I did not know, but I was seized by the conviction that I was on the right trail. My mother and Kirk had been there—but there had been another one as well. And perhaps it was the third who had fired the gun. The third who had come secretly along the hillside, and escaped as secretly, so that none of those at the picnic above had any realization of his presence. Clarita had lied.

I couldn't bear to think of this any longer. I must

empty my mind, think of something else—let anything that chose come to me. Absently, I added shading to the foliage of the sketch, then flipped over to another page and let my pencil move as it wished upon the paper. I hardly realized what I was drawing until the shape and look of Gavin's face began to emerge on the paper. When I saw what I was doing, I stopped at once, but now I couldn't stop my treacherous thoughts. The face I had drawn would have been the one he'd shown me that afternoon, when I sat beside him on the bench and he had held my hand as kindly as he'd done when I'd been a child. That, I reminded myself, was not his true face. He would fight for Eleanor with her grandfather, and he would shut me out, condemn me for being something I was not. Roughly I scratched over the lines I had drawn, and closed the book, put it aside.

As I undressed and made ready for bed, I felt emotionally drained. I could no longer think clearly, and I didn't know what my next move must be. There was no one to whom I could turn for counsel. If I told anyone the thing that had come to me, all of them would be against me. Perhaps even Sylvia. Only Paul would welcome eagerly anything I had to tell. He would use every crumb and give me no counsel worth having. He might even lead me in some wrong direction. What was I to do?

I turned out the lights and slipped between the sheets, drew up a blanket. The high mountain air was cool and Santa Fe nights were wonderful for sleeping. But I lay awake and listened to the house. It did not creak and groan in quite the same way that old wooden houses do, but there seemed a whispering of movement abroad. The lower bedrooms of the others were in an addition which had long ago been built onto the house. Only my grandfather's room and my own were isolated from the others.

Once I thought I heard footsteps on the narrow flight of stairs that mounted to my upper room. I tensed myself on one elbow, listening to the darkness with all my being. But there was no further sound. Either the

stairs themselves had created in the changing tempera-
ture, or someone sat on the steps, patiently waiting
for me to relax and go to sleep. Or to rise out of curiosity
and go to some dangerous rendezvous?

I couldn't bear the suspense of not knowing, and after
a while I left my bed and went softly to the door. It opened
quietly upon the stairs that led down to the room that
was an extension of the living room. Moonlight found
its way through deep windows, touched the light patches
of Indian rugs on the floor, flung the furniture into jet
shadow. It also silhouetted the stairs. No one crouched
upon them. But nevertheless, there was movement.

In the room below one of the shadows moved. It did
not dart, but moved slowly, with great stealth. Moonlight
did not reach to my place at the head of the stairs and
the moving shadow seemed not to sense my presence. I
had no impulse to cry out, to ask who it was. I was
filled with a dread curiosity. I had to know what was
meant by this action. At least the shadow was not creeping toward Juan Cordova's room, though I had the feeling that if there was danger, it was not to me.

Maddeningly, the moon went behind a cloud and the
chiaroscuro of the room was wiped out. Now there was
no light and dark, but all was shadow. I could no longer
distinguish movement, though there seemed a faint whisper
of sound as if something drifted across the room below.
Then I heard the soft creaking of a door and knew that
the night visitor sought the patio.

I turned quickly back to my room and ran to a window in the thick adobe wall. I climbed into the embrasure so that I could see directly down into the patio.
The moon was still hidden, but there was starlight, and
in the patio a single lamp burned on a standard. I could
just make out the slow movement of that stealthy figure
as it followed the path downward toward the little house
at the far end of the garden. Lights were out now at
the Stewarts' and there was no one down there to hear
or see. But if there was a tampering with the lock, the
alarm would go off. This I knew. Unless the person

who stole toward Grandfather's precious collection had a key. He had come from inside the house, so he might well have one.

I had to rouse someone. This might be another trick to be played upon Gavin, like the one with the stone head. No matter who it might be, our thief must be exposed. He would be trapped if he let himself into the little house and we could catch him there. I must call someone so that the culprit could be discovered.

I put on my robe and for the sake of quiet crept barefoot down the stairs. The door that led into the bedroom wing stood open, and a dim lamp burned on a small table, lighting the long hall with its closed doors on either hand.

Time was slipping by and I couldn't wait. Clarita's room was nearest and I turned the knob slowly, gently, so there was no sound. I didn't want to rouse the house so our thief—if that's what he was—would be alerted to escape. Softly I pressed the door and a wedge of darkness opened before me. The dim light from the hall gave me little help. I could barely make out Clarita's bed across the room, but there was no sound of breathing, and I could make out no mound of sleeping body beneath the covers.

Gathering my courage, I ran across the room in my bare feet. Clarita was gone from her bed. So it was she I must follow, and I needed no help for that.

I left the hall with its other sleepers, and ran through the living room to a patio door, where I let myself outside. The area still lay in shadow, with the moon hidden, but now the patio light had been turned off. Nothing stirred. No shadow moved along the walk, and all seemed to be quiet down near the building which held the collection. Nevertheless, someone had come out here. Alarm stirred in me. The very quiet seemed menacing.

Bricks were cold to my feet as I stepped outside and started down the walk. The faint rush of sound behind me came without warning—only another whisper in the night. There was no time for me to turn, to protect myself. Searing pain struck me across the shoulders and then came again and again, slashing furiously, so that I stumbled and fell to my knees, half stunned, trying vainly to escape the flailing whip. My own screaming split the night.

The blows stopped as suddenly as they'd begun, and there was an outcry from farther along the walk, the sound of a fall. I crouched dazed on my hands and knees, aware only of stinging pain. In the house lights flared on, but it seemed an age before Gavin came running down the walk. He paused beside me but I waved him on.

"Down there! Someone fell!"

He went past me and I heard Juan's choked voice. "The whip!" he moaned. "It was the *disciplina!*"

I managed to stand, to move toward the place where Gavin knelt beside my grandfather. But before I had taken three steps, I saw the thing that lay in my path, its three leather prongs outflung on the tile.

From the house Eleanor came running. She flung herself upon the old man, uttering cries of alarm. Where was Clarita? my stunned mind questioned, and I looked around to see her tall figure in the lighted doorway that led from the patio. She neither moved nor cried out, but waited while Gavin and Eleanor helped her father back to the house. Then her words reached me clearly.

"Go and phone for the doctor, Eleanor." There was no emotion in her tone.

The three moved past me, with Juan faltering between them, and I saw that he was fully dressed and wearing a heavy leather jacket. Perhaps that had spared him what I had suffered. Clarita let them by and then moved toward me, but before she could ask questions I spoke to her.

"I went to your room," I said. "You weren't in bed."

She ignored that. "Are you hurt?"

"A little," I said.

"Then come inside," she ordered, and turned back to the house.

Awkwardly, I reached back to touch my throbbing shoulders, but when I would have followed her, a voice spoke to me out of the lower shadows. Paul's voice.

"Can I be of any help, Amanda? What seems to have happened?"

I didn't trust him. The *disciplina* still lay at my feet and I picked it up with repugnance. The cruel thongs that would have lacerated bare flesh hung limp in my hand as I held it out.

"This belongs to you," I challenged.

He came toward me and took the whip questioningly. "So it does. There was another theft from the store today. My Penitente display has been rifled. This whip was taken, and so was the figure of Doña Sebastiana from her cart. But what's the whip doing here?"

"That's what I'd like to know," I said. "Someone struck me with it and then struck my grandfather, knocking him down on the walk. How could anyone be so cruel?"

Sylvia came running through the gate from the other house, a coat flung over her night clothes.

"Paul—what is it? I heard voices—someone screamed."

He said, "Go back to bed, Sylvia. I'll be along in a moment."

He was stroking the thongs of the whip gently across one palm, but as the moon came out from behind its cloud, his eyes were fixed on me with bright curiosity. By moonlight all he needed were the pipes and a cloven hoof.

"Who did this, Amanda? Who do you think did it?"

"I don't know," I said dully. I wasn't going to tell him about Clarita being out of her bed, or of my hearing sounds from the living room. I didn't want to talk to him at all. As I turned toward the house, he let me go, and I didn't look back until I reached a glass door. Then I looked around to see that both Paul and Sylvia were gone, and the whip with them.

Inside, Juan Cordova lay weakly on a leather couch in the living room, and Clarita was holding a wine glass to his lips. Eleanor stood by, her eyes alive with excitement rather than concern, and when they met mine across the room she gave me a smile filled with malice.

"What happened, Amanda? Were you whipped too? You see what can happen to you if you don't go away from Santa Fe!"

Gavin was kneeling beside Juan, talking to him quietly, and he looked up sharply at Eleanor. "What do you know about this?"

"I?" Her reproach was exaggerated. "Do you think I would ever injure my grandfather?"

The old man roused himself and pushed Clarita's glass away. "It was not Eleanor. She had nothing to do with this. Amanda, you were struck down first—did you see who it was? I had just come from the passage that leads to my bedroom when I heard you scream, and then he was upon me. In the darkness I couldn't see the attacker."

"Nor could I." I went closer to his couch. "I heard something but I couldn't turn in time to know who struck me. When the whip first lashed me I stumbled and fell, and I didn't see what happened clearly. I think someone rushed past me, but I was dazed."

He sighed and closed his eyes. "Whoever used the whip was strong. I have enemies, enemies."

"Are you going to call the police?" I asked.

Except for Gavin, they all looked at me as though I'd uttered some obscenity.

"There will be no police," Juan Cordova said harshly, and Clarita nodded dark agreement.

Eleanor laughed. "We never call the police, dear Amanda. There is too much guilt among us. Who knows what a policeman might turn up?"

"That is not the reason," Juan said coldly. "The papers are too much interested in Cordova scandal. It is not good for the store. There is nothing to be done anyway, since the culprit has escaped. We will handle this ourselves."

My eyes met Clarita's and she stared me down boldly, disdainfully, not caring what I thought. Where she had been, and why Juan Cordova had gone outside, I didn't dare ask, but Gavin had no compunction about asking direct questions.

"Why were you in the patio at this hour?" he demanded of Juan.

The old man answered readily. "I couldn't sleep. When I looked out the window I saw someone down there. Since there have been thefts, I feared for the collection. By the time I came outside, someone had turned off the outdoor light. I was starting down the path when I heard Amanda scream." He paused and seemed to draw a certain dignity about him, as though he would not allow himself to appear old and ill and half blind. "I would have gone to her aid. *Naturalmente*. But there was no time before I too was struck down."

Eleanor's voice had a little rasp in it when she spoke and she surprised us all. "You know very well who used that whip, don't you, Grandfather?"

The old man gasped softly, and at once Clarita was at his side. "Let him alone, Eleanor. This is no time for your teasing."

The doorbell rang, and Gavin went to let the doctor in. Clarita rose from her knees with quiet dignity and went past me to greet him. And in passing she spoke one word to me in a deadly whisper.

*"Cuidado,"* she said, and went to take the doctor's coat and invite him in. Dr. Morrisby was a small man, gray-haired and in his mid-fifties. He came in shaking his head and scolding Juan gently.

"In trouble again!" he said. "Can't you keep my patient quiet, Clarita?"

No one answered him. Gavin explained in as few words as possible that we had an intruder on the grounds. When the doctor had assured himself that Juan had not been seriously injured, spared by his heavy jacket, Gavin asked him to have a look at me.

He came upstairs to my room. "A bad business," he said as I lowered my robe. "The Cordovas have an attraction for violence. I attended your mother at the time of her death."

There were tender welts across my upper back and shoulders from which my light robe had hardly shielded me, but at his words I had no further interest in my own hurt.

"Do *you* think she committed suicide?" I asked him flatly.

He drew up my robe gently over the sore places and turned away to write a prescription for ointment. There was the matter of putting his glasses on and taking them off—all delaying tactics, I suspected—before he answered me. When he did his voice was kind, thoughtful.

"Doro was my patient from the time she was quite young. She had a gift for happiness. When she loved, she loved with all her heart, and sometimes she claimed that her heart was broken. But I doubt that she ever hated, and she always recovered. I believe that she loved your father in a more adult way than she'd ever loved that boy who died, and she was happy with him. It was hard for me to understand why she would take the action she did, or to believe that she would kill herself."

I thanked him warmly, and his eyes were pitying as he said good night.

"I will give this prescription to Clarita, so she can have it filled for you," he said, and went downstairs.

Alone in my room, I sat on the bed for a few moments, thinking about the doctor's words. And of that warning Clarita had whispered to me: *Cuidado!* In spite of Juan's belief that the real attack had been aimed against him, I didn't believe it. I was the one whom the attacker had meant to frighten. Juan had been lightly struck, so that he supposedly would not be able to identify my assailant. But Eleanor, who read her grandfather with a cool and calculating eye, believed that Juan had known who it was.

There *had* been someone on my stairs. The sounds had been intended for me to hear. Perhaps they had been bait to make me curious and entice me into the patio. It would not have been Juan down there in the living room, since he had his own passageway to the patio, if he chose to be secretly abroad.

Someone was growing afraid. Someone who wanted to warn me away from Santa Fe before I remembered too much. Was it that shadowy third one who struggled in the mists of my memory, and would not make himself known? What had Clarita said earlier about a death march? That it had begun again, and that she'd heard the footsteps before, when my mother had died? But Clarita was given to the ominously mystical.

Anyway, nothing further was to be gained by puzzling over all this now. I slipped off my robe and went to bed somewhat gingerly, trying to favor my shoulders. My thoughts would not stop their churning, however.

Downstairs Gavin had been kind to me again. He had been concerned for my hurt. But of course his kindness had been impersonal—simply the sort of thing he would extend to anyone who had been injured. It did not mean that he thought differently about me, or was ready to retract the harsh words he'd flung at me earlier in the evening.

Tears that I resented were wet against my pillow and I found that my teeth had begun to chatter with a reaction of nerves. I could feel the lash of the whip—intending to hurt, intending to warn. Warn of what might come next if I didn't go away?

I was so alone. There was no one to whom I could turn with confidence. The fetish had been the first hint of warning. Now it was growing worse. And I must keep my own counsel, lest he who was afraid be forced into more dangerous action. Or she? Clarita? Eleanor? But Eleanor wouldn't care about the past. She had been only ten when my mother died.

I tried to think of Gavin's hand holding mine, comforting me. I could remember the feeling of his fingers about my own, and that was all I wanted. If he loved Eleanor, it didn't matter—if only he would befriend me for a little while.

Sleep came while I was clinging to that memory—and at once I began to dream about the tree. But this time I was strong enough to sit up in bed and fling off the nightmare. When next I fell asleep, sore and exhausted, my dreams were harmless, and I couldn't recall them when I awakened to morning sunlight.

There was a stiffness to my back and shoulders when I got out of bed, but I could tell by the bathroom mirror that the red welts were less marked. If I stayed, I would live to face the next attack, I thought wryly. *If* I stayed. Was it worth it to risk what was now becoming a more determined warning to me to go away? I didn't know. Doroteo Cordova Austin seemed a faraway stranger to me this morning, and I was simply the daughter who did not know her—and who was afraid and terribly uncertain.

No one was at the table when I went to breakfast, and I ate very little. Coffee was warming and savory, and I began to make a plan for my morning. I needn't decide at once whether to stay or to go. I must give my mind time to quiet so that I could choose wisely. Whatever happened, I didn't want to run away in a panic—and have to live with an act of cowardice for the rest of my life. So this morning I would paint. I would go out into the street and find a vista that appealed to me, and I would give myself to catching it on canvas.

Decision helped. When I left the table and started toward my room, I felt momentarily eased. From the foot of my stairs, I could look through into the living room, and I saw that a bustle was going on. Clarita was there, directing Rosa, and plumping up the small henna cushions strewn across the couch. She looked up and saw me, nodding indifferently.

"How is my grandfather?" I asked.

"Overly stimulated." She shook her head in disapproval. "He wants to come downstairs to sit for a while. And he wishes to see you."

I stayed where I was, waiting. After a moment, she sent Rosa away and came toward me.

"And you? Did you sleep? How are you feeling this morning?"

"Sore and stiff," I said. "Does anyone know what really happened?"

"My father feels that he has enemies. Someone got into the patio last night while he was there. You were in the way."

"I certainly was. But what were you doing up?"

Her head went back at such blunt questioning, and she made an effort to stare me down. When it didn't work, she went back to her cushion plumping, and surprised me by answering.

"I knew my father was up and about. I was concerned for him."

Whether this was the truth or not, I didn't know. She had not come outside quickly, as had Gavin and Eleanor.

"I'm going out to paint," I told her. "Do you suppose my grandfather still has an old easel he could let me use? I brought none with me."

"There is one in the storeroom. I will get it for you."

"Thank you. I'll collect my gear and then come down and talk to him."

She nodded stiffly. "I have the prescription Dr. Morrisby ordered for you. You cannot apply it yourself."

She insisted on coming with me to my room, and while I lay on my bed, she smoothed the ointment matter-of-factly over my shoulders. She had neither sympathy for me nor compassion, but she would do her duty to a guest in her house.

When she'd gone, I changed to slacks and a sweater, and picked up my sketchbook. By the time I went downstairs, Juan Cordova was stretched out like a recumbent emperor upon the leather couch, and Clarita was nowhere in sight. She had kept her word about the easel, however, and it stood propped near the door.

# XIII

Rosa knelt before the hearth tending a fire of white piñon logs. Their pungence filled the room and I knew this was a scent out of my childhood—the scent of Santa Fe, of New Mexico, of the Southwest.

Juan Cordova seemed in a strangely benign mood, considering what had happened to us last night.

"How are you feeling?" I asked, sitting beside him in a chair near his couch.

He waved my query aside with a careless hand, perhaps because of Rosa's presence. "The thing I come downstairs for, Amanda, is this fire. Not only the warmth, but the fragrance. I remember it from my boyhood—out at the *rancho*."

"I remember it too," I said. "It's unforgettable."

"Odors breed memory. You are beginning to remember this room?"

But I wasn't. There were no flashes to remind me that the very young Amanda had ever been here.

He went on conversationally. "You know it was the women who built the adobe fireplaces in every house in the early days. And it was the women who polished the inside walls to a gloss, rubbing them with sheepskin on their hands."

Rosa stood up and regarded the narrow mantel over the fireplace. With a quick movement she stroked the ledge and brought her finger away gritty, shaking her head. There was always dust in Santa Fe.

"There's nothing more," Juan told her, and she gave us a quick smile and ran off to another part of the house.

"I am too rough for them," Juan Cordova muttered. "I am not defeated yet. They wait for me to die. Perhaps they try to hurry my dying. But I am still alive. And you, Amanda? It is you I am concerned about. Through no fault of your own, you have been drawn into our troubles."

"I'm all right," I assured him. "But I don't understand what happened. Or why it happened."

Even when he was lying down, his look could be fierce, intimidating. "It is not necessary for you to understand, but I think you must go away, Amanda."

"That's not what you said yesterday. I haven't forgotten the way you tried to use me against Eleanor and Gavin. They're both angry with me now, and for no fault of mine."

His soft laughter recalled how he had disconcerted us all, and he was not above enjoying the memory. Then he saw my face and sobered like a naughty child. But he was not a child in any sense, and I didn't like the pretense. I listened to his words in distrust.

"You must go away, Amanda, because it is no longer safe for you here. You are becoming involved in what you do not understand."

"Because I'm beginning to remember too much?"

He dismissed my words. "We have been over all that. There is nothing to remember that will serve your mother now. I have faced that fact long ago. I have tried to go along with this pretext that there is something you might remember that would exonerate your mother. I would like to believe that too, but I have had to face reality long ago. Now you must face it. So you must leave, because there may be danger for you here."

"But if there's nothing of importance for me to remember, how can there be danger? You contradict yourself."

"No—danger, if there is any, lies in the present. Because of what I may do with my will. Danger because of—Doña Inés."

"That's nonsense. Danger from whom—Eleanor, Gavin, Clarita?"

He flushed at what he must have regarded as my impertinence in contradicting him, but he let it pass.

"You do not understand these matters. I feared I might force some risk upon you, but I did not think it would come so quickly, or be so vicious. Now you must go away."

"Then you do think last night's attack was meant for me, not you?"

He repeated obstinately, "You must go away."

And, as obstinately, I resisted. "Not yet. You can put me out of your house, of course, but unless you do, I'll stay awhile longer. You brought me here, and now you must put up with me. I think I'm coming close to something."

"I did not know what a true Cordova I was bringing here," he said with surprising mildness, and I had to relent and smile at him. At once he held out his hand. "That is better. A dark brow does not become you. You give me pleasure when you smile. I am reminded of the portrait of Emanuella."

He was beguiling me, but his falcon's look did not match his tone. I began to gather up my painting gear, preparing to leave him.

"Wait," he said. "If you will not go away at once, then there is something you can do for me tonight."

"If I can." I was immediately cautious.

"Last night, while I lay trying to sleep, someone came and stood beside my bed, watching me. When I reached for the light, this person went away."

"Clarita, perhaps?" I said. "She was concerned for you last night."

"Clarita knows she must announce herself when she comes near me. She knows I will not be secretly watched.

But then there was the attack later in the patio, when I got up, being unable to rest because of concern for my collection. There are those who plot against me, Amanda. But I cannot see the face of my enemy."

This all seemed a little fanciful. There was no one who could get to him except the members of his household, and I could not see one of them threatening him seriously. He was quite capable of weaving fantasies in order to prevail upon my sympathy.

"What is it you want me to do?"

"I am no longer able to drive a car. I can go nowhere without being taken, so I cannot do this for myself. You will go to the store for me this evening."

"Go to the store?" I echoed. "To CORDOVA—at night?"

He went on calmly. "In the daytime you would be seen, your action noted. Surprise is on my side. Slip out of the house quietly, so no one will know you have gone. I will order a taxi for nine o'clock. It will wait for you where our road turns into Camino del Monte Sol. I will give you a key. Two keys."

He fumbled in the pocket of his robe and as he held out the ring I took it from him reluctantly.

"One is to the back door of the store. It will also deactivate the alarm. Let yourself in and go upstairs to the cabinet of Toledo swords. The second key will open it. There is a carved wooden box on the floor of the cabinet. Bring it to me. And tell no one."

The keys were cold in my fingers and I did not like the feel of them. Nor did I in the least like the prospect of going into that place at night when no one was there. It was eerie enough in the daytime, and too much had happened to me.

"You are not afraid of an empty store?" he challenged me.

"Of course I am. After last night, I don't want to go anywhere that's empty and dark. Why don't you send Gavin?"

"How far can I trust Gavin? How far can I trust any of those who work against me? You I can trust because you want nothing of me. You must do this for me, Amanda. And of course it will not be dark in the store. Certain lights are left burning all night. And no one will know you are going there."

His strong will compelled my own, bent me to his way, as he had done before. There was no affection between us, but perhaps there was a certain respect.

"All right," I said. "I'll do as you wish."

His thin lips twisted in the semblance of a smile, and once more I sensed triumph in his dominance over me.

"*Gracias, querida, gracias.*"

"What's in the box you want me to bring you?" I asked.

"When you bring it here to me, perhaps I will show you. But it is a Pandora's box and you are not to open it yourself. Promise me that."

"I promise," I told him, though I wondered what possible difference it would make if I knew the contents.

"Good. Then you may go about whatever you want to do with your day. I will sit here for a time where the fire can warm my bones."

"I'm going out to the street to do some painting," I said. "Clarita has found your old easel for me. I'll take a sandwich and not bother anyone for lunch."

He nodded as though his thoughts were already far away and I knew he was again deep in his own concerns and fear. But what he was afraid of I didn't know.

The morning was bright when I let myself out through the turquoise gate and walked along the dusty edge of the road, looking at adobe walls with their hand-rounded tops, and at the low houses behind them. Hills rose close by, while farther away were the snow-peaked Sangre de Cristos, and I wondered what it was like up there in the snow, far above the pines

There was little traffic on this blind road, and I found a sheltered place in the shadow of a poplar tree where the sun would not shine upon my canvas. There I put up my easel. I had brought several small canvas boards in my sketchbox and when I'd set one of them in place,

I made a finder of my hands to separate the picture I might want from its surroundings.

A portion of winding road with an adobe wall following it, an open gateway with a low house and a poplar at its door—these seemed right for composition and reflected this part of Santa Fe. I might put a small hill into the background as well. With that feeling of anticipation mingled with uncertainty about my own ability that often came to me when I began to paint, I squeezed coils of pigment onto my rectangular palette. This would be a picture of sunlight on adobe, and that was tricky to catch. You achieved sunlight by suggesting it to the eye, not by trying to color it in as an entity in itself. This could be accomplished by the exaggeration of contrast—by using both the highest and lowest values, and touching in highlights with a judicious use of white. I liked oils for sunlight because natural light penetrated and was refracted, so that the surface had a luminous effect—as though one mixed sunlight into the oil paints themselves.

When I had sketched quickly with charcoal, I went to work, and everything but the scene before me faded away. I could forget about Gavin, and even about that moment last night when a whip had slashed across my shoulders. None of that had reality in this sunny scene, and the hours slipped past as I worked.

There was the familiar smell of turpentine and the paints themselves, all mixing with the warming scent of the sun upon adobe—like sun-baked pine needles. Yet the air was cool and comfortable. I concentrated intensely, lost in a quiet joy because I was doing what I liked best to do, and nothing else existed. The picture was coming to life on canvas, and I thought it would not be too bad. I wasn't sure I'd caught exactly the right hues for adobe, but the effect was close. I'd been right about a touch of veridian green for the shadows of the houses. Burnt sienna seemed right for a patch of dried grass, and cadmium red, light, to touch in the poplar's shadow at the bole of the tree.

I was so far away from everything but my canvas that I jumped when a soft voice spoke behind me.

Jarred back to reality, annoyed at being interrupted, and aware of a crick in my neck and the weight of the palette on my thumb, I looked around at Eleanor. When I'd seen her in the gallery last evening, she had been furiously angry. Yet here she stood, a slim figure in jeans and white blouse, with the medallions of a silver concho belt slung low on her hips, smiling as though there had been no flaring anger between us. I didn't trust her, but I decided to go along with this suspiciously amiable mood and see if I could find out what lay behind it.

"How are you feeling, Amanda?" she asked.

I moved my shoulders gingerly, not wanting to remember.

"I'm all right."

She regarded me intently. "Who do you think used that whip last night?"

"I'm not trying to guess," I said. "Do you know?"

"Perhaps *I* can guess."

"Then you'd better tell your grandfather."

She changed the subject abruptly, studying my canvas. "I wish I could do something like that."

"Anybody can paint," I said, offering her the usual cliché.

"I don't think that's true." Eleanor stood back to look at my picture. "Not to do it as well as you can. Or as those artists did who painted the pictures in Juan's collection."

I laughed as I stroked in a bit of cadmium yellow. "Don't mention me in the same breath. I'm hardly in that class."

"Don't be so modest! I can't paint, but I've looked at paintings all my life, thanks to Juan. I didn't expect you to be so good."

With my brush poised in the air, I turned to look at her in surprise. Her fair hair was caught back at the nape of her neck with a torn blue ribbon, her pale bangs were ruffled, and her face was devoid of all make-up, so

hat it looked guileless and surprisingly young. I had
never seen her like this before, and I was instinctively
on guard. When the Cordovas chose to disarm, they
could be all too convincing.

"Do you care if I stay to watch?" she asked, and
dropped onto a patch of dry grass by the roadside, not
waiting for my assent. I turned back to my work, hoping
that she'd soon grow bored and go away. But she seemed
in a mood to talk, and though I didn't encourage her,
she wandered amiably into words as though we were the
best of friends.

"I understand you went out to the *rancho* yesterday.
Did Gavin tell you anything about the place?"

"A little," I said.

"It used to belong to Juan's father—Antonio Cordova,
our great-grandfather. He should have been a Spanish
don. He always claimed that Spain was the mother
country, and that Seville, not Madrid, was the historical
capital of the Americas. It was Seville which sent out
the explorers and the missionary priests."

For me, this was a new family name I hadn't heard
before.

"Did you know Antonio Cordova?"

"He died before I was born. But I've heard about
him all my life. Clarita used to tell me stories of her
grandfather. He was furious when his son married an
Anglo woman—our grandmother Katy—and moved into
Santa Fe to start a store. Clarita says Juan had to be
enormously successful to prove to his father what he
could do. It's too bad that Antonio died before CORDOVA
became as famous as it is today. You went through the
store too yesterday, didn't you?"

"Yes—it's impressive." I tried to concentrate on my
painting. The scene was coming rather well, in spite of
Eleanor's interruption.

"Someday CORDOVA will belong to me," she said and
there was a hint of defiance in her words, as though she
dared me to disagree.

I didn't pick up the bait. "It will be a big responsibility. It's a good thing you have Gavin to manage it and buy for it."

She jumped up and moved off a little way, then came back to me, kicking at the dirt with one stub-toed shoe.

"Let's not talk about Gavin."

I shrugged and went on with my painting.

After a moment or two she tried a different tack. "Clarita says you found that old turquoise mask out at the *rancho* and brought it home. Why?"

"Because I remember it. It made some connection in my mind with—with what happened."

Excitement kindled. "That's lovely! Paul will want to hear about this. What did it make you remember?"

"Nothing. Except that I was afraid. Sylvia says when they were all children, they used to play Blind Man's Buff with the mask at the *rancho*."

"Yes. Clarita's told me about that. One day when Kirk was wearing the mask, he caught Doro and took it off and kissed her. Clarita saw, and she was still angry when she told me the story. In those days she wanted Kirk herself, and she resented the fact that he liked Doro best. Of course she got over him later. He wasn't the love of her life."

"Who was?"

"Don't you know?" she asked slyly.

I wasn't going to play games. "Anyway, my mother ended by being in love with William Austin," I reminded her.

"That's not how Clarita's story goes. She thinks that Doro was still in love with Kirk when he came back after being away for all those years."

I said nothing more. I had no wish to argue such points with Eleanor, and I didn't know why she was talking about any of this.

"When Gavin drove you out to the *rancho* did you go through Madrid?" she asked. In the local manner she put the accent on the first syllable of the town's name.

"I don't know. Why?"

"He may have taken you by the other road. You'd know if you went through Madrid. It's a ghost town now, though it was once a thriving mining town. There are Cordova roots out there, and it would be a perfect place for you to paint. If you like, I'll drive you out there sometime."

"Thanks," I said, and gave her a direct look. "Why are you feeling better about me today? You were pretty angry with me yesterday."

"How suspicious you are, Amanda!" Eleanor's violet eyes gave me a wide look of innocence that did not convince me. "We're cousins, aren't we? So isn't it time we got acquainted?"

"Who do you think used that whip last night in the patio?" I returned her own question with a suddenness that made her blink.

For a moment she only stared at me. I went on. "Paul says several things were taken from the Penitente display."

"I know. He told me. Doña Sebastiana still hasn't turned up. But I don't know why anyone should want to attack Grandfather."

"I don't believe anyone did. I think I was the one they were after. He was struck down so whoever it was could get away."

She regarded me coolly, appraisingly, her earlier pretense of amiability gone. "Then I should be very much afraid, if I were you, Amanda."

"Why? Because I'm coming close to something revealing?"

"Aren't you?"

I told her then—told her I'd remembered that there had been three figures struggling together the day when my mother had gone to meet Kirk, and not two as Clarita claimed and everyone believed.

She listened with a bright avidity that I found chilling. Yet I'd felt I had to tell her. She would spread this around, of course. She would tell Paul and perhaps Clarita. She might even tell our grandfather. And now I might be in greater danger than ever. But this was the only way I knew in which to bring that hazy third figure into the open where he could be recognized.

She gave my painting another glance of pretended interest, and then said a casual *Hasta la vista,* and went off toward the house. Though it was past noon, the sun seemed a little less bright, and the air a trifle more chilly.

I moved about, stretching and flexing my fingers. Then I sat down on a low adobe wall and ate my sandwich, drank from a thermos. To go back to the house would break my mood even more than Eleanor had broken it, and as soon as I could I returned to my work and let it absorb me.

Only once after that did I surface, returning to the thought of the Cordovas with a jolt. In spite of my preoccupation with my work, and the successful distraction it offered, the thought of tonight and what I'd promised to do for my grandfather was not as far away as I would like. His plan still repelled me and I wished I hadn't agreed to something I didn't want to do. I had let his will overpower me again. When I returned to the house, I would simply tell him I'd changed my mind. I no longer felt safe and protected by adobe walls, and I had no intention of frightening myself further with the errand he had set me.

Coming to this decision gave me a sense of relief, and now I could paint the afternoon away, nearly finishing what I'd started. Sometimes it took days to complete a picture, but today I'd worked long and steadily and accomplished a lot.

I scraped my palette, dipped my brushes in turpentine and wiped them and my hands on the paper towels I'd brought along instead of paint rags. My sketchbox would hold a wet canvas without smearing it, and I packed everything away and returned to the house.

Clarita met me in the living room, and she seemed in something of a fluster. "Father is coming down to dinner tonight, Amanda. And we are having company. Sylvia

THE TURQUOISE MASK        213

and Paul. Sylvia was over just now and my father invited them. So put on a good dress and come down on
time."

She looked as though some ordeal were facing her,
and I think she might have rebelled if she could. I
wondered what had given rise to this sudden party, and
the unusual factor of Juan Cordova coming down for
dinner. But Clarita rushed off toward the kitchen to
supervise preparations, and there was no time to ask.

When I reached my room, I took out my painting and
set it in the embrasure of a window where it could dry
in the air. I liked the look of my adobe walls and winding road, yet it was not a sentimental picture. There
was a certain starkness about the hot sky and baking
earth. It was not really a Santa Fe picture, but one that
suggested the oasis of a village in desert country in mid-
summer—a timeless scene. A brown-clad brother who
was new from Seville might come riding up that road
on a burro at any moment. Perhaps I would even paint
him in. A glow of satisfaction was my reward. This was
the first of my New Mexico paintings, and I knew
there would be more. I had a special feeling for this land
that lent emotion to my brush.

Painting had brought relaxation from tension for a
time, but it had tired me too, and now I might lie
down and rest before dinner. My room was cool and
dim with late afternoon light, and I turned toward the
bed, about to throw back the coverlet—only to stop in
surprise. Slightly mounded, something lay beneath the
covers—something with a vaguely human form.

A tremor of warning went through me, and with it
came that awareness of something menacing and secret
that I'd first felt about this house. With my deepest
senses I knew what the house knew—and there was
terror all about me. Yet still my conscious mind told me
nothing.

With an effort, I managed to fling back the covers
and stood staring at the thing that grinned back at me
from the pillow. All of last night's horror re-engaged me,

and I could almost feel the sting of that three-pronged whip across my shoulders. Doña Sebastiana stared at me with hollow eyes, and bared, grinning teeth in her skull's head. Her bow and arrow seemed pointed at my heart and it was her bony figure which made the slight mound beneath the covers.

I ran to my door and called shrilly for Clarita. She heard me and came running up the stairs, to stand beside me, staring at the thing on the bed.

"*La Muerte,*" she said softly. "The carts are rolling. The footsteps are coming nearer. The death march."

If I listened to her I might go a little mad too. I grasped her by the arm and shook her roughly.

"Stop that! I won't be frightened by such tricks. I won't be threatened. This is Eleanor again, isn't it? Just as the fetish was Eleanor!"

"And do you think it was Eleanor who whipped you last night?" Clarita whispered. "Do you think it was Eleanor who whipped her grandfather?"

"Juan must be told about this," I said, and moved toward the door.

At once she blocked my way. "No. He has borne enough."

I pushed past her and ran down the stairs. Juan was no longer in the living room and I went up to his balcony and looked into his empty study. Then I stepped to a window and looked down into the patio. Only a little way off he lay in a lounge chair with a pillow under his head and the late afternoon sun warming him. But even as I found him, Clarita came outdoors, and I saw agitation in the way she bent above her father. She had reached him first, and I couldn't know what she might be telling him. Nevertheless, I must see him for myself.

When I went out to the patio she was still there, but though she faced me with a bitter anger in her dark eyes, Juan saw me, and there was nothing she could do when I dropped to my knees beside his chair. There was no way in which Clarita could stop me from telling him what I had found in my bed. He closed his eyes at my outpouring, but he heard me through before he spoke. Then he opened his eyes and looked at Clarita.

"Leave us, please," he said.

She was reluctant to obey, and for a moment I thought she might take a strong enough stand to oppose him. But old habit ruled, and she bowed her head so that the blue earrings swayed at her jawline. When she'd gone into the house, Juan spoke to me.

"You will go away soon, Amanda," he said weakly. "Tomorrow we will arrange for your plane back to New York. The risk is becoming too great. I should never have brought you here, but I had thought this was one way to stop Paul Stewart from trying to use you for his book. Here we could protect you from him. Or so we thought."

It was time to tell him. There was no longer any secret about what I knew, since I'd told Eleanor.

"There were three on the hillside when my mother died," I said. "I don't know who the other was, but there were three figures struggling together."

Weakness seemed to leave him, and he sat up in his chair and reached for my wrist with strong, thin fingers. "This is what Katy tried to tell me before she died. This is what I would not believe."

"Do you know who it could have been?" I asked.

He stared at me, not answering, and his fingers hurt my wrist. "It's too late to do anything now," he said. "I will not have all that old tragedy resurrected again. What is done is done."

"To protect the living?" I said.

He flung my hand away from him as though the touch of it had become suddenly distasteful. "To protect you. Doro's daughter. You must leave here at once."

"I won't go," I said. "Not now when I am coming so close to the truth. Don't you *want* to know, Grandfather?"

The weakness was upon him again. "I am old. I cannot bear any more. Tonight there will be a little party I have planned for you in farewell. And after dinner

you will slip away and do for me what I asked. I am in
danger too, Amanda, and only you can help me now.
Then we will talk again about your returning to New
York."

I rose from my place beside him without answering.
His dark, fierce eyes watched my face, and I think he
saw my opposition, my disbelief in *his* danger.

"I have told Clarita to take that—object from your
bed and give it to Paul Stewart when he comes tonight.
It must be returned to the display in the store. We will
meet again at dinner, Amanda."

I walked slowly back to my room. I didn't know
whether I would go away or not, but I knew now that
I would have to do as he wished and carry out the
mission he had set for me later tonight. Perhaps it was
the last thing I could do for him.

Doña Sebastiana was gone from my room, but Rosa
was there changing the sheets and pillowcase. I was
grateful to Clarita, for I'd have felt a repugnance to
touch the sheets where that figure had lain. Rosa's eyes
looked big and a little frightened, and I knew she must
have seen what had been hidden in the bed. She made no
attempt to talk to me, but hurried with her work, and
escaped as quickly as she could—almost as though an
evil spell had been laid upon me and she didn't want to
come too close.

I lay down on top of the covers and tried to rest.
I wanted nothing more of terror, of threat. Perhaps it
would be better to do as Juan Cordova wished, and go
away. But I knew that my life could never be the same
again, and always there would be the unanswered questions and the memories of Santa Fe and this old house.
There would be memories of Gavin, too, but I couldn't
help that. I was never able to put him completely from
my mind. Where was the borderline between being whole
of heart and foolishly in love? I might rage against him
when he angered me, yet a part of me yearned toward
him, and that made me angry with myself. There must
be a way out of this tunnel.

When it was time to dress, I did so with care, since this might be my last night in the Cordova house. Perhaps whatever occurred at tonight's dinner party might help me make up my mind. I must watch for some answer.

I had brought one dinner frock with me. It was an eggshell white, with long sleeves that fell in points over my wrist, a long slim skirt with a slit to one knee, and a rounded neckline. The lines were simple and it was without decoration, so I pinned my Zuni brooch near the neckline and clipped on my mother's earrings. No matter whom they might upset I wanted to wear her little birds tonight. My lipstick was a light mandarin—not too pale, and I left my eyes alone. Men weren't fond of heavy eye shadow—that was a female choice of make-up— and tonight I dressed for Gavin. Never mind whether I had any good sense or not. Very soon now I might never see him again.

When I went downstairs a little late, I found them having drinks in the living room—all except Gavin, who was missing. Eleanor wore black in contrast to my white, with a diagonal of fringe across the front, like a Spanish shawl, and she had piled her hair high upon her head, graced with a Spanish comb and a flower, and plastered down her bangs in spit curls. There were pearls about her neck, and at her ears, and she looked stunningly beautiful. Apparently recovered from his earlier weakness, Juan sat near the fire, and could hardly take his eyes off Eleanor for pride. She need not, I thought, worry about losing her fortune to me. His look approved my own appearance when I entered the room, but it was Eleanor who held his real affection.

Clarita, surprisingly, wore a long robe of claret velvet, trimmed with an edging of old gold, and her earrings were great golden hoops. I found myself staring at her, seeing for the first time that she could be a remarkably handsome woman when she chose not to efface herself. Sylvia Stewart was thoroughly modern in a powder blue tunic and trousers, and Paul had pleased himself and worn a comfortable plaid jacket with a southwestern bolo tie.

I wondered where Gavin was, but no one mentioned him.

Though Paul's attention often wandered to Eleanor, he shortly attached himself to me, and I knew he'd probably had her latest report about my elusive memories. He drew me aside and tried to probe a little, and when I had nothing more to tell him, he grew insistent.

"I've always been sure that something was kept off the record that day," he told me. "And you're the one who knew what it was, Amanda. Are you sure you haven't found the answer?"

Intent, his yellow-green eyes seemed to demand the truth from me, and I found myself resenting him more than ever.

"Perhaps it would help if we could know exactly where you were that day," I said, deliberately baiting him. "You told me that you and Sylvia were coming along the upper road together on the way to the picnic, but Sylvia says that she was alone that day."

He stared at me fixedly for a moment, and then laughed aloud, so that heads turned to look at him.

"So you'd like to tie me into it," he said. "Do you think I'd really want to write about a murder I'd committed?"

"I don't know," I said.

"Sylvia must have forgotten." His words were casual

I let the matter go. "Anyway, I'm not sure of anything—except that they all want me gone."

"I can see why. They want you gone before you turn their comfortable lives upside down to any greater extent. I've heard about the will. Eleanor was pretty furious for a time, but she seems to have calmed down I advised her to."

"It won't matter," I told him lightly. "I'll probably be gone by tomorrow."

"So they're sending you away?"

"I haven't decided yet," I said, and moved off toward Juan Cordova, where he sat on the leather couch near the fire.

He nodded to me and I saw his gaze flick to my ear

ings, but he did not tell me to take them off, as he
ad done before. Nor did he attempt to engage me in
onversation. I suspected that he was more tired tonight
han he wanted us to know and was concentrating on
is inner forces so that he could get through the eve-
ing.

Paul had returned his fascinated attention to Eleanor,
vho was thoroughly alight in her black gown, moving
nce more like a dancer, her long fringes swaying as
hough she played a role, and as though her dance might
e mounting to a climax. Not only Juan Cordova watched
er, and Paul, but Clarita too, and I saw the pride of
naternal possession in those dark eyes. To Clarita,
Eleanor would always be her child. But Clarita watched
Paul too, with a certain fondness born, I wondered, of
ong ago love?

Oddly, Sylvia, who usually fitted in anywhere, was on
he outside tonight. She stood a little apart from the
thers and watched them all as though she held a seat
t a play in which she wanted no active part. When I
vas able, I moved quietly to her side.

She looked at me with a start that told me I hadn't
een one of those she studied. "Why tonight?" she said.
"Why a party *tonight?*"

"I suppose because I'm expected to leave tomorrow.
But you were looking at them so strangely. Tell me
vhat you see."

"Calamity." She grimaced. "That's what Eleanor is—
alamity. She's like Doro in that. She won't be happy
ntil she blows everything sky high."

"Did my mother really want to have that effect?"

"Perhaps not consciously. But she never saw what
vas coming."

"Is that why Gavin isn't here tonight? Because of
vhat Eleanor might do?"

"But he is here," she said.

I looked past her and saw him in the doorway. With-
ut defense, our eyes met across the room, and for an
nstant I saw his light. Whether my own betrayed me in

return, I didn't know, and he looked away at once, his guard immediately raised. Clearly he was surprised by the party.

Clarita went quickly to welcome him and explain, and I suspected that they'd deliberately not warned him ahead of time, lest he stay away. So one more factor of disruption had been introduced into the room.

Strangely, it was Clarita who pulled everything together as we went into the dining room and took our places at the table. She dominated the room quite magnificently in her claret red gown, and I saw Eleanor watching her in astonishment. Something had enlivened Clarita and given her a strength I had not seen before. By way of contrast, Juan seemed to shrink to a lesser size, and the usual hubris he radiated was gone. If it hadn't seemed impossible, I might have thought that my arrogant grandfather was afraid of his elder daughter.

It was Eleanor, however, who dropped the first pebble into the pool and started the ripples widening across already muddied water.

"I happened on an interesting fact today," she announced. "Have any of you remembered that this is Kirk Landers' birthday?"

Sylvia gasped softly and Clarita flashed a look at her.

"No, it is not," Clarita said.

With an effort, Juan Cordova reached for his wine glass, ignoring his daughter. "There was a time when Kirk was very dear to us, as you are, Sylvia. Why should we not remember a lost son with a toast?"

I had the feeling that he was defying Clarita in some way, and perhaps tormenting Sylvia.

Eleanor caught up her glass at once. "You give the toast, Sylvia."

Juan nodded benignly at his foster daughter, appearing more like himself. "We are waiting, Sylvia," he said.

Looking about to dissolve in tears, Sylvia did not touch her glass, but only sat there, shaking her head miserably. "I—I can't. Eleanor is being cruel."

"Let me then," said Paul, and that bright green gleam was in his eyes as he raised his glass. "To one we all miss. To one who died too soon and too young. To Kirk Landers!"

I remembered that those two had quarreled, and knew this for mockery. Juan and Eleanor raised their glasses. Gavin looked angry and did not touch his. Nor did I touch mine, since I'd never known Kirk Landers except as a small child, and I had too many questions in my mind. Clarita reached for her glass last, as though she forced herself—and knocked it over. In the ensuing distraction, with cries for Rosa and the process of mopping, Sylvia jumped up from her place and ran from the room.

Gravely Juan and Eleanor clinked each other's glasses and sipped wine, their eyes meeting in affection. Then Juan glanced at Clarita.

"You had better go to Sylvia," he said.

Clarita faced him down the length of the table. "No! I have no comfort to offer anyone. This was a cruel thing to do. A mockery, as you know very well."

"I'll go to her," I said, and slipped from the table.

She had run into the living room and flung herself full length on the leather couch. The scent of piñon wood was pungent on the air. I went to sit beside her, touching her shoulder gently. "Don't be upset. Eleanor is heedless."

"She's utterly cruel." Sylvia took several deep breaths to quiet her emotion, and looked up at me tearfully. "This isn't Kirk's birthday, as she knows very well. This is the anniversary of the day he died."

I stared at her in dismay. I hadn't known. I'd never known the exact date. Then this was also the anniversary of my mother's death.

"Why would Juan"—I faltered—"why would he gather us for a dinner on such an anniversary?"

"I don't know, I don't know!" Sylvia cried. "Perhaps to torment someone. Perhaps to remind. Perhaps really only because he's sending you away tomorrow."

"Then let's go back to the table. I want to go back, so I can watch."

"No!" Sylvia cried. "Don't wake up the sleeping. Don't call back the ghosts!"

I stared at her. "You always surprise me. When I first met you, I thought you were worried about something, but I also thought you were contained and controlled. I thought you were the unruffled type."

She sat up beside me, suddenly defiant. "I am. I must be. God knows I've practiced long enough!"

I pounced on the word. "Practiced—what do you mean?"

"Nothing, nothing. Let me alone, Amanda. If you'll wait for a moment till I run to the bathroom and wash my face, I'll go back to the table with you."

"I'll wait," I told her.

She hurried off, brushing against the end table as she went. The ugly tarantula fell off into my lap and I picked it up and replaced it on the table with repugnance. I remembered my thought that Juan Cordova was omnivorous. Tonight he had joined with Eleanor to prove that fact. If Sylvia was right, he had meant to disturb someone, and he knew very well who that someone was. But whom would he protect, if he knew the truth? Clarita, perhaps. Sylvia, possibly. Paul—surely not.

I heard Gavin's steps as he came into the room, regarding me gravely. "Is Sylvia all right?"

"She's pulling herself together. She'll be back in a moment."

"Juan says you're going away tomorrow."

"Juan doesn't know. I haven't decided."

"It's best if you do go," he said. "What happened last night was meant for you, no matter what Juan believes."

"Yes, I think so too."

"And it may happen again—and be worse."

"Do you know who it was?"

He was silent, and I knew the answer. Gavin believed

that his wife was behind the attack upon me, but he would not say so.

"Please believe me," I said. "I don't want anything from Juan in his will. He hasn't changed it yet, and I don't think he will. Eleanor is his darling."

"Eleanor is the daughter of Rafael—a son he thoroughly disliked. You are Doro's daughter."

"I'm not the one he cares about," I said. "I've been watching the way his eyes follow her. There's no danger to anything she wants. He'll take nothing away from her. And I need to stay. Gavin, I'm close to the truth of what happened. There are cracks in the surface. They're widening."

Sylvia came back in time to hear my words. "You mustn't stay now. I urged you to go in the beginning, but now everything is much worse. What can it matter to you, Amanda, whether some buried 'truth' comes out? What good will it do your mother if it only harms someone still living?"

"I don't know the answer to that. I only know that I must stay."

She gave me a long, despairing look and started for the dining room. Gavin waited for me, as relentless as Sylvia, and I went with him.

Salt had been sprinkled on the wine stain and a padded cloth mounded beneath it. Clarita looked strained, nervous, and no longer able to carry off the wearing of her handsome gown. Juan, on the contrary, was himself again. If anything, he looked renewed by what had happened, and he and Eleanor were talking to each other animatedly. Eleanor glanced around as we took our places at the table.

"I'm sorry," she said, mockingly contrite. "Grandfather tells me that I'm wrong about my dates. So I apologize. Anyway, he's feeling much better these days, and I've coaxed him into taking a little outing with all of us. Tell them, Grandfather."

While Clarita served the meal with hands that shook a little, Juan spoke to us cheerfully. "It has been too many years since I have been out to the *rancho*. So we are all going there one day soon. We will drive out in the morning, have lunch, and come back in the late afternoon."

"I don't think——" Sylvia began, but he shook his head at her gently.

"You too, of course. And Paul. It will be like the old days. It is unfortunate that Amanda will not be here, but otherwise it will be a family party."

I put my hand lightly on his arm. "But of course I will be here. I'm not going away yet, Grandfather."

Around the table heads turned toward me, eyes were fixed upon my face, and I had the feeling that one of those who stared was angry and perhaps dangerously frightened. But I looked only at Gavin. His face was cold, shutting me out, condemning me.

Eleanor laughed softly. "Then we'll all be together. What fun, Amanda! If only Kirk and Doro and Grandmother Katy could be there too, our party would be complete."

She was once more stepping upon dangerous ground, but no one said anything, no one reproached her frivolity. After that the meal turned into an ordinary dinner, even though I sensed awareness, watchfulness below the surface. Once more I had time to think ahead to the errand Juan had planned for me. And to be again afraid of what I must do. I had no taste at all for an excursion into the dark reaches of the store at night. Now even less than ever.

# XIV

Though it was Saturday night, the plaza was quiet by nine o'clock, and few people were about on the streets. Most of these were wandering *turistas*.

I paid off my taxi near the plaza, since, when I was through with Juan's errand, I could go to the Fonda del Sol and phone for another. As I walked quickly toward the store, I could hear sounds of gaiety from the direction of the Fonda Hotel, but there was no one in sight when I walked down the side street and around to the back of CORDOVA.

The key Juan had given me slipped easily into the lock, but I hesitated for a moment before I pushed open the door. If I'd had any choice, I would have preferred to turn around and go home right then, but the thought of Juan Cordova's displeasure forced me to open the door. He had told me that lights were left on in the store overnight, and I found them dim but welcome as I stepped inside and closed the door softly behind me.

At once I was in an alien world, cut off from all I knew. It was a shadowy world of faint light and no sound. The daytime bustle was gone with the flow of customers on the main floor. The quiet was so intense that it was as if my coming had caused the great open space of the store to hush and hold its breath, waiting for me to make some move. At night this place had a life and being of its own—the entity that was CORDOVA seemed alive.

I stood very still in the center of an aisle near the back door and listened. The smothering silence seemed without boundary. Scents of leather and sweet grasses came to me, mingling with other exotic odors that were closed into the store at night. But I mustn't stand here, I thought, listening for some whisper of sound, waiting for an imaginary footfall. Last night's attack upon me had undermined my courage, and I was sharply aware that while someone could come to my aid quickly in the patio, here no scream of mine would ever be heard and no one would come if there was danger.

But this was nonsense. Who but Juan knew that I was here? I wasn't a child to be afraid of the dark and a strange place, and I must get this over with quickly.

The nearest aisle led to the front of the store, and I followed it, walking with light steps so as not to disturb the sleeping hush. Near a lighted window I stood for a moment looking out into the street where nothing moved.

When I turned toward the stairs that led to the floor above, I had again the strange feeling that, for all the quiet about me, the store had a living spirit of its own. This was the beating heart of the thing which ruled the Cordovas, and would rule me if I let it. All about me rich stacks of merchandise were piled—offerings on a temple's altar. And the gods of the temple lurked just out of my line of vision, waiting for sacrifices.

I shook myself impatiently and started up the stairs. If there was anything here to fear, it would be living, not imaginary, and I did not feel that anyone was here. Juan had not wanted my mission to be known, so no one could be lying in wait for me, ready to strike.

The great cavern of the first floor continued to lie breathlessly still below me as I mounted the stairs. Only the creaking of wooden steps broke the blanketing silence and seemed startlingly loud. At the head of the stairs, behind glass, the figure of the flamenco dancer glimmered at me in dim light. She looked as though she might burst into movement at any moment and I could almost hear the beat of wild music. I was reminded of Eleanor tonight in her high comb and swinging fringe.

As I left the stairs, the upper floor seemed suddenly a maze, a labyrinth in which I no longer knew my direction. When a cold hand touched mine, I stifled a cry, before I realized it was only the mailed glove of a set of Spanish armor, standing lifesize beside me. I hadn't seen the armor before. I hadn't come this way. Where had Gavin led me so that I had found the cabinet of Toledo steel? I no longer knew the course I had taken and I could recognize no landmarks.

Confused by the dim aisles, with the lighting up here even fainter than it was downstairs, I moved haltingly. The clinging silk of a Spanish shawl brushed my arm, and I tried to remember where I had seen those splendid shawls.

This wouldn't do at all. I stood still, trying to regain my sense of direction, and listening in spite of myself to the utter silence. Or was it silence? Had a faraway door creaked open? Had I heard a whisper of voices? Were those feet upon the stairs? I was not imagining this time.

Laughter that sounded like Eleanor's crashed suddenly through the upper reaches of the store, echoing to the high ceiling. Because my knees weakened, I grasped a nearby counter to steady myself and shake off the alarm that swept through me. Now I could hear someone running on the stairs, hear another pair of feet coming after her, another voice speaking.

Paul Stewart's voice!

"The display is over here. Have you brought the whip?"

"Of course," Eleanor's voice replied. "And you've brought the Lady. Let's fix up the display and then explore. I wonder if all these things have a life of their own when no one is watching? I've never been here before at night."

"Nor have I," Paul said, sounding less enthusiastic.

It was all right, I told myself. They didn't know I was here. For some odd reason—probably Eleanor's whim—they had brought the Penitente things here tonight to return them to the display. I had only to be quiet and wait, and they would go away, never dreaming I was present in the empty store. Why I felt it vital to keep my presence secret, I wasn't sure, but I knew I wanted neither of them to discover me.

They made no attempt to be quiet themselves. I heard the showcase opened and the sounds of rearrangement as Doña Sebastiana was restored to her place in the stone-filled cart. In fact, they were making enough noise in the quiet store so that I could move again myself, under the cover of sound. When I reached the place where my aisle met a cross aisle, I looked carefully around.

Now I could see it. The case of Toledo swords was a tall cabinet, rising above others in its vicinity, and I made my way toward it, stepping softly. I had slipped my second key into its lock, when Eleanor's voice halted me to listen intently.

"How did you like the way I managed to plan a trip to the *rancho?*" she asked.

Paul's laughter held approval. "You handled it perfectly. The old man fell right in with what you wanted."

"I thought I could coax him. Do you know what he told me before tonight's dinner? He said we could use the fact of the date to make someone worried and uncomfortable. But the only one who went to pieces was Sylvia. I wonder why? Do you suppose she's worried about you?"

"Worried about me?" Paul repeated her words evenly.

The taunting little laugh came again. "Why not? You and Kirk hated each other, didn't you? Isn't it possible—" Perhaps something in Paul's expression stopped her, for she broke off.

Now she seemed to back down. "Oh, don't think I care about what happened that day. I'm interested in *now*. Amanda's getting around Juan, and I don't like it. But when they all go out to the *rancho*—perhaps tomorrow if I can work it—they'll be out there for most of the day. Then it won't matter what Juan does about his will. I don't like that trust he's set up for me anyway. I want money in my hands—so I can be free of Gavin, free of them all."

"Come here," Paul said.

There were faint sounds that were not of struggle, and I suspected that he was embracing her, kissing her. Silencing her? Poor Sylvia, I thought, and disliked Paul even more intensely than before. I no longer wanted to wait for them to go. All I wanted now was to get the box I had come for, and escape from the store before those two discovered me.

I turned the key and the cabinet door creaked faintly as it opened.

"What was that?" Eleanor said.

She and Paul were quiet, listening, and I kept very still. After a few moments their attention returned to the display, and when there were sounds again I reached quickly into the bottom of the cabinet to find the flat case Juan had told me to bring him. My fingers touched the carving on the lid as I drew the box out. When I closed the cabinet door, it creaked again, betraying me.

"I'm sure I heard something," Eleanor said. "Let's look around."

They were moving in my direction, and I dropped below the level of the nearest counter and crept in the direction of what I hoped was the stairs, carrying the box with me. Since they made no attempt at secrecy in their approach, I could tell where they were, and it was easy enough to keep out of their way.

The flamenco dancer loomed above me and I found the stairs. But try as I would for quiet, the ancient wood groaned under my feet, and I heard Eleanor cry out again.

"There *is* someone here! The stairs are creaking!"

I ran down without trying for stealth, and found my way toward the back door. Eleanor and Paul had left it open, but there was a light outside, and I knew I would be silhouetted against the outdoors if I stepped into the doorway. The stack of great wooden Santa Fe doors offered me a hiding place, and I stepped behind their shelter, clutching Juan's carved box to me.

Across the store, the two ran down the stairs, and I heard Eleanor whisper, "Whoever it is must be down here. Hush, Paul. Don't make any noise."

Now they were both as silent as I, and I lost track of their location. At any moment they could creep upon me, and I quivered at the thought. Eleanor would not share her secrets readily, and neither would Paul. I had heard too much. Perhaps I'd better chance the door and escape into the narrow side streets of Santa Fe. There would be less chance of their catching up with me then. Moving as softly as I could, I stole toward the escape of the open door. The stuffiness lessened, and a hint of breeze came through the doorway, welcoming me. I crept toward the opening.

There was a single instant of awareness before it happened—an instinctive premonition of danger, so that I ducked my head just as the blow fell, and I was spared its full, deadly impact. Crashing lights on a wave of pain went through my brain as I sank into oblivion.

For a long time the darkness behind my eyelids seemed to pulse with a beating of pain. Faraway voices seemed to be discussing my plight. Someone was calling my name, calling me back to pain that I wanted to escape.

"Amanda, Amanda, Amanda," the voice urged, insisting on my return.

The mists cleared slowly and I seemed to be floating in some dim void where my only contact with reality was the sound of my own name being repeated over and over. I opened my eyes to dim light and a face bending over me.

"That's better," a voice said. "You're coming round now."

Gradually the misty weaving of my surroundings steadied and I could see Paul Stewart kneeling beside me, with Eleanor standing just behind him, her face shadowed in the dim light of the store.

"Can you sit up?" Paul asked me. "We'd like to get you home, Amanda."

As he drew me to a sitting position, memory drifted back. I recalled being in the store, remembered the Penitente case and Paul and Eleanor—and my errand for Juan. Feebly I moved my hands about, concentrating only on the latter, seeking the carved box I must take to Juan—as if it were more important at the moment than anything else. The case lay under me. My hands found it and drew it from beneath my body, while Eleanor and Paul watched.

"What were you doing here, Amanda?" Eleanor demanded. "Who struck you down?"

*Didn't you?* I wanted to ask, but the throbbing increased and silenced me as I got to my knees, and clutched at Paul, steadying myself.

"Someone tried to kill me," I said. "Didn't you see who struck me?"

Eleanor shook her head, all her mockery gone. Paul leaned over and picked something up from the floor.

"Quetzalcoatl," he said, and held up the brass figure for me to see. "The Plumed Serpent—one of the Aztec gods. He's made a good bludgeon."

How much of this was acting? I wondered. Eleanor moved her head and light caught the glitter of excitement in her eyes.

"But who would hide in the store and strike you down? We heard you fall, but there was no one here when we reached you. What did you come here for, Amanda?"

I found that my legs would hold me, and my head

was clearing. The throbbing lessened as I righted myself. Gingerly I felt the back of my head and discovered a rising lump. But there seemed to be little blood, if any, and I knew I had spared myself the full force of the blow by moving at the moment it fell. All I wanted now was to get away from these two. I could trust neither one. Either might have struck me down. But my arms were weak and the box I clasped dropped to the floor with a clatter.

At once Eleanor leaned to pick it up. "What's this? What are you taking away from the store?"

With an effort, I reached for the box, but she drew it away and set it on a counter. There was no way to stop her as she pressed the clasp and raised the lid. The interior of the box was lined with midnight blue velvet, its contents wrapped in a chamois skin which Eleanor unwound, revealing a slender dagger with an ornate handle.

There was a roughness in Paul's voice when he spoke. "What do you want with that, Amanda?"

For just an instant I thought of saying that I needed it to protect myself against someone who'd strike me on the head with Quetzalcoatl, but that would do no good. Secrecy was no longer possible.

"Juan Cordova asked me to bring him the box," I told them. "I didn't know what was in it."

Eleanor whistled softly, looked at Paul. Then she replaced the weapon in its wrapping and closed the box, gave it back to me.

"I suppose you'll have to take it to him," she said. "But I don't like this at all."

Paul held my arm as we went out the door, and Eleanor ran ahead to open her car. I was helped into the back seat, where I slumped into a corner. We drove home without incident, and no more questions were asked. It was good to breathe deeply of the night air, and my headache faded to a dull throb. I didn't try to think of anything.

When we reached the house there was a hasty,

whispered consultation between Paul and Eleanor in
the front seat. Paul helped me out and waited long
enough to see whether I was able to walk. Then he told
us a quick good night and cut through the patio to his
own side gate, while Eleanor took my arm and steadied
me through the living-room door.

"Shall I help you up to your room?" she asked.

I shook my head. "Not now. I'm going to see Juan
first. He asked me to come to him when I got back."

For a moment Eleanor looked as though she might
say something more—perhaps ask for my silence, perhaps ask how much I'd heard of her conversation with
Paul—but she must have known it would do no good,
for she shrugged and made a slight grimace.

"I'll go get Clarita. She'll want to have a look at that
lump on your head."

I tried to tell her not to bother, but she went off, and
I moved reluctantly toward my grandfather's study. I had
no wish for long explanations. All I wanted was to sit
in my room and try to recover myself. But there was
no help for it—I had to face Juan Cordova.

He was lying on his couch, waiting for me.

"I've brought the box," I said, and put it into his
hands.

He sat up, almost fondling the case, his fingers
moving in appreciation over the carved lid.

"I know what's in it," I said. "Why did you want
the dagger?"

He made a sound of annoyance and opened the box.
With careful fingers he unwrapped what lay within and
held it up by the handle, forgetting me for the moment
as light caught the blade in a bright flash.

"There is no better steel than that of Toledo," he
murmured. "And this handle is of fine Toledo Damascene.
I purchased it myself in a shop there many years ago."

"Why did you want me to bring it to you?" I persisted.

With a suddenness that startled me, he thrust the
dagger beneath his pillow on the couch. "I do not mean

to lie here helpless, defenseless. But I told you not to open the box, Amanda."

"I didn't open it," I said. "Eleanor did." And I told him that she and Paul had been in the store, apparently to return the Penitente things to their display case, and that I had been trying to escape without their discovering me when I was struck.

He was silent for a long time after my account, his gaze fixed on the wall beyond my head. When he spoke his face seemed to collapse into the fallen lines of despair.

"What am I to do? Where can I place my trust? Which one of them did this to you, Amanda?"

"I don't know whether either of them did," I said.

"But who else would go to the store? Amanda, this is no longer a choice you can make. You are not safe in this house."

"Because the one who killed my mother is afraid of me?"

He made a choked sound. "No one killed Doro. She died by her own will. It was Kirk Landers who was shot."

"You believe what you want to believe!" I cried. "You won't be shaken from your own stubbornness."

He looked at me with pain in his eyes, but as I started to say more Clarita burst into the room in an agitated state. She was dressed in black again, with only one of the gold hoops she'd worn at dinner still gracing an ear.

"What is this, Amanda? My father has told me of this foolishness in sending you on an errand to the store at this hour. Now you have been hurt. And I suppose you have come crying back to him?"

"That's enough!" Juan said sharply. "I wish to know all that happens. There are to be no secrets held from me."

"Isn't it time you went to the police?" I asked.

Both Clarita and Juan made sounds of repudiation.

"I will not advertise our troubles in the newspapers," Juan insisted. "We have been through all this before."

Clarita bowed her head in agreement. "Come with me,

Amanda, and I will look at your bruise in a good light. It must be bathed and perhaps bandaged."

"Go with her," Juan said. "We will talk more tomorrow, before you start for home."

"Right now this is my home," I said, "inhospitable as it seems to be," and I followed Clarita out of the room.

She led me to a bathroom where she opened a medicine cabinet, so thoroughly annoyed that she spat angry little cries as she took out what she needed and examined the back of my head.

"Why must you be where you should not be? Why must you provoke trouble? You will be killed if you continue like this. You must heed my father and leave Santa Fe tomorrow."

"Who is it that wants to kill me, Aunt Clarita?" I asked softly.

She dabbed roughly at the lump on my head with cotton dipped in disinfectant, and the skin must have been broken because it stung.

"Ask no more questions. Close your eyes. Close your ears. Be quiet until you can get away."

"What did you do with the diary pages, Aunt Clarita?"

Again her hand on my head was rough. "I don't know what you are talking about. Stand still. I must fix a patch over this spot."

I stepped away from her, declining to have my hair stuck up with a taped patch. "The lump isn't important."

She gave up in further annoyance, but she was not through with her questions. "He told me he'd sent you to the store, but what did he want you to bring him?"

"You'll have to ask him yourself," I said. "Or ask Eleanor. She knows."

Clarita flicked her hands at me in dismissal. "Eleanor is being wronged. But go to bed now. Here—I will give you something to help you sleep."

"Perhaps I'd better stay awake," I said, though I accepted the pills from her.

"As you please," she said.

I started toward the door, leaving her to put away

her bottles and bandages—but then I turned back.

"Where did you lose your gold earring, Aunt Clarita?"

Her hands flew to her ears and I knew that she was unaware that one was missing. "I'd started to undress," she said. "I haven't been away from the house, so it's undoubtedly on my dressing table."

"Undoubtedly," I said, and went out of the room, leaving her with a look on her face that I didn't like.

I took the capsules she'd given me to my room, but I didn't swallow them, nor did I go immediately to bed. Instinct told me that my senses must not be dulled artificially. I needed to be alert, lest there be some further move against me. Though probably I was safe enough now. No one was likely to attack me in my room.

I went to turn down the covers of my bed and stopped with my hand on the spread. The Zuni fetish lay against the pillow. It was the same one I had found before, and which Eleanor had taken away to return to the exhibit in the store. The small, heavy stone with its rudimentary carvings of the legs and head of a mole, its bloodstains and its thong binding of arrowhead and turquoise beads, all were the same. Now I knew I would not sleep.

This was too much. Somehow it seemed the last, shattering straw, as frightening as the whip and the blow on my head. It meant that whoever threatened me would not let up for an instant. The hunter was close on my trail, and he wanted me terrified.

I paced about my room with the ugly little stone in my hand, and found there was no order to my thoughts. There were only desperate questions in every direction in which I might turn. And now there was constant terror as well.

When the knock came on my door, I dissolved into trembling despair. My room was remote from the others. There was no escape from it except down the narrow stairs where this visitor, whoever it was, must stand. The knock came again, and a voice. Gavin's.

"Amanda, are you there?"

Relief swept through me and I ran to open the door.

It didn't matter that he was displeased with me, that he distrusted me, I simply clung to him, shaking so that my teeth chattered.

He held me quietly, impersonally, and it was enough that his arms were about me and that I loved him, however hopelessly. He, at least, would let nothing harm me. He was not involved in any of this plot.

His warmth and closeness soothed me, and my shivering stopped, my chattering teeth stilled. I became all too aware that his arms merely supported me, and that it was I who continued this embrace. I stepped back from him, still feeling shattered but in better control of myself.

"I—I'm sorry," I faltered. "I just—let go for a moment."

"I know." His voice was kind. "Clarita has told me what happened to you in the store. I came to see if you were all right."

"She—she gave me some sleeping pills, but I don't want to take them. I'm afraid to go to sleep. Look!"

I held out the fetish to him and his eyes seemed to cloud as he looked at it.

"It was there on my bed," I ran on. "Where someone also put the death-cart figure."

His composure seemed to crack a little as he took the fetish from my hand.

"Eleanor," he said. "She likes to play such games. I'm afraid there's a cruel streak in her—as there is in Juan. But she's unlikely to take any serious action."

I wasn't sure about that, and I walked away from him to a window and looked down into the patio. Nothing moved in bright moonlight. A single light burned at the Stewarts' house. Someone was taking serious action. I just didn't know who it was.

"I don't know what to do," I said.

He didn't answer me directly. "It's not terribly late. Put on your coat and come with me. I'll take you for a drive and make you sleepy without pills."

I turned from the window with a feeling of unreasonable joy. All my emotions were exaggerated tonight—out of bounds. Of course I would go with him—anywhere, and gladly.

While I wound a scarf around my neck and took out my coat, Gavin stepped to the window embrasure where I'd propped my small painting to dry.

"May I?" he said, and drew it out.

I froze with my coat still on its hanger. Here was more emotion. I couldn't bear it if he thought poorly of what I'd done.

He held up the canvas in both hands and studied my brilliant scene of village road and stark hot sky.

"It's good," he said, and I breathed again. "It's very good. You've painted your own feeling into your pigments, as a true painter should. You must show this to Juan."

He put it aside and came to help me with my coat, and I was awkward about finding the sleeves because I was too happy to concentrate on mundane matters like putting on a coat. Gavin liked what I had done, and my feelings were off on a new and joyful path. I had to make an effort to contain myself and not bubble with foolish happiness like a child. For me, just then, only the moment existed, and I would not look ahead or use my wits. I would not look behind. It was enough to be with him, and I asked for nothing more.

No one saw us as we went downstairs and out to the garage. I got into the front seat beside Gavin, and he eased the car onto the narrow road, where I'd done my painting in a time that seemed utterly remote from now.

"There's a full moon tonight," he said. "I know where I can take you."

We followed the quiet streets of Santa Fe and then turned onto a side road that led off toward the mountains. Before long the highway began to rise, winding and climbing into the Sangre de Cristos. Our headlights cut the darkness and the moon shone down on forests of ponderosa pine, with stands of aspen still above us.

Gavin knew the road well and he drove with con

fident skill. I let myself relax beside him, breathing the night scent of pine trees which had warmed all day in the sun. The world was all the more intensely beautiful because of my unreasoning happiness. If only this drive could go on forever, I would be content and ask for nothing more.

Once or twice Gavin glanced at me as though my mood puzzled him and he might be wondering what had become of all my fears. It was colder now, but the air was bracing and nothing could chill me. When we came to a lookout place, Gavin pulled off the road and let me gaze over the lights of Santa Fe, sparkling at our feet, and off to the faraway lights of The Hill— Los Alamos. I let beauty hold me. I would have liked to paint a night picture of this—something I'd never attempted. Again Gavin was watching me, rather than the scene he knew so well.

But he said nothing, and in a few moments we started up the mountain again. There were patches of snow in the crevices now—white and shining, with shadows of indigo. We were climbing in low gear, and suddenly the tall trees gave way to scrubby growth, and we were in the open below the snow peaks. Santa Fe was no longer in view. A dark building rose on our right and we could see the framework of the ski lifts climbing to the fields above us. Nothing moved. Deep silence lay over the peaks. Again Gavin stopped the car and we got out into invigorating cold. Our breath frosted on the air and I wrapped my scarf about my head to keep my ears warm.

Gavin held out his hand to me and I took it easily as we walked about the open area where cars would park for the winter skiing. His hand was as warm as mine was cold, and once he stopped to chafe my fingers. The moon had an icy radiance and this was a world far removed from threats of violence, from the darkness of murder. There was no evil in this clear air. Happiness was a mountaintop at night and the companionship of Gavin Brand.

As we turned back to the car we ran, our hands still clasped together, though when he reached the car he did not open my door at once, but just stood looking at me for a moment. Then he drew me into his arms in hungry despair.

"I knew from the first that you spelled trouble," he said ruefully. "I meant to make you dislike me, distrust me."

"I don't do either," I said with my cheek against the rough cloth of his jacket.

He turned my face up to him and kissed me with a tenderness I'd never known before. "What am I to do about you?"

It had happened to me—just as it had once happened to my father and his Doroteo—and I had no wish to struggle against it. This was a natural force which would go its own way, and there was no stopping it. My quiet joy had heightened.

"Let's never go back," I said with my cheek against his jacket. "Let's just go away and make a life of our own."

His arms tightened about me, though he didn't answer my foolish words. Down in Santa Fe the Cordovas waited for us, and there nothing had been settled.

"*You* must go away," he said at last. "Your safety means everything now. Juan is going to be angry, and so is Eleanor."

I could think of nothing but my new love. "You aren't going to do what Juan wishes, anyway," I pointed out. "Can't we stay together?"

He released me and opened the car door, waited until I was in my seat, and then walked around to the driver's side. When he was behind the wheel he turned the engine key, switched on the heater, and we sat for a little while in silence, not touching each other. I knew there was nothing more I could say or do. I had declared myself without reservation, and whatever happened now would be up to Gavin.

"I don't know whether I can make you understand,"

he said. "It's true that I've told Juan I want to get out of this marriage, just as Eleanor does. But it isn't a simple matter and I can't cut off the past with a sharp knife."

"Do you still love her a little?"

He slipped an arm behind me on the back of the seat. "I love you, even though I wish it hadn't happened. But once I loved her a great deal, and I haven't entirely got over my feeling of responsibility for her. She can be heedless. Juan knows that. He knows that I've kept her on a steadier path than she might otherwise have followed."

"If you leave her now, will he put you out of the store?"

"It's likely. But that isn't what matters most. I want to see her land on her feet and not destroy herself."

"With Paul Stewart?"

"Paul will never leave Sylvia. He's roamed a bit before this. Eleanor is too sure of herself, too sure that the world revolves around her. She can't help that. It's what Juan has taught her. But she may be in for a shock with Paul. There are matters which must be settled before I can be free. You came here in the middle of turmoil. Will you go away and wait for me?"

"I'll wait as long as you like. But I won't go away. I can't go away now."

He put the car in gear, backed around and started down the mountain. We drove in low gear most of the way, and this time we didn't stop to look at the view. Once Gavin tried helplessly to say something, but only broke off. Not until we reached the Cordova garage did he pull me to him again, and I clung a little tearfully as he kissed my mouth and my wet eyelids. But there were no more words to be spoken and I understood that a wall not of our own making rose between us, and until it was leveled, he could not be wholly free to come to me. I could only wait until all the problems were solved, even though they were problems I didn't wholly understand. Of course they would be solved—I must believe in that. It was all I had to hold onto.

The Cordova house was asleep when we left the car in the garage and went inside. Gavin did not touch me again, and his look was bleak when we said good night. I went to my high room and took the capsules Clarita had given me. I'd plunged from my high peak of joy, and I wanted to go quickly to sleep and for a little while to think about nothing.

# XV

The next morning was Sunday, and when I went down to breakfast they were all gathered at the table, except Juan. Clarita had been up and out to early Mass, and she greeted me guardedly, inquiring about my head. The lump was there, and it was tender, but not unduly painful. I found myself speaking in a subdued manner, as though a heavy restraint lay upon me.

There were polite murmurs from Eleanor and Clarita when I said I was feeling better. Only Gavin was silent, and after a single searching look, he didn't glance at me again, so that I had the feeling that during the night his burden had increased. Clearly depression rode him this morning, and it did not bode well for our happiness.

No one discussed last night's occurrences—as though in that direction quicksand lay which none of them wanted to test. I had brought the Zuni fetish to the table with me, and when I'd taken my place I pushed it across to Eleanor.

"I think you must have left this in my room," I said. "I thought you might want it back."

Gavin raised his head and stared at her, but Eleanor only laughed.

"Since it keeps turning up, I'll keep it for a lucky

243

piece," she said, and set it beside her place, neither acknowledging nor denying any part she might have had in placing it in my room.

Clarita spoke to me. "Juan has phoned to make a reservation for your flight to New York. Sylvia will drive you to Albuquerque this morning. There is a local plane, but the trip is apt to be bumpy, and this will get you there more comfortably in plenty of time. You must pack right after breakfast."

They were all looking at me, including Gavin, and I raised my chin obstinately. "I'm not ready to go."

Clarita began to fuss, but Eleanor cut in, silencing her. "In that case, Amanda, you can come with us on our visit to the *rancho*. Juan is feeling fine today, and he wants to go. You'll come too, won't you, Gavin? Since it's Sunday?"

She had put on a pretty, pleading look, and though he responded with no warmth, he agreed to make the trip. I suspect that, like me, he wondered what she was up to.

"We'll bring Sylvia and Paul along as well," Eleanor rushed on. "It will be like old times out at the *rancho*. We'll wake the place up."

Her excitement seemed real enough, but its cause was faked. Something she had no intention of revealing motivated Eleanor, and as I buttered crisp toast, I wondered what this exodus meant. Last night at the store she had been plotting about it with Paul, but I had heard nothing worth reporting to Gavin or Juan.

Only Clarita seemed against making the trip. "I do not wish to go," she said, looking the picture of black gloom.

Eleanor was after her in a flash. "Why not, Aunt Clarita?"

"I do not care for that place."

"Because of its memories?" Eleanor persisted.

"Perhaps I will stay home today."

"No!" Eleanor cried. "I won't let you stay home. You never have any fun, and this will be good for you. Please come with us, Aunt Clarita."

She left her place and ran to Clarita's side, coaxing and cajoling until the older woman gave in, sighing.

"Very well, *querida*. But I have a feeling that no good will come of this. Old ghosts should be allowed their quiet."

Eleanor threw a sharp glance at me. "Amanda doesn't think so—do you, Amanda?"

"Perhaps the old ghosts have no quiet," I said. "But if you think they're stirring out at the *rancho*, I'd like to be there to meet them."

Eleanor's eyes were bright with some secret malice. "Then it's settled!" she cried. "We're practically on our way."

After breakfast there was a flurry of preparation. Clarita reluctantly canceled my plane reservation. Sylvia was called and asked to change her plans and come with us. It developed that Paul wanted to work on his book today and would not give in to any coaxing. This latter fact alerted me, yet there was still nothing to give me a clue as to Eleanor's intent. I would simply have to wait and keep my own watch for anything untoward that might happen. I felt as though I were marking time, waiting for some unseen explosive to go off and perhaps damage all of us. Perhaps even Eleanor, who held a torch to the fuse.

This morning I was no longer as sure of myself as I had been last night. What had happened on the mountain seemed distant and unreal, especially in the face of Gavin's remote air and his lack of effort to speak to me. It all seemed part of a dream, rising to false heights of joy that inevitably meant a later plunge to despair. For the last year or so I had managed to move on a fairly even plane emotionally, without extremes of happiness or sorrow. It was safer that way. Since last night, however, my feelings had taken on a quicksilver quality and were all too ready to dart about, changing their character from one moment to the next, running the scale from high to low. Now a sense of foreboding haunted me, and the barrier was there that I could not see beyond. The barrier between Gavin and me.

Back in my room I tried to cheer myself by putting on my favorite beige slacks and a buttercup-yellow blouse, but the sunny combination seemed to mock me in the mirror. That was when I had another bad moment. The plan for going out to the *rancho* had made me think of the mask again, and I opened the drawer and rummaged under the clothes where I had hidden it. The mask was gone.

I looked in several other places, lest my memory had played a trick on me, but the mask was no longer in my room. In the end, I gave up my search and went downstairs, but the fact that it was missing seemed ominous. The mask had meant something to me, and someone, clearly, did not want me to have it.

There were six of us going on the trip, and it had been decided that we would take two cars. Juan and Clarita and Eleanor would go in one, with Eleanor driving, while Gavin would drive Sylvia and me. Except for Paul, who stayed behind with his book, we all assembled near the Cordova garage as the cars were backed out. Juan was brought downstairs last, and he leaned on Clarita only a little as she helped him into the back seat of Eleanor's car. Some quickening force seemed to possess him this morning, and he had come thoroughly to life.

I stood well back in the garage, watching them settle Juan in his place, not projecting myself to his attention. He gave me a single look of annoyance and I looked away at once. He was displeased with me because I wouldn't leave, and there was nothing I could do about it.

Something on the garage floor caught my eye as I stood there, and I bent to look more closely before I picked up the fine hoop of gold that was Clarita's matching earring. How it came to be in the garage when she had gone nowhere last night, I didn't know.

I went to her just as she was about to get into the back seat with Juan. "Your earring," I said. "I just found it there in the garage."

She snatched it from me impatiently and without a thank-you, dropped it into her handbag. All her attention was given to Juan, and she had no time or interest for me. Or perhaps it was just that she had nothing to say to me, and wanted to attempt no explanation.

In Gavin's car I managed to sit on the outside, with Sylvia in the middle. Last night's dream was far away and he was so much on guard against me this morning that I couldn't bear to sit next to him.

Sylvia had heard sketchily from Paul what had happened to me at the store, and she was full of questions, which I answered rather shortly. Strangely enough, she did no speculating as to who might have struck me. She seemed to have more concern about the fact that Eleanor had coaxed Paul into going to the store at that hour to restore the Penitente display, and I knew that she was worried about her husband.

Eleanor was already on her way ahead of us and she was driving as fast as usual, so that we did not even catch a glimpse of her car during the trip. Gavin drove more moderately, but he kept to the top of the speed limit and I sensed the nervous energy that spurred him.

In a way, I was glad to be going out to the *rancho* with all of them this morning. I would have a chance to observe the Cordovas in a familiar atmosphere that might recall old actions, might lead to revelations. I had no knowledge then of what Eleanor might be planning.

When we reached the hacienda and went inside, we found Juan and Clarita in the long *sala,* Juan sitting before a lively fire of piñon logs, and Clarita hovering about, trying to make sure he was comfortable. The brief rebellion that she had instituted last night when she wore the dress of claret velvet, had vanished, and she seemed to be Juan's serving maid as always. Only when she looked at me did she stiffen with displeasure—perhaps because I had found her earring where she did not want it to be found.

Eleanor had disappeared, and no one knew where she had gone.

"The *rancho* is home to her," Juan said when Sylvia inquired for her. "She knows every corner."

"So do I," said Sylvia. "Let me show you about the place, Amanda."

Gavin had matters concerning the store to discuss with Juan, and he had no time for me this morning. I went with Sylvia, back into the dark reaches of the house, where narrow passageways with plastered walls led to series of rooms. The house had been built all on one floor, and it meandered into small, rather dark rooms packed with ancient and often shabby furniture. I had seen a little of it with Gavin.

"You should have been here in the days when they used to entertain out here," Sylvia said. "Juan and Katy loved to have house parties, and they would fill every room with guests. In those days there were enough horses for everyone to ride who wanted to, and Kirk was the best rider of them all. Juan used to say that Kirk should have been his natural son, instead of Rafael, who did nothing but disappoint him. Kirk took up the Spanish ways and made them his own. He had that wild streak that Juan admires and he might have been one of the Cordovas, instead of a foster son. When he and Doro died, Juan lost a son as well as a daughter."

I'd had only glimpses of Kirk before and I listened with interest.

Sylvia had opened the door to a small, rather cell-like room, which had been denuded of most of its furnishings. With one exception, there were no hangings on the walls, or rugs on the floor, and the single, narrow wooden bed was stripped to its springs, a table by the window was bare, and the bureau void of ornament. The single exception hung against the wall just over the head of the bed, and it was a large duplicate of the little *Ojo de Dios* I carried in my purse.

"I gave him that," Sylvia said, her eyes on the red and black and yellow strands of wool wound outward from the central Eye of God. "A lot of good it did him!"

She wandered idly to the tall dresser and pulled open an empty drawer. If this had been Kirk's room, I wanted to miss nothing, and I went to stand beside her. The drawer was empty, and she slammed it shut, opened another. This time there was an old newspaper inside, and Sylvia drew it out curiously and opened the pages, exclaiming as she spread them on the bare table.

"That was the year!" Sylvia said softly.

I knew what she meant. It was the year of the tragedy, but an earlier date. Sylvia turned to the second page and her hand was arrested on the paper. I saw why. Smiling at us from center page was a photograph of a young man in an elaborate costume of tight trousers, white shirt, short embroidered jacket and broad sombrero caught under his chin with a strap of leather thongs.

"Juan sent to Mexico for that *charro* outfit for Kirk," Sylvia said. "And he wore it as though he'd been born to silver and leather and embroidered braid. He was as good a horseman as Juan, and when there was a fiesta he rode his own palomino."

Her voice was low, lacking emotion, as though she thought aloud, without any awareness of me, standing beside her.

The photograph showed him full length, smiling arrogantly into the camera, and his narrow, full-lipped face was as handsome as the face of any man I'd seen. But there was something about it—something I couldn't quite put my finger on. . . .

"You can see why women were mad about him," Sylvia went on in that same even, rather dead voice. "Doro and Clarita were only two out of many. Though they were the two closest to him. I think Juan always wanted him for Doro, because that would make him doubly his son."

"But I thought Juan sent him away so he couldn't marry her?"

"That was mainly Katy's doing. She persuaded Juan

that Doro was too young. Katy loved Kirk, but she didn't want Doro to marry him. So the arrangement, supposedly, was that he would go away for a few years. Juan got him a job in South America—Ecuador— since he spoke Spanish well and would feel at home. He was to come back to Santa Fe in a few years and then marry Doro, if they both still wished it. When he did return, of course, Doro had married your father, and Kirk was furious. Doro was more beautiful and fascinating, and Kirk fell in love with her all over again. He still thought Doro would run off with him, and I don't think he was ever convinced that she could love someone else. Anyway, he was on their hands again, and since he knew horses so well, Juan put him in charge out here, and he worked on the *rancho* until the day he died."

I studied the faintly insolent young face in the picture. It wore a confidence that was supreme—as though he knew very well that women and horses would obey him. There was no heartbreak in his eyes, but there seemed a steely determination.

What was it that bothered me about his face? As though I had seen it somewhere before—as though, somehow, I knew Kirk Landers very well.

"He doesn't look like you," I said to Sylvia.

"Of course not. He wasn't related to me by blood. He was my stepbrother. I'm glad we weren't alike."

A cool note had come into her voice and I threw her a quick look. Until now I had taken it for granted that she had been fond of her stepbrother, but the tone of her voice seemed to repudiate him.

"What did you think of him?" I asked. "As a sister?"

"I detested him. He was cruel and thoughtless and selfish. He hurt Doro more than once, and he played with Clarita because it amused him to. Because I wanted Paul, he was against Paul, and he nearly killed him in that fight they had. If he'd lived, he might have come between Paul and me."

She folded the newspaper roughly with hands that

showed mounting emotion, and almost ran out of the room. I stood for a moment longer, looking about me, trying to get the measure of the man my mother had loved when she was young and before she had met my father. But if there was a haunting presence here, it told me nothing.

There was one thing, however. I thought I recognized the *charro* costume Kirk wore in the picture. Those were the same garments which had been stuffed into that box with the mask and diary, and which Gavin had taken from me without explanation. I remembered wondering why at the time, and now I wondered again.

Since Sylvia had given up guiding me about the house, I found my way back to the *sala,* and found her kneeling before the adobe hearth, warming her hands at the blaze as though something had chilled her to the bone. Clarita sat a little apart in the room, where shadows hid her face, and I had a sense of her watching and listening presence, as though she wanted to be there without calling attention to herself.

Gavin stood up as I came into the room to make a place for me between him and Juan, and my grandfather smiled at me tightly, still not forgiving my obstinacy.

As I sat down, he pointed to a space at one side of the rounded adobe chimney. "That is where the turquoise mask always hung when the children were small, Amanda. We must bring it back and hang it there again."

"It's gone from my room," I told him. "I'd put it into a drawer, but someone has taken it away."

Gavin looked at me sharply. "More tricks?"

"I don't know," I said. "I'm just as glad to have it out of my room, because it haunts me. But I didn't take it away myself."

Maria came to tell us that our lunch would be served in the dining room.

Juan asked where Eleanor was, and Maria said she was looking through old cartons in Señora Cordova's former room. Maria would call her to lunch.

The dining room was long and narrow, and so was the dark wooden table with its woven straw place mats. High-back chairs with cracked leather seats awaited us, and dark paintings of somber Spanish scenes hung upon the walls, none lighted clearly enough to be appreciated. Arched windows set in deep walls looked out upon the courtyard of parched, dry earth.

"I used to hate this room when I was small," Sylvia said. "It never made me feel like eating. I used to expect one of those figures from Grandfather Juan's pictures of the Inquisition to come walking in, all hooded and threatening."

"This is foolish," Juan said. "There was always good conversation here, and laughter and fine wine. The hacienda is rich in Spanish tradition."

Maria lighted creamy white candles in candlesticks of pewter and the flames dispelled the gloom a little. We did not wait for Eleanor, but were served tacos with a delicious meat filling, though a little hot with chili for my taste. There was Spanish rice and *sopapillos* —those pillowlike puffs of thin bread, which I especially enjoyed.

We were halfway through the meal when Clarita, who sat at the end of the table facing the door, gave a sudden cry and put her napkin to her lips. Sylvia stared at the door, turning so white that I thought she was going to faint. From where I sat, Juan's chair blocked the door, but I saw the grim look on Gavin's face, saw him push back his chair.

Juan, made aware by behavior around the table that something was happening behind him, twisted about and stared toward the door. A lithe figure in dark blue moved into view, and I saw the tight suede trousers, trimmed down the sides with tarnished silver buttons, the short jacket ornamented in white braid and embroidery, a white sombrero topping the whole—and I saw something else. Where the face should have been beneath the rolled brim of the sombrero, was a blue mask, its features formed of silver and turquoise, the mouth rounded in an "O" that seemed a silent scream.

Clarita cried out—a single name, "Kirk!" and covered her face with her hands.

Sylvia said harshly, "Don't be silly—it's Eleanor!"

The figure in the *charro* costume pranced a little, sweeping the sombrero from her head in a bow, whirling about the table as she showed herself off.

I could hear the screaming when it began, and I covered my ears to shut out the terrible sound. I didn't know until Gavin came around the table and shook me gently by the shoulders, that it was I who screamed.

"Stop it, Amanda, stop it. You're all right," he said.

Juan spoke for the first time. "Take off that mask, Eleanor. You are upsetting Amanda. What is this prank you are playing? What are you trying to do?"

Eleanor flung aside the sombrero and unfastened the mask, laying it on the sideboard. Her own face was a mask in itself—a mask of heightened excitement and cruel curiosity.

"What do you remember, Amanda? What do you see?" she urged me tensely.

Before Gavin could move to stop her, she came around the table and knelt beside me in her tarnished silver and leather.

"Look, Amanda, look!" she whispered, and pointed to the breast of the jacket. There were dark stains across the heart, brownish where they touched white braid, and the material had been broken by something that had left a scorched hole.

I had stopped screaming, but I was trembling so desperately that I clung to Gavin to keep my hands from shaking, and I buried my face against his heart. He held and soothed me gently, and there was a silence all around the room. Clarita was the first to break it.

"Oh, wicked, wicked!" she cried to Eleanor. "Sometimes you are as wicked as he was." And I knew she meant Kirk. I had never before seen Clarita angry with Eleanor.

Sylvia pushed back her chair and walked out of the room, without a look for anyone, as though she had need to recover privately. Only Eleanor and Juan continued to stare at me, with Gavin there beside me, holding me to him, smoothing my hair, whispering softly to calm me. I clung to him and wept, not caring who saw me, or what they might think.

"You have outdone the Cordovas," Juan said at last to Eleanor. "I suggest that you go and get into your own clothes. Then have Maria wrap those things in a parcel and bring them to me. They must be disposed of. I did not know they had been saved."

"My mother saved them," Clarita said in a choked voice. Now she was watching me too, weighing what she saw with a look as dark as Juan's.

Eleanor paid no attention to Juan, still playing her cruel role. "I remember, if you don't, Amanda, though I didn't see what happened. Kirk was wearing this very *charro* outfit when he came to meet Doro on the hillside that day. I'd seen him in it before at fiestas, and I saw him that day, too, when they carried him up the hill afterwards. I saw the blood, just as you did, Amanda, but I didn't go to pieces over it the way you did."

Her eyes were bright with defiance of her grandfather, of Gavin, of all of us. She snatched up the sombrero and put it back on her head, taunting me, and when I closed my eyes against the sight, I could still see, vividly, that figure with the great sombrero on its head, and the turquoise mask covering its face. But I knew it was Kirk I was seeing, not Eleanor. Kirk ripping the mask from his face and dropping it to the ground, so that it fell beside me. I could almost hear him speaking to my mother, threatening her. Yes, I could remember the voice—rough and threatening. And I could almost see her frightened face. She was crying out, "No, no!" as she struggled with an adversary. There was a blast of sound and I saw the dreadful, staining blood heard the crash of her body, falling endlessly. Afterwards everything went blank and I could remember only that

I was sitting on a bench with the blue mask in my hands, staring at that terrible cottonwood tree which seemed to my young eyes the spirit incarnate of evil.

Gavin was holding a water glass to my lips. I sipped weakly and the vision faded. Sylvia had made a supreme effort to recover herself and she returned to the dining room. Her hands drew me away from Gavin, her voice whispered to me softly.

"Let it go, Amanda. Don't try to bring everything back."

I wanted only to continue clinging to Gavin, but he had stepped back, to leave me to face Sylvia's ministering. When I put a hand to my face I found it wet with tears, and I felt exhausted.

Eleanor was still there, still prying and intent. "You've remembered, haven't you, Amanda? Tell us what you saw!"

Weakly, I moved my head from side to side. "No— it nearly came clear, but not completely. I can remember Kirk. I can remember my mother's fright. But nothing else—nothing."

Someone sighed as if in deep relief, and when I opened my eyes I saw it was Sylvia. But it was Eleanor I must look at now. Look at and recognize. Because now I knew. I knew why I'd sensed familiarity in the photograph of Kirk Landers. His picture had looked like Eleanor in this very mood.

Strength began to flow through me, and I pushed Sylvia away. Eleanor and Kirk—why? I stared at Juan and at Clarita, and I saw vestiges of resemblance to Eleanor there. But Kirk had not been related to the Cordovas at all. Or that was what Sylvia had told me. So why?

Juan had not moved from his place and now he spoke down the table. "Perhaps you will feel better, Amanda, if you finish your lunch."

I looked with distaste at the food on my plate, and Clarita rose from her place. "I will get her some soup from the kitchen." She spoke without liking for me, without sympathy, though she would minister to me.

Eleanor, still defying her grandfather, slipped into her chair at the table and began to eat hungrily, still dressed in Kirk's Mexican *charro* costume, with that dreadful powder burn and the brown stains on the front. But now Juan had recovered his own inner power and this time when he spoke to her his voice crackled.

"You will eat nothing more until you have changed your clothes," he told her. This time she did not dare to disobey. Her defiance melted and she slipped from her place like a scolded child and ran out of the room.

Clarita returned shortly with a cup of heated broth, and I drank it gratefully. Eleanor came back as I finished, changed into her own slacks and blouse.

Gavin said, "I'll take you home now, Amanda. You've had enough."

"Then I'll come with you!" Eleanor cried.

"No," Gavin said. "You will not."

Juan looked at Sylvia, and she said, "I'll drive back with you, if I may, Gavin."

He nodded to her shortly, and we went out to the car. At the table Juan, Clarita and Eleanor sat like images, watching us go.

This time Gavin placed me next to him in the car, and Sylvia sat on the outside.

"Juan is furious," Sylvia said nervously. "He wants you to stay with Eleanor, Gavin. He won't stand for—for you and Amanda. You've floored us all, I must say."

I knew they had seen plainly how I felt. It was my own fault, my own weakness. And I didn't seem to care.

"There's not much he can do about it," Gavin said grimly.

"He can fire you."

"If he wants to. But he still needs me."

I knew I should murmur something about being sorry, apologize for giving my feelings away so thoroughly, but I didn't want to. I leaned my head against Gavin's arm as he drove, and once he reached over to stroke my cheek, so that I knew he wasn't angry with me. I

loved him so much that I couldn't bear it. Yet when we
had driven a few miles in silence, I knew there were
things I had to ask.

"I know now why that picture you showed me of
Kirk seemed familiar," I said to Sylvia. "He looks like
Eleanor."

"Kirk?" Gavin sounded surprised. "I've never thought
that. But then, I can't much remember what Kirk looked
like."

"You're imagining it," Sylvia said with a lightness I
couldn't believe in. Whatever the truth was, Sylvia
knew.

"Was Juan Kirk's father?" I asked bluntly.

Gavin exclaimed and Sylvia seemed to choke on the
words she'd been about to speak. "Oh, no, no, of course
not!" she cried.

"Then why did Kirk have the Cordova look?"

"He didn't have!" Sylvia insisted heatedly. "Not at
all, Amanda!"

I paid no attention. "If he did inherit it, then Kirk
and my mother might have been half brother and sister,"
I said.

Sylvia shook her head vehemently. "You're going
down a completely wrong road. There was nothing like
that. Kirk was my stepbrother."

"Then tell me the truth," I said.

She only shook her head again, denying knowledge of
anything, denying my claim that Kirk had the Cordova
look in his face.

I went on, thinking aloud. "If Doroteo had wanted
to marry Kirk and he was really her brother, then Juan
couldn't have allowed that, could he? What if it was
Juan who came along that hillside? Juan who killed
Kirk?"

"And pushed his favorite daughter down the bank?"
Sylvia was derisive.

"What if Clarita lied about what she saw from the
window?" I went on. "What if she has protected her
father all these years?"

"Don't!" Sylvia cried. "Amanda, don't. Juan was ill that day. Katy had put him to bed. But if you want to know something, Clarita was never anywhere near that window from which she claimed to be looking. All her avowals to the police were false."

I turned my head to stare at her, and so did Gavin. Sylvia was looking straight ahead at the highway that rushed toward us, with the rooftops of Santa Fe in the distance, and the mountains rising beyond.

"Are you making this up?" I asked.

Once more she had turned as pale as she'd been when Eleanor came prancing into the dining room in Kirk's costume.

"I'm not making anything up. Paul saw her that day. He saw her outside the house where she couldn't have seen a thing on the hillside. And she's been lying ever since."

I remembered that Sylvia had earlier given away the fact that she and Paul had not come to the picnic together that day.

Gavin asked the next question. "Then why didn't Paul go to the police with what he knew?"

"He chose not to. He was sorry for Clarita. She'd gotten over her young crush on Kirk by that time, just as Doro had. It was Paul she was in love with, and she'd begun to see Kirk through Paul's eyes. She knew he was thoroughly bad."

I leaned my head back against the seat and closed my eyes. It was as if a picture I had been looking at for some time had suddenly shifted in character, and all the recognized brush strokes now meant something new and different.

I couldn't bear to think about it any more. Far ahead the snow crests glistened in the sun and I remembered what it had been like to be up there among the peaks last night, alone with Gavin. How clean and pure the snow had seemed under the moon. How clear and simple love had seemed then. Now it was neither. Yet somehow another corner had been turned and Eleanor had put herself outside of Gavin's consideration. I wondered what she would do now. She might be amusing herself with Paul, she might be eager for a divorce, yet I had the suspicion that she would not easily release to a rival something she had once owned. If Gavin loved me, she would hate me for that very fact.

I could cope with nothing more. I let myself go limp, forced my mind to empty. No one spoke in the car, though now and then Gavin threw me a concerned glance. There was no strength in me to reassure him. Eleanor's prank had wrung me out emotionally and all my ability to think and feel had been washed away. I was numb, and I didn't want painful sensation to return.

When we reached the empty house, Gavin held me close for a moment that might have been comforting if I could feel anything, and then turned me over to Sylvia. She came up to my room with me and offered to stay for a while.

"I'll be all right," I assured her. "I just need to be quiet and—and catch my breath."

In a way, Sylvia was more disturbed than I in this unfeeling state. She moved restlessly about the room, and I had the sense that she didn't want to go home to Paul right away. In fact, she admitted this after her third round of the room.

"Paul will want to know everything that happened, and I—I don't want to talk about it. What Eleanor did was dreadful. She believes it will drive you away and still help Paul with his book if she can stir things up, but I don't think they should be stirred up. Forget about today, Amanda. Let it be."

This was the old song that Sylvia was forever singing, and I wondered at her deep concern.

"I haven't any other choice," I said. "I'm very close —but I'm not there. And until the fog clears completely, there's nothing I can do."

She stopped her pacing and stood beside my bed. "If it does clear, what will you do?"

"I don't know," I said. "How can I even guess? I

suppose I'll go to Juan if what I remember clears my mother."

"I'll tell Paul you can't remember," Sylvia said. "I'll tell him not to pay any attention to Eleanor."

I closed my eyes, only wanting to be alone, and in a little while she went away. When her steps had stopped echoing on the stairs, I lay quiet on the bed, listening to silence. After a time it was broken by the arrival of the other three. I heard Clarita helping Juan to his room, and when I got up and looked out the window, I saw Eleanor running across the patio toward the Stewarts' gate, and I knew she was losing no time in talking to Paul.

When I lay down again, I managed to fall asleep, and I didn't waken until Rosa came up my stairs bringing a tray Clarita had sent up to me. It was a simple meal of soup and cheese and fruit, and I managed to eat it, as I could not have done a full dinner. When Rosa came to take the tray away, I lay down again, more awake now, more alive, yet still unsure of what it was I must do next.

The room darkened, and the light in the patio came on, throwing a slight radiance against one window. I lay in the dark and thought of Gavin and wished myself into the future, when all problems might be solved and I could be with him for good. If that time ever came. The present returned to me sharply when I heard Juan calling my name.

When I went to open my door, I found him at the foot of the stairs, his back to the lighted room, so that I could not see his face.

"Come down to me, Amanda," he said softly.

A deep breath gave me a semblance of courage, and I went down the steps. Whatever I expected in the way of chiding did not come.

"I want you to do something for me," he said, and held out a ring with two keys.

I took them from him, my look questioning.

"There's no one else I can send," he told me. "I'm

too weary to walk down there tonight, and my eye-sight can't be trusted. I want you to check the collection for me."

"Check the collection?" I echoed.

"Yes. We've been away most of the day. I always look at it immediately after being away. I want you to be my eyes this time. I want to know if everything is all right."

"But I won't know if anything is missing," I objected. "I should think Gavin—"

He gave me a dark look. "Not Gavin. It isn't necessary to check everything. There is just one thing that matters —the Velázquez. I want to make sure it is safe. I have worried about it all day."

"But someone nearby would have heard the alarm if it sounded, and you'd have been told."

"Not necessarily. Don't argue, Amanda. Just go out there now. And then come to me in my study."

I looked reluctantly at the keys in my hand. "All right, I'll go." At least it was something that he didn't mean to lecture me now.

"You remember? The burglar alarm key first. Then the other. And when you come to me, follow the passage from the patio, so no one will see you. The door is open."

I nodded, and he turned back toward his room, lean-ing heavily on his stick, as though all his strength had been used up in our day's excursion.

I let myself out to the patio through the living-room door. No one was about, and I turned down the flagged walk to the building with its peaked redwood roof. Using the keys in proper succession, I let myself in the door.

With curtains drawn as always, it was very dark inside. I found a switch at the right of the door and turned on the indirect lighting. Scenes of Spain sprang to life along the walls, but I paid no attention to them, walking rapidly toward the alcove at the back. There I touched the switch that lighted Velázquez's painting of Doña Inés.

It took only a moment to assure me that the picture was safe. I stared at that strange, indented face of the stunted woman with the dog at her feet, then turned off the light and returned to the main room. As far as I could see, nothing had been disturbed. There seemed to be no vacant places on the walls, or on any of the shelves which held carved figures and ceramics.

Once more the painting of Doña Emanuella caught my attention and I stood before it, trying to see in that bright face with the sulky mouth the image of my mother. If only she had lived. Not Emanuella, but Doroteo. She had cared about me as Grandmother Katy had cared about her daughters. As my father had cared about me. None of the other Cordovas would serve. I had been seeking a mirage to expect anything from them.

But now there was Gavin. The thought of him warmed and comforted me, and I tried to tell the Doroteo I saw in the picture that at last I had someone of my own, as she had had. Someone who loved me. But she only smiled her tantalizing smile, and I knew Doroteo had not been like the girl in the picture.

Dreamily I switched off the lights and went outside. Paul Stewart stood waiting for me in the patio. He was the last person I wanted to see, but there could be no escaping him now.

"I saw the light as you went in," he said. "I wondered who was there."

I locked the door and reactivated the alarm. "Juan gave me the keys. He was worried about the Velázquez."

"I'm sure no one has touched it," Paul said. "I haven't been far from my typewriter all day. I'd have heard any disturbance."

"That's what I assured Juan," I said, and started past him.

"Eleanor told me what happened today," he went on. His eyes had that pale green light I didn't like, and I knew he must have praised Eleanor for her wild prank.

"She didn't succeed," I said coolly. "I've remembered

nothing more. But she managed to upset everyone. It was a dreadful thing to do."

Paul paid no attention to my disapproval. "Will you promise me one thing—if it all comes suddenly back in your memory, will you tell me first?"

"Of course I won't. Why should I?"

"It might be better for everyone if you did," he said quietly, and turned away to disappear through the gate in the wall.

I watched him go and then walked slowly toward the entrance to the passageway to Juan's rooms.

The door was unlocked, as promised, and I let myself into the narrow tunnel. A pool of light thrown by the bulb at this end illuminated the beginning of the stone-paved way, but it grew darker near the steps at the far end, and for a moment I hesitated. Too much had happened to me lately. But as I paused, the door of my grandfather's room opened in the distance, and he called to me.

"Is that you, Amanda?"

I answered him, and moved along the passageway. He had stepped back from the doorway, and it was empty when I climbed the steps and entered the bedroom. It too was empty, but lighted, and I averted my eyes from the agony of the man in the painting who burned endlessly at the stake.

Juan awaited me in his study and he wore a long brown robe with a monk's cowl thrown down at the back. For a moment I stared at him in dismay because he looked all too much like one of the dark, hooded figures which circled the fire in the painting.

But he was waiting for me, and I went into the room and dropped the keys on the desk before him, and watched as he put them away in a drawer.

"I don't think anything has been touched," I told him.

He seemed to relax in visible relief and his hands unclenched where they rested on the desk before him. He was obsessed by the Velázquez painting and I wondered if that was good for his peace of mind.

"Why don't you send it back to Spain?" I asked.

"No! Not in my lifetime."

"But you say you can't see it clearly any more."

"I can see it with my inner eye. I can see it with my mind and my heart, and I can touch it with my fingers. It is my greatest pleasure."

"It would never have been Katy's greatest pleasure," I said. "I think Katy believed in what was human."

"If Katy had lived, much would be different in my life," he said. "Now a picture becomes important."

"It isn't even a very beautiful picture," I objected. "I'll agree that it's magnificently painted, but there's a sort of horror about it. I prefer the picture of Emanuella."

"Then that painting shall be yours. I give it to you now. Let me keep it upon that wall while I live. Afterwards, it is for you to own. I will put this in writing."

At once I was on guard. Juan Cordova was not a sentimental man, nor given to gestures of generosity. This was an attempt to win me.

"Thank you," I said quietly, and moved toward the door.

At once he stopped me. "Wait. Sit down for a moment, Amanda."

The lecture would come now, I thought. Because of the way I'd betrayed my feeling for Gavin. But he surprised me.

"What happened today? What came back to your memory?"

"Nothing. I remembered seeing Kirk in that *charro* costume wearing the mask. Why do you suppose he wore it?"

"Katy believed it was because Doroteo used to adore him when they were younger and he dressed like that. And they used to play some game of flirtation with the mask. So he wanted her to remember that time. He wanted her to run away with him. Which she would never have done."

"Yet someone came along the hillside and shot him.

Not my mother. I've remembered that much. I know it wasn't Doroteo."

I heard a choked sound behind me and turned in my chair to see Clarita standing there. She looked outraged, indignant.

"Of course it was Doro! I saw it with my own eyes—"

I stood up to face her. "No, you didn't see anything, Aunt Clarita. I learned that much on the drive home today. Paul saw you outside the house. You couldn't have been anywhere near that window when it happened."

Juan reached across his desk and caught me by the hand.

"What are you saying? What do you mean?"

Clarita uttered another choked cry, put her hands over her face and fled from the room. The pressure of Juan's fingers forced me back into the chair.

"You will explain yourself," he said.

I repeated what Sylvia had told us in the car and Juan listened to me with a stunned expression.

"All these years I have believed her," he said. "Why did she lie—if she was lying? Why?"

"To protect someone, I suppose," I said.

With difficulty he roused himself and released my hand. "Go and find her. Bring her here to me, Amanda. And then leave us alone."

He had forgotten all about Gavin, and I went away in relief. The living rooms of the house were empty, and I went into the bedroom wing. I tapped on Clarita's door and when she didn't answer, I opened it and looked in. Her black-clad form lay stretched upon the bed, and I thought for a moment that she was weeping. But when I spoke her name, she sat up and stared at me with dry, ravaged eyes.

"What do you want? Haven't you done enough damage for one day?"

"Your father wants you. He said I was to bring you to him at once."

She waved her hand at me in dismissal. "I will go to him. There is no need to bring me."

As I knew very well, when Juan gave an order, he meant it literally, and I stayed where I was. After a moment she got up from the bed and came toward me.

"Why did you lie?" I asked her softly. "Who was it who went along the hillside that day?"

For just an instant I thought she was going to strike me. Her thin hand with its flashing rings came up, but I stood my ground and it fell back to her side just short of my face.

"You are like your mother," she whispered. "You ask for killing."

Then she pushed me aside and went out of the room. I followed her to the foot of the balcony steps and watched until I saw her go into her father's study. When the door closed, I fled to my own room and got ready for bed.

I felt more than a little frightened. The corner into which I'd painted myself seemed to be narrowing. Before long there would be no way in which I could turn. All my motions were automatic as I undressed and got beneath the covers. Gavin seemed very far away.

# XVI

That night a dream wakened me. It was not the dream of the tree, but it was so vivid, so horrible, that I sat up in bed and turned on my bed lamp. My small travel clock showed three-thirty. I tried to recall the details, but they were already fading. Something about a dog. Something quite dreadful about a dog. But there was no dog in this house, nothing to make me dream about one. I had not had a dog as a pet since I'd been a child in my aunt's house in New Hampshire.

I slipped out of bed and went to the window where I could look down into the patio. The usual night light burned, and I could see the pale glimmer of adobe and redwood at the far end, but nothing moved down there. All was blank and empty.

Suddenly I remembered.

Of course. *She* had been in the nightmare too. It was the picture of Doña Inés with her dog that had made me dream. She had been part of the nightmare. Looking at the painting again had disturbed me. But what was it about the dog? There had been something —something eerie, something monstrous. I couldn't remember.

I went to the other window and stood with a cool

wind blowing in upon me. Once more I could see moonlight shining on the snow peaks. Night hours were the worst. They would always be the lonely time—the time when courage fades and I am sure that nothing in my life will ever come right. Now something dark and threatening seemed to menace me, and Clarita's words echoed in my ears.

"You ask for killing," she had said.

But I didn't want killing, I wanted to live—as my mother had wanted to live. Because now there was Gavin. Yet there could be no turning back. I had gone too far. Eleanor had gone too far. There was no safety anywhere, and I had to live, somehow, until it was over.

Questions were sharp in my mind. Where had Paul really been at the time Kirk had died? Where had Clarita been? For that matter, where had Sylvia been at a time when she was angry with her stepbrother for quarreling with Paul?

I managed to sleep a little, and there were no more dreams that I could remember in the morning. I rose early and found only Clarita at the breakfast table. Her hair was not smoothed as usual, and for once she wore no earrings. It was as if something in her had begun to give up. I wondered what had passed between her and Juan, but I was not likely to know because she barely spoke to me. Indeed, I think she hardly saw me there at the table.

Eleanor didn't appear at all, but Gavin joined us, and Clarita did not speak to him either. A restraint lay upon all of us, and though Gavin looked at me with concern, he made no attempt at conversation.

Not until I was about to leave the table, did he make his suggestion.

"Amanda, will you come to the store with me this morning? I've already phoned Paul and he'll join us there. We can't let the matter of the attack on you pass without some investigation. Perhaps we can reconstruct a little and find an answer. I'll also ask the salesgirls to check on whether anything is missing from their stock."

"What if it was Paul who struck me?" I said. "Or even Eleanor?"

Gavin sighed. "Anything is possible. But that's all the more reason why we have to make this effort. We'll both keep our eyes open for leads."

Clarita rose gravely from the table and went away toward her room without comment. I thought of her earring on the floor of the garage.

"Perhaps we should take Clarita with us," I said.

Gavin dismissed that as idle humor and looked at me down the table. I wanted to be in his arms, and I knew he wanted me there, but we both held back. Quick, stolen embraces under the roof of this house were not what either of us wished. Ahead of us were the mountains which had to be climbed. Higher than the Sangre de Cristos.

Paul met us at the store, as planned, and we went through a mock-up of all our actions of that night. It came to nothing. Paul seemed more than eager to help, but I didn't trust him, and I sensed a secret mockery behind all he said and did. Gavin and he were carefully polite to each other, but the enmity between them showed, and if Paul Stewart had come to the store with something to conceal, it was still carefully hidden by the time we left.

Only one thing of any consequence happened during the hour we spent wandering the aisles of CORDOVA —and that occurred inside my own head. I began to worry again about my dream of the night before. What was it that disturbed me about Doña Inés and her dog? I began to wonder if the dog in the painting could have something special to tell me. The thought brought with it an impatience to get back to Juan's house, and to somehow have another look at the collection.

Luck played into my hands. When Gavin drove me home, and then went back to the store, Rosa met me at the front door and told me that Clarita had taken my grandfather for a drive. That left the field clear.

The moment Rosa went about her work at the far end of the house, I ran up the balcony steps and entered Juan's study. The drawer of his desk was locked, as I might have expected, and the keys to the collection were there, where I couldn't get them. While I was wondering what to do, I heard a sound that froze me. A sound that came from Juan's bedroom.

I could have escaped. I could have fled out his study door and gone to another part of the house without being seen. But I had to know who stirred in his empty room while Juan was away. It took only a moment to drop down behind his long sofa and crouch there perfectly still.

The sound that came from his bedroom was one I recognized. It was the closing of a door. Someone had come up the passageway from the patio and let himself into Juan's bedroom. A moment later there were steps into the study and the sound of a drawer being unlocked and opened. I peered around the end of the couch and saw Eleanor standing there. Her key was in the lock of the very drawer I had wanted to open, but she was not taking out the collection keys—she was putting them back.

From the living room, Rosa called to her, and Eleanor closed the drawer hastily and went out to the balcony to answer. I lost no time. In a moment I had the drawer open, the collection keys out, and had closed it again. When Eleanor came back to lock the desk and take away the key, I was once more hidden.

When she removed her key from the desk drawer, she didn't linger, but went quickly out of the room, leaving by way of the balcony. I sprang up and hurried after her. When I reached the bedroom wing, I was in time to see her go through her own door at the far end of the hall. I tapped on the wood, and after a moment's hesitation she called to me to come in.

I stepped into a room that was entirely Eleanor's, and I knew she didn't share it with Gavin. Curtains and spread and rug were of soft colors that complemented her gold and cream. But I gave the room no more than a glance. It was Eleanor who held my attention.

She stood upon a pale blue scatter rug in the center of the floor, and I could see that she was still nervous. Her fingers played with the silver medallions of the concho belt slung low on her hips, and her eyes studied me with a wary regard.

"Why did you have the keys to the collection?" I asked.

She brushed a hand over the dishevelment of her blond hair. "What are you talking about?"

"I saw you just now in Juan's study when you put them back. Perhaps you wanted to know about the Velázquez too? You needn't worry. It hasn't been touched. He sent me to check."

She laughed and seemed to relax a little. "Good for you. If you must know, I was a bit worried and I had a look myself. Perhaps he infects us all with his concern about his great treasure."

"Would you keep it as he does—if it were yours?"

"Of course not." She answered easily. "I'd sell it on some black market and be rich for the rest of my life."

"Surely it ought to go back to Spain," I said.

"And if he writes you into his will, you'll send it there?"

"He won't do anything of the kind. He'll never take away what is yours. And I don't want anything he can give me—except the truth about my mother."

"As if you'd have anything to say about it!" She sauntered off the island of the rug and dropped onto a low ottoman, clasping her hands about her knees. A frown drew her brows together as if in puzzlement, and her mouth pursed quizzically. "Are you really like that, Amanda? Do you really care so little about money?"

"I can always earn money. Not a lot, but enough for what I need."

"And I suppose you're counting on Gavin anyway?"

"There isn't anything in Santa Fe that I count on."

She ducked her head down to her clasped hands for

an instant, and when she brought it up again she was smiling at me in a manner more friendly than I'd seen until now.

"It doesn't matter, Amanda. I don't want him anyway. Once he thought I was marvelous—but somehow he got over that. As I got over how I felt about him. But let's not talk about Gavin."

She rose from her stool and came swiftly toward me across the room. I stiffened, and she saw and laughed ruefully.

"You don't trust me at all, do you, Amanda? Not that I can blame you. That was an awful thing I did yesterday. I didn't really understand how it might affect you. Juan has been scolding me."

She seemed surprisingly contrite, but I knew she still didn't understand the effect she'd had on me. Eleanor lacked the faculty of empathy, and she would never understand how other people felt. What she had done could not be erased by an apology, and I turned toward the door. Before I had taken two steps, she was after me, clinging to my arm.

"Amanda, let me make it up to you. I told you I'd drive you out to Madrid one of these days so you could paint. Let's go now. Besides, there's something I want to show you out there—something you ought to see."

"What?" I asked bluntly. I had no desire to go with her anywhere, least of all to an empty ghost town.

"Something about your mother, Amanda. There's something out there I've never shown anyone. But I'll show you now, and it will answer a lot of your questions."

"Do you mean you know the answers?"

"Some of them."

"Then tell me here and now. We don't need to go anywhere."

Her hands moved in a helpless gesture. "You'd never believe me. You have to be shown."

I hesitated for a moment longer, thinking of the keys to the collection, a lump against my thigh in the pocket of my slacks. But Juan was away and perhaps he would not look for them for a while. And I could do what I wanted to do when we came home from Madrid. Inés and her pet could wait.

Eleanor saw indecision in my eyes, and she smiled at me with that charm I had seen her exert before. "Get your painting things, Amanda. You can have all the time out there you like."

"I'll just take my sketchbook," I said, and hurried off toward my room.

"Meet you in the garage," Eleanor called after me.

I picked up a sweater and my handbag with the sketchbook in it, and hurried down to join her. I'd made up my mind and I didn't dare linger to weigh whether what I was doing was sensible or not. In any case, Eleanor was unlikely to try anything in broad daylight, while I was watching her.

When I was beside her in the front seat, she wheeled the car a bit wildly out of the garage, and turned around in the street with a squealing of tires. It was as though she wanted to get away as quickly as possible. Without our being seen? I wondered.

Just before we pulled away, Clarita drew up in her car, with Juan Cordova in the front seat beside her. They both stared at us in surprise, and I leaned in the window to shout to Juan.

"Eleanor's driving me out to Madrid. I'm going to do some sketching."

Our car pulled away so fast that I wasn't sure they'd heard me, and Eleanor looked sulky.

"Why did you do that? You shouldn't have told anyone we were going out there."

"Whyever not?"

"You'll see," she snapped at me.

The narrowness of Canyon Road and its traffic slowed her down, but once we were out on the highway, turning south, she let out the car, going faster and faster, well over the speed limit. I wondered how many tickets for speeding she collected in the course of a year, and how she had managed to keep her driver's license. Los

Cerrillos, with their individual humpy hills, seemed to move toward us rapidly, and I could see the Ortiz Mountains rising beyond.

"It's wonderful to get away!" Eleanor cried, her sulkiness gone. "Don't you feel sometimes that Grandfather's house smothers you, walls you in?"

"I've felt that," I agreed. "But I'm surprised you feel that way."

"Of course I feel that way. Juan, Gavin, Clarita—all of them want to hold me down, keep me in a prison. But I'm going to escape. I'm going to show them all!"

She was becoming increasingly keyed up as we left Santa Fe behind, and I was filled with a growing uneasiness. I couldn't imagine Eleanor settling down and waiting for me quietly while I did some sketching, and my puzzlement as to why she was really bringing me out here grew. Once or twice I protested her speed, and she would heed me for a mile or two, and then press her foot on the gas pedal again so that the wind would whistle by. I hoped that Madrid was not far away.

Some twenty miles or so out of Santa Fe we found ourselves on a canyon road, and I saw ahead the houses of a town dotting a slope of hillside. Eleanor slowed the car.

"Here we are. Take a good look at it, Amanda. This is our history too. Once a great-uncle of ours ran a coal mine here, and we still own some property. But it's a dead town. As dead as the Cordovas."

Slipping past the car windows, the gray houses on the slope were derelicts. There was no adobe here, and all the houses were built of splintery gray frame. They stood with broken windows and sagging doors, looking drearily out upon nothing. Eleanor drove on slowly, until more weathered, unpainted houses lined each side of the road, with others crowding behind in what had once been a fair-sized town. She was right—this would be something to sketch and paint.

"Thousands of people lived here once," Eleanor said, slowing the car to a crawl. "That was when the mines flourished. A million tons of coal came out of just one seam in this area, and thousands of people flocked in. I've heard Juan tell how at Christmas time the ridges, the houses, the canyon sides were covered with lights at night. But now it's all dark and dead. A true ghost town. Like ours has been turned into a ghost family, Amanda."

Pulling the car off to the side of the road, she set the brake, opened the door and jumped out. Then she came around and opened my door.

"Come along! We've arrived, and there's something I want to show you before you start sketching.

Suddenly I didn't want to go with her. Crowding all about on the hillside, the ghost houses seemed inimical. They didn't want their sleep disturbed. They didn't want to be reminded of the life they no longer led. But Eleanor had already run across the scrabble of dry grass at the side of the road and was wandering in among the houses as they ranged above us.

"There's a sign that tells us to keep out," I called after her.

She turned and waved an arm at me, beckoning. "Who's to see? Besides, we belong here. We're ghosts too, aren't we? The ghosts of the great Cordova family!"

I got out of the car and followed her uneasily as she wound among the irregularly set houses, running ahead, pausing now and then to make sure I was coming.

The place set its spell upon me, and I almost forgot my cousin. I climbed broken steps and looked past a sagging door into a bare room, where floorboards had buckled and something brown scurried down a hole in the corner of a room. I backed away hastily, and after that limited myself to staring through broken panes of glass into long-abandoned interiors. Only the sound of my own steps disturbed the sleeping hush.

Ahead of me, Eleanor waited, the canyon wind blowing her bangs and lifting the tendrils of her long fair hair. I could feel the gusts on my face, and it was a chill gray wind that had nothing to do with the blue sky overhead, and bright New Mexico sunlight. It was a wind that belonged to the sleeping Madrid.

"These are the houses where the miners lived," Eleanor said. "The Cordova house was much grander, but it's long gone. It burned down one night, and no one ever knew how the fire started. Everything we touch turns to ashes."

With an effort I tried to resist her, tried to resist the very mood of the town around me.

"CORDOVA is hardly a pile of ashes," I said. "I suspect that it will always keep you nicely."

"Hush!" she whispered. "Don't laugh at them, Amanda. Don't make any sounds to wake them. They're all asleep and it's best to let them stay that way."

Unwilling to accept her fantasies, I tried to shut away the eerie sound of her voice. If I came here to paint, I might be willing to enter into such a mood, but I had no desire now to stop and sketch, and my growing feeling was that I'd like to turn my back on this place and go quickly away.

Ahead of me Eleanor moved on again, and I called after her.

"Let's go back. I've seen enough. I can sketch a bit in the car, and perhaps come here another time to paint."

Eleanor stepped from shadow into bright sunlight and flung out her arms. "Can you imagine what it's like at night, Amanda? I wonder if all the old ghosts come out and dance by moonlight? I'd like to be one of them. Maybe I am one of them."

I wasn't a child to be frightened by ghosts, but the uncanny mood which ruled her touched me. I'd had enough of Madrid, and I turned about and started down the hill, picking my path between the derelict houses, staying away from broken windows and empty doorways. At once Eleanor shouted to me, forgetting her own edict of silence.

"Wait! Don't go back yet, Amanda. We're almost there. You haven't seen what I can show you. You want to know about Doro, don't you?"

Her shouting roused a clacking of echoes among the bare, stark houses, as if they too shouted in protest at my departure, rattling their skeleton bones. I had begun to think that all her earlier talk about my mother had been pretense to get me out here for some reason that might put me at her mercy in this dead place. But she had come to a halt beside one of the gray houses where there were still panes of glass, where dark green shades had been drawn before all the windows, and the steps had been repaired, though unpainted.

She beckoned to me. "Come," she said, and I surrendered, turning about to climb the hillside and stand beside her. "Go in," she directed. "I've unlocked the door. Go in."

She spoke with the authority of Juan Cordova, and I found myself obeying. I climbed the three gray steps and put my hand on a cracked china doorknob.

"Open it," said Eleanor behind me.

I turned the knob and stepped into a strange world. At once she came up the steps and closed the door, so that we were shut together into a room that came out of the long ago.

In this place of abandoned dwellings and empty rooms, this room was completely furnished. There was wallpaper sprigged with blue cornflowers, instead of whitewashed walls, and at the three windows of this main room hung blue and white crisscross curtains. There was a wide brass bed, a small table with a marble top, a wooden rocking chair, and an easy chair upholstered in red plush. True, the wallpaper hung in strips in one corner, the curtains were limp and gray-hued, a nest had been built by some animal in the center of the blue bedspread, the brass bed knobs were tarnished, the red plush chair was worn shiny in the seat and raveled across the back, and there were cobwebs everywhere. Yet this room had been used and left furnished.

"Why?" I said. "Why?"

"Doro and Kirk fixed it up like this when they were

young—before Kirk went away, and Doro met your father. Clarita says they brought pieces of furniture from the hacienda, and bought other things. Doro made the curtains, which is why they're lopsided. It was their hideaway. When Juan and Katy thought they were at the *rancho,* well chaperoned, they would come here. What a romance they must have had!"

"But why has it been left like this? Does Juan know?"

"Probably. He knows everything. But he's shut it out of his consciousness. He won't accept what he doesn't want to accept. A love nest for Doro and Kirk was never in his picture. Katy knew, Clarita says, and she just locked it up after Doro and Kirk died. Clarita found the key to Katy's things one time, and when I was in my teens she brought me out here to tell me about her younger sister and the wicked young man she loved. Wicked in Clarita's lights."

Stirring up dust wherever I moved, I wandered about the room, aching a little for the broken romance my mother had suffered, even though I wouldn't be here if it had continued.

"Of course she never came here any more after Kirk went away and she met your father," Eleanor went on. "When they were both dead, Clarita brought your father here and showed this room to him. She said he had to understand about the woman he had married, so that he would take his daughter away from the Cordovas and never come back again."

The marble of the small table felt chill under my hand, and I whirled around angrily. "It's Clarita who was wicked. What a dreadful thing for her to have done!"

"She had to make him understand why Doro had killed Kirk. He wouldn't believe in their love until she showed him this."

"Clarita has no business calling anyone else wicked!"

Eleanor's smile was enigmatic and I didn't like the way she looked, or the fact that she'd brought me here.

Apparently the house had two rooms, for a second door opened at the back. It was ajar and to help regain my composure I left Eleanor, to walk through it. There was a rusty enamel sink under a window, and ancient pipes, a bare wooden table and two rickety chairs. No effort had been made to fix up the kitchen and if there had been a stove, it had been removed.

In one corner stood a small battered trunk, and I went over and raised the lid. Only emptiness and a lingering odor of mothballs greeted me. Except for one thing. I leaned over in surprise and picked up the tiny bonnet made of yellowed satin and lace—a baby bonnet which lay in the bottom of the trunk. The uneven stitches told me that Doroteo had made this too, but if she had made it for me, how had it come to this place on which she'd never looked back?

When I'd closed the trunk, I carried the bonnet into the other room to show Eleanor.

"What do you make of this?"

Eleanor had no interest in baby clothes. She was watching me with something electric about her that made me uneasy.

"Amanda," she said, "do you believe the old stories about the Cordova curse that came down from Doña Inés? Do you think there's a strain of madness in all of us?"

Her eyes were alight with some excitement I did not like, and there was no kindness, no friendliness in her smile. Perhaps there was a little madness in all of us. Even in me, who had thought herself outside the reach of the Cordovas.

She went on softly, while I moved about the room again, trying to shake off the spell she was weaving.

"I wonder what she was really like—Inés? I wonder how she felt when she stood beside that bed in the middle of the night with the blood of her victim staining her hands and her gown. Was Emanuella afraid of her then?"

There was something insidious about her words, about the very tone of her voice. I had to face up to her and I mustn't let her frighten me.

"It was you behind that fetish I found in my room both times, wasn't it?" I said. "And you who put Doña Sebastiana in my bed? Was it you, too, who used the whip in the patio and—"

"And struck my grandfather down?" Eleanor cried.

"He wasn't hurt. And perhaps you used the brass statue of Quetzalcoatl in the store?"

As she stared at me, her face looked utterly white beneath the frame of her long hair. "I haven't been as clever as all that. The fetish, yes. And those tricks on Gavin with the stone head and other things. Aunt Clarita helped me because we both wanted him in wrong with Juan. But they were silly attempts and they never worked. I didn't do any of the other things, and perhaps that was my mistake, Amanda."

Her eyes were fixed upon me so intently that I felt myself held by her gaze. Yet I knew I must get away from her. Something was building. If there was madness, it was activated now, and I could believe nothing she said except that she meant me harm. I dared not turn my back to her, and I began to move stealthily backward toward the door, a step at a time. She didn't seem to notice because she was looking around the room. Her attention fixed itself upon a narrow, splintery board that had fallen from the molding of a window, and with a quick, darting movement she sprang toward it, picked it up with both hands. I could see the rusty nails protruding from one end as she fixed me again with the bright excitement of her look.

"So you thought you would take my inheritance, Amanda? And now you want to take Gavin. But you aren't going to, you know. There's no place to run to. This will be worse than a *disciplina*, Amanda. If I choose, you may never leave this little house where your mother used to come. It might take them years to find you. And when they did, you'd look like Doña Sebastiana in her death cart."

I couldn't stand there and wait for her to come toward me, to strike me. I had to be quicker than she was—I had to get away. Whirling toward the door, I made a dash for it, tearing it open, flinging myself down the steps—and straight into the arms of Gavin Brand.

# XVII

Gavin held me, steadied me, and for a moment I clung to him in helpless relief. There was no movement in the room behind me, and when I had control of my legs, I turned and stared at Eleanor.

She held the splintered board in one hand, and she was laughing. "Oh, Amanda! I really frightened you, didn't I? You were such a sitting duck, I couldn't resist. Gavin, where on earth did you spring from?"

He answered her coldly. "Juan saw you and Amanda taking off in your car with all that wheel squealing, and he was worried. When Amanda called out that you were going to Madrid, he had Clarita phone me to come after you."

Eleanor flung down the board with a violent gesture. I could imagine her with the whip that she'd denied.

"Please—I'd like to go," I said to Gavin.

He put an arm around me and walked away from that small, haunted house, leaving Eleanor to its ghosts. More than ever, she was my enemy now, and there was nothing I could do about it. In Gavin's car I put my head against the seat back and closed my eyes. I could sense his anger with Eleanor as his hands grasped the wheel and he turned about on the highway. But he was angry with me too.

"Why did you go with her? Why did you trust her?"

"She said she would show me something about my mother," I told him. "And she did. Did you know that room existed? Did you know my mother used to come there with Kirk?"

"I didn't know. Clarita told me where to look. But what good does it do for you to know?"

I was still holding the yellowed lace bonnet in my hands and I help it up for him to see. "Perhaps this is *my* Cordova madness. That I want to put together all the pieces about my mother."

I folded the bonnet and put it away in my bag. Whatever I learned seemed to add more questions, never to answer them. I couldn't even be sure whether Eleanor had meant me real harm, or only wanted to vent her spite by frightening me.

"The way never opens," I said miserably.

Gavin didn't answer, and I knew it was closed for him too as the wedge between us grew wider. He would be happy with me only if I went away, as would my grandfather.

As we neared Santa Fe, I thought again of the keys in my pocket. I must visit the collection before Clarita or Juan knew I was home, and now Gavin must come with me.

We entered the city with silence growing between us, and there was nothing we could find to say. When we reached Canyon Road, I asked him to come with me out to the collection, and told him something was troubling me about the picture. He parked the car and we entered the patio through the garage. If anyone saw us, at least no one called out.

When we reached the building with the peaked roof, I gave the keys to Gavin and he opened the door. We stepped into inner darkness and stood for a moment listening. There was no sound anywhere, not indoors or out. He led the way through dimness to the alcove at the back and turned on the switch for the lamp above the Velázquez. In an instant the painting was flooded with light.

Doña Inés looked down at us with her strange, demented eyes that now seemed a little like Eleanor's eyes as I had seen them in a ghost town that morning.

It was not the dwarf who interested me, however, but her dog. The animal lay at her feet—silver gray, with its forepaws outstretched, its hound's ears cocked and pointed.

"Look at the dog!" I cried to Gavin. "Velázquez never painted a dog so clumsily."

Now that I was paying careful attention and not taking something for granted, other details sprang to view. The tiny hand of the dwarf, curled against her breast, the face itself, all were subtly wrong. The very texture of the master—never to be matched—was missing.

"This was never painted by Velázquez," Gavin agreed.

"We've got to tell Juan!" I reached for the switch and turned off the light. When we'd locked the door, we hurried toward the house together.

We found my grandfather in his study and he fixed me with a cold look as we burst in. "Was it you who took my keys, Amanda?"

I placed them on the desk before him, but when Gavin would have spoken, I put a hand on his arm.

"When you used to paint," I said to Juan, "did you ever learn by copying old masters?"

"Yes, of course. I visited museums in various countries, and I made many copies. It's a good way to learn. When the Velázquez came into my hands, I made a copy of that. Probably it is still around somewhere, if you'd like to see it. Though I did the dog badly—I was never good at painting animals."

Gavin and I looked at each other. Clarita had heard us talking and she came upstairs to the study.

"The Velázquez is missing from the collection," Gavin

said. "The picture that's been hung in its place must be the one you painted long ago."

The old man did not move or speak. He sat frozen at his desk, his eyes fixed upon Gavin. Clarita made a soft, moaning sound and sank into a chair, though it seemed to me that she was watching her father warily.

"Surely this is the time to bring in the police," I said to Gavin.

He shook his head. "There'd be a tremendous uproar and publicity. The painting might be taken away, if it was recovered."

"Exactly," Juan said coldly. "Which I will not have. As long as I live it is mine. What happens later does not matter."

"Then how can you recover it?" I asked.

"I will recover it. Where is Eleanor?"

"We left her in Madrid," Gavin said. "I got there in time to prevent her from tormenting Amanda."

Juan looked at me. "This is why I sent Gavin after you. I didn't want her to do some reckless thing that might injure her."

"She might have injured me," I said dryly.

"Why did you go with her, then?"

Clarita began to utter little sounds of distress, as though she wanted to prevent me from speaking, but I answered him without heeding her.

"Eleanor wanted to show me something out there. Do you know that the house where my mother and Kirk used to meet is still there, and that a room in it is furnished?"

"What are you talking about?" Juan's fierce, dark gaze pinned me, demanded the truth from me, but before I could go on, Clarita broke in.

"Please, please—it is nothing. I can explain everything."

Juan turned that dark look upon his eldest daughter. "You have had to do too much explaining today. Do you remember what I told Katy? Do you remember that my order was to have that house torn down, and everything in it destroyed?"

For just an instant before Clarita bowed her head, I saw the look of malice she turned upon him, and I knew that if Juan had an enemy to fear, it was Clarita. But she answered meekly enough.

"Yes, I remember. But my mother would not do it. Everything else of Doro's had been destroyed or disposed of. Only this was left, and my mother wanted to keep it. Though Doro never went there after Kirk left Santa Fe."

"Then it is to be destroyed now," Juan said. "I will not have that place left standing."

I broke in. "But, Aunt Clarita, she must have gone there at some time after he left. Because of this."

I opened my handbag and took out the bonnet of yellowed lace and dropped it on the table before Juan. As he stared at it blankly, Clarita gasped, and a strange thing happened. She left her chair, and it was as if she left her body, her former spirit. As I watched in astonishment and some dismay, she became the woman I had seen briefly at the dinner table—the woman who had worn claret velvet and comported herself with the arrogant confidence of a Cordova. Even in her habitual black, she seemed now to grow in stature—and in subtle menace.

"No," she said. "Doro never returned to Madrid." She reached past me and picked up the bonnet, stood looking at it in her hands as though it fascinated her. Then she held it out to Juan. "Do you remember this, my father?"

He stared at the small scrap of lace and satin with an air of dread, and he did not answer her. After a moment she went proudly out of the room, carrying the bonnet with her.

Juan made no effort to stop her, and as she had grown, inexplicably, he seemed to shrink in his chair. The lines in his face grew more deeply etched. Paying no attention to either Gavin or me, he stood up and crossed the room to his long couch. I expected him to lie down upon it, but he did not. Feeling beneath the pillow, he reassured himself that something was there, and returned to his desk. I knew he had searched for the dagger.

"My enemies gather," he said dully. "Go now and leave me. I must think. When Eleanor returns, send her to me."

Though Gavin might have stayed to argue, he accepted the edict when I did, and we went down to the living room together.

"What is happening?" I cried, and Gavin shook his head unhappily.

"I don't know, Amanda. Except perhaps about the painting."

"You know what's happened to that?" I asked in surprise.

"I can guess. But I'm not going to make any wild accusations. We'll wait until Eleanor comes back from Madrid."

However, she did not return to the house for the rest of the day. Gavin went to the store, and my grandfather remained alone. As did Clarita in her room, without going near him. I wondered what had transpired when he had accused her of lying about being at that window.

By midafternoon, I decided that I must talk to someone, and the logical person was once more Sylvia Stewart. Without telling anyone where I was going, I ran down through the patio and let myself into the next-door yard. Across the Stewart *portal* the living-room door stood open. I called out Sylvia's name, but had no answer. Yet I could hear a light, clicking sound coming from Paul's workroom.

No matter what I was interrupting, I had to find Sylvia, and I stepped to the door and looked in. Paul was nowhere in sight, but his wife sat at the desk. The sound I'd heard was the idle tapping of a pencil as she drummed it on the desk, but she didn't know I was there, so absorbed was she in the yellow second sheets before her. Her brown head was bowed over the manuscript, her lips slightly parted as she read with excitement.

It was necessary to interrupt, and I spoke softly so as not to startle her. "Sylvia?"

Nevertheless, the startling was extreme. She dropped her pencil and jerked around to face me, a bright flush rising in her cheeks as she stared at me.

"I'm sorry," I said. "I did call out when I came in the door from the *portal,* but you didn't hear me."

Her dazed look told me she was still far away, though the flush in her cheeks indicated that guilt of some sort was surfacing.

"I thought you were Paul!" she cried. "He'd have a fit if he knew I was reading his manuscript. But he got a phone call a little while ago and went out, so I took this chance."

"Is that his book about Southwest murders?" I asked.

"Yes. And the chapter about the Cordovas is going to be all right." For some reason she seemed tremendously relieved. "I was afraid he would stick too closely to the facts, but he's fictionizing again. It will be all right."

When she turned back to the pages, I stepped close to her chair to look over her shoulder, but at once she flipped the sheets face down.

"No, Amanda. I can't let you read this unless Paul says so. It's one thing to pry when I'm his wife, but something else when it comes to letting other people see."

She pushed away from the desk and turned off the typewriter lamp. "Let's go where we can be comfortable. What's been happening? You look thoroughly keyed up."

I couldn't let the matter of Paul's book go so easily. "If he fictionizes—when he's dealing with facts—won't he chance trouble from Juan Cordova?"

"Perhaps not. He's glamorizing Doro and making out Kirk a villain. I don't think Juan will object to that."

While I trailed her back to the other room, she waved me into a chair and flung herself down on a couch with bright canary pillows tossed among the brown.

"Can I get you something to drink, Amanda?"

"Thanks, no. Why are you so relieved about Paul's book? What did you think he'd write?"

With an elaborate effort, she busied herself finding a pack of cigarettes, offering it to me, tapping one out for herself when I refused—all the while plainly marshaling what she would say to me.

"After all, that whole affair is pretty thin ice, isn't it?" she said. "If Paul were clumsy, he might crash us all through into freezing water."

"What do you mean?"

"Oh, nothing much. If it's what you're curious about, he isn't making anything of that brainstorm you had about a third person appearing on the hillside. Though he is doing quite a thing about the frightened child and her loss of memory."

"I don't like that," I told her. "And perhaps that third person will come clear."

With a shrug, Sylvia blew smoke into the air. "I'm afraid he's given up asking you. What's wrong, Amanda? Has something happened to bring you here?"

"I just wanted to talk. Sylvia, what do you know about a house the Cordovas own out in Madrid?"

Her eyes widened as she stared at me. "Don't tell me that place is back in the picture?"

"Eleanor took me there today. She said my mother and your stepbrother used to meet there."

"That's true enough. Fixing up the house and trying to keep it secret was one of Doro's wilder fantasies. And Kirk had as wild a streak as she had, so he went right along with it. I warned him that there'd be an explosion if Juan Cordova ever found out. And of course there was. Doro was his darling and he loved Kirk like a son. But they were both too young, and he was a proper Spanish father. So he packed Kirk off to South America and put Doro into Katy's care as though she were a nun. Which she certainly wasn't."

"And then he ordered the house destroyed?"

"Yes, he wanted all evidence of their affair wiped out."

Her nervous smoking made me even more edgy and I wished she would put down her cigarette. Ever since I'd first met Sylvia, I'd known that some deep worry was eating away inside her, and I still wanted to know what it was.

"What do *you* believe?" I asked her. "Do you think it could have been Juan on that hillside, angry with Kirk because he'd come back to bother Doroteo?"

"Maybe it was!" Sylvia pounced on my words so eagerly that I knew she didn't believe in them. Why should she want me to go down a side road, unless there was something she wanted to hide?

"You don't believe that," I contradicted. "Because Juan wouldn't have minded their marrying if Doro hadn't been so young. He was fond of Kirk, but wanted to give them both time to grow up and know their own minds. Katy urged that too. And they were right. Because she forgot about your stepbrother and fell in love with my father. But there's more I wanted to talk about."

I hesitated, wondering whether to tell her about the whole dreadful episode with Eleanor. When I'd decided not to, I went on.

"While I was poking around out in that house, I found an old baby bonnet my mother must have made for me. But when I brought it home and asked Clarita about it, she behaved strangely. She said Doro had never gone back to that place after Kirk left. So who took a bonnet of mine out there and left it?"

Sylvia ground out her cigarette with another of her nervous gestures. "Clarita was lying. Doro did go back. She went back for one last time. Clarita was with her. But I won't talk about that, so you needn't ask me. Let it alone, Amanda."

How often she had said that to me—"Let it alone." But I would never let it alone now, though I didn't press her at the moment. There was another question I wanted to ask.

"Sylvia, who was it that found Kirk's body, and then my mother's? Why has no one ever told me that?"

She stared at me without answering, and I went on.

"It was Paul, wasn't it? He wasn't with you on the road, as he let me think earlier. After he saw Clarita away from the house, he came along that path by himself—and found them both. It was he who raised the alarm, wasn't it?"

"Why do you think that?"

"You're stalling," I said. "I remember his being there."

The words seemed to echo through the room and dash themselves against the white painted walls, astonishing me as well as Sylvia.

"You—*remember?*" Sylvia repeated softly.

In strange confusion I tried to examine the thing that had just come to me. I seemed to see a man rushing about, calling people, trying to be helpful. He was a younger version of Paul.

"I think I remember. Something is coming back to me."

"The third one in the struggle?" The words were almost a whisper.

"I don't know."

Suddenly I didn't like the way she was looking at me— no longer in her half-jesting, easy manner, but with something inimical in her eyes. I stood up and moved toward the door.

"Thanks for letting me talk, Sylvia. I'll run along now."

She was not like Eleanor. In spite of the way she looked, she might have let me go without a word to stop me, but I stopped myself, pausing in the doorway.

"Did you know," I said, "that Juan's Velázquez has been stolen? The painting of Doña Inés is gone from the collection. An old student painting of Juan's has been put in its place."

The pallor that had replaced her earlier flush was alarming. She looked so sick and faint that I stepped back into the room.

"Are you all right? Can I get you a drink of something?"

But as I had always suspected, Sylvia was a woman of strength when she had to be strong. She sat erectly on the couch and stared at me without blinking.

"I'm perfectly all right," she said. "Why shouldn't I be?"

I put her to no further strain, but went out the door onto the *portal*. When I turned and looked back, she was sitting exactly as I had left her, staring after me, and I knew she would do so until I was out of sight.

The gate in the wall stood ajar, and I went through it and back to the house. I'd been given no answers to anything except the one fact that Paul Stewart had found Kirk's body the day he had been shot.

Eleanor had still not returned, and she did not appear during dinner or later in the evening. With Paul gone too, I wondered if they had met somewhere and were plotting together. Perhaps they were already busy trying to sell the Velázquez on some black market. If Eleanor had given him the keys, Paul could have spirited it out of its frame and made the substitution the day we were all out at the *rancho*. It seemed clear now that this must have been why Eleanor had wanted us away from the house, and why Paul had stayed home. But how was anything to be proved? Eleanor wanted money in her hands, and this could be a way to get it, as well as a daring escapade of the sort that would be to her liking. In a way, she was only taking what belonged to her, since she would inherit the painting anyway. But the injury to Juan Cordova was great—perhaps because he too suspected what had happened, as undoubtedly Gavin had. And Clarita? She knew Eleanor best of all, and I remembered her little performance of shock, during which she had watched her father warily while she was moaning in distress.

In any case, since that moment when she had picked up the bonnet she had become the woman who had worn claret red the night of Juan's party. She had finally come out of her room, and she moved about the house with her head high—clearly in command. I heard her telling Juan that he'd had a difficult day and he had better go to bed early. A role of authority she would never have dared assume toward him earlier. I saw him again that evening, though only to tell him good night, and he seemed a weary and beaten man. For the first time I had a feeling of sympathy for him, but I would not insult him by showing it. As Clarita's strength increased, his own faded.

Gavin did not appear at all, and I had no idea where he was, or exactly how things stood between us. The climate of the house was uneasy, and all my early dread of it seemed to have returned, so that I moved quickly and kept an eye upon the shadows. Something must be done, and I must do it. But what? And what, if anything, did the sudden flash of memory I had had about Paul mean?

I took some books up to bed and read for a while before I fell asleep around eleven o'clock. I'd placed a chair under the knob of my door, since I had no lock and key, and I knew that anyone who tried to enter would have to waken the house as well as me. So I could fall asleep without fearing an intruder.

It was after one in the morning when a sound woke me. It had been distant—not at the door of my room. I left my bed and ran to remove the chair from beneath the doorknob. Was Juan abroad again? There was a sound from the living room, as though someone hurried through it. Going toward Juan's room?

I put on a robe and slippers and went softly down the stairs. Everything was quiet, and there was no sound from Juan's room. Perhaps I had been wrong, but it might be better to rouse Clarita or Gavin, so we could investigate together.

When the scream came from the direction of the

balcony outside my grandfather's room, it shattered all silence. That was Eleanor's voice. After the first cry of fright, I could hear her screaming, "No, no!" hysterically.

Clarita and Gavin came in moments, but I was the first one up the balcony steps. Juan's study was dark and as I fumbled for the switch, the scene sprang to life to show Eleanor, fully dressed, standing beside Juan's desk. Evidently he had been sleeping on the couch, for it was covered with rumpled bedclothes, but now he stood grasping Eleanor by one arm, and he held the Toledo dagger in his other hand.

"He was going to stab me!" Eleanor wailed. "I felt the knife!"

The old man tossed the dagger onto the couch and reached for Eleanor with both hands.

"Hush, *querida,* hush. I would never hurt you. But when I heard someone come close to my couch, I grasped the dagger and sprang up. I thought you meant me injury. I didn't know until I touched you who it was."

She pressed her head against his shoulder, still sobbing, clinging to him, letting him smooth her hair, comfort her. She was no longer the woman I had seen in Madrid. Since those moments when she had threatened me, all the venom had gone out of her, and the adventurous spirit with it.

Clarita stood proudly back, somehow giving the impression that she could take charge if she chose, but did not wish to.

Gavin waited for only a little of Eleanor's sobbing. "What were you doing here in the dark?" he asked her. "At this hour?"

She hid her face against the old man's shoulder and would not answer. One hand flicked behind her, and I heard a tinkle that was familiar. When I picked it up from the carpet and held it out, the ring of keys was still warm from her hand.

Gavin took it from me gingerly. "What did you want with these, Eleanor?"

Again she would not answer, and Juan Cordova

looked at us over her head, recovering some of his authority.

"Let her be. I have frightened her badly. I left my bed to sleep here, so my enemy would not find me where expected. I did not know it was Eleanor—but thought it was someone who meant me harm."

"Was it you who came that other time and stood by Grandfather's bed?" I asked Eleanor.

She recovered herself slightly so there was a hint of defiance in her voice. "I came once before. I didn't think he knew."

Again Gavin tried to question her. "Where have you been? We've been looking for you since early afternoon."

This time she chose to reply. "I stayed in Paul's study. He let me stay there while he worked. Not even Sylvia knew I was there. I didn't want to see any of you."

This, I knew, was a lie. Paul had not been in his study. But Sylvia and I had. So why this stealthy visit to Juan's study, and why the filching of his keys?

"Come, Eleanor." Clarita spoke with decision. "You have caused enough trouble today."

"Go with her," Juan said, and Eleanor walked away from him and let Clarita put an arm about her shoulders. Her eyes looked a little glassy, whether from tears or because she was staring so fixedly at nothing, I couldn't be sure.

Juan returned to his couch and picked up the dagger, thrust it once more beneath his pillow. "No one will get to me," he said. "You can see that I am able to protect myself."

"Against what?" Gavin asked. "Against whom?"

The old man did not answer. "Tell Clarita to stay away," he said, and settled himself beneath the covers. Gavin helped to pull up the blanket, but at Juan's request we did not turn off the lights when we went away.

Gavin put his arm about me as we descended to the living room. "Are you all right, Amanda?"

"I don't know," I said. "I feel as if I were walking a ridge with a precipice on either side. Walking it blindfolded. Perhaps I'm the one playing Blind Man's Buff behind the turquoise mask. If I could take it off, I'd see everything clearly. But I can't remove it. If I look into a mirror I'll see it on my face."

"No, you won't," he said, and turned me about gently to face the fireplace.

I saw it then—where someone had hung it against the rounded chimney. The mask looked out over the room, and I shivered, turning away from it, clinging to Gavin.

He held me close, kissed me. "I've wanted to tell you," he said. "I'm leaving this house late tomorrow. I'm taking the first steps."

Cold waters seemed to close over my head. His presence was my security. No matter which way I had turned, he had been there to guard me. The steps he was taking had to be—yet now I would be vulnerable, open to any one of them who wanted to attack.

"I want you out of this house too," Gavin went on. "And you will be soon. But for the moment you'll be all right. I've talked to Clarita."

I looked up at him. "Clarita?"

"Yes. I've made her understand. She doesn't approve of divorce, but she knows that neither Eleanor nor I can be held any longer in this marriage. Juan can't have his way, and I think in a sense she's glad to oppose him. But now she'll watch out for you. I doubt that there'll be any danger from Eleanor again. In fact, now that you've faced them all down, I don't think anyone will try to threaten you."

I didn't know this for sure. I didn't know it at all, but he had never believed in what I was trying to prove. That someone else had killed Kirk, and not my mother.

He raised my chin and kissed me again, not tenderly this time, but roughly, so that I felt a sense of rising storm in him—and liked it. Here was a man who would respect me as a person—some of the time. And he would dominate me some of the time, so that I might have to fight him for my own existence. If I chose to fight. Perhaps I wouldn't always, and yet I knew that he would never hurt me when my defenses were down. And he would always want me to paint—so the rest didn't matter.

He turned me about and faced me in the direction of my room. "Go back to bed. You've stood enough for today."

Without looking back, I fled up the stairs to my room. Once more, I propped the chair beneath my doorknob before I got into bed, and then I went quickly, deeply, sweetly to sleep.

In the morning it was Clarita who awakened me, rapping sharply on the door and demanding that it be opened to her. I slipped out of bed and removed the chair, so that she could come into the room prow first like a battleship in full array.

"Gavin has talked with my father, and he has gone to the store for the last time today," she told me. "From now until the time you leave, you are to go nowhere without me. Gavin wishes it to be so."

I remembered a gold earring on the floor of the garage, and was silent, making no promises. Perhaps Gavin trusted her, but I did not. Yesterday I had seen Juan afraid of her and I knew it was against her he would defend himself with that dagger.

"What plans have you made for today?" she demanded.

"None. Perhaps I'll paint for a while here in my room. I have a picture to be finished. Perhaps I'll spend some time with my grandfather if he wants to see me."

"He will not want to see you. He is ill today. Dr. Morrisby has already come and he wants him to be very quiet. The last few days have been too much for him."

"I understand," I said meekly, not trusting her.

"Our doctor has had two visits to make here," she went on. "Sylvia is ill as well, and staying home from her shop. I have already been over to see her."

I could guess what might be wrong with Sylvia. She hadn't taken lightly my word that the Velázquez had been stolen. I suspected that she knew very well that her husband and Eleanor were involved, and today she had gone to pieces. But I said none of this to Clarita, merely murmuring my sympathy.

With a regal nod, Clarita went away, and I marveled at the change in her. Always she had been kept under the thumb of Juan Cordova. But now somehow their roles had been reversed, and I had the feeling that while he was afraid of his older daughter, she was no longer afraid of him. The change, I suspected, was more psychological than real, and it had something to do with that baby bonnet.

When I had breakfasted alone and returned to my room, I set up Juan's easel. My room that had once been Doroteo's was high and light, and would serve me well. When my painting of an imaginary desert village was in place, I set out the colors on my palette. I knew exactly what I was going to do to finish the picture. Coming up from the end of that narrow, winding road I would paint a burro, and on his back would be riding a Franciscan brother in a brown robe, with a knotted white belt about his waist. I could see him vividly in my mind, and he would add exactly the right touch to my ageless New Mexican painting.

But when I went to work, that rare and mysterious magic which sometimes occurs took over. One never counted on it. One worked with or without it. But sometimes when it came the work prospered beyond the means of an artist's talent, and he surpassed himself. Sometimes he even painted what he had not at first intended. It was like that now, and I knew the colors on my palette were wrong. I scraped them off and started fresh because accumulations of wrong colors could be a distraction and a discouragement.

The burro was not a burro. It was a palomino. And the man who rode it was not a Franciscan brother, but a Mexican *charro* in dark blue suede, with silver buttons and white braid and a broad white sombrero. He rode jauntily up into the foreground of my picture, his left hand light on the reins, and his face—tiny though it was—was Eleanor's.

I worked intently for an hour or more. The figure was small, not dominating the scene, but done in greater detail than its surroundings. And all the while I was telling myself something—something I knew with my feelings, but not with my conscious mind.

When the figure in dark blue riding his spirited horse was completed, I picked up the painting and carried it carefully downstairs. There were three people I wanted to show it to—Sylvia, Clarita and Juan. Strangely, Eleanor didn't matter. That inner thing that had caused me to paint was still ruling me, and it must be obeyed. First Sylvia—whether she was ill or not.

Clarita was not about, and I was glad to postpone that confrontation.

This time I found Sylvia Stewart lying in a deck chair where the sun slanted across the *portal,* a light Indian blanket tossed over her. She greeted me without pleasure and I told her I was sorry she wasn't feeling well, and asked if Paul was home.

"I've done a picture," I said. "I'd like you to see it."

She nodded languidly, and I turned the small canvas about. Sylvia stared at it with no great interest, and I brought it close so that she could focus on the rider of the palomino. At once she closed her eyes and turned her head away from me.

"You've caught the way he used to look," she said helplessly. "How did you know? That jaunty air of Kirk's, the expression on his face."

"I painted Eleanor," I said. "You weren't telling me the truth out at the *rancho*—none of you was telling the truth. Juan was Kirk's father, wasn't he? Kirk was Eleanor's uncle. The Cordova likeness is there in all of them."

Sylvia opened her eyes and stared at me. "You don't know, do you?" she said. "You truly don't know."

I remembered Paul saying those very words to me before, when they had concerned my mother.

"Hadn't you better tell me?" I asked.

"No. Never. It's not up to me."

She would be adamant, I knew. There was granite in Sylvia when she made up her mind.

"There's something else," I said. Carefully I set up my painting against a table, where nothing would smudge the wet portions. "There's the Velázquez."

She made no attempt at evasion. "What about it?"

"Do you think Paul and Eleanor have taken it away to sell?"

With a deep breath that seemed to strengthen her, she sat up and threw off the blanket. "I don't think so. Let's go and see."

"Did they tell you about taking it?" I asked, following her into the house.

"No. I guessed after you were here. And I checked to make sure. They didn't worry about how well they hid it."

Crossing the living room, she opened the door of a closet and rummaged about inside. When she didn't find what she was looking for, she dropped to her knees and padded about into the corners and over the floor with her hands. There was alarm in her eyes when she looked up at me.

"This is where Paul must have put it when he rolled it up. It was here yesterday."

Neither of us had noticed that the typing in the room beyond had stopped, and neither was aware of Paul until he stood behind us at the closet door.

"Put what?" he asked.

Sylvia didn't trouble to look up at him. "The Velázquez," she said from her creeping position.

I saw his face change. The green in his eyes had an angry glitter as he leaned over to grasp his wife's arm and pull her to her feet. Sylvia cried out and began to rub her arm when he released her.

"What are you talking about?" he demanded.

She continued to rub, but she answered him with spirit. "Oh, Paul, you're better at this sort of thing when it's done on paper. I'm sure everyone has guessed by now about your plotting with Eleanor. I suppose it was safe enough, because Juan would never punish her. But what have you done with the painting? You couldn't simply take it away and sell it. Not as quickly as this!"

Pushing past us both, he searched the closet himself. When he couldn't find the rolled-up canvas on the floor, or standing in a corner, he pushed things off the shelves, turned everything upside down and emerged at last in a rage.

"What's she trying now?" he demanded, and walked to a table where a telephone stood. In a moment he had dialed the Cordovas' number and was talking into the receiver. "She must be there, Clarita. Do look for her."

The phone at the other end was put down and for a time there was silence. Sylvia and I sat on the couch, waiting, not looking at each other. Paul's face was dark with anger and I would not have liked to be Eleanor at that moment.

"Everyone's guessed by now," Sylvia told him. "There's nothing you can do but return the painting. Why did you do this wild thing anyway?"

He turned his angry look upon her, and she winced away. Then Clarita was back on the line, and Paul listened.

"Thank you," he said in a dull voice, and hung up. "Eleanor can't be found. Her car's in the garage, but she's nowhere about. And apparently the Velázquez has disappeared with her. I suppose she could have taken a taxi. I suppose she could be halfway to Albuquerque by now."

"Then it's not your responsibility," Sylvia said. "There's nothing Juan can do about it, if Eleanor has the painting. You're lucky if you can get off so easily."

He rushed out of the room and onto the *portal*, his eyes searching the patio, the area about the house, as though he might still discover her. By chance his look fell upon my painting—and was arrested. He picked it up to hold it at arm's length, studying the small adobe village, the cottonwood trees, and winding road with that small meticulously painted figure riding up it.

"Why Eleanor?" he asked me.

"It's not supposed to be Eleanor," I said. "It's Kirk."

He stared as if the picture hypnotized him, but when he spoke, it was not of my work.

"No, she hasn't skipped out and taken the painting with her. I think I know what she'd do. Yesterday we were together awhile, and she was vacillating, uncertain —not like herself. She mentioned once that she'd like to go out to Bandelier again, to think things through. She has some sort of affinity for the place. This time she must have taken a taxi all the way—to throw us off by leaving her car behind."

"Then I hope you all let her go," Sylvia said fretfully. "She only does it so someone will chase after her and plead with her to come home."

"That's not what she wants," Paul said grimly. "But this time *I* am going after her. I'm going to bring her back."

Sylvia was up from the couch in a flash, flinging herself upon him, "No, Paul, no! Don't go now while you're angry. Wait awhile—wait!"

I stared at her in surprise, but Paul paid no attention. He was already heading for the garage. When I had picked up my painting, I left without either of them noticing me. It didn't matter. What Eleanor did now, or what happened to the Velázquez, no longer interested me. My own direction was clear. I could mark Sylvia off the top of my list. Clarita was next.

All was dim and quiet in the bedroom wing, and the first door—Clarita's—stood open. I paused on the threshold to call her name, but there was no answer. Just as I was about to leave, something I saw stopped me. A yellowed streamer of satin ribbon hung from beneath the lowered lid of a camphorwood chest.

In a moment I was across the room, lifting the lid of the chest. The baby bonnet lay on top of the piled contents, and something else lay there too. Eagerly

I reached in to pick up the top sheet of a sheaf of papers. Fading script seemed to spring at me from the page, and I saw the ragged inner edge, where the sheet had been torn from a book. All the pages beneath bore similar tears. So it had been Clarita out at the *rancho* that day, speeding away in a car, Clarita who had tumbled Katy's room in her search, and torn out the diary pages. Here beneath my hand lay Katy's words, and the answer to everything.

I began to read, standing where I was, following down the page the strong handwriting now so familiar to me. The words dealt, not as I had expected, with the day of Doro's death, but with reminiscence. She had been writing of the past.

> *It rained all that day. When I remember it, I always think of rain beating on the roof of that little house in Madrid. It was all we could do to climb the slope of hill and get her to the cabin because her time was already upon her. Clarita came with me, and old Consuelo, who knew about such matters. We boiled water for sterilizing, and listened to her moaning. All the while Clarita muttered angrily. I tried to hush her, but that day she was made only of anger against both of them. I did my best. My darling was frightened and needed affection, and I could give her that at least. She was my youngest and I had no blame for her, no anger in me. But we all knew Juan must be dealt with after it was over.*

I'd reached the bottom of the sheet, and I set it aside in the chest and picked up the next page. I knew what the baby bonnet meant now. It had never been intended for me. I wasn't born until five years later.

"What are you doing with my things?" The low, deadly voice spoke behind me and I whirled around.

Clarita's lips were pale, her eyes blazing, but I had to face her without wavering.

"I'm beginning to see," I told her. "My mother went back to that cabin to have her baby, didn't she? The baby who was born five years before me."

With a violent gesture, Clarita snatched the paper from my hands and tossed it back in the chest. She slammed down the lid, nearly catching my fingers beneath its edge. She wouldn't have cared if she had broken my hand, and I felt far more afraid of her than I had of Eleanor in Madrid. But there was no Gavin now to rescue me, no one about in this empty wing.

"You meddle," Clarita said, and her voice held its deadly level. "You've been meddling ever since you came here."

Carefully I moved away from the chest, edging toward the door. All this had happened before, in another place and another time, but this time the intent was more dangerous. Nevertheless, I had to face her, I had to know.

"It was you in the patio with the whip, wasn't it? Even to whipping your father, whom you hate. It was you in the store, wielding that brass statue of Quetzalcoatl. You'd kill me if you could because of all the hatred in you. For me and for my mother. Why? Because she was the favored one always?"

Her eyes never left mine, her expression never changed, but she stood utterly still, and there was a difference— as though all life and hope were seeping from her. Now a great deal was coming clear to me. By the time I'd reached the doorway, she still had not moved, had not tried to stop me. In a moment I would be free to escape her. But there was even more to be said.

"Now I understand about you and my grandfather. You had to bend to whatever Juan wanted because Eleanor has been like a daughter to you, and you knew he could disinherit her to spite you, if he chose. But after she took the Velázquez, you knew she would have money enough for the rest of her life, and you wouldn't bow to him any longer. The turning point must have come when you held that bonnet in your hands and you thought of what all of you had been through. So you weren't afraid any more. He had too much pride of family to betray what had happened. But I know now who came along that hillside with a gun in hand. You hated Kirk by then, didn't you? Not only because he wouldn't look at you when you were younger, but also because of what he'd done to your sister, and thus to Juan and your family."

With an effort, Clarita managed to break her frozen posture, and she made a lunge toward me. But I was already gone from the doorway, running down the hall and into the main house. I left my painting behind. It didn't matter now. I understood about the thing some hidden consciousness had told me, and there would be no need to show my work to Juan. What Katy had written changed all that.

I ran across the living room and up the balcony steps to Juan Cordova's room. I didn't know how much he had discovered over the years, or how much he knew now, but he had to be told all the truth, and at once.

With both his hands flat upon its surface, he sat behind his desk. His skin looked gray and his eyes sunken. An inch away from his fingers lay the dagger with the Damascene handle, and he was staring at it. Because I knew Clarita would follow me, I burst into words that were not altogether coherent.

"I've seen what Katy wrote in her diary!" I cried. "Clarita had the missing pages hidden away in her room. So I know about the baby that was born in Madrid. I know everything."

He did not move or look at me. He was a very old man and life was nearly over for him. It would not be possible for him to bear very much more. I was suddenly sorry that I'd burst in on him so explosively, but I had had to before Clarita could do something drastic. She was already there behind me in the doorway, though she didn't cross the threshold but merely stood there in silence.

Juan must have sensed her presence, for he raised his

eyes slowly from the dagger. When he spoke his voice was low and hoarse.

"What have you done, Clarita?"

His elder daughter extended her hands in a gesture of despair. "It is not what I have done. It's this one—this viper you have brought into your household!"

"Where is Eleanor?" Juan asked, ignoring her spite.

Clarita was silent again.

"Bring her to me," Juan said. "I must speak with her at once. I will tell her everything myself."

"No—no!" Clarita took a step toward him. "She will never forgive me. Or you. She will never forgive the deception."

"I will tell her," he said dully.

"I'm afraid you can't tell her anything for a while," I put in. "Paul Stewart thinks she's gone to Bandelier again. He's gone after her. Because of the Velázquez. They took it, you know. They plotted its theft between them."

When he chose, Juan's eyes could still blaze as fiercely as Clarita's and he turned that searing look upon me, so that I winced beneath it, and drew back. But he only waved me aside.

"Paul has gone to Bandelier—after Eleanor?" Life seemed to return to him. With no evidence of weakness, he stood up from his desk and walked toward his daughter. "Then you will take me there. We must follow them at once. The Velázquez must be recovered, and Paul must not be alone in that wilderness with Eleanor."

"But, Father—" Clarita began, only to have him hush her fiercely. "At once. You will drive me."

He went out of the room and she hurried to help him on the steps. It was clear that his will was once more ascendant, and he would have his own way. I didn't wait to hear them leave the house, to hear the starting of the car, but picked up Juan's phone and dialed CORDOVA's number.

When Gavin's voice came on, I told him quickly that Eleanor had gone out to Bandelier and Paul had gone after her. That now Juan was forcing Clarita to drive him there. I attempted to tell him nothing more, since there was no time, and he responded with blessed speed.

"I'll get out there," he told me. "I'll be leaving at once. Juan shouldn't be making that drive."

When I heard the click of the phone, I hung up and went slowly out of the room. There was nothing I could do now. The wheels were turning without me, and they couldn't be stopped or swerved from the course they would follow. I didn't know what would happen to Clarita now, or how what she had done all those years ago would affect all our lives in the present. The coming hours would be anxious ones, but at least Gavin would be there, and he would search for Juan and the others. Once more Eleanor had turned us all toward Bandelier.

# XVIII

As I moved through quiet rooms, I remembered that this was Rosa's afternoon off, and the house was empty. No one was nearby except Sylvia, in the next house. Now if I chose, I could return to Clarita's room and read the rest of those diary pages. But I had no desire to. I felt a little limp. The full story would come out now, and it could wait. It was enough for me to know that Doroteo Austin had never been guilty of murder. Why and how she had died, I still didn't know, but perhaps her spirit could rest, now that all the truth would be known.

Only Doroteo's own quiet room could offer me solace, I thought, as I climbed the stairs. I wanted to be quiet and understand, not only what had happened on that hillside, but all the ramifications of that secret birth in the little ghost town of Madrid.

My door stood open as I had last left it, and I walked unsteadily into the room. In reaction to wildly spent emotions, my legs felt rubbery, and I wanted only to lie for a while on my bed and let the earth spin around me. But someone had been there, for a long roll of canvas lay upon the bed.

It took me only a moment to partially unroll it from

the bottom of the painting until Doña Inés' small feet, and the feet of the dog which crouched beside her came into view. With hands that shook, I unrolled farther until the full figure of the dwarf was displayed. This was the real Velázquez—fragile, precious—though how it had come to be left on my bed, I didn't know. Eleanor must have put it there.

Behind me I heard the faint swish of sound, and turned just in time to catch the movement of the bedroom door as it swung shut. I whirled about—and faced my cousin Eleanor. No—my sister Eleanor.

She wore her jeans and concho belt, and she stood with one foot crossed jauntily over the other, and her arms akimbo.

"Hello, Amanda," she said, her head tilted in cocky defiance. "How do you like my turning honest woman and giving back the painting?"

I glanced toward the bed and then at her. "I thought it must be you. But why—why?"

"I'd have preferred to return it to its frame," she said. "I went out yesterday to see if I could do it by myself— when you caught me putting back the keys. Then last night I tried to get the keys from Grandfather's desk, but he caught me. And he hasn't been out of his study all day. So I thought I'd leave it here before I went away."

"Away where?"

"I don't know. I've been packing. Perhaps I'll go out to California as a start. Gavin can get his divorce. And afterwards if Juan wants me back, perhaps I'll come. After everything has simmered down and he's forgiven me for what I've done."

I couldn't wait any longer. It was necessary to tell her what I knew.

"You started something in Madrid yesterday."

"Yes, I know. I couldn't live with myself very well afterwards. I've done other things, but I've never seen myself as vicious before. But now I know what I can be like. The Cordova heritage—from Doña Inés."

"That's foolish. Anyway, the Madrid episode is over. What matters is that bonnet I found out there. It wasn't one Doro made for me, Eleanor. It was one she made for you."

Her look was more curious than shocked. "Well, go on," she said. "Tell me the rest."

I explained then about my growing awareness of the way she and Kirk resembled each other, though I'd gone down a wrong road at first in seeking a relationship. I told her about my painting and what I'd found in Clarita's room when I went to show it to her. As well as I could remember it, I quoted the page I'd read from Katy's diary.

She heard me out thoughtfully, surprisingly calm. "So Doro and Kirk were my parents. And that makes me your half sister, doesn't it? How strange, Amanda. You don't know how strange. Sometimes I've felt so remote from my parents. I didn't seem to be anything like them. When they died, I was secretly a little shocked because I didn't care enough. When Juan knew I'd been born to Doro—and I'm sure Katy would have told him at once—he must have found a way to get Rafael and his wife to take me as their own. And then, when they died, he and Katy took me themselves, and raised me in the same house with Doro. I always felt close to her, and I was sad when she died. It's funny though— I don't remember Kirk at all. When you came here I was jealous of you because you were Doro's daughter. Remember what I said about the portrait of Emanuella out in the collection? That none of her belongs to me? I was lying. I wanted to belong to her and to Doroteo. And now I do. But I must be like Kirk too. It isn't all Cordova wildness."

I heard her out, not entirely trusting, not able to accept this new mood. She had meant me so much harm, and I didn't believe in lightning changes.

Softly she began to laugh. "Wait until Paul hears all this! What wonderful material for his book. What a story it will make!"

This was the normal Eleanor. "You mustn't tell him!" I cried. "Think of Juan!"

"Of course I'll tell him. Juan can't stop me. I'll go and tell him now."

I remembered then. "You can't. When Clarita couldn't find you in the house—because you were probably up here where she wouldn't look—he decided that you'd gone out to Bandelier again. You might as well know he's furious with you, and he's gone out there to find you. To get the painting back."

Her laughter increased. "Oh, lovely, lovely! I'll go after him and confront him with a few things."

I sighed. "Thanks to this idea of Paul's, Clarita and Juan have gone out there too—because Juan doesn't want you there with Paul. And I've called Gavin, so he's followed them. Though I think it's Juan he's worried about. Grandfather seemed beaten and old this morning."

Eleanor, who had hardly been able to contain her laughter, suddenly stopped. "I'll go right away and call off the search."

There was certainly nothing amusing about this wild goose chase. I remembered the rage in Paul's eyes, and I didn't like to think of Eleanor out in that wild place, confronting him, as she very well might.

"Don't go," I begged her. "There's no point now."

"Oh, yes there is." The laughter was gone, but she was still lightly amused. "Think of them all searching that place for me, and not finding me. We can't have that. If I'm the treasure they're hunting for, I'd better be there."

She was on the stairs now, running down. I doubted this new, sweet concern, but I went after her.

"I'll go with you. Just give me time to change shoes."

For a moment she hesitated, looking back at me, then she nodded. "I'll wait."

I ran up to my room and changed into slacks and walking shoes.

When we were in the car on the way to Bandelier, I

became aware of a further change in Eleanor. She was no longer amused, no longer pleased with the idea of confronting them all and making them look foolish. Something had happened in her thinking to sober her and give her a strange edge of anxiety between the time when I'd left her to change my clothes, and when I'd joined her in the garage.

All desire to talk had left her, and she drove at her usual high speed, but with a new urgency, so that it was not merely as though she tried to escape something, but as if she was thrusting herself toward something that frightened her badly.

Only once did I try to question her on the way, and then she behaved as though she didn't hear, or at least had no intention of answering.

A memory returned to my mind while we were traveling—of Sylvia the time I'd spoken to her of Eleanor's father. She had given a strange answer that I couldn't fit with what I knew of Rafael. Of course! Sylvia had been speaking of Kirk. So Sylvia knew.

When we reached the open space in front of the Visitor Center at the park, Eleanor at once checked the other cars. All were here, and we had gone only a little way on foot along the trail before we ran into Gavin.

He hadn't found the others yet, and he was clearly surprised to see Eleanor and me together. I explained about the mistake and apologized for sending him out here. He brushed my words aside. "It's Juan I'm worried about. He looked pretty bad this morning and he shouldn't be wandering around out here, even though Clarita is with him."

I wondered how much protection Clarita would be in any case, but there was no time for explanations now. It was best to find those two right away. Paul I didn't care about.

It was decided that Gavin would take the lower trail that followed the stream through groves of trees along the floor of the canyon, while Eleanor and I would take the path that led upward past the caves along bare, unwooded rock. At least we had no need to look into the caves today. There would be no one hiding in them.

Eleanor started off by rushing ahead of me, and I was hard put to keep up with her. Once I called out and asked her to wait for me, begging her not to go so fast. She astonished me by turning to show me a look of anxiety that was not far from tears and thoroughly unlike Eleanor.

"We've got to hurry!" she cried. "They should never have come out here—never. I don't know what will happen. If only we could find Paul."

Paul was the one I cared least about, but after that I didn't try to control Eleanor's hurry. We stumbled along the cliff path, sometimes slipping on rocky surfaces in our haste, running when we found a level space, holding onto rough walls as we helped ourselves through tight passages cut from rock. We met no one, nor did we see anyone in the glimpses we had of the lower trail far below us.

Across the canyon, on the steep, wooded cliffs opposite, no trails were visible, though there must be those that climbed among the trees. But it was unlikely that Juan or Clarita, or Paul, for that matter, would be up there. They would expect to find Eleanor at an easier level.

On a space of trail where there were steps up and down, and a narrow walk hugged the cliff, Eleanor rushed ahead of me again. New York city canyons hadn't prepared me for clambering over New Mexico rock at this altitude, and I stopped for a moment to catch my breath, watching her slim figure silhouetted against the cliff ahead of me, where she stood at the top of steps carved into the rock. She seemed frozen in a position that was unnaturally still. I hurried to join her in that high place. The moment I brushed her arm, she whirled and ducked back down the trail.

"I don't think they've seen us. Quick, Amanda, get out of sight. Let's climb into one of the caves."

I stayed where I was, protesting. I wasn't afraid of Clarita out here in the open, with Juan behind her. "But why—why?"

"Clarita's down there, and she'll have seen you by now. Juan must be with her."

I glanced up the trail from where I stood, and saw Clarita looking up at me. We both turned away at the same moment, and I rejoined Eleanor, out of sight.

"Clarita saw me," I said. "But she turned back. Why don't we go and meet them?"

"No, no!" She grasped my arm and fairly dragged me toward a ladder that led to the lip of a deep cave. She pushed me up the ladder and scrambled after me as I crept into cool darkness.

"Keep your head down and lie flat," she directed.

There was no denying her urgency and I stilled my questions and obeyed. *I* knew what Clarita had done, but surely Eleanor didn't.

We lay close together on the stone floor and there was a smell of rock dust in our noses, the hardness of rock fighting our flesh. Beside me, Eleanor lay with all her senses alert, listening, every muscle in her body strained to hear some betraying sound.

"What is it?" I whispered. "Clarita won't hurt us out here. All we have to do is stand up to her. There isn't any gun this time."

"I know, but now I'm afraid," she said. "I'm terribly afraid. Amanda, while you were changing your clothes, I went into Clarita's room and read the pages of Katy's diary. I had to read about that baby in her own words. But then I read farther. I read about the day of the picnic."

"I didn't get to that," I admitted. "But it doesn't matter. I know because I confronted Clarita there in her room. But she's beaten now. She can't hurt us. Let's go out and—"

Eleanor pulled me back roughly. "Wait—I'll look. Stay here. Stay down."

She crept to the lip of the cave, where she could

look out and down the trail. Then she scrambled hastily back to me.

"Now we know the enemy," she said. "It's not *we* who are in danger, Amanda. It's *you.* Only you. Keep quiet. Don't make a sound."

For a moment or two I lay beside her as still as she wished. But I couldn't believe what she said, and if I was careful I could see out for myself nearer the lip of the cave. I could hear someone moving about on the trail below, hear a murmur of voices. Then footsteps went past, and I crept closer to the edge in order to look over. Behind me Eleanor caught hold of my foot, tried to pull me back. But I was close to the ladder now and I wrenched away. The small struggle dislodged a chip of rock and sent it skittering over the edge to the stone path below.

That alarmed me, and I too lay still, listening. There was no sound at all. Behind me Eleanor, perhaps shocked by the clatter of the falling stone, was equally still and her hand was no longer on my foot. After a moment I crept to the top of the ladder and looked down. Looked down upon Kirk's white sombrero that was rising toward me up the ladder. Before I could move back, the rolled brim tilted to reveal the face beneath, and I stared directly into the turquoise slits of a blue mask.

In the flood of terror that followed, I tried to slide backward into the depth of the cave. But the blue mask, thrust toward me, was coming up the ladder, evilly intent beneath the brim of the white sombrero.

In an instant everything flashed back from that other time, and I cried out, knowing the truth, remembering that day on the hillside, remembering the loved face, and the gun that had spat death for Kirk Landers. Remembering Doroteo struggling, trying to save Kirk as she fought her father, then losing her own balance, falling down the bank to lie dead in the arroyo.

All this in a moment of memory.

Behind me Eleanor cried out. "No, Grandfather, no!"

The man on the ladder snatched off sombrero and mask and I looked down upon that fierce falcon's head —and the face of death. One thin hand thrust out to clasp my arm and hold me there.

"So you have remembered everything—and you have destroyed everything for me. You have injured me with my daughter's daughter. Because of you she must know what should never have been known. It is the end."

I saw the upward flash, saw the dagger in his right hand, and tried to roll away from him. But his grasp held me with a madman's strength. There was no way to escape that upheld blade. Then Eleanor was upon me, pushing me, rolling me aside in the instant that the knife rose to its height and came swiftly down, tearing into human flesh. There was blood again, and I was sharply aware of the figure on the ladder—Juan Cordova's terrible face looking up at us for an instant before he teetered and fell backward on the rock below. In the same instant I saw Clarita coming back from one end of the trail, and Gavin running toward us from the other.

But only Eleanor concerned me now—her soft moaning, and that bloody wound in her shoulder. My sister, who had saved me. Clarita came past Juan and up the ladder to kneel beside us. At once she ripped off Eleanor's cotton blouse and used the unstained part of it to stanch the blood. Gavin was bending over Juan Cordova on the path.

"Eleanor will be all right," Clarita told him. "You must go and phone for an ambulance."

Gavin stood up. "Juan is dead. I'll go to the Center and phone at once."

When he'd gone, I spoke to Clarita. "Eleanor saved me. But now I remember it all. It was Juan who shot Kirk. But I still don't understand why."

Clarita answered me evenly, without emotion. "It is time for the truth. Now you must know. There must be an end to hating. It is not your fault, though I too have hated you. When Kirk came back to Santa Fe and learned that Doro had borne his child, he threatened to go to William Austin with the whole story unless Doro ran away with him. She came to meet him on the hillside that day to tell him she would not, even if he ruined her marriage. But she told her father first of Kirk's threat. Juan was in a rage, and he took a gun from Mark Brand's room and came along the hillside to threaten Kirk. His anger was so great, and when Kirk laughed at him, he shot and killed him. Doro fell while she was struggling with him to get the gun away."

"I know," I said and heard my own choked voice as though it were someone else's. "Did you see it from that window after all?"

"No. I was away from the house, where Paul saw me. But afterwards Juan called me to his room and told me what I must say. He told me that not even Katy was to know the truth. But mother was too wise for that. He did not tell her, but she forced the truth from me. She had to go along with my story to save her husband, and she never let him know she knew until she was dying. However, she had written it all down in her diary, so as to keep a record. After you came I went out to the *rancho* to get those pages and hide them from you."

"Why didn't you destroy them?"

She gazed at me coldly. "Because it was necessary to hold something over my father's head. He ruled me, and I bowed to him because he threatened to disinherit Eleanor—who was like my own child—if I did not do as he wished."

"And the whip?" I said. "That time in the patio? And the brass figure in the store?"

"He wanted to drive you away. You were becoming too dangerous, and to him you were not Doro's first-born—Eleanor was. He feared to have her learn the truth of her birth and discover that he had killed her real father and caused her mother's death. Eleanor was the only one he loved left alive. It was he who made sounds that would lure you into the patio that night where he could use the whip, and then pretended the attack upon himself. I drove him to the store that other night, and he went inside alone, looking for you. And found you. But it was I—because he ordered it —who brought him the whip and the Pentitente figure. I who placed Doña Sebastiana in your bed. I too wanted you to go away. It would have been better for you as well as for my father. Yet the real guilt lay in the past, and not with you."

I looked down at my grandfather where he lay with that fierce visage turned upward toward the sky. Beside him lay the sombrero and the turquoise mask. I went down the ladder and picked up the hat to lay it gently over that unguarded face.

"Why did he bring the hat and the mask here?" I asked Clarita. "And the dagger?"

"He wanted to frighten Paul so that he would stay away from Eleanor. My father was always given to the dramatic. He knew Paul would remember those things from that other time on the hillside. And the dagger would threaten him. But when I saw you above us in the trail, he was not far behind and he saw you too. So he used his masquerade in another way."

I pressed my hands over my face and began to weep softly into them. I wept for us all, and because of my lost, foolish dream of finding a family. Surprisingly, Clarita put a hand on my shoulder.

"*Pobrecita*," she said. "Do not cry. It is over now."

I took my hands away from my wet face. "But you —you seemed to grow stronger, even today."

"As he grew weaker, he began to fear me more. When he saw that bonnet you brought from Madrid, I thought I could control him. It reminded him of all I could tell if I chose. I was wrong. Much of this is my fault— because I did not speak out and stop him."

Eleanor had lain weak and silent, listening to us, making no sound, and now she reached for Clarita's hand. "It doesn't matter that Doro and Kirk were my parents. *You* are my true mother."

Clarita bent to caress her as though she had been a child, and there were tears in her eyes.

The park men came with two stretchers, and Juan and Eleanor were carried back to the Center to await an ambulance. Clarita followed them. Gavin and I waited until they were gone. Then Gavin bent to pick up the blue mask.

"What shall we do with this?" he asked.

I took it from him. Stepping to the edge of the trail, I flung it out into a growth of cactus and chamiso far below. When it had fallen out of sight, I put my arm through his and we walked back to the Center together. I never wanted to see that mask again.

Paul was waiting for us, and his eyes were alive with excitement. He had his story now—the full, lush story that would make his book. Or so he thought. Later that evening Sylvia ended his dream. She told him quietly that she would leave him for good if he used one word of the Cordova story in his writing, ever. And Paul did not want to lose Sylvia. She had known about Doro's baby, known who Eleanor was, but Sylvia had always feared that Paul might have shot Kirk, and she was terrified lest this come out. She could see Paul playing with fire in writing his book, though perhaps disguising his role even further. She thought that if Clarita had guessed, she might have protected Paul out of old affection.

When the ambulance had gone ahead, and Clarita, Eleanor, and Paul were gone on their separate ways, Gavin and I followed in his car. I lay weakly back in the seat with my eyes closed until I felt the car stop. When I opened them I saw we were at a lookout point and that the bare opposite wall of the canyon stood up with all its stark striations markedly visible in the intense New Mexico light.

There was no need for words. Gavin's arm held me with my head against his shoulder. The sun had shone on all my terror for the last time. But it would be a long while before I would forget that moment when I had looked down into the eyes of the turquoise mask.